S0-ACM-289

Dear Reader:

It is my pleasure to present yet another captivating novel from bestselling Allison Hobbs, a "Queen of Erotic Fiction." Now with her seventh novel, *The Climax,* Allison brings back two women, Kai and Terrelle, and their obsession with one man, Marquise. It is the follow-up to the bestselling *Insatiable* and will keep you engrossed as the twisted tale takes you on a ride from Philadelphia to California to the backwoods of South Carolina.

I first met Allison at the Baltimore Book Festival several years ago and was immediately impressed with her talent. Not everyone has a natural writing ability but Allison was born to create masterpieces such as the one you are about to read. She is ever positive and determined, much like myself, and will go far in this industry as her next four books are already scheduled for publication.

She is the author of *Double Dippin',* *Dangerously in Love,* and *Pandora's Box;* all published by Strebor Books. Allison took on the genre of "paranormal erotica" with *The Enchantress* and in *A Bona Fide Gold Digger,* Allison spins a seductive tale about the alluring Milan Walden, her secret sex life and her quest for wealth.

Thanks for supporting Allison's efforts and for supporting my imprint, Strebor Books. I am overwhelmed by the legions of avid readers who genuinely appreciate not only my personal work but the works of the dozens whom I publish.

Now sit back and get ready for another erotic adventure with Allison Hobbs.

Peace and Many Blessings,

*Zane*

Publisher
Strebor Books
www.simonsays.com/streborbooks

ALSO BY ALLISON HOBBS

*A Bona Fide Gold Digger*
*The Enchantress*
*Double Dippin'*
*Dangerously in Love*
*Insatiable*
*Pandora's Box*

ZANE PRESENTS

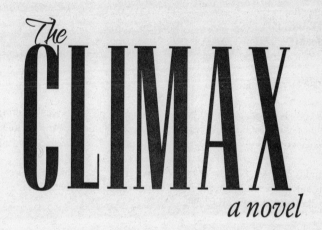

# The CLIMAX

*a novel*

# ALLISON HOBBS

## STREBOR BOOKS

NEW YORK  LONDON  TORONTO  SYDNEY

DOUGLASS BRANCH LIBRARY
Champaign Public Library
504 East Grove Street
Champaign, Illinois  61820-3239

Strebor Books
P.O. Box 6505
Largo, MD 20792
http://www.streborbooks.com

© 2008 by Allison Hobbs

This book is a work of fiction. Names, characters, places and incidents are products of the author's imagination or are used fictitiously. Any resemblance to actual events or locales or persons, living or dead, is entirely coincidental.

All rights reserved. No part of this book may be reproduced in any form or by any means whatsoever. For information address Strebor Books, P.O. Box 6505, Largo, MD 20792.

ISBN-13 978-1-59309-184-2
ISBN-10    1-59309-184-2
LCCN 2001012345

First Strebor Books trade paperback edition February 2008

Cover design: www.mariondesigns.com

10  9  8  7  6  5  4  3  2  1

Manufactured in the United States of America

For information regarding special discounts for bulk purchases, please contact Simon & Schuster Special Sales at 1-800-456-6798 or business@simonandschuster.com

FOR
MY FATHER,
STERLING J. HOBBS

# ACKNOWLEDGMENTS

Zane! Zane! Zane! The Queen of All Media. Thanks for sharing your shine!

Charmaine Parker, Publishing Director of Strebor Books. There are no words to adequately express the depths of my gratitude for your many acts of kindness over the years. New York and Cosmopolitans. I had so much fun with you and cousin Debbie.

When I became a part of The Strebor family, I believe there were only about five or six authors. My, how the family has grown! I want to extend a welcome to some of the new members, whom I've had the opportunity to meet: Janet Stevens Cook, Caleb Alexander, Che Parker, Nikki Jenkins, Marsha Jenkins-Sanders, and Sonsyrea Tate Montgomery.

Dywane D. Birch—Your writing is off the chain. Your intelligence and wit have me in mad literary love.

Jessica Holter—Condom Kingdom was the shyt! Thanks for inviting me.

Tina Brooks McKinney & Tina R. Hayes—The road to South Carolina was long and hard, but we did it, y'all.

Rodney Lofton—Your presence at my signing in Norfolk, VA was really the icing on the cake.

Anna J.—I have so much love and respect for you, my Philly sistah of the pen.

Nakea Murray—I've shouted you out in print before, but I can't sing your praises loud enough.

Navorn S. Johnson, editor of this novel and three previous titles. Thanks for making my words sparkle on the pages.

Kimberly Kaye Terry & Delilah Devlin, I was tryna be lazy, but you two made me step up my game. Thank you for the sisterhood. I'm really lovin' our literary ménage-à-trois!

Black Horizons Books and my girl, Xanyell Smalls.

Black & Noble Books, Broad & Erie, Philadelphia, PA. Thank you, Hakim and Tyson and the entire Black and Noble family.

Tasha & Ron of Waldenbooks, Military Circle Mall, Norfolk, VA. Thanks for making my signing so much fun!

Elmer and Daphine Marcus of Norfolk, VA. (This married couple read together and I'm told they have many nights of unspeakable freaky pleasure while reading my sexy stuff!)

I want to give a special shout-out to my SJNH Readers & Friends: Yvonne Williams, Kia Gary, LaTricia Brown, Jewel Everly, Elizabeth Stewart, Janet Stewart, LaToya Mann, Catalina Starling, Beverly Perez & her mom, Maria, Michael Booker, Janice Robinson, Nicole Llewellyn, Domingo Moody & my buddy, Stuart. Thank you all for embracing me and being so kind while I was passing through.

Thank you, Yona Deshommes, Publicist, Atria/Simon & Schuster. I appreciate the radio interviews and events you hooked up for me.

Monique Ford, personal publicist, feisty road dawg & sassy sistah friend.

Shari Reason, you're like a daughter to me. You definitely have my heart.

Thank you, Karen Dempsey Hammond. My sister, my confidante, my best friend forever.

Hugs and kisses to my brood: Kyndal, Korky, Kameron, Keenan, Kha'ri, Kareem, and Kapri.

# Chapter 1

To the observer, it seemed Terelle Chambers was locked inside herself, unaware of her surroundings. Her caregivers at Spring Haven Psychiatric Hospital hand-fed her, manually moved her limbs, and even toileted her, but they treated Terelle dispassionately as if she were an inanimate object—something that required care. Her affliction, persistent catatonia, had robbed the young woman of even a glimmer of her former personality.

Aside from occasional sorrowful whimpers and anguished moans—fleeting echoes of a tormented inner world—Terelle had not uttered a coherent word in two years.

However, although she appeared to have retreated from the outside world, Terelle was keenly aware of touch, taste, smells, and sound. Her thoughts and memory were jumbled and disjointed but she was able to distinguish among the smells and voices and even the touches of the doctors and nurses who briskly performed their duties on her behalf without emotional attachment.

Awakened by the sound of footsteps approaching the bed where her rigid body lay, Terelle was instantly comforted by the feelings of compassion and love that emanated from the person who had entered her room and was now standing over her.

*Saleema*, she thought as a smile formed in her mind. She would have greeted her dearest friend with a hug if her unmoving arms and clenched, contracted fists would agree to such a gesture. She wished she could remember how to speak the word, *hello*, but the technique required to form clear and audible words escaped her.

Terelle inhaled deeply, trying to draw in her best friend's fragrance. But instead of the pleasant hint of Saleema's perfume, Terelle recognized a masculine scent. She gasped in alarm.

Long thick fingers tenderly stroked her cheek, calming her. The fingers inched upward and caressed the soft hair that curled at her temples. Terelle knew this person—this man. She recognized his touch—his essence. Was she still asleep? Was she lost inside a dream?

The squeal of the bedrail being lowered sounded much too real for this to be a dream, but in her heart she knew a dream was all this could be. Terelle's lashes fluttered as she struggled to raise eyelids that felt too heavy to lift. The struggle ceased when she felt the weight of his chest pressing down upon her breasts. He kissed her cheek.

"Terelle," he whispered her name. "You gotta get better, babe." He squeezed her closed fist. "This ain't the way it was supposed to go down." His voice caught. She heard him taking in deep breaths. She felt his raw emotions. His sorrow. And his love. "I miss you."

Marquise! Terelle wanted to look in his face, but she knew if she opened her eyes, he'd disappear as he did at the end of every dream. She could only be with Marquise during slumber, so she allowed herself to relax, praying to remain blissfully asleep forever.

"I know you got the strength to come up outta this," he said, stroking her hair. "You can't give up. We still can have a future together. Me, you, and Keeta."

*Markeeta! Oh God, my poor baby.* She'd been enjoying the time spent in dreamland with Marquise long enough. It wasn't right for her to remain in her inner world just to be with him. She had to get well for Markeeta.

"You can't give up like this." He caressed her arms and her hand and then leaned down and kissed her lips. The sensation of their hearts beating together nearly took her breath away. When she felt his lips touch hers, Terelle easily accepted that her life on earth had ended and she was finally reunited with her beloved. No dream kiss could feel like this. Had she died—was she in heaven?

"All that shit with that other broad wasn't about nothing. Didn't you listen to the message I left on your answering machine?" His voice sounded choked. "I gotta go," he said suddenly and then abruptly pulled away.

*Wait! Don't leave me*, she wanted to shout but couldn't get the words out.

"I love you, girl. But I can show you better than I can tell you," he told her, speaking words that were uniquely his.

*Oh, Marquise. I'm not dreaming. It's you. It's really you!* Tears moistened and unsealed Terelle's closed eyes. In an act of sheer determination, she willed the muscles in her neck to cooperate. Forcing her head to turn, she managed to catch a fleeting glimpse of a very tall man pacing quickly toward the open door. *Marquise!*

His name was on her tongue, but she couldn't make a sound. From the depths of her soul, she drew on the memory of the mechanics required to produce coherent sound. She tried to shout his name, but the sound that issued from her lips was an unintelligible whimper. Determinedly, she tried again and this time his name came out in a loud and clear shriek, *Marquiiiiiiiise!*

But instead of being comforted in Marquise's loving arms,

Terelle was held down by several pairs of strong hands, trained to restrain the chronically mentally ill.

The next day Saleema Sparks sat at Terelle's bedside. Saleema gazed anxiously at her best friend, but Terelle did not acknowledge her. As usual Terelle was mute and wore a blank expression.

Holding Terelle's limp hand, Saleema pleaded, "Talk to me, Terelle. Why won't you say something? The charge nurse called last night. She told me you spoke. She said you screamed for…" Saleema swallowed. "She said you screamed for Marquise." She squeezed Terelle's hand imploringly and gasped when she felt a slight movement in Terelle's fingers. Saleema's eyes, shining with hope, flashed upon Terelle's face.

Terelle's vacant look was replaced by a grimace as she struggled to emit sound.

"Terelle! You're back! I know you are. Oh, my God; I gotta get a nurse," Saleema said excitedly as she pushed herself forward, prepared to rise. Terelle's fingers wiggled urgently.

"No?" Saleema asked. "You don't want me to get the nurse?"

One side of Terelle's face twitched as she uttered a gurgling sound. Saleema looked into Terelle's eyes. Terelle blinked rapidly. "Okay, I understand. You don't want me to get a nurse. But I don't know what to do. Are you in pain?"

"Maaar," Terelle uttered with great effort.

"Markeeta?" Saleema said, nodding. "She's fine, Terelle. Keeta's beautiful. Four years old and smart as a whip. I've been taking real good care of your baby. I love her like I would my own but I make sure she knows you and…" Saleema's voice faltered. "I show her pictures of you and her daddy," she said in a voice filled with emotion.

Tears slid down Terelle's cheek. "Oh, my God. You're crying. But that's a good thing," Saleema said as she snatched a tissue out of box on Terelle's bedside stand. She wiped the tears from Terelle's eyes. "Your tears mean that you hear me. You understand everything I've told you." Tears now welled in Saleema's eyes. "Oh, Terelle. I missed you so much." She bent down and gave Terelle's prone body an awkward hug. "I'm so glad you're back." Then Saleema, unable to keep her emotions in check, began to sniffle. She reached over and grabbed another tissue to wipe her own eyes.

"Maaarq...," Terelle said again. Saleema knew all along that her friend was referring to Marquise. But instead of acknowledging Terelle's attempt to speak her deceased fiancé's name, Saleema spoke animatedly about Terelle's daughter, Markeeta.

Exhausted from the effort of trying to speak, Terelle closed her eyes. Saleema sat holding Terelle's hand until her friend drifted off to sleep. Looking back at Terelle with concern, Saleema quietly left the room.

Saleema barged into the charge nurse's office. "I want Terelle to have speech lessons."

"Well, she's been evaluated and unfortunately, despite her breakthrough last night, Terelle's still not responsive. I'm sorry," the nurse said sincerely. "Terelle is not a candidate for speech therapy."

"Excuse me!" Saleema held up her hand in an exaggerated motion, which informed the nurse that she was not pleased. "The last time I checked, my name was written at the bottom of the check this hospital gets for taking care of Terelle Chambers. Don't get it twisted; I'm not asking for anything. If she can't get speech therapy here then I'll take her to another hospital—a better one." Saleema whirled around and strutted away.

"Ms. Sparks," the nurse blurted. "I didn't mean to offend you. I'm only reporting what the speech therapist wrote in her evaluation note."

Saleema stopped abruptly, turned around. "You people told me that Terelle would never have meaningful or conscious interaction with her family or friends. That's what the doctors said, right?"

The nurse nodded.

"Wrong! My girl is interacting her ass off—blinking, moving her fingers—trying to communicate with me. So do your job. No more tests. Call in a speech therapist who knows what the fuck she's doing—"

"Ms. Sparks, that language isn't—"

Saleema held up her hand. "Don't be criticizing my language. I can talk any way I want. The way y'all misdiagnosed Terelle, you shouldn't even be concerned about no cuss words. You better hope I don't call my attorney and have him slap this place with a malpractice suit."

"I'll have another speech therapist evaluate Terelle."

"No, I'm not trying to hear that," Saleema said, wagging a finger. "No more evaluations, no more tests. The next time I come up in here, that therapist better be doing her job; I want her working with Terelle and giving her some real speech lessons. Ya heard?" Deliberately intimidating the now obviously frazzled nurse, Saleema threw out her arms in a flagrant combative gesture, glowered at the nurse, and then sashayed out the door.

# Chapter 2

After reading an article on DNA, Kai Montgomery had an awakening. She'd come to realize that the narcissistic and unscrupulous conduct that had ultimately led to her unjust incarceration was not her fault. Her bad behavior, she'd learned, was genetically inherited. Her biological mother, a conniving and completely immoral human being, had passed on defective DNA. Her mother had diligently visited her long enough to deceive Kai into believing she could help her get the justice she deserved. Once she'd obtained her daughter's banking information, the bitch absconded with the money Kai had stashed in a safety deposit box.

Now equipped with a clearer understanding of herself, Kai decided it was time for an abrupt halt to the martyr persona. She would no longer passively accept her prison sentence. She'd been behind bars for two years and quite frankly, enough was enough. Sure, she'd done some vile things to a lot of people, but it wasn't as if they didn't deserve to feel her wrath. Spending the rest of her life in prison for a murder she didn't commit went beyond poetic justice.

She did not kill Marquise Whitsett, yet she was convicted of the crime and sentenced to life in prison. Kai refused to rot in jail for the rest of her life. Doing time was hell. Everyone thought that prisoners' needs were met by the state. That was a crock! Survival behind bars was dependent upon financial security.

Kai's adopted parents provided her with money to make purchases from the commissary, but what they gave was just a drop in the bucket compared to what they owed her. She'd deal with them one day. It was only a matter of time before she got out and got even!

Her scheming birth mother had informed her that her adoptive parents felt so embarrassed by the scandal of her murder conviction, they'd disinherited her and skipped to southern California. Providing her with only a post office box in Santa Barbara, her crafty parents made sure Kai could never contact them directly.

Someday, someway, she'd find her neglectful parents, but in the meantime, her thoughts of exacting revenge on people whose whereabouts were unknown were frustrating and unsatisfying. So she turned her thoughts to her most recent sex partner, a hot male prisoner named Mookie. Mookie reminded her of Marquise. Like Marquise, he was a real rough rider—tall, with a deep dark complexion, handsome features, and best of all, Mookie was well hung. *Mmm!* Just thinking about Mookie made her kitty purr.

With intense sexual images running across her mind, Kai wrote Mookie a graphic note. It was time for another rendezvous. Knowing just the person to make the delivery, Kai folded the crude lined paper, ripped from a composition notebook.

Kai found Taffy in the kitchen stuffing her face instead of stacking trays. "Whassup, Taffy," Kai said. She'd had to adapt to prison life, including speaking the vernacular.

"Hey, Kai!" Taffy's round face swelled into a big, expectant smile. A while back, Kai had considered riding Taffy's tongue, but there were some gross rumors about the girl that made Kai steer clear. Anyway, Mookie was handling things now and quite frankly she was bored with having her pussy licked.

Taffy had finally taken a hint and stopped pestering her, but Kai knew the pathetic pig still had the hots for her, so she had to conceal her contemptuous superiority and handle the situation delicately. "I need you to get a note to Mookie for me," Kai said casually. "He's supposed to be hooking me up with a big-time attorney to handle my appeal."

"I thought you didn't have no money for a lawyer," Taffy said suspiciously.

"I don't. Mookie told me that the lawyer would take my case *gratis*," Kai said, slipping into her natural pattern of intelligent speech. But remembering that she was talking to a damn-near retard, she explained, "Um, the lawyer will work on my case for free. He'll accept a few favors for pay." Kai gave Taffy a conspiratorial wink. "You know—I'll have to give up some booty," she further explained. "I wrote dude twice but he ain't wrote me back yet." Damn, Kai hated talking like an uneducated idiot, but when in Rome…

"Uh-huh," Taffy said, inhaling food instead of chewing it.

"You know, Mookie has a cell phone," Kai continued, sensing Taffy required more detailed information. "I want him to make a call to that lawyer."

Men in prison had it going on. Their thuggish attitudes and muscular bodies had everyone from fat lonely girls on the outside to female inmates as well as correctional officers on the inside drooling over them. The women in their lives made certain male inmates kept their gear up and had access to cigarettes and drugs, and plenty of money on their books. Many male inmates even had internet access. Nurses and social workers were always willing to exchange sex with the gorgeous hunks for a little computer time.

Female inmates, on the other hand, had to pretty much scratch and scrounge and eat a lot of pussy for material gain. Fortunately, though Kai had been on the receiving end of oral sex with women, she'd never reciprocated. Thanks to the pittance she received from her parents, she'd never had to.

Forcing Kai to keep her company while she ate, Taffy changed the subject, and Kai had to endure the delay.

"Did I ever tell you we used to be able to work in the kitchen with the men?"

Kai shook her head, knowing Taffy was going to tell her a drawn-out tale.

"Yeah, girl, we used to work side-by-side with the men until this chick got pregnant by one of the male inmates. After that they had to separate us."

*Why is she telling me this? What the hell do I care?* Kai wanted to slap the shit out of Taffy, but instead of showing annoyance, she wore an impassive expression.

"Anyway, that chick sued the state for millions."

"Millions?" Kai lifted a brow. Sounded like something she would have done but she wouldn't have enjoyed having to get pregnant for the money. Getting an abortion would have been on the top of her list, but still, she knew she would loathe the idea of something growing inside her. Yuck!

"Yeah, that bitch got a fat bankroll off the state," Taffy said as she wiped sweat from her forehead with the back of her plump hand. Her other hand shoveled food into her mouth. Her eyes kept darting to the back of the kitchen, where several workers rattled pots and pans.

Taffy was a tray runner, a job that required her to distribute food trays to the female inmates. Overweight inmates like Taffy loved having that position because they were able to eat the food from the extra trays. Tray runners picked up the food trays from the men's areas of the correctional facility also. Though separated by a metal gate, the tray runner was able to pass the men notes from female inmates. A tray runner could make exchanges of cigarettes and even drugs, all for a price of course.

Kai toyed with the note in her hand. "Look, if you get this note to Mookie, I can get you a perm kit or something."

Taffy glared at Kai, and Kai was immediately sorry she had blurted out the offer of a perm kit. According to prison gossip, Taffy was so broke when she first came in that she ate some girl's foul-smelling pussy in exchange for a perm kit and ended up having to get treated for gonorrhea of the throat.

"Mookie ain't even here no more!" Taffy spat, her moon face etched in animosity.

"What do you mean, he's not…" Kai couldn't continue. Feeling a sudden bout of nausea and vertigo, she backed against the wall to steady herself.

"Your man Mookie is the one who got that girl pregnant. It took her a couple years to get the money. But she's a rich bitch now. She paid off Mookie's restitution. I heard she picked him up in a fly-ass Maybach yesterday. Bitch rode up to the gate with their little son strapped in a car seat. Yeah, Mookie and his bitch is two thorough-ass niggas. The bitch played the system and Mookie played *you!* Big time," Taffy added with her face twisted in a sneer.

Kai gasped. She took in so much air, she choked. Coughing, she clutched her chest while tears burned her eyes. It was outrageous that someone as intelligent as she had been outsmarted by an ignorant thug. A poorly educated, practically illiterate convict and his ride-or-die chick had conned the system. Gagging and coughing from the shock of the unwelcome news and feeling humiliated beyond belief, Kai couldn't keep her thoughts from turning to Marquise and his ghetto-trash girlfriend, Terelle—the psycho bitch who had really killed him.

"Need a drink of water?" Taffy inquired. Her darting eyes gleamed with something Kai couldn't quite detect. Was it triumph? A second too late, Kai recognized that it was malevolence that danced in Taffy's eyes.

As if on cue, two female inmates emerged from the shadows. Their smoldering hostility was almost palpable.

Knowing she was about to be ambushed, Kai opened her mouth to scream. But Taffy threw her heavy body across the table, then reached out and clamped a beefy hand over Kai's mouth, muffling the sound.

The three women, undoubtedly brawlers from birth, easily dragged Kai's bucking and thrashing body into a secluded pantry. Kai kicked and twisted to no avail. Amid institutional-sized canned goods, large sacks of flour, and corn meal, Kai was pinned down. Taffy removed her hand but it was instantly replaced by the dry and calloused hand of one of her brutal assistants.

"Did y'all know this bitch thought she was too good to have sex with me?" Taffy asked her cohorts. She folded her arms across her chest.

"For real?" one of the women asked, sounding personally offended.

"Whatchu gon' do 'bout this stuck-up bitch," inquired the other inmate. "I say she needs her face fucked up real good."

Eyes wide with terror, Kai shrank back. Taffy glowered, her folded arms tightening as her anger mounted. Now filled with a sufficient amount of rage, Taffy sauntered over.

Kai wondered whether the crazed inmate would draw a crudely formed dagger or brandish a butcher knife or some other dangerous form of cutlery accessed from the prison kitchen. Trembling in horror, she imagined the pain and agony of having her beautiful face carved and disfigured. Oh, Jesus! She needed help. Where were the fucking C.O.s?

But instead of hovering over Kai with a shank, Taffy began to peel off her prison-issued uniform. "Bitch, I ain't nevah want to eat you out. I was just messin' wit your head. I heard you was a freaky bitch so I was runnin' game so I could get you somewhere by yourself."

Kai blinked in confusion.

"Oh, don't get it twisted, bitch. You real cute and everything, I could fuck the shit outta you— but see, I'm loyal to the 'hood." Taffy pounded a balled fist against her heart. "Bitch, I represent southwest. That shit that went down with my niggas wasn't cool. I grew up with both of them," she said, emphasizing her last words with three powerful punches to her open palm.

Both of whom? And what the hell had gone down? Kai would have asked if she were permitted to speak.

In response to the baffled look in Kai's eyes, Taffy replied, "Marquise and Terelle! Them was my niggas, bitch. You killed Quise and fucked Terelle up for life."

The information that passed Taffy's lips was far worse than Kai could have ever imagined. The chubby tray runner had never let on that she knew Marquise or Terelle. Kai had never suspected that the woman had a personal vendetta against her. The conniving food addict had listened with feigned compassion when Kai first met her and had professed her innocence.

Trumped again by yet another vulgar hood rat, tears of defeat fell from Kai's eyes and wet her captive's hand. Were all the inhabitants of the ghetto educated in the school of treachery and deceit?

The hand that covered her mouth pulled away and balled into a fist. As quick as a lightning flash, a pair of knuckles crashed against Kai's face. "This crying bitch got her nasty snot all over my hand," the rough-skinned inmate told the other two. Using Kai's abundant head of curly hair, the inmate wiped the mucous off her hand.

Kai's mouth was uncovered and wide open but she couldn't scream. Her jaw felt unhinged. She was certain she saw stars. But her ordeal was far from being over. Taffy had taken off her prison garb and now squatted over Kai's face.

"Crying ain't gon' do you no good," she informed her struggling victim. "My girl told you she was gon' fuck up your face, but she forgot to add that *I'm* gon' *pussy-fuck* that pretty face."

As Kai feebly fought against her attackers, she instantly regretted having wasted so much time doing cardiovascular exercises in the prison gym. She preferred being slender and fit, but at this moment, she could have used some extra strength and would have gladly welcomed a set of powerful arms that rippled with manly muscles. If this travesty wasn't an isolated event, if a series of horrific physical confrontations would take place for the duration of her prison experience, she'd have to incorporate heavy weight-lifting into her workout routine.

Grinning, the ugly inmates held her down firmly. As Taffy's vagina hovered over Kai's face, the stench of sweat and urine was so overpowering, it curdled Kai's stomach. "HEEEEEELP!" Kai tried to scream, but the word came out raspy and slurred.

In an instant, Taffy lowered her putrid pussy, connecting it with Kai's open mouth. Intertwined in Taffy's pussy hairs were bits of toilet paper that stuck to Kai's tongue. Thick, smelly secretions oozed from Taffy's rank vagina and into the mouth that Kai was unable to close.

# Chapter 3

There was a box in her room that emitted loud noise and had brilliantly colored, fast-moving images inside. But she couldn't make out the images or remember what the box was called.

A woman Terelle had never seen came into her room to talk to her. Terelle kept her eyes focused on the shiny object the woman held in her hand. The object looked familiar.

"You're staring at my pen," the speech therapist said, sounding amused.

*Pen! I remember that.* Terelle was grateful for the information. Her memory loss was frustrating, there were a million unformed questions in her mind, but she was determined to relearn all the information she'd lost.

"Can you say 'pen,' Terelle?"

She could hear the word in her mind but she'd forgotten how to coordinate her lips and tongue to produce the sound. But with the same determination that she'd used to speak Marquise's name, she instructed her brain to transmit the information to her mouth. Her tongue felt thick—too heavy to lift. But Terelle persevered. "Paaaah." She heard herself and was greatly disappointed. She tried again. "Puuuuh." The second attempt sounded worse than the first. Now angry and fueled by that anger, but rejecting the notion of giving up, Terelle opened her mouth wide. Something that felt like a powerful *click* went off inside her head. "Pen," she was able to say clearly, stunning herself and the speech therapist as well.

Her eyes shot toward the box that had baffled her.

"TV?" the therapist asked.

She remembered instantly. "Television," Terelle said with ease. If she could, she would have pointed to all the unknown objects in her range of vision, but she didn't have to. The therapist began rattling the names.

"Bed," the woman said, patting the side of Terelle's bed. "Picture," she exclaimed and pointed to a floral print that hung on the wall.

After teaching Terelle the names of objects, the therapist began listing the parts of the body—ears, nose, fingers, toes—helping to rekindle Terelle's memory.

Atop the bedside table was a framed photograph of Terelle's daughter, Markeeta. Despite her cloudy memory, she'd never forgotten Markeeta. With her eyes locked on the image of the daughter she hadn't seen in person in two years, Terelle formed a coherent sentence. In a voice barely above a whisper, Terelle said firmly, "I want to see my daughter."

After the therapist rushed from the room to report Terelle's progress, Terelle, determined to make her body function, willed her muscles, joints, and tendons to move. She wiggled her toes and fingers. She lifted her hand a few inches from the bed but it dropped down, uselessly. She tried again and again until she could finally lift both hands and ball her fists.

The power of love could work miracles. It didn't make sense, but Marquise was alive. How, what, and why didn't matter. For the sake of her family, Terelle had to dig deep and get herself together.

Smashing through the set of double doors that led to a row of administrative offices, Saleema stopped at the first open door. "Where is Terelle Chambers?" she bellowed. "Her room is empty and nobody knows shit!"

"Who?" asked a befuddled secretary, looking up from her computer screen.

"Oh, this is a bunch of bullshit," Saleema remarked, incredulous. "You don't know where Terelle is? She's paralyzed, so she damn sure didn't walk outta here." *Oh, Lord, what am I gonna do if they tell me Terelle is dead.*

"Miss, I don't know—"

"Hold up, hold up," Saleema said, shaking her head and waving her hand. "If I don't get some information in about two seconds…" Her heart pounded with anger and trepidation. Saleema found it hard to speak. She muttered expletives and then took a deep breath to calm herself down. Quelling the fear that Terelle had died, she gathered her wits and spoke as calmly she could. "I swear to God…I'm about to flip," Saleema spoke slowly and menacingly.

The secretary stole a glance at the computer monitor, her fingers clicking against the keyboard.

"Yo! Stop whatever that is you're doing and listen to what I'm saying. Terelle Chambers is a patient here. She's not in her room, the nurses don't know shit, talkin' about they just came on duty. But fuck all that—"

Offended by the profanity, the secretary grimaced.

"And fuck you, too," Saleema shouted, responding to the secretary's disapproving scowl. "Now if you don't want me to turn this goddamn place out, get on the phone and get me some answers."

The secretary quickly snatched the phone out of the cradle, pushed buttons and started talking fast. "Yes, I'm trying to locate a patient. Her name is Terelle Chambers." The secretary listened intently to the person on the other end of the phone.

Saleema smiled to herself. She'd learned how to speak and behave in a dignified manner and did so when she conducted business with her clients. But experience had taught her that nothing motivated difficult people as effectively as getting real loud and ghetto on their asses.

"Oh, she's in the sunroom?" the secretary said, turning to Saleema with a big smile.

*Now, that's what I'm talkin' about!*

"Thanks," Saleema told the woman. However, the secretary had worked her nerves so badly, Saleema made sure there wasn't a trace of gratitude in her voice.

She approached the facility's sunroom, prepared to cuss out whoever had the audacity to take Terelle from her room without permission. That stupid person could have caused Saleema to have a heart attack. *It's a wonder I didn't pass the fuck out when I saw Terelle's empty-ass bed.*

Shaking her head at the stupidity of some people, Saleema entered the sunroom. Her eyes swept the large, avocado-colored gathering place. "Terelle!" she screamed when she spotted her friend, who was amazingly sitting upright in a wheelchair facing a window that overlooked a courtyard with lush green trees, tranquil ponds, and bubbling fountains.

Maneuvering between wheelchairs and recliners, Saleema nearly tripped as she hastily dashed toward Terelle. Dropping to her knees, Saleema wrapped her arms tightly around Terelle's waist. Soothingly, Terelle patted the top of Saleema's head.

"You're not paralyzed?" Saleema asked, lifting her head from Terelle's lap.

"No, not anymore," Terelle said in a whispery voice.

"You can talk!" Saleema shrieked with glee. Her girl had miraculously recovered; Saleema's joy was immense and without measure.

A woman sitting next to Terelle smiled at Saleema. "You must be Saleema. I'm Catherine Alexander, Terelle's speech therapist. Terelle has made amazing progress."

"I see. Thank you," Saleema said sincerely. Her eyes pooled with tears.

"Oh, I can't take any credit. Terelle did this all on her own."

"When can I take her home?" Saleema asked, rising from her kneeling position.

"Well...Terelle needs a lot of rehab therapy. But that's something you should be discussing with her doctor. Due to this significant change in her physical and mental status, I'm sure the clinical team will meet with you soon and discuss discharge planning."

"No disrespect, but I'm not worrying about that clinical team." Saleema turned her attention to Terelle. "Are you ready to go home, girl?"

"Not yet," Terelle answered softly. "But I want to see Markeeta."

"Listen, I'm going to give you two some privacy. I'll be seeing you tomorrow, Terelle. I'll tell your care nurse that you're in the sunroom. Nice meeting you, Saleema." Smiling, the speech therapist waved good-bye to Terelle.

Terelle waved back and whispered, "See you tomorrow, Cathy."

"Terelle, I prayed for you to get well. Me and Keeta prayed every day for this moment. She's going to be so happy to see you—to talk to you. She's in school right now; I got her in a fancy private school. She's smart as shit. So, look I'm gonna bring her by tonight. Right now, I'm gotta run out and buy you some new loungewear. Styles have changed, girl," Saleema said, laughing. "Like me, Keeta's a fashion diva. She won't appreciate reuniting with a mother dressed in played-out gear." Saleema was so animated and giddy, she was talking fast and gesturing extravagantly.

Terelle chuckled.

"Ooo, girl. It's so good to hear you laugh." Saleema bent over and hugged Terelle again.

"Saleema." Terelle spoke directly in Saleema's ear.

Saleema broke the embrace and studied her friend's face.

"Marquise is alive. He was here—with me."

Saleema's joy instantly disintegrated. Her pleasant expression cracked into a dreadful frown. She couldn't bring Markeeta to see Terelle. Sure, Terelle could move a little and she could speak, but the words that had just spilled from her lips were crazy. *Damn, I knew this shit was too good to be true.*

Saleema knelt again. She held Terelle's hand. She straightened her shoulders and took a deep breath. "Marquise wasn't here, Terelle."

"I saw him, Saleema. He kissed me."

"No, Terelle. Marquise is dead," Saleema insisted. "You shot him."

"I remember *everything*. It was an accident," Terelle whimpered.

"Yes, it was," Saleema said softly, her voice distant as if she were back in the parking garage the day Marquise was shot. "You were aiming for that yella bitch he was cheating with, but you shot Quise by mistake. He's dead, Terelle. And you have to move on for your daughter's sake."

Terelle shook her head. "He's not dead! I have to tell Markeeta that her daddy is alive. He wants us to be together."

*Aw shit. My girl's worse off than I thought.* Terelle was still delusional; there wasn't a chance in hell that Saleema would allow Terelle to tell Markeeta that her dead father wanted them to be together as a family. Damn shame that Markeeta would have to be kept far away from her mother. Hell, for all Saleema knew, Terelle might be planning some kind of murder and suicide plot so she and Keeta could be reunited in death with Marquise.

"Terelle, I can't let you upset Keeta with that crazy talk. I don't want to hurt you, girl, but I'd be slacking up on my duty if I didn't do what's best for Keeta. And personally, I don't think it's wise to let her visit you without supervision—"

Terelle's eyes widened in disbelief. "You can't keep Markeeta away from me. I'm her mother!" she shrieked.

"Terelle, I wouldn't deliberately hurt you for nothing in the world. You know I want you and Keeta to be together, but I can't let her see you if you're gonna be trippin'. Listen," Saleema said softly. "I'll bring Keeta tomorrow—on one condition."

"Oh, it's like that?" Terelle stared icily, her voice was steel. "Okay, what's the condition?"

Saleema hesitated. Unable to look her friend in the eyes, she spoke with her eyes downcast. "You can't bring up Quise's name." It hurt Saleema to her heart to cause her best friend this degree of pain. But she was doing it for Keeta.

Breaking into Saleema's musing, Terelle cleared her throat. "Marquise said he left a message on my answering machine—"

Saleema's eyes bugged out; she nearly choked. She thought back to the day she heard Marquise's last message. She tried to erase his voice, but she found out later, while listening to Terelle's other messages, that in her haste and grief, all she'd done was fast forward the tape. And she still had the old tape locked in a safety deposit box. But how could Terelle possibly know? She shot Terelle a look of bewilderment.

"Marquise is alive," Terelle repeated. "Now, bring me the tape."

onvinced her jaw was broken, Kai put in two requests to have her injury treated at the prison's infirmary. Both requests were denied. Apparently, nothing that was less than life-threatening qualified as an emergency situation behind prison walls. The pain was excruciating and unrelenting. It hurt to open her mouth. It hurt when she tried to close it. It hurt to chew. It hurt to talk. And it hurt her—no, traumatized her— every time she ran into Taffy and her two cohorts.

That very morning as Kai and a stream of fellow inmates lined up for the standard prison-cafeteria breakfast, the barbaric trio sauntered over. As Kai collected her tray—a cold pack consisting of cereal, milk, and bread—and turned to make her way to her table, Taffy blocked her path.

"Lemme get that tray," Taffy demanded. There was a chuckle in her voice but her eyes were deadly and cold. "You can't eat nuffin with your jaw cracked and everything." Preening for the crowd of onlookers, Taffy gestured excessively.

She was absolutely right. Kai couldn't eat and had no qualms about giving up the unappetizing meal. Being that it was painful to speak, Kai handed Taffy the tray without uttering a word.

Insulted by her silence, Taffy leaned back in indignation. "Oh! You gon' act like you don't know me now?"

Even if she were inclined to speak, Kai couldn't respond. Her jaw was not functioning; it felt out of alignment.

"Oh, aiight, it's like that now. You knew me pretty good when you had your tongue stuck up my hole." Boisterous laughter followed that remark.

Angry and humiliated, Kai maneuvered around Taffy. She wanted to run, but in prison there was no escape. Desperate for assistance, she looked in the direction of the two guards who were supposed to maintain the peace. Engrossed in a personal conversation, the male and female correctional officers on duty, didn't give Kai as much as a glance.

Up to this point, Kai had made the best out of prison life. Having an overactive libido and a kitty cat that preferred the feeling of a stiff dick made it difficult for her to rely on other women to fulfill her sex needs. Over the past two years, never once did Kai have to coerce anyone into giving her oral pleasure. Dozens and dozens of female inmates lined up to lick her cat. Kai's kitty was in such high demand, there were numerous times when the horny female prisoners fought over the opportunity to give her head. So where were all her adoring pussy lickers now that she could use some backup?

The sad answer came to Kai as she sat down at the cafeteria table. Her relationship with Mookie had made a lot of women extremely jealous. No amount of pussy licking, finger fucking, or clit bumping could compare to Mookie's good-fucking dick. During the time that Mookie had been serving it up, Kai was forced to ration out her goods, allowing the horny, pathetic women only limited access to her pretty kitty.

Now seated at the table, Kai searched for a degree of compassion in the faces of her tablemates.

"Payback's a bitch," snarled Sasha, a manly, well-muscled, brown-skinned woman who used to write Kai desperate love letters daily.

Kai took another look around, but was met with hateful glares and looks of disgust. Distraught, she dropped her head, anxiously twirling a lock of curly hair. She was damaged goods, befouled and tainted by Taffy. No one would help her. And now with Mookie out of the picture, what the hell was she supposed to do about her sexual needs? Masturbate? *Of course not!* That was a preposterous notion. With a prison filled with hard-up, over-sexed women, why should she have to resort to self-pleasuring?

A sudden stirring made Kai raise her head. Taffy and company were headed toward her table. Hoping that a lack of acknowledgment would make them go away, Kai quickly lowered her head.

No such luck. Taffy slammed the ill-gotten breakfast tray down on the table. She grabbed a handful of Kai's hair and yanked her head up. "Who you think you are? The prison princess or somebody?" Taffy broke out in malicious laughter and then tightened her grip on Kai's hair, giving Kai's head two hard yanks. The head yanks were nothing compared to what the jostling of her head was doing to her jaw. Tears of pain clouded Kai's eyes.

"See, that's your problem, bitch," Taffy ranted. "You think you too good to associate with us. You acted so high and mighty, you had bitches taking numbers just to taste your pussy." Taffy released Kai's hair.

"I got an announcement to make." Taffy cleared her throat meaningfully. "Y'all shouldn't let her pretty face fool you," she told the onlookers who appeared riveted by the hostile encounter. "She ain't nuffin but a stone-cold slut. A nymphomaniac. I ain't lyin'! Bitch had all y'all thinkin' she didn't believe in eating pussy. That was game." Taffy curled her lips in disgust. "This bitch was grubbin' on my pussy like she was at Red Lobster. Sucking so hard, I thought she was trying to suck out my ovaries and shit. Bitch got a tongue so long, it scared the shit out of me. I ain't lying. She was diggin' up in my coochie so damn deep, felt like it was all up in my stomach." Taffy observed the incredulity on the faces of her audience. "I ain't lyin'," she repeated and held up her right hand in earnest. "Shit felt so good, my legs got to shaking and the next thing I knew, my thighs was clamped around the bitch's face so tight I heard something go *crack!* I was like—dayum, I done broke the nympho's jawbone. "

At this point, Taffy had the whole room, including the correctional officers, convulsing in loud guffaws. "But hold up, y'all," Taffy told her amused audience. "Even after I felt her jaw break, I couldn't stop workin' it." Taffy gyrated lewdly, demonstrating how she molested Kai. "But, check it, y'all—that shit was feelin' too damn good to stop. Wasn't nothing gon' keep me from getting mine. I ain't release her face from my death grip 'til I busted about three or four big-ass nuts."

Though Kai tried her best to block the sound of the roaring laughter, she couldn't. The sound reverberated all around her, echoed inside her head. How she loathed Taffy and the other two callous attackers. The pair who had restrained her while Taffy had sexually abused her reminded Kai of salivating hyenas.

"Hurry up and get your jaw fixed so you can give me some brain, too," said one of the hyenas. "Can't they wire it at the infirmary?"

"Probably," the other hyena replied. "But she owes me some brain, too." The grinning hyena hunched over and cupped her crotch as if it ached to be satisfied.

"How y'all figure that shit?" Taffy blurted.

"We helped you get yours, now it's our turn."

"Y'all trippin'. The other night was payback for Terelle. That bitch still owes me for Marquise. Shit, the way she killed my nigga, she gon' have to come out of pocket and bankroll a bitch. Y'all feel me?" Taffy asked the room at large. Another eruption of raucous laughter indicated that every person present had taken sides with Taffy, which prompted her to take her threat up a notch. "What they call that shit, you know when you have to come out of pocket for some rank shit you did? Oh, yeah… restitution! I'm gon' stay on that ass 'til she pays off the restitution she owes me for fuckin' with my southwest niggas."

The bizarre scenario had taken a grotesque turn. Had Kai been able to open her mouth, she would have shouted, "*I did not kill Marquise Whitsett*," at the top of her lungs. She'd screamed her innocence inside the courtroom but she'd been found guilty. Wasn't it bad enough that the judicial system had failed her? Now a demented prisoner, who was not even a blood relative of Marquise Whitsett or Terelle Chambers for chrissakes, was demanding restitution of all things! Could her life get any worse?

"Whatchu did to Quise is gon' cost you some money *and* some brain," Taffy told Kai. "But I ain't feelin' no quick shot in the dark in the back of the kitchen." Taffy shook her head emphatically. "Naw, baby. Not this time." A teasing light danced in Taffy's eyes as she tangled her fingers in Kai's hair. "Me and you gon' need some long-term, private playtime." She spoke in a low, seductive voice. Then Taffy threw a glance at the two correctional officers. "Can y'all see about making her my new celly?"

*Her celly!* Kai felt her chest constrict in fear. A feeling of dread consumed her. Her life had most definitely taken a turn for the worse.

"We could probably work something out, ain't that right, Porter?" said the boxy female correctional officer to her partner, a lean male officer. Porter had a boyishly handsome face with a neatly trimmed mustache. Based on his wholesome appearance, Kai hoped he'd have some degree of honor—of humanity and come to her rescue.

"For a price," Porter replied, dashing Kai's hope. "But she's out of commission," he said, focusing his gaze on Kai. "What's the point in keeping her in your cell if she can't do anything?"

Kai felt at once hopeful and disgusted by Porter's logic.

"Her mouth might not be working, but ain't nuffin wrong with her pussy," Taffy told Porter sassily. "Me and her gon' have to bump pussies all night 'til she gets herself together."

Amazingly, Porter nodded as if Taffy's warped reasoning made perfect sense. Kai felt ill as she listened to Taffy's and the correctional officers' scheme. Revolted by the thought of having to suffer the stench of Taffy's vagina again and terrified to the point of feeling nauseous, Kai's hand flew to her mouth, but not soon enough to stop the gush of vomit that spewed across the table, splattering a few of her tablemates.

"No, the fuck she didn't," shouted a furious inmate, as she gawked at the reddish-colored vomit that had landed on her arm.

"We need to stomp that nasty bitch," another female inmate cried out as she grabbed a napkin and wiped a bit of gook off her neck.

Now faced with the double threat of being handed over and locked in a cell with Taffy as well as being stomped by a mob of vomit-covered inmates, Kai felt herself growing faint while the angry crowd jeered her. Through the haze, just before her vision dimmed, she saw the bloodthirsty looks on their faces.

Kai suddenly slumped over and then tumbled out of her chair, passed out cold on the hard, concrete floor.

Kai regained consciousness inside the prison infirmary. She was handcuffed, which wasn't surprising, but to her astonishment she lay atop an examining table, naked beneath a coarse white sheet. The handcuffs were painfully tight and she had no idea why she needed to be nude to have her jaw examined. Still, Kai appreciated being spared the horror of being thrown like a piece of meat into a cage with the ravenous Taffy. And she was exceedingly grateful to finally receive the medical attention she desperately needed.

A rotund figure wearing a white lab jacket entered the room. "Oh, great. You finally decide to wake up," said an annoyed, pudgy, middle-aged man who Kai assumed was the staff doctor. He was totally gross-looking with greasy, thinning, dark-gray hair that was pulled back into a ridiculous ponytail. "My shift is almost over, but I suppose I have time to give you a quick pelvic exam." The doctor gave a long, tired sigh.

*Pelvic exam!* Kai gawked at the doctor in alarm. Her eyes darted about anxiously. Frantic, she blubbered unintelligibly, trying to convey that she didn't need a pelvic exam; she had a broken jaw, dammit. Couldn't the quack of a doctor see that her face was swollen? What the hell was wrong with the idiot?

Ignoring Kai's expression and murmurs of panic, the doctor flung off the top sheet. That single action caused the overweight man to breathe heavily. His blotchy, hanging jowls shook. His belly, which hung over his belt, quivered considerably. Looking like an ill-tempered Santa, the doctor peered at Kai with intense blue eyes and then patted her mons pubis. "Spread your legs," he told her in a grumpy voice.

Slowly and determinedly, Kai tried her best to communicate her problem, but the doctor didn't even make an attempt to decipher the gibberish that spilled from her lips.

Without bothering to snap on a pair of surgical gloves, the doctor squeezed lubricant into the palm of his bare hand. With his other hand, he tapped Kai's kneecap, continuing his unreasonable insistence that Kai spread her legs. "I guess it's hard on you girls to have to go so long without an intimate relationship with a man," the doctor said, sounding illogically sympathetic. "I guess I'm pretty much the only male you girls can legitimately have any type of sexual contact with. Now, spread your legs," he repeated irritably.

Deciding an abusive pelvic exam was preferable to having to deal with a pack of bloodthirsty inmates, Kai parted her thighs for the perverted prison doctor.

The doctor inserted a well-lubricated finger. Though Kai was completely appalled by the loathsome physician, an unexpected moan escaped her lips after the disgusting doctor inserted his thick finger, twisting and snaking it inside her vagina, giving her immense pleasure. The incredible sensation of his undulating finger served as a temporary painkiller for the prolonged aching that emanated from her lower jaw.

Kai rode the doctor's finger. As if it were a dick, she clenched her walls around it and lifted her hips to take in more. Moaning, she thrust forward, encouraging the doctor to drive his chubby finger in all the way to the hilt.

Perspiring and panting as if he were giving Kai a hard fuck, the doctor's paunchy jowls and belly shook as he pounded Kai with his finger. "You dirty prison bitches are so sneaky. You pretend to be sick so you can get in my examining room and suck my cock. Is that what you want to do?" he demanded as he gave Kai a hard finger thrust.

Unable to speak, and inexplicably aroused even more by the doctor's obscene insults, Kai could only grunt in response. She arched her back and shuddered as knives of pleasure ripped through her.

The doctor hastily withdrew his finger while Kai was still in the throes of an orgasm. She could have smacked him for that. He sniffed the finger that glistened from Kai's secretions. "Smells clean, but I can't take any chances. You could be afflicted with genital warts or herpes. And your mouth… well, let's just say that orifice can be as germ-ridden as a filthy vagina. Guard!" the doctor bellowed.

A stone-faced C.O. whom Kai had never seen and who apparently had been waiting in the corridor, hurried inside the examining room.

"Unlock the cuffs."

The guard cut a suspicious glance at Kai.

"It's okay. She's not going to give me any trouble," the doctor assured the correctional officer.

The tall, black man walked across the small room. He had ordinary facial features, but an extraordinary physique. He appraised Kai's naked body with unmasked lust before he unlocked the handcuffs. Kai had considered grunting out an S.O.S. to the correctional officer, but judging by the brazen, lingering look the man gave her, it was clear that he and the doctor were in cahoots.

"I'll call you when I'm done," the doctor told the correctional officer. At the doctor's orders, the C.O. left the room.

At the sound of the closing door, the doctor quickly unzipped his pants and released an erect penis with pre-cum bubbling out of the tip. "He's ready." His words were accompanied by rapid, lustful breaths. He was breathing so hard, Kai thought the stout doctor was in the throes of a massive heart attack.

"Use your hand," the doctor panted. "Lube it up," he told Kai in gasping breaths as he reached for a container of lubricant. "Work him over good." The doctor glided his own hand over his shaft, his eyes glinting in lustful expectation.

It only took a few squishy strokes to get the doctor off. Just before he spurted out cum over Kai's closed fist, the doctor's eyelids fluttered; his eyes actually rolled to the back of his head. What a despicable degenerate!

"By the way, I examined your jaw while you were knocked out. It's dislocated. I guess you hit that concrete floor pretty hard," he said knowingly. "You're lucky it wasn't fractured or broken. Since you girls love to do each other such bodily harm, instead of bringing you here for treatment, the state should throw you all in a pit and let you battle to the death. Like the gladiators," he said with a chuckle.

Kai's attitude toward the doctor quickly changed from disgust to appreciation when he said, "Sit still so I can reposition your jaw." Firmly, he held the mandible on both sides, pushing gently downward and rocking backward until a loud popping sound indicated Kai's jaw was back in its proper position. "There you go. You're as good as new," he told Kai cheerfully.

Surprisingly, Kai could open and close her mouth with ease.

"Thank you!" she said earnestly, appreciative that she no longer had to grunt like an animal when she attempted to communicate. The sound of her clearly enunciated words was music to her ears.

"No point in keeping you overnight. I'll let the guard escort you back to your cell."

Kai's expression of elation shifted to sheer panic. She had no desire to go back to the cell block to be mauled by Taffy and company. In fact, now that Kai was out of pain and could think straight, she intended to stay in the safety of the infirmary for as long as possible.

"But my face…it's still swollen. And it hurts," she complained, rubbing her swollen cheek.

"We can apply an ice pack for an hour or so. But I can't keep you here much longer than that. Guard!" the doctor barked again. The buff correctional officer materialized in an instant. Checking the time, the doctor looked down at his wrist. "I'm allowing the patient to apply an ice pack to her injury. Escort her back to her cell in an hour." The doctor hastily retrieved an ice pack from a small refrigerator and tossed it to Kai.

"Sure thing, doc," the correctional officer said to the staff doctor as he quickly retreated from the room.

# Chapter 5

S aleema was stunned when Terelle demanded that she bring the tape. She had no idea how Terelle knew about Marquise's last words—his final declaration of love. She scanned her memory, trying to recall if she'd blurted out the secret while her best friend was comatose. No, she would have never uttered a word about the tape. So, why had she kept it for the past two years? Why had she gone so far as to transfer it from tape to CD? *For Terelle*, Saleema reminded herself. If Terelle woke up and seemed strong enough to handle it, she had planned to let her friend know how much Marquise really loved her and Markeeta. Saleema gave a sigh. Well, the no-good cheating bastard *claimed* that he loved them, she thought cynically.

Saleema had figured that hearing Quise speak of future plans that included her and Markeeta might be a comfort to Terelle. She knew her best friend would be more than willing to forget all the emotional torture Marquise had caused her. She'd forgive him for being the lying, cheating, whoremonger he'd been.

Saleema grimaced at the memory of her and Terelle gasping in shock as they witnessed Marquise shamelessly eating that half-white bitch's pussy. He'd done it right outside in the darkened parking garage. It was too much for Terelle. Hell, it was too much for Saleema, which was why she shoved her gun into Terelle's hand. Terelle was aiming for that high-yella slut, but she'd shot and killed Marquise, her fiancé, by mistake. Unable to deal with reality, Terelle had a mental breakdown. She'd been a damn vegetable for the past two years and Saleema was forced to helplessly watch her friend deteriorate.

As far as Saleema was concerned, both she and Terelle had paid in full for their part in Marquise Whitsett's death. And that Oreo bitch, Kai Montgomery, had gotten exactly what she deserved, life in prison. Saleema felt no remorse for Kai's unjust imprisonment. That man-stealing slut deserved to serve two lifetimes for fucking up Terelle's life.

Last night, when Saleema downloaded the CD to an iPod, so Terelle could listen in private, she could only pray that her best friend wouldn't relapse after hearing Marquise's last words.

"Good morning," Saleema greeted Terelle, who sat in a chair near the window in her room.

Terelle gave Saleema a half-hearted, "Hey."

"How're you feelin' today?"

"Fine," Terelle said dully.

"I talked to your Aunt Bennie. She's so excited, she wanted to come to see you right away, but I figured you weren't ready for any company so I pretended that you were still pretty bad off. I told her to wait a week or so. Is that okay?"

Terelle nodded. "How's my mom? Does she know?"

"No, she doesn't know. She's pretty much the same, still hitting the pipe, in and out of rehab. She's been missing for a coupla weeks, but you know Miss Cassy, she'll turn up sooner or later."

Terelle winced in memory at the awful beat-down she'd given her mother when her mother told her Marquise was dead. *I'm sorry, Mom.* Despite her inability to love Terelle more than she loved drugs, Cassandra Chambers was still her mother and Terelle loved her unconditionally. If the day ever came when her mother wanted to live life clean and sober, Terelle would welcome her into her life with open arms. "Where's Markeeta?" Her voice caught when she spoke her daughter's name.

"In school; I'll bring her tonight."

Terelle nodded. "Did you bring the tape?"

Saleema pulled the iPod from her crystal-pink Juicy Couture handbag. Silently and against her better judgment, she helped Terelle adjust the iPod ear buds. If Terelle had a relapse, she'd only have herself to blame. She should have erased the damn tape when she had the chance, Terelle would have been fine with old photos of Marquise.

With nervous eyes fastened on her friend, Saleema swallowed hard and then tapped Play.

*This is Quise.*

The first three words of Marquise's last recorded message sent shockwaves through Terelle's system. Blinking back tears, she listened to her beloved's voice.

*I know you mad, babe. You got every right to be. But believe me, I got a good explanation for all the bullshit I done put you through. Babe... look...this is the deal. I got involved with this crazy jawn. She's rich... but she's scattered like a muthafucker. I'm talkin' fatal attraction crazy. She been threatenin' to have both of us locked up. She been talkin' all kinds of crazy shit 'bout that damn watch. Yeah, I lied about the watch. I told you the Jamaicans gave it to me. But check this...she thinks she can buy me. So, I'm gonna run some game and act like I'm wit it. Tonight we gon' pick up this fly-ass truck I talked her into*

*buyin' for me. I woulda had it yesterday, but it wasn't ready. She paid
for it in cash and I made sure she put it in my name. I want you to pack
up yours and Keeta's shit 'cause after I git the keys to the truck, we gon'
be the fuck out. We can drive down south somewhere and start all over.
Fuck Philly. Philly don't offer a nigga nothin' but jail time or death.
I'm tired of bein' a fuck-up; I'm through lyin' and cheatin' on you. It's
a wrap, babe; count on it. I'm a family man now; I'm through wit the
streets. You hear me, babe? I said it's a wrap; I swear on my life. I love
you. But you know me…I can show you better than I can tell you. Put
on something sexy, aiight? I'll be home tonight.*

Tears streamed down Terelle's cheeks and by the time she
pressed Stop, she was sobbing. "I told you he's alive, Saleema.
He told me he left me a message on my answering machine."

Saleema raised a doubtful brow.

"If Quise didn't tell me, then explain how I knew about the tape,"
Terelle wondered aloud, sniffling and swiping at her wet cheeks.

Saleema shook her head. "I don't know. I've tried to make
sense of all this." Saleema shrugged. "You know I don't believe
in no supernatural, hocus pocus bullshit, but the only conclusion I can come up with is maybe Quise's spirit came to you in a
dream or something." She threw up her hands, exasperated. "I
really don't know what to think, Terelle."

Terelle turned tear-filled eyes on Saleema. "You know me,
Saleema. You know I'm not crazy. Yeah, I flipped out over Quise.
Mentally, I let go. With everybody trying to convince me that
he was dead when I knew in my heart he wasn't, I guess I just
snapped."

Saleema nodded solemnly. "Terelle," she said in a whisper.
"You told me you remembered shooting Quise, now you're saying he's alive."

Terelle nodded. "Yes, I remember what I said and I remember hearing the shot and seeing him fall." Terelle took in a deep breath. "It's a miracle; Quise is alive." She shuddered at the wonder of it all and then her expression hardened. "I was so mad at him. Marquise was…" Her speech faltered as she recalled the hot anger that coursed through her when she remembered what Marquise was doing to that uppity social worker, Kai Montgomery. "I remember that I was trying to shoot that…"

"…that bitch," Saleema filled in.

"Yeah. That bitch." It was a painful memory. Tears brimmed in Terelle's eyes at the reminder of Marquise down on his knees, giving Kai oral sex. "But I forgive him," she uttered. "Through all the hell Marquise put me through, the lying and cheating, I never stopped loving him. Not for a second. And I've never once doubted that he loves me. What I feel for him—the kind of forgiving, unconditional love I've always had for him—is something I don't expect anyone to understand."

As she replayed Terelle's words in her mind, Saleema fell silent for a few moments. "If he's alive like you say, then why is he acting so weird and everything—slipping in and out of here like a ghost? That's creepy, not like Quise at all. The Quise I knew would have come through like gangbusters, demanding to see you. He would have turned this place out if anyone had the nerve to tell him he couldn't."

A tiny smile curved the corners of Terelle's mouth as she pictured her thoroughly thugged-out fiancé causing a commotion. "I don't know why he's acting so mysterious, but it definitely has something to do with him needing people to believe he's dead," she said, mystified and shaking her head. "But believe me, the next time he comes through, I'm going to be wide awake, waiting for him."

❖❖❖

Though Terelle was expecting Saleema and Markeeta, their entrance caught her off guard, left her breathless. Overwhelmed by seeing her daughter in the flesh, Terelle pressed her hands against her chest. Her heart pounded in excitement and threatened to burst with pride. Markeeta had grown into quite the little lady. At four and a half years old, she was dainty and appeared to possess a quiet, prim demeanor. There was a dignity, a maturity about her that defied her four and a half years.

"This is Markeeta," Saleema announced brightly.

"Oh, my God! Look at my big girl," Terelle exclaimed. "Come here, baby." Ready to embrace her daughter, hug her tight and cover her face with kisses, Terelle held out wide open arms.

But Markeeta didn't rush into her mother's arms; she remained by Saleema's side. "Hello. It's nice to meet you, Terelle. I hope you're feeling better," Markeeta said to her mother.

"That's your mother, don't call her by her first name," Saleema chastised Markeeta. Stubbornly stoic, Markeeta didn't correct herself.

Markeeta's words were carefully enunciated and well expressed, far surpassing what Terelle would have expected from a four-year-old, but she was saddened by the lack of emotion in her daughter's crisp tone, and heartbroken by Markeeta's unwillingness to call her Mommy. But what could she expect? Markeeta didn't remember her. She felt no attachment to her mother. Markeeta had spouted polite words—stiff pleasantries one would bestow upon an overly affectionate, distant relative.

Terelle looked her daughter over, taking her in completely. She was still the spitting image of her father, but she was even more beautiful than she'd been as a toddler. Under the guardianship of Saleema, as expected, Markeeta was swathed in designer kiddy apparel. From the fancy bows in her hair down to her shoes, she was the height of fashion. She even had an expensive-looking handbag draped over her shoulder.

"Well, Saleema. I have to give you credit. My daughter is dressed to the nines." Terelle chuckled, trying to break up the tension in the room—tension that she'd created by expecting Markeeta to overlook her two-year absence and embrace her as if she'd been gone for only a few days.

"Yeah, she's rocking a Juicy Couture dress," Saleema bragged, and pointed to Markeeta's extremely cute, rose-colored cotton knit dress. "Her shoes and bag are Prada, of course," Saleema added.

Terelle gazed down at her daughter's feet and sure enough, the metallic strap on Markeeta's Mary Janes boasted the Prada label.

"You dress a four-year-old in Prada!"

"Sure do. But Keeta isn't just cute eye candy. She's being educated at an exclusive private girl's school. My godbaby has brains, beauty and a killer wardrobe."

Other than Markeeta's remarkable resemblance to her father, there wasn't a hint of the toddler Terelle had left behind. Feeling out of the loop of her daughter's life, Terelle was overcome with envy and far too threatened by Markeeta's attachment to Saleema to fully appreciate the remarkable job Saleema had done in raising her child.

As if detecting Terelle's feelings, Saleema gave Markeeta a pat on the back. "Go give your mommy a hug," she prompted.

Hesitantly, Markeeta took the few steps to the chair by the window. Terelle pulled her daughter into her arms and hugged her so tight, she had to release her for fear she'd crack her baby's tiny rib cage. In the short duration of the embrace, Terelle inhaled her daughter's hair, took in her familiar scent. Amazingly, her child not only looked like Marquise, she also smelled like her father.

# Chapter 6

The correctional officer locked the door to the examining room. Being turned over to the hot C.O. was the kind of punishment Kai could get into. With her jaw back to normal and the pain substantially lessened, a good fuck would calm her nerves. She had every intention of spending the night in the safe environment of the infirmary and had no doubt the C.O. would give in to her demand. After all, she wasn't any ordinary prisoner. She was Kai Montgomery, stunningly beautiful, even in prison garb and with badly-cared-for hair. After a good night's sleep, she'd be able to strategize a defense against Taffy and company. She'd have to remind the C.O.s on her cell block that siding with Taffy would garner them only chump change at best. She'd remind them that she was an heiress, the privileged daughter of a renowned surgeon. Since no one knew that Kai's biological mother had absconded with her funds and they certainly had no idea that her wealthy adoptive parents had disinherited her, she'd bribe them with promises. Oh hell, she'd give them a portion of the monthly miserly allowance her parents kept on her books. Compared to that of the other prisoners, her monthly pittance was a king's ransom.

Kai allowed her gaze to wander over the C.O.'s body. Her

imagination ran wild and the corners of her mouth curled devil-ishly as she imagined concrete thighs with a long, juicy dick swinging between them.

Kai held out her wrists in mock surrender. "Aren't you gonna cuff me, Mr. C.O.?" she asked, her voice sultry.

"My name's Jason, baby. In answer to your question, naw, I'm not gonna cuff you right now. We can get into something kinky later," the correctional officer said, his eyes sparking with sexual interest. When he unbuttoned and removed his shirt, Kai was reminded of both Mookie and her Marquise. Like Mookie, the man was buff to the bone with bulging muscles that rippled down his shoulders and arms. His skin was a smooth dark chocolate that appeared to be the exact shade of brown as Marquise's.

To her sheer delight, Jason was as well hung as both Marquise and Mookie—the only two black men she'd ever been sexed by. Kai was mesmerized by the sight of his dark throbbing man-hood. She pinched the rosy tips of her sensitive nipples to see if she was dreaming.

He stroked his dick, which amazingly lengthened right in front of Kai's appreciative eyes. "By the time I start filling you up with all these inches, you're gonna start screaming and want to dig your nails in my back, grip the sheets, or hold on to something. I know one thing, you're gonna be glad I let you have full use of your hands," he bragged as he got on the bed and straddled Kai.

Still moist from being finger-fucked, Kai didn't want to bother with foreplay. Preparing for a magnificent joyride, she took a deep breath and opened her legs wide.

Jason wasn't just a lot of talk. Nor was he just another big dick. He was a master of the bedroom, or in this case, the examining room. He was giving Kai such a superb work-over, the sensation of his thickness inside her was like a live wire pressing against her raw nerve endings, inciting her to release a series of soft moans and then loud cries of pleasure. He rocked her body, pumping it with pleasure until ripples of ecstasy flowed through her, making her thrust wildly, jerk, and scream.

"Be quiet," he cautioned and placed a firm hand over Kai's mouth, muffling her sounds of passion. And though he successfully muted Kai's screams and moans, the creaking of the examining table was a dead giveaway that something more than a medical procedure was taking place in the room.

When Kai felt the beginning of an orgasm, she reflexively pulled Jason closer. Now in the throes of a massive climax, her body trembled and shook beneath the guard's severe pounding. He picked up the pace, his breathing became labored as he drove himself into her furiously until his swollen length was embedded deeply inside her. Kai wrapped her legs around his waist, locking them together groin-to-groin, making sure the C.O. felt her shuddering, clenching spasms. Groaning in blissful agony, Jason released a splashing flood of molten juices.

Finally spent and glowing in the aftermath of good sex, Kai sighed in complete contentment. Jason's chest heaved up and down as he lay on his side, a fine sheen of perspiration covering his muscular body.

Determining that a show of affection might garner additional rewards, such as a pass to the infirmary whenever she needed to escape from her cell block, Kai turned to Jason and ran her hands over his steely shoulders and chest. She smoothed away the moisture from his cheeks and forehead and began to cover his face with tiny kisses.

Pulling back from her kisses, he propped himself up on an

elbow. "You ready to get kinky?" he asked, with an intense look in his eyes.

Always in the mood to get her freak on but also desiring to linger in the infirmary for as long as possible, Kai responded with a sexy wink.

"Okay, but we're gonna have to find another spot. The cleaning guy comes here around this time every night," he said, glancing quickly at his watch. "Put your jumpsuit back on," he said, grabbing his uniform.

Kai's heart dropped. She didn't want to leave the seclusion of the infirmary. But she didn't want to be caught by a nosey cleaning man and get sent back to her cell, either. Her eyes did an unenthusiastic sweep and landed on her prison garb, which had been tossed in a corner on the floor. She preferred nudity to the orange fashion disaster that lay in a crumbled heap. Reluctantly, Kai put on the jumpsuit and held out her wrists to be hand-cuffed.

"I know somewhere we can go that's real cozy. Nobody around," he said, trying to get Kai back in the mood. "You can make all the noise you want."

Kai laughed. "I wasn't the only one getting loud in here," she teased. "You were pretty noisy yourself."

"You're right," he admitted. "That's why we have to go to a different location. I know a real quiet place." His lips slowly spread into a devilish grin. "Who knows, I might want to try something new. Fuck it, I might as well get real and tell you about my fantasy. You seem like someone I can trust."

Extremely interested in what the C.O. was about to confess, Kai nodded enthusiastically. "You can trust me," she said, encouraging him to continue.

"Well, I have this fantasy…" He paused, a sly smile played at the corner of his lips. "I don't know if my urges would be considered sick…"

"What?" Kai blurted, overcome by curiosity.

"In my fantasy, a female prisoner overpowers me, grabs my weapon, and orders me at gunpoint to put on the cuffs—" He shook his head incredulously, as if he couldn't believe he'd divulged his deepest secret.

Kai's eyes lit up like she'd just uncovered the secret of the Holy Grail. Now, this was the kind of fantasy that she would truly enjoy enacting. Visions of freedom flashed across her mind. If she played her part convincingly, there might actually be an opportunity for her to get her hands on Jason's weapon. She exhaled excitedly at the thought of carrying a loaded gun and blasting her way out of the hellhole that she'd called home for two torturously long years.

Gleefully, Kai accompanied the guard out into the corridor. Provocative images of escape and revenge filled her mind and put a malicious smile on her face.

Two seconds later, they bumped smack into Herman, a corrections officer who worked the evening shift on Kai's cell block. At the sight of Herman's stern face and knowing what his presence represented, Kai's smile slipped away.

"Hey, whassup, Herman," Jason greeted him, his expression sheepish.

"'Sup, man. Damn, if I knew you were bringing her back to the block, I could have saved myself a trip," Herman said agitatedly.

*Back to the block!* Kai froze; she was so afraid, she could actually feel the color draining from her face. Hoping to hear Jason voice a strong objection, Kai immediately turned toward him, but his nonchalant expression made her stomach sink.

"I feel you, man," Jason replied, sucking his teeth and shaking his head. "The communication in here ain't shit." Jason pulled out his key ring and removed his set of handcuffs from Kai's wrists. "Well, here you go. She's all yours, man," he said and nudged Kai toward Herman.

Kai tried to quickly gather her thoughts and arrange them into a coherent and convincing plea, but with the distracting sound of Jason's clinking cuffs, Kai went into fight or flight mode. Her words came out sounding disjointed and crazy. "Wait a minute! You can't do that. I'm not a regular prisoner. Tell him, Jason. Tell him we had a deal…"

Jason and Herman exchanged a knowing glance, a silent acknowledgment that Kai was a kook.

"You can't do this to me," she shrieked. There was more than a hint of insanity in her voice. Possessing a flair for the dramatic, Kai snapped her head back, grimacing as if she'd taken a brutal blow to her injured jaw. Covering the slightly swollen side of her face with her palm, Kai drew in a long breath and released a screech. "Help me! Oh, God! I'm in agony. The pain is excruciating. My jaw hasn't been treated. It could be broken! I can sue the state for malpractice," she blurted hysterically. "You can't send me back to my cell before my jaw's been X-rayed." Kai's pleading eyes darted desperately to Jason. "You know the doctor said I need to stay here overnight," she yelled, imploring Jason to pipe in and corroborate the story she'd concocted on the spot.

"Man, I don't know what the fuck shorty's talking about." Jason shrugged and gave Herman a look that said Kai was certifiably crazy.

"You talkin' a lot of shit for somebody who claims to have a broken jaw," Herman said disgustedly as he unhooked the handcuffs that dangled at his side and tried to snap them onto Kai's wrists.

"Leave me alone!" Kai shrank back. Roughly, Herman jerked her forward. Kai struggled with the husky guard, but he quickly overpowered and cuffed her.

"Ow! They're too tight," she complained, switching her frantic glance from Jason to Herman.

Jason wouldn't meet her gaze. Herman popped her upside the head. "Shut the fuck up, bitch! I heard enough from you," Herman boomed, and then tightened the handcuffs to the point of practically cutting off her circulation. He then gave Kai a hard push.

She stumbled forward a few steps, almost falling, but managed to steady herself. She twisted around to face Jason. "Don't let him take me back there. Do something!"

Seizing Kai by the arm, Herman yanked her toward the stairwell.

She spun around quickly. "Tell him what the doctor said," Kai pleaded with Jason as she struggled to break from Herman's grip.

"The doctor said to take your ass back to your block," Jason replied with a smirk.

Any vestige of hope vanished. No amount of theatrics, bribing, or bartering was going to change this outcome. Kai would soon be in the arena with her vicious tormenters. There was no way she'd let them see her quivering in fear. Composing herself, Kai shook her curls into place, straightened her shoulders, and walked back to her block with the dignity of a queen. Her beauty and privileged background, she told herself, made her a tragic figure much like Marie Antoinette. Yes, she now knew exactly how the badly maligned and misunderstood queen must have felt while on her way to the guillotine.

# Chapter 7

*Oh, no!* The atmosphere was wrong. Every muscle in Kai's body tensed as Herman escorted her down the wide cream-colored corridor with cells on both sides. She looked around in bafflement. This was not her wing. "I thought you were taking me back to my cell," she murmured, frightened by the possibility that her worst nightmare might be coming true. "You can't..." Kai stammered, but Herman pulled her along impatiently. A few minutes later, he stopped in front of a cell with none other than Taffy waiting inside.

"Good looking out!" Taffy told Herman.

"Yeah, make sure you keep the noise down," he advised.

"We gon' take care of business on some real hush-hush shit, ain't that right, baby?" Taffy said and winked at Kai.

"You can't leave me in here with her. I have rights. My father is a wealthy man. When he's through with you, you'll be locked behind bars for life!" Kai ranted at Herman.

"Shut the fuck up!" he shouted, raising his fist. "Keep on running your mouth and I'm gonna let her celly come and help her out. Is that what you want?"

Not relishing the prospect of being double-teamed by Taffy and her cellmate, Kai shook her head hastily.

Being thrown inside a lion's den would have been no less terrifying than being locked inside a cell with Taffy. Though she wore a convincing mask of sanity, Kai had never been emotionally stable; she'd always known that she was hanging on to a thread of rationality. With the urgent need to escape this horrendous situation, Kai gladly welcomed the badly needed and long overdue psychotic breakdown that was slowly overtaking her.

"Take your clothes off and lay your ass down," Taffy ordered, inclining her head toward the bottom bunk.

Kai repressed a strong impulse to run around in circles, screaming like a banshee. She betrayed no sign that she had reached a quiet hysteria that presented as peaceful surrender as she began to undress. Her expression was stoic as she complied.

It was senseless to plead for mercy, to scream at the top of her lungs for help. Any attempt to draw attention to her plight would be futile. No one was going to rescue her, no one cared, and there was no point in putting up a fight she couldn't win. The only way out of this unbearable ordeal was to let go of the precarious hold she had on her last thread of sanity.

"Umph, umph," Taffy muttered, leering at Kai as she lay nude and vulnerable on the bunk.

Taffy tore off her prison garb and quickly joined Kai on the lower bunk. Lying beside Kai, she caressed her face and ran her fingers through Kai's mop of curly hair.

"We ain't gotta rush 'cause ain't nobody coming in here 'til just before shift change in the morning," Taffy said while trailing a finger across Kai's lips. There was a happy lilt in Taffy's voice as if she had given Kai the best news of the day.

Then her expression became serious and her voice went from soft to gruff. "I had to give that C.O. and his friends a lot of cake to have a private pajama party with you. So you know I won't hesitate to put my foot up your ass if that's what it takes to make you fuck me right," Taffy threatened, her eyes narrowed menacingly. "You heard me?" she added harshly. Then her voice softened. "If you would stop acting like you too good for somebody and hurry up and choose me for your woman, we could both enjoy ourselves on the regular. But for now, we just gonna relax, take our time, and give each other a whole lotta pleasure." Taffy bent her head; her puffy, unattractive face loomed over Kai. "You a pretty muthafucker, you know that?"

Kai wanted to scrunch her face up into a fierce scowl and defiantly jerk her head away from Taffy's foul, hot breath, but fearing harsh repercussions such as a smashed jaw, broken teeth, or busted lips, she nodded in agreement. Yes, it was tragic but true; her unquestionable beauty was now a curse, making her a target for an uncouth heathen like Taffy.

Taffy stuffed a plump finger inside Kai's mouth. "Suck it! That shit turns me on."

*Ugh!* Merely hearing such a deplorable request warranted an instant and complete nervous breakdown. Miserably, Kai sucked Taffy's finger and eagerly awaited the first sign that she'd fallen over the abyss into insanity. But nothing happened. She was still cognizant and very much aware of the repugnant act she was forced to do.

Taffy's name suggested chewy candy, sweet molasses. Her finger, however, had nothing in common with her name. It tasted bitter. Unclean. Disgusting.

"Mmm," Taffy moaned softly as she slipped her index finger in and out of Kai's mouth while she gyrated against Kai's crotch. Taffy withdrew her slimy finger and replaced it with her tongue.

The thick, slimy tongue tasted far worse than the finger. Feeling the need to buy time while she waited for her well-deserved mental collapse, Kai pretended to be aroused by her tormentor's kiss. She faked hard breathing as Taffy passionately snaked her sour-tasting tongue inside Kai's mouth. It was a revolting act, but keeping Taffy sexually engaged was preferable to enduring any more bodily harm.

She wondered how her break from reality would manifest. Would she flip out of the bed and go into convulsions, kicking and twitching while frothing at the mouth? Would she quietly succumb to absolute darkness, or would her body suddenly go rigid and catatonic from the trauma of being forced to participate in such a despicable kiss?

Taffy became so worked up, she broke the kiss and announced breathlessly, "Damn, girl. You look good; you kiss good—umph! You gon' have to suck my pussy real quick. I need something to take the edge off, feel me? But when you get to my clit, I want you to lick it real slow and sexy, know what I mean?"

Thrilled at the prospect of having Kai eat her pussy, Taffy scooted excitedly toward Kai's face. "I ain't never mess around with a woman 'til I got in here. Now, I'm hooked! After I bust a nut, I'm gon' take my time with you—make sweet love for hours. And after we get our sexy on, we gon' cuddle up for a while, then I'm gon' let you pop some of these pimples on my back." Taffy twisted around slightly, revealing patches of dark, hardened bumps near her shoulders and the center of her back.

Kai's face contorted in disgust as she considered the revolting options Taffy had just presented. Meanwhile, Taffy worked her groin up to Kai's chin, brushed her pubis against it, and then reacquainted her pussy with Kai's lips.

"Eat my pussy," Taffy whispered cajolingly. She gyrated against Kai's mouth, her slimy slit forcing Kai's lips to open. Taffy's pussy made thick, squishy sounds while emitting an odor more rank than Kai remembered from the previous sexual assault.

Heaving, Kai recoiled. Anything that smelled that bad had to be infested with a plethora of STDs. Repulsed, Kai pressed her lips together tightly. At any moment, she was about to become violently ill. Having only recently recovered from Taffy's brutality, Kai was deathly afraid of the much larger woman.

"Eat my pussy!" Taffy demanded. Her voice, low and guttural, was more insistent. Her command rang in Kai's ears. Still, no amount of fear could persuade Kai to insert her tongue inside Taffy's reeking pussy. It was absolutely out of the question. In her mind, she cried out against another sexual assault. She couldn't do it. She wouldn't do it, dammit. And that was emphatically that!

Knowing that Taffy would delight in delivering a vicious beat-down, Kai's survival instinct took over. She became acutely aware of the only weapon available—her teeth.

It didn't occur to her that she had finally toppled over the edge of sanity as she savagely bit into Taffy's flesh. She didn't know or care which part of Taffy's vagina her teeth sank into. *Eat my pussy!* Kai was operating on survival instinct alone as she savagely chomped into the soft, mushy vaginal flesh. *Eat my pussy!* Now, unconcerned about contracting an infection, Kai was giving Taffy exactly what she asked for.

Too shocked to scream, Taffy gave a surprised gasp. It was a throaty, croaking sound. Taffy began to squawk as her body jerked, but Kai mercilessly ground her teeth into the soft flesh, tasting blood as she tore away and spit out a piece of Taffy's labia.

Finally able to inject strength into her vocal cords, Taffy gave a sharp yelp, which quickly escalated to a long and loud scream. Unfortunately for Taffy, she'd paid the prison guards to turn a deaf ear to any sounds that might emanate from her cell. Her anguished cry went ignored. The correctional officers, assuming Kai was crying for their help, ignored the yelling and went about their business. One flipped through a magazine and the other roared into a cell phone, engaged in a heated argument with his wife.

Incredible pain tore through Taffy's groin, briefly immobilizing her. Fearing for her very life, Taffy sat up and swung punches at Kai's head. But because she was weakened and disoriented by the agony of having her genitalia maimed and mangled, Taffy's aim was off. Most of her punches didn't connect and those that did were cushioned by Kai's abundant, curly hair. Kai hardly felt the few flimsy blows to her head.

Snarling and growling, Kai bit into the clit she'd been ordered to lick, mauling it viciously.

"Bitch, you fuckin' crazy!" Taffy exploded in pain, her eyes huge at the sight of her blood trickling down the sides of Kai's face. Taffy kicked, wriggled, and thrashed, but like a rabid animal, Kai growled, salivated profusely, but didn't let go. Locking jaws like a pit bull, she put a steely hold on Taffy's clitoris. Kai briefly released the tight clamp she had on Taffy's sensitive bud and then quickly switched from her strong back teeth to her razor-sharp front teeth, tearing off the hood—the thin, protective, outer layer of flesh that covered the clitoris. With all the raw nerve endings of her clitoris exposed, Taffy let out a screechy cry, and then passed out cold.

Having lost her connection with reality, Kai continued the one-sided fight, mauling and mutilating the unconscious woman's vagina. She was oblivious to the fact that something had exploded inside her head and she was finally in the throes of the psychotic breakdown she'd longed for.

The hard, pounding sound of running feet grew louder and closer, but Kai was too caught up in the macabre feast to care. The sound of astonished murmurs and the loud echoing clang of the cell door banging open did not deter her. In fact, it prompted her to deliver more damage. Kai climbed atop her semi-conscious prey and even more viciously tore at the mauled mess that had once been a vagina.

Herman stopped in his tracks. With his mouth hanging open, he observed the slaughter taking place. Rivulets of blood poured from Kai's mouth and streamed down, pooling between Taffy's thighs, staining the battered mattress. "What the fuck!" he shouted.

A female C.O. raced behind Herman. "Goddamn!" she shrieked as she stopped, frozen in place as she witnessed Kai chewing Taffy's vagina. "Oh, dear God! That rich girl's eating her alive. It's a fuckin' bloodbath in here. She's literally eating Taffy's pussy!" The woman covered her mouth, repressing an urge to retch.

The female guard swiveled around and looked toward the corridor. Instinct told her to call for backup, but she couldn't. Questions would be asked. Who had taken the Montgomery woman from the infirmary to Taffy's cell? The female C.O. was in cahoots with Herman and that meant her job was on the line. She and Herman would have to take care of the gruesome situation by themselves.

Despite the presence of the correctional officers, Kai continued the grisly attack. Like a starved beast, she growled as she ripped into Taffy's vulva, biting ferociously and spitting out bloody chunks of flesh.

Repelled and terribly afraid of Kai, who was obviously totally mad, the female C.O. stood close to her male counterpart. Herman had easily wrestled Kai into handcuffs and had forced her into Taffy's cell earlier that evening. Now, despite his muscles and masculine strength, he couldn't break the hold Kai had on Taffy's vulva.

As she began to regain consciousness, Taffy trembled and moaned as Kai held her mangled vaginal flesh tightly between her teeth, ripping what was left to shreds.

Having no choice, Herman produced a canister of pepper spray and delivered two full blasts to the part of Kai's face that was visible.

Kai yelped and rolled off Taffy. She placed her hands in front of her blood-smeared face to protect her eyes from the burning spray. Unfortunately, Taffy's mutilated genitalia were also in the line of the peppery fire. Howling like a tortured animal, Taffy regained full consciousness.

# Chapter 8

B raced against the sink, Terelle gazed into the bathroom mirror and pulled a brush through her impossible tangle of long, wild hair. The hair that curled at her temples, giving the appearance of sideburns, hadn't been trimmed in two years. The hair on her arms, legs, and her head was out of control.

Saleema stood in the doorway of the small bathroom. Her concerned gaze traveled the length of Terelle's body. "When you're feeling up to it, we can go to a black-owned day spa and get pampered. You need a perm, girl. And a fly hairstyle. That ponytail you've been rocking for the past decade ain't gon' get it," she said teasingly. "We'll get you a hot wax job for all that body hair, too. All that crazy hair on your arms and legs is—"

"Marquise always liked the hair on my—"

Not wanting Terelle to go there, Saleema cut her off. "You're wolfin' real bad, girl." Saleema's musical laughter broke the tension that was about to fill the air the moment Terelle spoke Marquise's name. "But seriously, you're making a lot of progress, Terelle. You've improved so much, the social worker here has arranged a discharge planning meeting."

"When?" Terelle asked excitedly.

"Next week. You're expected to attend."

"Discharged to where?" Her voice took on a troubled tone. She'd been so focused on proving that Marquise was alive, she hadn't given much thought to making arrangements for her own future.

"That's what we're going to discuss. You and I have to have a serious talk."

"I guess me and Keeta could go stay with Aunt Bennie until I get myself together."

"I'd invite you to stay with me, but there's something I haven't told you yet."

Terelle gazed at Saleema expectantly. "I can tell you've changed, Saleema." There was no judgment in her tone. She'd simply made a comment.

"For the better, I hope."

"Yes, for the better. You don't seem to have that angry edge anymore and you talk…" Terelle paused to contemplate her next words. "Well, for one thing, you don't cuss like a sailor anymore," she said with a chuckle. "You talk like you've been taking speech classes or something."

"I have. Elocution lessons to soften my ghettoese. I backslide from time to time, but I try to go easy on the Ebonics, too. I quit the business a long time ago. But I'm a kept woman."

Terelle gave her friend a curious look.

"Had to," Saleema explained. "For Keeta's sake. I couldn't represent my girl at her snazzy school, talking like I'm straight from the 'hood."

A look of worry clouded Terelle's face. "I'm not going to be able to keep Markeeta in that expensive school."

"Come and sit down, Terelle," Saleema said softly. "We need to discuss Markeeta."

Taking cautious steps, Terelle crossed the room and sat in the chair near the window. Tears had started forming in her eyes. "Please don't tell me you don't think I'm capable of raising my own daughter?"

"Of course you're capable. You were the best mother..." Saleema's voice trailed off. The word *were* rang loud and clear.

"I could still be a good mother. I just need time."

"I know. Anyway, I've been involved with a very wealthy man. I get more dough from my sugar daddy than I earned running my own outcall service."

"You were running a service for tricks and hoes?"

"Yeah, but that's in the past. My sugar daddy, Franklin, recently dropped a bomb on me. He's divorcing his wife and wants to marry me. As much as I enjoy being single, I'd be a fool to turn down his offer. Being legally entitled to Franklin's dough puts me in an entirely different class. Besides, it might even be nice to finally settle down."

Terelle nodded, finding it hard to imagine Saleema settling down with anyone.

"That's what I want to talk about. Franklin and I are planning to move to the Cayman Islands. That's where he stashed most of the money he hid from his wife. Uh... well..." Saleema stammered, "Markeeta's not ready to live with you. She has to get used to you again, Terelle." Saleema shifted uncomfortably. "I don't think she could handle it if I left without her. I plan to take Markeeta with me. You're welcome to visit her a couple times a month or whenever...you know, until you get back on your feet."

"Are you crazy? You're not taking Markeeta to some damn Cayman Islands. She's staying right here in Philly with me. In fact, tell that social worker to move up the date for that discharge meeting. I'm ready to get out of here today! Me and Keeta will stay at Aunt Bennie's until I can hook up another apartment…a two-bedroom, so Keeta can have her own room. With me and Quise both working, maybe we could keep Markeeta in that school."

Saleema snorted at the mention of Marquise's name. Wagging a finger and reverting back to her old mannerisms, Saleema rotated her neck for emphasis. "Let me tell you something, Terelle. I've made a lot of sacrifices to raise Markeeta. I was the best guardian I knew how to be." Saleema drew in a deep breath. "Now, this may sound harsh, but I've got to look out for Markeeta's best interests. I'm her legal guardian and I'm not about to let you traumatize her with all your crazy talk about Marquise being alive."

"Legal guardian! I didn't sign any papers—"

"You didn't have to. You weren't capable of making decisions. Listen to me, Terelle. I love you and I love Markeeta. But you're a grown-ass woman and Markeeta's an innocent child. You made the decision to love Marquise at all costs, even at the cost of losing your daughter and your mind."

Terelle sat up straight. "You're blaming me? Like I deliberately checked out of reality? I was sick!"

"Heartsick over losing Marquise. And the way I see it, even after his death, you're still trippin' over him. I can't subject Markeeta to your obsession with Quise."

"You heard the tape!" Terelle shouted.

"That tape doesn't prove shit. You probably dreamed it."

"Oh, so now I'm psychic. I dreamed about something I didn't know existed."

"I can't explain how you knew about the tape, but I do know that Markeeta is not going to live with you until you get a grip."

"You can't keep me away from my child."

"I have to. You're not thinking about what's best for Keeta."

"Being with her mother is best for Keeta."

Saleema didn't speak. Her silence was a disquieting indication that she was pulling together thoughts. Thoughts that she would soon put into words that would not be pleasing to Terelle's ears.

"You're my girl. And I love you. But I'll do whatever I have to do to protect Markeeta."

"Protect her from what? Me?" Terelle leaned forward, her face contorted in pain and confusion. The deep lines of worry seemed to instantly age her. "I love my daughter," Terelle murmured as she slumped back in her seat.

Saleema sighed. "I know you love her, Terelle. I know you do," she repeated. "But you're not thinking rationally. You know I wouldn't keep you away from Markeeta if I didn't think it was best, but if you're not going to provide a healthy atmosphere for her…"

Propelled by a sudden flash of hot anger, Terelle sprang out of the chair and onto her feet with the agility of a gymnast. "I see playing mommy has gone to your damn head! In case you forgot, you are not Markeeta's mother—I am!" she shouted, poking a finger into her chest. "I'm not going to let you and one of your tricks kidnap my baby and drag her off to some damn island."

Saleema flinched at the low-blow reference to her past profession but she recovered quickly. Rising off the bed, Saleema twisted her face into a scowl. "That *trick* and I will see your ass in court. That's right, I'll take it there. And trust me—I'll win!"

# Chapter 9

At first it seemed pathetically absurd that instead of being carted off to the mental ward, Kai was thrown into solitary confinement, a punishment intended to have a profound negative effect on the prisoner's psyche. But after being isolated inside the small room referred to as "the hole" for a week, Kai decided the experience wasn't nearly as bad as she would have imagined. In fact, she rather enjoyed viewing the hustle and bustle of prison life through a five-inch square window. Inmates who passed by the solid steel door of the concrete vault that confined her often gave Kai the finger, shook their fists at her, and mouthed profanities.

Though the guards had warned Kai that there was a price on her head for mutilating Taffy's vagina, Kai had no fear of the inmates who anxiously awaited her return to prison population. Filled with a new sense of power and invincibility, Kai feared no one. She simply had no desire to rejoin the masses. She felt content inside her three-walled concrete world. She embraced the solitude. Her only regret was that she had no memory of the bloody massacre she'd reigned upon Taffy, no gory images to envision and relive. Damn!

According to a guard who had befriended Kai, Taffy's vagina

was so badly mangled; she'd need reconstructive surgery to make it come close to resembling a vagina again. The prison didn't pay for cosmetic procedures, so it appeared that Taffy was going to have to get accustomed to a clit-less, lip-less, stinky-oozing twat.

In the guard's own words, Taffy was still in the prison hospital, stinking up the place. She had to wear an adult diaper to catch the foul secretions that oozed from her mutilated pussy. She urinated from a tube placed in her stomach. Hospital staff couldn't stand being near her for more than the few moments they could tolerate holding their breath.

It was doubtful, the guard concluded, that Taffy would ever enjoy sexual relations with a man or a woman again unless she got her hands on a whole lot of dough and provided gas masks along with the high price she would have to pay a potential sexual partner.

Obviously the experience had traumatized Kai, causing her to block it from her memory. Had she been allowed to spend some time on the prison psychiatrist's couch, had she been able to unburden herself of the misfortune of growing up biracial in a white world; if she'd been allowed to vent about her first and only encounter with her disgraceful, conniving, bitch of a biological mother; had she been able to release her inner turmoil, the sense of powerlessness she'd felt when she was convicted of murder; had Kai been able to speak at length on the weighty responsibility of having an overactive libido that required the constant sexual attention of both men and women to keep her mildly satisfied; and had she been able to talk about all the factors contributing to her anger, anxiety, her fears—maybe a proper diagnosis could have been made.

Over the past week, she'd had ample time to ponder her mental condition, but the correct diagnosis deluded her. Schizo-phrenia? No, she wasn't delusional, she didn't hear voices nor did she hallucinate. Bipolar disorder? Kai wrinkled her nose and shook her head. She wasn't a manic depressive, laughing and giddy one minute and down in the dumps the next. Fuck it! She didn't need a label. Plain and simple, she was just fucking psy-chotic. She'd be damned if she was going to rack her delicate brain trying to come up with a medical term for her particular type of craziness.

Sooner or later, she'd be released back into prison population and Kai pitied the idiot who considered her stunning beauty an invitation to molestation. If the inmates thought her altercation with Taffy was atrocious, wait until they got a gander of what she had in store for the next tough bitch who wanted a piece of her.

Surprisingly, her next dispute was not with another inmate, but with her attorney, the same bungling attorney who had failed to prove her innocence during her trial for the murder of her ex-boyfriend, Marquise Whitsett.

"I'm being released?" Kai asked incredulously.

The lawyer nodded. "Yes, in a couple of days, you're going to be released."

"Just like that?" Kai snapped her fingers for emphasis. "Why?"

"You're being set free and you wanna ask why?" The attorney chuckled and shook his head as if Kai were a silly adolescent.

"Yes, I want to know why! I also want to know who's responsible for this massive screwup?" Kai spoke through clenched teeth, her facial features hardened, imploring the attorney to stop his nonsensical laughter and take her seriously. "I'm an innocent victim and I've been left to rot in this place for two years… I want compensation!" she shouted. Worked up to the point of rising from her chair, the cords in her neck stretched and taut, Kai ranted, "I demand one thousand dollars for every day I was incarcerated."

"Whoa, whoa." The attorney held his palm out defensively. "I think you better satisfy yourself with being released. As far as fighting for any type of compensation…" He paused, scratching his head. "You'd have to come up with a retainer fee. That's an entirely different matter. That's something that has to be approved by the senate. I must inform you that it's highly unlikely that you'd receive more than your annual earning as a social worker. What was that? About thirty-five thousand a year? I could try to get the two years' wages you lost, but it's doubtful that you'll get anything." The lawyer shrugged. "We can try, but as I said, I'll need a retainer."

"You greedy, incompetent bastard!" Kai spat. "I wouldn't pay you one thin dime to represent me. I demand another lawyer."

The attorney began stacking papers and stuffing them into his briefcase. "Fine," he said, in a tone a parent might use with a petulant child. "Suit yourself. Go right ahead and slow down the wheels of justice. I was just trying to tie up the loose ends of this case. But, suit yourself," he repeated. "Find a pro bono attorney or—God forbid—a public defender. Switching lawyers will put you on ice for another couple of months."

Being confined needlessly for even another day was beyond comprehension. Kai had a swift change of heart. "Okay, since my parents already paid you, I guess you can represent me, but I'm really curious—who killed Marquise? Was it his fiancée, Terelle?"

"Beats me. I'm only doing what I was told to do—file a motion for your release."

"Told by whom?"

"Uh, the uh, the feds," the lawyer stammered.

"What feds?"

"Look, it's not really clear. Not even to me. My best guess is that there wasn't enough evidence to convict."

"Your best guess," Kai said mockingly. "That doesn't make sense. Lack of evidence or not, the jury definitely *convicted* me. Or is it just my imagination that I've been sitting in this hell hole for two long years?"

"With all due respect, Ms. Montgomery, if I were you, I'd try to stifle some of that sarcasm when you stand before the judge. I don't think he'll take too kindly to your derisive comments and lack of appreciation. If you want to pursue monetary compensation, I'd advise you to wait until after you've been released."

The attorney rose and left. Kai was at once befuddled and elated. She was going to be released. Yippee! But why? What information had been uncovered? And why was her impending release shrouded in secrecy? Unable to come up with a plausible answer, she decided that the enforcers of the law had finally determined that Terelle Chambers had killed Marquise. Being that the deranged young woman was mentally incapacitated, Kai wondered if the trigger-happy ghetto girl was now handcuffed to her wheelchair. It would serve her right for screwing up Kai's life the way she had.

After listening to an hour-long session of legal mumble jumble that never revealed Marquise's killer, Kai stood before the circuit judge. She was dressed in the same outfit she'd worn to court on the day of her sentencing. Her wild hair had been tamed with mousse and a hairbrush and pulled into a tight bun.

"Motion granted. You're a free woman, Miss Montgomery."

"May I ask His Honor a question?" Kai requested. She heard her attorney groan loudly and out of the corner of her eye, she saw him roll his eyes toward the ceiling.

"Go ahead," the judge said, injecting patience into his tone.

"May I ask who committed the crime for which I was accused and convicted?"

"That question remains unanswered, Miss Montgomery. We now know that it was not you. And on behalf of the city of Philadelphia's District Attorney's office, we all would like to extend a heartfelt apology."

The bailiff removed the shackles from Kai's wrists and ankles. Prosecutor Russell L. Jones extended a congratulatory hand. "I'm proud to say my office worked tirelessly to correct this travesty in the justice system."

"Fuck you, very much," Kai said mockingly. The coarse words issued from her lips in a sweet, musical tone. "The city of Philadelphia is going to pay dearly for my unjust incarceration. I want compensation for the abuse and loss of dignity I suffered behind bars—"

"Your Honor," Kai's attorney interrupted. "Excuse my client's outburst." Dramatically expressing his embarrassment, the attorney shook his head and let out a loud groan of exasperation. "I've already explained to Miss Montgomery that—"

"You're fired!" Kai spat at her stupid attorney. Directing her attention to the judge, she said, "I'll be back to collect my millions, armed with a qualified attorney."

"The court understands that you've been dealt an egregious violation of—"

"Oh, shut up," Kai uttered disrespectfully. As she haughtily pranced out of the courtroom, Kai sent scornful glances to all the members of the judicial system who had the audacity to cast sympathetic smiles in her direction.

Victoriously, she waltzed into a waiting elevator and minutes later, Kai stood outside the courthouse on Filbert Street. She took in a huge breath of fresh air. Freedom was sweet, but having limited funds, she was unable to totally bask in the joy of it. In addition to being dissatisfied with her finances, Kai had quite a few personal axes to grind.

She didn't know who to deal with first. Melissa Peterson, Terelle Chambers, or Dr. and Mrs. Philip Montgomery?

Melissa Peterson, Kai's biological mother, had swindled her out of her savings and deserved merciless retribution. Her birth mother was somewhere in New York, exactly where was anybody's guess. That lowlife prostitute had probably already spent every dollar she'd extorted from her daughter.

Kai knew without a doubt that Terelle Chambers, Marquise's so-called fiancée, had coldly and calculatingly, pulled the trigger of the gun that killed him. After the murder, Terelle pretended to lose touch with reality and was conveniently placed in a loony bin, leaving Kai to take the fall. Kai got a physical rush just thinking about getting her hands on the ghetto gun moll. She pondered how a catatonic woman would react to a stinging slap across the face or a swift kick in the abdomen. Would physical abuse snap Terelle out of her self-imposed stupor? Kai shrugged. It really didn't matter. Ending Terelle's worthless life was the only kind of justice that Kai would find satisfying.

Kai's adoptive parents, Dr. Philip Montgomery and his wife, Miranda, didn't appreciate having their good name tainted. Embarrassed by Kai's imprisonment, they disassociated themselves from her by packing up and relocating. They were chillin' in California, intending to never set eyes on Kai again. Yes, her loving adoptive parents—the two people who had raised her from infancy—had kicked her out of their lives with the pious disdain of two Catholic priests exorcising a demon from their midst. Kai imagined they were living even more luxuriously in California than when they had lived on Philadelphia's prestigious Main Line.

Assuming Kai would be locked up forever, the Montgomerys had pulled some legal maneuvers and stolen the millions her adopted paternal grandmother had left in a trust fund for Kai. The greedy sonofabitches had added Kai's multi-million dollar trust fund to their already huge bank account.

The Montgomerys were the farthest away in distance, but they had the financial means to restore Kai's lavish lifestyle and fund her quest to settle her score with Terelle Chambers and Melissa Peterson.

Kai had given that slimy Marquise Whitsett most of her cash on hand a few days before he was killed. While incarcerated, her biological mother had tricked her out of the money she had left in her safety deposit box. There was only one hundred and ten dollars in the slim Gucci wallet she was carrying on the day she was sentenced to live out her life in prison. She wouldn't get very far with that measly amount of money.

The need for vengeance against those who had wronged her was as powerful as the urge to fuck. Kai's vaginal muscles contracted at the thought of having her kitty cat invaded. She hadn't had sex since she and the backstabbing C.O. named Jason had fucked inside the infirmary. At this point, any fair-to-large-sized dick would do. Being the natural-born daughter of a lowlife whore, Kai assumed she was predisposed to sell her body for cash.

Getting paid for the sex her body craved would be a bonus. Though she detested her birth mother, in a weird sort of way, Kai was grateful for the mutant play-for-pay genes her slut of a mother had passed on to her. With her looks, killer body, and corrupt DNA, Kai would easily earn some fast cash for a first-class ticket to California. Once she located her horrible parents, she'd dispense the appropriate punishment as well as retrieve her trust fund from the two thieves.

The Pennsylvania Convention Center was only a block away from the court house. Conventioneers typically stayed at the Marriott hotel. Kai sashayed a few blocks over to Twelfth and Market where the hotel was located. The doorman at the Marriott welcomed her. She glided inside and spotted the bar. A rowdy crowd of inebriated men, whom she assumed to be convention-eers, would provide easy pickings.

## Chapter 10

Terelle Chambers and Saleema Sparks attended the discharge planning meeting at Spring Haven. Being of sound mind, Terelle affixed her signature to a stack of release forms. Though Terelle was able to walk out of the mental hospital without the assistance of a walker or cane, there was no expression of joy on her face, no attempt to put some spring into her faltering steps. It was the day both women had been waiting for, but the mood was somber instead of celebratory.

"Aunt Bennie's waiting for you in the parking lot," Saleema said quietly.

"You knew I'd want to see Keeta. Why didn't you bring her?"

"I wanted to but—"

"You thought I'd try to kidnap her or something?" Terelle asked sarcastically. "I can't walk fast enough to grab my child and try to make a run for it, you know."

"She didn't want to come," Saleema reluctantly admitted.

Terelle stopped in her tracks. "What?"

"I told her that you were getting out today and you'd really like to see her," Saleema said with tired patience. "Keeta's little lips started trembling and then she broke down in tears. I picked her up, kissed her, and asked her what was wrong…" Saleema looked intently into Terelle's pained eyes. She took a deep breath and then somberly delivered the bad news. "Markeeta said she doesn't like you. She said she's scared of you and that you…"

"What?"

"She said you smell funny. But I told her you don't stink. It's the place you're in. I told her some people go to the bathroom on themselves and need to get changed," Saleema spoke rapidly, as if trying to get the painful words out of her mouth as quickly as possible. "She asked if you go to the bathroom on yourself and I told her, no, you don't. But Markeeta said she heard Aunt Bennie tell someone that it broke her heart that you had to wear a diaper…"

"I was in a coma or something. I'm continent, now. I'm okay."

"I know that. But Markeeta started screaming and begging me not to give her to you." Saleema shook her head mournfully. "I know hearing all this has to hurt like hell. I'm so sorry, Terelle."

Badly stung by Saleema's report, Terelle was momentarily silent and then pulled herself together. "Markeeta's just a child; you could have reasoned with her," Terelle said angrily. "You should have put her mind at ease and told her she misunderstood Aunt Bennie. You wouldn't like it if I co-signed some mess like that if you had a child and she wanted to know if *you* wore a damn diaper. That's not something you admit to a four-year-old about her mother. Damn, Saleema, I shouldn't have to tell you this." Terelle peered at Saleema, waiting for an indication that Saleema understood and agreed with her, but Saleema gave her a blank look. Terelle pressed on. "It seems like you're encouraging Markeeta to think of me as some crazy, pissing-on-herself monster. I think you want her to be afraid of me."

"That's not true," Saleema protested. Her eyes and mouth were wide with indignation.

"Then why does it feel like you don't have my back anymore? Why does it feel like you're trying to steal my daughter?" On the verge of tears, Terelle's voice cracked. Her eyes became moist and red but she was determined not to give in to tears.

Terelle's attention was suddenly drawn to two honks of a car horn in the parking lot. She turned away from Saleema. Quickening her unsteady gait as best she could, she hurried toward Aunt Bennie's blue Honda.

Saleema easily caught up to Terelle. She gripped her friend by the shoulders and forced her to turn around. "I didn't turn Markeeta against you, Terelle. I had your back every step of the way and you know it. Markeeta is a part of *you*; that's why I love her so much. And that love makes me want to protect her the same way you would protect her if you were thinking with your right mind—"

"I am thinking with my right mind! Stop calling me crazy!" Terelle shouted.

"Then stop acting like you're crazy. Why would you want to uproot Keeta from her comfortable home and take her to live with you and your weird-ass aunt?" Saleema nudged her head toward Aunt Bennie's Honda. "You know I'm not with that dyke shit Aunt Bennie's into. It's not the kind of thing Keeta should be around. Seeing two women hugging and kissing would freak her out!"

"Listen to the pot calling the kettle black. You turned tricks for a living, but I never said you couldn't be around Markeeta."

"If you really thought the way I was making my money was so bad, then you shouldn't have let me come near Markeeta. You're such a hypocrite. Now that I know how you felt about me, I guess you only allowed me in your daughter's life because I helped you take care of her. Shit, Keeta stayed rocking designer gear from the day she was born." Indignant, Saleema waved a long finger in the air. "I dressed your ass, too and I gave you dough to send Quise when he was locked the fuck up. You reaped a helluva lot of benefits from all the tricks I turned."

Terelle turned slightly from Saleema and held up a finger, signaling Aunt Bennie to give her a moment. Aunt Bennie got back inside the car. Terelle returned her attention to Saleema. "After all we've been through, Saleema," she said and then paused. She felt angry, heartsick, and weak. So weak, she found it hard to speak. It took all her strength to push out her remaining words. "This is so unreal." She spoke softly, with her head down, as if speaking to herself. Then, lifting her gaze, she spoke directly to Saleema. "No one could have ever made me believe that *you* would hurt me like this."

"I'm sorry, Terelle. This is so fucked up. But you have to understand, I'm not trying to hurt you. I have to do what I think is best for Keeta." Saleema reached for her friend, tried to hug her, but Terelle drew back. With shoulders slumped, Terelle, twenty pounds lighter than her former self, moved slowly, pitifully toward the waiting Honda.

Two federal marshals—Dwyer and Hughes—sat in an enclosed waiting area inside Union Station in Washington, D.C. Posing as travelers, the men pretended to read newspapers while casting sly glances at a young black man who was seated in an adjacent waiting area.

Extremely tall and lean, the young man wore a red-and-black fitted New York Yankees cap with the brim pulled low. He glanced frequently down at his wrist and then, as if doubting that his watch had the correct time, he shot a curious look at the station's digital time display. His right foot, covered by a gleaming white Nike sneaker, tapped impatiently as he waited to board a train en route to Philadelphia.

A few minutes later, there was a gate announcement that the train to Philadelphia would be arriving in five minutes. Lithely, the young man sprang from his seat and joined a line of passengers waiting to board the train. He towered over the other travelers, standing out like a bright red flag. Seeming suspicious of being watched, he tugged on the brim of the red cap, pulling it down farther as he disappeared through the gate.

Dwyer, a stocky man of medium height with a thick neck and a stomach that hung over his belt, closed and folded his newspaper. "There he goes. He's out of compliance."

"Again," added Hughes, who was rather nondescript other than having reddish facial hair.

"I guess he thinks sporting a New York cap instead of advertising his home team is a brilliant disguise." Dwyer ran an exasperated hand over his forehead and through his wheat-colored hair.

"He sticks out like a sore thumb. But, hey, it's his life he's risking. We can't protect him if he insists on breaking security guidelines."

"How many times do we have to hammer it into this guy's head?" Dwyer paused pointedly. "No one has ever been harmed under our watch! When that bullet with his name on it finds its way to his skull, it won't be because we didn't do our job."

"I don't even know why the program bothers to help certain people. You can tell right off the bat which guys are gonna benefit from the program and which guys are gonna blow their cover," Hughes complained.

"Yeah, we should let them serve whatever time they need to

serve, pull 'em out of jail to testify at the trial, and let them suffer the consequences of being a snitch. Trying to protect the younger fellas is a waste of taxpayer's money. Instead of appreciating the protection, they get antsy. Living on the edge must give 'em some type of rush."

"It's like they have a death wish or something." Hughes's eyes were narrowed in seriousness as if he'd made the most profound statement of his life.

"I don't know about that," Dwyer disagreed, loosening his stifling tie. "If you ask me, the risk takers are plain stupid. They lack intelligence. Too stupid to know they're not invincible. It takes having the bad guys show up unexpectedly at their mother's doorstep to show them they're not so slick after all."

"Yeah, you have a point. What galls me is that they think they're smarter than us. He should know we have to keep our eye on him until after the trial."

"He's even more stupid to think he can slip past the bad guys."

The Amtrak heading for Philadelphia gave a loud whoosh as it pulled out of the station.

"It's your turn to write the report," Dwyer said.

"Just my luck!" Hughes gave a sigh. "Doesn't he realize he could get jail time for leaving his assigned state?"

"Yeah, but he'll be more forthcoming at trial if he's a free man."

Hughes nodded. "I'm gonna make a suggestion that we relocate Marquise Whitsett. Being this close to Philly is obviously too tempting."

"We should send him somewhere like Boise, Idaho. The racial makeup there is something like ninety-two percent white and less than one percent black. We should unleash our boy in Boise and give that lily-white community a big dose of urban culture." Both marshals broke up laughing.

"The best part of that idea is giving those marshals in Boise something to do besides talking about potatoes." Hughes wrinkled his brow. "What else is Idaho known for?"

"Beats the hell out of me," Dwyer said, eyeing the food court. "Speaking of potatoes... feel like stopping for a bite?"

"Why not?" Hughes said dryly. The two men wound their way through the throng of commuters, locals, and tourists as they moved in the direction of the food court.

*Chapter 11*

Kai released her curly hair from the tight band and shook it free. Along with her financial security, her haute couture wardrobe, and her sanity, the two-year stint in prison had also taken away the luster from her hair. Her coiled tresses, no longer expensively coifed, had become a dullish brown. Giving her dry curls an arrogant flip, Kai Montgomery strode into the hotel bar with her carriage erect, her head held high, her nose turned up in the manner of a haughty heiress.

Kai was spared having to waste time scanning the dim room in search of a mark. The mark spotted her. Pointing a finger at an empty barstool next to him, a casually dressed, ordinary-looking white man beckoned Kai with a quick smile and a wink.

Accepting the offer, Kai gave him a curt smile and a nod.

"How ya doin', gorgeous? My name's Parker... what's yours?" Parker had an annoying Boston accent.

"Hmm," Kai pondered the question. "Tell you what. Call me Gorgeous. I like it."

The Bostonian laughed heartily. "Can I buy you a drink, Gorgeous?"

"Sure can," Kai remarked, as she positioned herself on the cushiony seat of the swiveling barstool.

"Let me guess…you like dry wine?"

He was right, but Kai did not intend to indulge in dry wine or any mood-altering elixir. Conducting business required that she keep her wits about her. She shook her head adamantly. "I'll have a raspberry-lime seltzer."

"Aw, you're no fun. First you refuse to give me your name. Now you're refusing to have a real drink."

"I can sit somewhere else, if you prefer." Kai gave Parker a challenging smile.

"Just kidding, gosh!" Parker looked toward the ceiling, his expression seeming to say, *where's your sense of humor?*

The bartender materialized suddenly. Parker ordered another drink for himself. Sounding apologetic, he also ordered Kai's non-alcoholic drink.

Taking small sips, Kai sized up the man who would fund her trip to California. She wondered how long it would take to separate the rather ordinary-looking man from a portion of his bank account. Driven by the image of the shock on her neglectful parents' faces when she showed up on their doorstep, Kai cut to the chase. "Horny?" she asked with a straight face.

Parker choked on his drink. "Gosh, you're really blunt."

"Why waste time?" Kai asked in a low, sensual tone. She enjoyed the role she was playing, mysterious woman without a name. Yes, the role suited her. For the moment. She'd hold off on the mentally disturbed aspect of her persona. She'd fully unleash *crazy* on her unsuspecting parents.

"You're a knockout…you know that?" Parker's mushy smile was a bit lopsided, informing Kai that he was feeling the liquor. He guzzled his drink and then beckoned the bartender for another.

"Do you want to fuck or do you wanna get kinky?" Kai boldly queried.

"Wow! You don't play around. Can we do both?" Parker inquired. Excitedly, he downed his drink. On cue, the bartender refilled his glass.

"Sure can." Kai forced a smile on her serious face.

Parker beamed and then quickly crinkled his brow in suspicion. "Are you… ? You're not a hooker, are you?" Parker stammered.

"I'm a businesswoman."

"How much do you charge?"

"Make an offer."

Parker raised his shoulders in a timid shrug. "Two hundred bucks?"

*Oh, crap,* Kai thought. "I'm insulted," she said with a sarcastic smile.

Parker's face flushed. "How much do ya want?" he whined, his speech slurred from too much liquor. Whiny, slurred speech and a Bostonian accent was an aggravating combination. Kai sighed. She needed at least a grand for air fare and incidentals.

"My prices start at one thousand."

Parker whistled in response.

"One thousand for an hour," she added firmly. Twirling a tendril of hair around her finger, Kai held Parker in an intense and unwavering gaze.

He retrieved a credit card from his wallet, beckoned the bartender. After paying the bar tab, he eased off the stool. "Do I get the full range, uh, you know, of services?"

"Sure do," she said coolly.

"I hope you're worth it." Parker attempted to sound humorous, but there was an undercurrent of irritation beneath his words.

Kai ignored the snotty remark. "Do you need to detour to the ATM? I don't accept credit cards." She gave a wry smile.

"ATM? No, I have cash," he muttered. Seeming unable to

decide whether he should agree to the steep price or mull it over with another drink, Parker stood awkwardly close to the bar.

"Great, you have cash!" Sealing the deal, Kai slipped her arm into his. "Let's get out of here," she whispered silkily.

"Good idea. Righto," Parker said uneasily.

*Righto! Oh, give me a fucking break.*

In his hotel room, Parker retrieved the money from a safe inside the closet. He counted out the amount Kai requested, handed it to her, and locked the safe.

Sitting in a chair next to the king-sized bed, Kai flipped through the bills. Satisfied that she hadn't been cheated, she folded the money and slipped it inside her purse.

"So what kind of convention are you attending?" Kai asked as she began stripping off her clothes.

Instead of getting on with the sexual aspect of the business transaction, Parker stood fully clothed with his eyes glued to Kai's bare flesh, awed by her naked beauty. A bulge began to form between his legs. Parker appeared to be in extreme discomfort and incapable of verbal expression.

Mildly disgusted by his stupid show of horniness and adolescent-like inexperience, Kai plopped down in the chair next to the bed. "Let me know when you're ready." She let out a sigh and examined her ragged nails. Perhaps she'd use some of Parker's money to get a manicure before boarding the plane to Los Angeles. Her eyes traveled down to her feet, which were badly in need of a pedicure. She scowled. Prior to being hauled off to jail, she'd always kept an immaculate appearance. Red-hot anger enveloped her. Oh, how she was going to make her parents pay for their atrocious neglect and thievery.

Parker dawdled. He stood awkwardly as if he had no clue as to what to do with a beautiful, naked woman. Irritated and impatient, Kai was seriously close to absconding with his cash. In her mind, she could vividly see herself dressing quickly, grabbing her purse, and racing out of the hotel room. Instead of the elevator, which could be brought to a standstill by hotel security, she'd use the stairwell for an escape route. After running down the numerous flights of stairs, she'd finally reach the ground floor and bolt out the door. Outside, she'd flee into the middle of Market Street, halting traffic while she waved her arms to flag down a cab.

Then, seated safely in the backseat of the cab, she'd look back in amusement at Parker, who, in hot pursuit and ridiculously clad in socks and underwear, would be red-faced and panting as he shook his fist as the cab roared away. Enveloped by exhaust fumes that plumed from the cab's tailpipe, Parker would be left in his drawers, choking and coughing in the middle of Market Street.

Kai emitted a spiteful chuckle as she tore herself away from the malicious reverie.

"What's so funny?"

"Oh, I was just thinking about something."

"Wanna share?" Parker sounded defensive.

"It's not important. By the way, you never answered my question."

"What did you ask?"

"What kind of convention are you attending?" She didn't really give a shit but hoped that engaging the moron in meaningless chatter would relax him and get the ball rolling. She was eager to honor her obligation and be on her way to tracking down her parents and recovering the money they'd stolen from her.

"Why do you want to know?"

Disgusted, she held up her hand. "Oh, crap! Forget it."

"Uh, I didn't mean to upset you. My profession is confidential, but you seem to be a trustworthy person."

Kai gave a loud sigh.

Parker chucked uncomfortably. "I'm here for the annual detective's convention. It was in New York last year. There's a lot more action in New York than here in Philadelphia."

"You're a detective?" Her eyes gleamed with interest.

"Uh… yeah."

"You're kidding," she said, regarding Parker with newfound respect. This was too good to be true! She'd picked up a fucking detective—a trained procurer of information! A private dick who could unearth hard-to-find assholes such as her biological mother! For that information, she'd fuck him until his toes curled and his eyes crossed.

"No kiddin'. Seriously. I'm a licensed private detective." The admission seemed to puff Parker's chest out an inch or two.

Parker didn't fit her image of a private eye. He looked too clean-cut and appeared way too naïve. He apparently didn't even smoke cigarettes. She imagined a private detective wearing cheap, wrinkled clothes, with eyes that were reddened from squinting through cigarette smoke as he sat for hours on end in a beat-up car, chain-smoking and drinking coffee while he was staked outside some dump of a motel.

"You can track down people who don't want to be found? You know, uncover their whereabouts—like get an exact address?" Kai shuddered with excited expectancy.

Parker nodded proudly, his bout of boyish shyness quickly disappearing. Suddenly bold, he pulled down his pants. There was a small bulge inside his boxers. Still, the fact that Parker was a private detective made her kitty twitch with excitement. What a stroke of luck!

Seductively, she slid to the edge of the chair and stood. Seconds later, she was pressed against Parker, caressing the little lump inside his boxer shorts. "Your cock seems really big," she lied with ease. "Can I see it?"

Grinning, Parker proudly peeled off his underwear. Kai stared in fascination. His tool was the smallest she'd ever seen. Hmm. He'd be the easiest fuck of her life. The thought of a quick fuck, cash, and obtaining the exact addresses of her enemies made her kitty warm and moist. Still, keeping her mind focused on her obligation to uphold her end of the bargain with passion and enthusiasm, Kai stroked the little dick. With her free hand, she steered Parker toward the bed. "Do you work outside of Boston?"

"Sure. I can pretty much track down anyone in the United States. I've even found people outside the States," he boasted. He propped his head up with two pillows and glanced down at his cock. "Is it okay to start with a blowjob?"

Kai nodded and licked her lips, giving the impression that sucking him off would be as delicious as indulging herself with a gourmet meal. She straddled him and quickly stuffed his miniscule cock inside her kitty.

"Hey! Not so fast," Parker complained. "I want you to suck me off first."

Kai pushed down on his rigid little dick. "Okay," she murmured in a feigned sexy tone. "I like sucking candy-covered cock. My kitty cat's dripping sugar all over your cock."

"Oh, God," Parker groaned. "I love it when a woman talks dirty."

"After I cum," she continued, whispering in a husky tone, "I'm gonna suck your cock like it's a giant sugar cane stalk."

"Agh!" Parker grimaced in ecstasy. Thrusting hard, he growled, "I'm fucking your cunt with my giant stalk!"

"Fuck me, Parker. Hurt me with your giant cock." She turned her face away to hide the gigantic grin that had spread across her face. Unbelievably, Parker was going along with the farce and referring to his ridiculously small cock as a giant stalk. *Crap!* There sure were a lot of kooks in the world. Maybe she wasn't as nuts as she'd thought. Maybe she was completely sane. She'd have to have herself thoroughly checked out by a qualified psychiatrist after she retrieved all her money. Knowing her exact psychiatric status would be useful information.

Parker pushed his mini dick in as far as it would go. Kai squeezed her pussy muscles, her walls struggled to grip the short shaft. Once the dick was secured, she began a series of quick grips and releases. She was a master at contracting her vaginal muscles.

"I can't hold it," Parker muttered pitifully.

His admission was music to Kai's ears. "Let it go, baby. Shoot your load. Fill up my sweet kitty cat."

"Agh!" he called out, humping fast, losing control.

"Yes, Parker, baby," Kai said soothingly, rubbing the soft hair on his head. "You're making my kitty screech. I feel like a nasty alley cat in heat," Kai added, knowing that the raunchiness of her words would weaken Parker's resolve.

"I'm cumming!" Parker yelled, alerting Kai as his cock flicked inside her cunt. The head pushed against her soft lining, intruding into sensitive, fleshy nooks and crannies that had gone untouched, unexplored for quite some time. Kai scrunched her nose in disgust. There was no pleasure in feeling his spasms and disgusting groans. But she had business to attend to.

She'd make it a point to locate a more useful dick before she left Philly. Perhaps she'd get a quick fuck in the hotel elevator after she left this detective asshole, or maybe the cabdriver who drove her to the airport could fill her cunt with some worthwhile and enjoyable cock. Finding good dick as well as pussy had never been a problem for Kai. But the one thing she definitely did not want was pussy. She'd had enough kitty licking from the female prisoners to last her a lifetime. No more bisexual exploits for this girl, she told herself as she felt Parker trying to ram her as if he truly possessed a useful tool.

Parker sucked in a startled gasp of air. Judging from his grave expression, Kai gathered that Parker considered his speedy ejaculation as a tragic event.

Too bad! The fuck session was over. She'd lived up to her end of the bargain. It wasn't her fault that her purring kitty rendered him a quick shooter. If he wanted her to stick around while he revived himself and reloaded—if he wanted to squirt some more sex juice inside her kitty—Parker would have to fork over more cash and most importantly, he'd have to provide some on-the-spot detective work.

Kai cut her eye over at the open laptop on the desk near the window. She wondered if Parker had the wherewithal to track down people over the internet. She hoped the way he conducted business didn't require him to physically dig up information. She didn't have time to wait while he tailed suspects, talked to witnesses, or scrounged around in the cloak of darkness looking for clues. All she needed was two residential addresses and the name of a particular mental hospital. And she needed the information ASAP!

As she mused, Kai felt Parker's little cock wriggling back to life. *Oh, fuck that!* Kai squirmed away, forcing his cock to slip outside her vagina.

"S'matter?" Parker whined in his nauseating Bostonian accent as he rolled on top of her. "I'm still horny."

Kai forced away the frown that had begun to form on her face. Somehow, she managed to manufacture a sexy smile. "You really worked me over," she said breathily. As if exhausted, she dramatically swept her curly hair away from her face. "I need to catch my breath; can you give me a minute?" She wriggled beneath him. Reluctantly, Parker rolled off her.

Kai nudged her head toward the laptop. "Can you work while you play?"

"What do you mean?"

"Can you get information online? You know, do some private investigating while I lick your cock?"

A broad smile revealed all thirty-two of Parker's teeth. "What do you need to know?"

Without disclosing her ulterior motives, Kai told him what she needed.

Parker crinkled his brow in thought. "Might take a day or two to get the scoop on your mom and dad out in California. Your, uh, who's the lady in New York?"

"Melissa Peterson. My birth mother." Kai managed to look forlorn. She even squeezed out a tear or two. "She's the scum of the earth, a lowlife prostitute, but she's still my mother and I want to find her."

Parker looked briefly uncomfortable. "Well, it might take some poking around to locate your mother and your, uh, other parents. I have a couple friends who owe me favors—they'll get me the scoop on your family members."

Kai flinched at the phrase "family members." She had no family. She loathed and detested Melissa Peterson and the Montgomerys.

"The young woman who's hospitalized here in Philly shouldn't present a problem. I can get her info in a couple hours."

Kai immediately envisioned herself holding a pillow over Terelle's face, snuffing out what was left of the murdering thug girl's worthless life.

"How much longer will you be in town?" Kai asked.

"I'll be here until Sunday."

It was only Tuesday. Hopefully, she wouldn't have to lay up with Parker for the next five days. But if necessary, she would. She'd do whatever it took to obtain the information she desperately needed. She'd fuck him, suck him, talk dirty, talk sweet—tell him whatever he wanted to hear.

# Chapter 12

T wice in the same day, Terelle awakened with a feeling of hopelessness and a tremendous sense of loss. Staying with Aunt Bennie and her girlfriend Sheila in the house that had once belonged to her deceased grandmother seemed like a dream—a bad dream. Aunt Bennie and Sheila went out of their way to make her feel at home, but Terelle couldn't get comfortable. She was in limbo. She might as well have remained in a catatonic state. This wasn't living; she was merely going through the motions.

The pre-catatonic Terelle would not have settled for the life she was now living. She would have been out pounding the pavement, finding a place for her and Markeeta to live.

Feeling bereft, Terelle sat on the edge of the bed. Bent over, she massaged her temples. The thought of Markeeta made her head throb. She eyed the bedside clock. It was almost one in the afternoon and she hadn't even combed her hair. Earlier that morning, she'd managed to accomplish some of the daily tasks of living, such as brushing her teeth and taking a shower. She'd even willed her weary legs to step into a pair of jeans. Saleema's jeans. Terelle was so painfully thin even Saleema's tiny jeans were swimming on her, requiring a tightly buckled belt. Being a size three looked good on Saleema, but Terelle looked like a bag of bones. Back when she wore a size twelve her curvaceous body, with her thick legs, full hips, and her big round butt, really filled out a pair of jeans. She'd love to get her weight back up, but with her frazzled nerves and poor appetite, it would be a long time before she got back to her normal size.

Terelle sighed. It was a disgrace to be sitting around in her bedroom late in the afternoon while Aunt Bennie and Sheila were toiling away at their places of employment, earning money that secured the roof over her head. But there was nothing to do. Aunt Bennie kept the house as neat as a pin; there wasn't a speck of dust anywhere. Because she was disabled, she couldn't go out in search of employment. The only thing she could do was, wait. Wait to hear whether her disability claim had been accepted. Wait for Saleema to allow her to have a visit with Markeeta. And wait for Marquise to resurface.

*Oh, Marquise! Where are you?* Feeling helpless, lonely, and unloved, Terelle held her head in despair. Marquise hadn't attempted any type of communication since the time he'd appeared at her bedside at Spring Haven. She pushed the thought of that night from her mind. It was her belief that he was still alive that had caused her current predicament.

Truth be told, Terelle was beginning to doubt herself. Maybe her illness had caused her to hallucinate. Had the voice she'd heard actually come from a living and breathing human being? Was it possible that she'd been visited by a spirit? No! She'd felt his lips, felt his heartbeat. She could recall every aspect as if it had occurred only a few seconds ago. But real or not, the sweetness of that memory didn't ease the pain of losing Markeeta. She yearned so badly for her daughter, it hurt. Physically. She couldn't eat, hardly ever slept. She was a bundle of nerves and constantly crying or on the verge of tears.

Maybe Saleema was right. Maybe her ability to make sound judgment was impaired. If she hadn't stubbornly insisted that Marquise was alive, she'd be with Markeeta and Saleema right now. Saleema would be lovingly assisting her in the gradual resumption of her role of mother to Markeeta. Saleema had always been there for her, through thick and thin. Whether Terelle was right or wrong, Saleema always had her back. Until now.

Terelle hugged herself. Being apart from her child was unbearable. In an instant, Terelle decided it was time to wave her white flag. She rose suddenly. She had to make a phone call to Saleema. She knew Aunt Bennie wouldn't mind her using the phone in her and Sheila's bedroom, since there was no phone in her room, but Terelle wasn't comfortable intruding on their personal space. She headed for the stairs to make the call from the phone in the kitchen. Terelle reminded herself that she'd have to convince Saleema that she'd come to her senses. Terelle didn't know what to think regarding Marquise, but she'd have to make Saleema believe that she finally had accepted the fact that he was dead. Terelle was willing to do or say whatever it took to get her daughter. Hell, she'd leave Philly, move to the Cayman Islands with Saleema and her trick if necessary. Whatever! It was time to end the pain. Firm in her decision, Terelle gripped the banister for support and slowly descended the stairs.

The doorbell rang. Her first impulse was to ignore it, but figuring it was the mail carrier with a letter from Social Security that required her signature, Terelle yelled, "Just a minute," and tried to quicken her unsteady descent. Going up and down stairs was more challenging than she'd realized. Despite her decision to call a truce with Saleema, Terelle still needed her own income. She couldn't afford to risk having her disability claim delayed. "Coming!" Terelle called out when she reached the bottom step.

As she paced across the living room, old programming kicked in. Having lived in the 'hood her entire life, Terelle knew that the possibility of danger always lurked nearby. Suppose a burglar, a serial killer, or anyone with malicious intentions who knew she was home alone was on the other side of the door. Cautiously, Terelle leaned toward the window and peeked through the blinds. She made a canopy over her head with a curved hand, protecting her eyes from the blinding rays of sunshine.

From her vantage point, she couldn't see a face; all she could see was a pair of male hands. She sucked in her breath and blinked rapidly in surprise at the dark-brown hands with distinctive long fingers. Surely, there were no other hands like those in the whole world. Quickly, she shot her gaze downward in a frantic search for more evidence. Her focus landed on a pair of white Nikes. Her heart hammered inside her chest. Then, it seemed all the breath left her body. She knew she wasn't hallucinating, and she hadn't lost her mind. Apparitions did not appear on the doorstep in the middle of a bright sunny day.

Terelle didn't require further convincing; she'd recognize those size twelves anywhere.

*Marquise! Oh, God, Marquise!* Her heart thundering in her chest, Terelle ran a nervous hand over her uncombed hair. There was no handy mirror nearby. *Oh, God! Oh, Jesus*, she thought anxiously. *How do I look?* She conducted a quick a mental check and concluded that she honestly didn't care.

Excited, delighted, and overcome with emotion, she stumbled against a leather ottoman near the front door, then tripped and fell. Infused with strength brought on by the sight of a pair of hands and a pair of Nikes that could only belong to Marquise, Terelle picked herself up and raced toward the door. Her heart was filled with such joy, she felt as if she were airborne.

With astounding dexterity, she swiftly unbolted a double set of locks and flung the door open wide.

Weak in the knees, she swooned when her gaze connected with the beautiful brown eyes that beamed down at her. Her eyes shifted to his lips. No one had lips like Marquise's. His incredibly full, sensual, brown lips began to spread, showing sparkling white teeth that gleamed a greeting. Any doubt that she was loved instantly vanished in the glow of his smile.

At first, she was paralyzed with shock. Then she cried out, "Marquise!" Her voice was a strangled shriek that bordered on hysteria. Terelle tried her best to hold it together, but she couldn't calm down. Her body shook. She trembled so badly, it was impossible to stand upright for a second longer.

With love-filled eyes, Marquise held out long, muscular arms. Without hesitation, Terelle tumbled into them.

He swooped her into his arms and cradled her. "Terelle! Baby! I love you, I love you, I love you, I love you," he murmured over and over, like a mantra. Using his foot, he pushed the door closed. "I missed the shit outta you. You know that, right?" His words came out sounding choked and anguished.

Terelle had a million burning questions, but she didn't dare speak. She was afraid the sound of her voice would jolt her awake from this wonderful waking dream.

Cradling her in his arms, Marquise glided across the room.

Enfolded in his warmth, Terelle could feel his breath breezing through her hair; she felt his heart beat against her flesh. She inhaled his wonderfully familiar body scent, an odor that was uniquely his—and Markeeta's. *I'm not dreaming; he's alive!* Overcome with a surge of emotions, Terelle murmured his name, tried to tell him how lonely she'd been without him, how long she'd been dreaming of this day; but being completely overcome with emotion, she couldn't form coherent words. She emitted garbled sounds, a mixture of happy shrieks and torturous whimpering.

"Shh! Shh! It's all right, babe," Marquise murmured. "I gotchu. I'm not going no where. I know Saleema's been taking care of Keeta…but I'm back and we gon' get our baby girl. Me, you, and Keeta gon' get as far away from Philly as we can."

Holding Terelle, Marquise lowered himself on the sofa. For a very long moment, Marquise was silent. In awe, he stared at her face. His roving gaze took her in from head to toe. Lovingly, he lifted her hand to his lips, kissed the back of her hand, her palm, her wrist, and her fingers. "I missed you so much. I'm so, so sorry for everything I put you through."

Terelle touched his face. Her fingers flitted against his skin lightly, as if applying pressure would cause Marquise to disintegrate—go *poof*—right before her eyes. Wordlessly, she gazed at him. She removed his red-and-black baseball cap. His long, thick braids were gone. His soft hair was cut close, revealing a mature, dark-brown face that was even more handsome than she'd remembered.

Terelle gazed at her man, her eyes conveying unconditional love.

Forgiveness.

And yearning.

She felt a sexual longing so sudden and so strong, Terelle had to restrain herself from reaching out and tearing off Marquise's clothes. She'd never had what she would have considered an overdeveloped libido, but in this moment, she was keenly aware of the void left by two years of sexual abstinence. The hunger was so powerful, she felt ravenous—sex-starved.

Terelle shuddered with desire. While her lust-filled eyes remained fastened on his handsome face, Terelle reached out. She ran a trembling hand from his strong jaw and down to his neck, touching tendons and veins, feeling his Adam's apple as it bobbed beneath her fingertips. She plunged her hand inside the neckline of his shirt, caressing his broad chest and muscular shoulders. To her delighted surprise, Marquise's slender frame had morphed into a powerfully built physique.

Briefly, she felt ashamed of her frail body, and then quickly thought, *fuck it!* Now that Quise was back, she'd finally develop an appetite and get her weight up in no time.

Excitedly, Terelle explored Marquise's developed shoulders and arms. Her fingers flitted down to his abdominals, caressing each isolated muscle of his bulging six-pack. Her eyes dropped to his growing erection. She drew in a sharp breath. At that moment, Terelle needed Marquise more than she needed the air she'd just inhaled.

Recognizing the look of raw sensuality that glowed in Terelle's eyes, Marquise worriedly bit down on his bottom lip. Uncertainty flickered in his eyes. "You been sick, babe. I don't want to hurt you. You sure you feelin' up to—"

Her eyes burned into his, cutting off his apprehensive utterances. "Yes, I've been sick. But you're here now, and I know you can heal me."

Still uncertain, he bit down on his lip.

"Heal me, Quise." Terelle's voice was low but demanding. The doctors had told her that a nutritious diet and the regular performance of muscle-strengthening exercises were essential to restoring her former health. Abstaining from sex had not been mentioned. As far as Terelle was concerned, sharing physical love with Marquise was the medicine that would give her instant and total health.

Boldly, she pressed her lips against his.

Marquise kissed her back, at first softly and hesitantly. Then, overcome with a hungry urgency, he captured her lips.

The sensation of his kiss, his masculine scent, and his big hands smoothing her hair and massaging her, incited her to want more. Terelle clung to Marquise. She traced his upper lip with the tip of her tongue, then softly nipped at his bottom lip with her teeth.

Her lips, now parted, invited him to slide his tongue inside. Terelle moaned as Marquise licked the moist lining of her inner cheek; his tongue brushing against her gums and her teeth. Aroused by Marquise's searching tongue, Terelle quivered. Simultaneously, her neck reclined and her lips spread wider, encouraging Marquise to explore her mouth, to absorb her essence.

As his tongue slid in and out of her mouth, something stirred inside Terelle, making her bolder, encouraging her to indulge her sensuality. Her hand traveled past his abs and stroked the bulge that throbbed beneath his jeans. She rubbed until his penis jerked involuntarily.

"Oh, babe," he uttered hoarsely. Transfixed by the look of love and lust on his face, Terelle couldn't take her eyes off Marquise. His eyes were half closed, his lips were slack with unbridled lust as he tore open her top. Marquise flung the cotton fabric to the floor, then unhooked her bra and bared her breasts. He cupped the small, saggy breasts that were once heavy and full and began kissing and sucking them with a fervor that told Terelle that in his eyes, her breasts were as plump and desirable as they'd been prior to her illness. Marquise's succulent lips tugged persistently on her nipples until they became so stiff, they ached with desire.

"Quise!" she gasped as his tongue tortured her dark pearls. Marquise gave a harsh rush of breath as Terelle's fingernails sank into his shoulders. "Fuck me, Quise!" she whispered desperately.

"You sure, babe? I don't wanna hurt you." His eyes held tenderness, and a loving concern she couldn't recall having ever seen in them before.

"Quise," she repeated, her voice urgent.

Obeying her command, Marquise unbuckled her belt and slowly lowered her jeans. He pulled them from around her ankles and tossed them on the floor, where they landed next to her top.

"Babe," he whispered as he repositioned her on the sofa. He pulled down her panties, revealing the door of her femininity. He rubbed her clit with the ball of his thumb, making it swollen and slippery. His longest finger penetrated, giving her a slow finger-fuck. Moaning loudly, Terelle arched her back.

Marquise lowered his head and brushed his face against the nest of downy curls that covered her mons. Rotating his neck, Marquise nuzzled his neatly trimmed beard, his nose, and lips against Terelle's tickling pubic hair.

Terelle felt a burning heat of passion. She was seized by a rush of sensation that made her moist and forced her to spread her legs apart.

"Mmm," Marquise murmured, as he sniffed her pussy. "I missed my baby's pussy." Enraptured, he groaned as he deeply inhaled her fragrant musky arousal. With his tongue, he tenderly separated her soft folds. Terelle gasped. She shuddered in delight. Marquise had never loved her with his mouth. Being on the receiving end of oral sex was a brand-new and unexpected pleasure. His big juicy lips pressed against her vagina were driving her crazy; had her talking shit and blabbering nonsensically. The sensation of his warm tongue teasing and tasting her womanhood gave her such extreme, never-experienced-before pleasure, she felt on the edge of delirium. With his finger, Marquise delicately pulled back the hood of her clit, then he stroked and caressed the exposed, tender flesh with his tongue.

Past delirium, Terelle turned her head from side to side. She bucked upward, pushing her pussy in his face, demanding tongue. Terelle was losing her mind. She wondered briefly if she would be carted back to Spring Haven, this time in a state of sexual rapture.

Marquise gently widened the space between her open legs. "You like that, baby?" he murmured in a husky voice as he entered her pussy with his firm tongue.

Terelle tried to say "yes," but could only squeak out a response.

Marquise drove his tongue in and out—fast at first and then he slowed the pace, leisurely licking away the honey that streamed between Terelle's legs. Terelle writhed and moaned in blissful agony. Alternately, Marquise sucked her swollen clit, licked the lining of her vaginal walls until her breath became choppy. Her blood roared through her veins.

Having Marquise's juicy lips pressed against her pussy seemed as surreal as an out-of-body experience. Though she wanted the incredible feeling to last forever, Terelle could feel her body vibrating, inside and out. She was about to explode. Unable to maintain even a semblance of self-control, Terelle gave in to the building orgasm. She screamed Marquise's name, her knees clamped against the sides of his face as her juices spilled. Her body quaked in long-overdue sexual release.

# Chapter 13

S he lay naked in the afterglow of a powerful orgasm, a gift from the only man she would ever love. Tears of joy watered her eyes. Marquise smoothed wayward strands of hair away from Terelle's face.

As if gauging the level of Terelle's energy, Marquise stared deeply into her eyes.

"Let's go upstairs," she suggested, responding to his unasked question.

He put his cap back on his head, picked her up, and carried her upstairs. Marquise didn't need to be pointed in the direction of Terelle's bedroom. It was the same room where they'd hastily unleashed their passion during their teens, when their hormones had raged. Terelle's childhood bedroom had served as their love nest even after they'd reached adulthood—before Marquise was sent to prison and before Terelle had found an apartment for them to call their own.

Marquise stripped out of his clothes. Seeing him totally naked sent electrical currents straight to her center. Marquise's muscular body appeared carved from dark chocolate. He looked so enticing, so deliciously edible, Terelle wanted to taste every inch of him. She wriggled downward, toward his rapidly growing black velvet erection. She wanted to suck his dick, deep throat him, so badly her mouth watered. She teased Marquise with the tip of her tongue as she circled the opening at the head of his dick, tasting his tangy pre-cum. Marquise, quivering with excitement, thrust forward. Terelle gave a soft moan as she felt his smooth knob push urgently past her lips.

Mmm, the taste. So salty and sweet. Eager for multiple sensations, Terelle pushed his dick out of her mouth and maneuvered herself farther down.

Marquise groaned as she rotated between licking and sucking his sac, rolling his balls around with her tongue.

"I love you, Marquise," she whispered. Her breath tickled his scrotum, driving him wild. She cupped his moist balls with one hand and grabbed his iron-hard shaft with the other. Rubbing his knob against her wet lips, Terelle moaned with the realization of how much she loved Marquise's dick. It was the only dick she'd ever sucked—ever fucked. The dick that now teased her lips had created life in her body.

"Don't fuck around on me anymore, Quise," she said, her voice taking on a threatening undertone.

"I won't," he gasped. "I promise, babe." Thrusting, aiming for her parted lips, Marquise struggled to get back inside Terelle's warm, moist mouth.

"This is my dick, Quise. I'm not sharing it no more. You hear me?"

"I hear you, babe. It's all yours. I swear to God. I'm a changed man. Being without my family for two years changed me. All that cheating is outta my system. "

Satisfied that Marquise belonged to her alone, Terelle opened her mouth to receive the dick she loved. As he slid his thick chocolate in and out of her mouth, there was no doubt in her mind that she'd die for his dick—kill a bitch and do time for his dick. *Bitches beware! Do not fuck with Marquise Whitsett unless you're prepared to die.*

Her distaste for guns was gone forever. She'd pull a trigger on a bitch in a hot second. And any pity she'd felt about the injustice of Kai doing time was quickly withdrawn. Kai should not have fucked with her family! Considering the damage she'd done, Kai had actually gotten off easy. But the next whoring-ass, man-stealing bitch that had the gall to wave her panties in Marquise's face had better be prepared to exit this earth because the next time Terelle pointed a gun and pulled the trigger, she would not miss. Her renewed anger at Kai Montgomery incited Terelle to apply more suction to Marquise's dick.

"Damn, babe. You gon' make me cum." Marquise placed his hands on Terelle's head and eased out. Grabbing her arm, he guided her upward. "I gotta get inside you, babe. I miss the shit outta that pussy," he moaned. He tugged at her arm, urging her to get on top. "Ride me, babe. Can you ride Daddy?"

*Fucking yes!* An hour ago, she'd had difficulty descending the stairs. Now, motivated by love and a mounting sexual desire, Terelle squatted over Marquise with the agility of a seasoned gymnast.

With a seeming will of its own, Marquise's dick snaked its way to Terelle's silky opening. Terelle pressed down, hungry for his hardness. Her pussy was wet and slippery from cunnilingus. The lips of her sex, slick and puffy, separated easily, accepting the head of his dick. She rotated her hips; her pussy muscles tightened around his throbbing shaft, taking it in inch by magnificent inch.

Marquise bit his lower lip; his face contorted as he fought the powerful urge to climax. Unable to stand the slow torture, Marquise took control. His massive hands gripped Terelle's slender waistline as he drove the full length of his hot flesh up inside her, filling her to the hilt. With his dick deeply embedded, he bounced Terelle up and down his pole.

Terelle took a long, deep breath, followed by short, sharp gasps. Her muscles clenched, she grit her teeth, and gave a husky sigh.

"You ready, babe?" he asked, recognizing the subtle signs that Terelle was close to another climax.

"I'm trying to hold back," she uttered helplessly. She could tell by the way his lips had become slack and his eyelids were squeezed shut that he, too, was on the brink of eruption.

Marquise suddenly pulled out. "Fuck it, I'm not ready to cum. Not yet. Been waiting too long." He eased her off him and lay her on her side. Slowly and gently, he slipped his dick in and out. Terelle's breathing became so ragged, she was so close to the brink, that Marquise withdrew his length, leaving in only the tip as he waited for her to regain her composure.

He kissed the back of her neck, massaged her shoulders. "You want it, babe?"

"Yes," she whispered.

"How you want it?" His voice was husky and rough as he penetrated, slipping in and out of her soft folds.

"Harder. I want it harder," Terelle demanded, panting.

Marquise repositioned her, pulled her on her knees, increasing the depth of his penetration.

"How hard you want it, babe? I don't wanna hurt you."

"Real hard, Quise. Fuck me hard," Terelle cried out, pushing backward.

Marquise obliged, slamming into her from behind. His moans,

low and deep, vibrated beneath her shrill screams. Love sounds.

As their passion crested, Terelle felt a clench deep within her. She could no longer deny herself release. "Cum with me."

Marquise's breathing quickened; he bucked within her. Together, they soared over the edge. The aftermath was violent; their bodies banged together, shuddering, convulsing, heartbeats hard and fast. The climax was peaceful; their breathing becoming even, their heartbeats slowing, merging as one.

Sweaty and spent, Marquise and Terelle needed to cool off. Marquise put his pants on and bounded down the stairs to get himself and Terelle a cold drink.

"Here you go, babe," he said when he returned to the bedroom. He handed Terelle a tall glass of fruit punch. Standing, he drained his glass and then plopped himself down on the bed beside Terelle.

"Thank you," Terelle said as she took the glass from his hand. Her voice, however, held no cheery gratitude. There was a serious quality in her tone. Her love-glazed eyes had turned clear and intense. Her lustful desires had been fulfilled and now that she was clear-headed, she needed answers to the burning questions that filled her mind.

"No matter where I was at, babe, I always came and checked up on you and Keeta. She's pretty like you, babe. She looks really happy with Saleema, but it's time to get our daughter back. Feel me? Look, I know Saleema's holding it down for us. Believe me, I've been keeping an eye on Keeta. Checking her out while she's playing at school. Scoping her getting in and out of the car with

Saleema. Listen, babe…that beef I had with Saleema is over. She came through for us. I give her mad props for the job she's doing with Keeta."

Everything Marquise said sounded good on a surface level, but Terelle had lots of questions. "What's the story, Quise?" Terelle took a swallow of the fruit juice and placed the glass on the nightstand. "You're talking about getting Markeeta back, but you're not explaining where you've been. Don't you realize everyone thought you were dead? My Aunt Bennie held a memorial service for you." Terelle closed her eyes, squeezing back tears. "I lost my mind over you…" She looked him in the eyes. "Why would you allow me to believe you were dead?" She lowered her head, fingers trembling as she pushed hair from her face.

"Look at me, babe." Marquise lifted her chin, forcing her tear-filled eyes to meet his. "I didn't have a choice. I was forced to go along with that sham—"

"Sham? What sham?" Marquise opened his mouth to speak, but Terelle cut him off. "You knew how I'd react to hearing that you were dead. How could you allow your family to be destroyed over some…some stupid sham?"

"Babe," he said softly, a warm light emanating from his eyes. "I was in deep trouble. I woke up in the hospital, shot in the neck…"

"The neck?" she wondered aloud. Terelle thought she'd accidentally shot Marquise in the head. Grateful there wasn't a bullet still lodged somewhere in his head, she murmured a prayer of thanks.

Marquise tilted his head, revealing a small, barely visible scar on his neck. Terelle grimaced at the scar she'd inflicted on the love of her life. She clenched her teeth to stop the confession from spilling from her lips. She didn't think she could bear to see his face when he found out she'd almost killed him.

"I didn't know what the fuck had happened," Marquise told her. "I was laying up in the hospital bed, a bullet hole in my neck, both legs broke. The Jamaicans shot me and that psycho bitch got scared and ran me over. The feds had the nerve to be all over my ass like I had committed a crime." He shook his head at the memory.

"Right after I came out of surgery, they handcuffed me to the hospital bed. Told me they had shorty in custody but instead of hitting her with attempted murder, they were going to slap her with a murder charge."

Puzzled, Terelle frowned.

"The feds told me that my probation violation was a serious offense. Drug laws were a lot tougher than when I got popped for drug trafficking. They said I could do a lot of time. Twenty years or more. They said since I was good as dead, I might as well cooperate with them. Now what could I do except go along with their bullshit. I didn't have a choice; I had to cooperate. But I knew, even under the influence of painkillers and white mutha-fuckas sticking a pen in my hand, forcing me to sign shit…I knew I'd find my way back to you. And Keeta." His voice cracked when he uttered his daughter's name.

"Drug laws? What do you mean, you had to cooperate? I'm not following this story, Marquise."

Marquise swallowed. "I was into some real dumb shit, babe." His Adam's apple bobbed repeatedly, his eyes became moist. "I was stupid. Lying all the time, cheating and disrespecting you. I disrespected you and my daughter when I messed around with that nut-ass chick, Kai…"

Terelle inhaled sharply at the mention of Kai's name. Up until this point, Marquise had been referring to her as "shorty" or "psycho bitch." Hearing Kai's name spoken from Marquise's lips made her want to throw a fit. But needing to hear the story, she managed to hold herself together.

"I'm sorry, babe. I know how bad I hurt you. Cheating was a bad habit I couldn't break. I never planned it; it just always seemed to happen. I was young and dumb. Hard-headed…"

"And selfish," Terelle added.

He nodded in agreement. "Yeah, real selfish. I knew I loved you with all my heart. But I never saw anything wrong with having something on the side. I got all caught up with Kai—"

"What does Kai have to do with the feds and drug laws?" Terelle interrupted, truly perplexed.

He inhaled deeply and seemed to drift on in thought. "It wasn't just about sex with her," he finally said.

Terelle flinched in pain. "Oh, no? What was it, then? Love? Were you in love with Kai?" Terelle asked, dreading Marquise's answer.

He emitted a sound of disgust. "Never that. It was about greed, babe. I thought I could use Kai for her money. Get the material things I couldn't afford to buy.

"I wanted to get my hustle on, make my own money, but the Jamaicans run Philly. They got the game on lock. I got tired of waiting around for them to let me handle some weight, so when I found out Kai was handling millions, I figured I'd roll with her for a quick minute—just long enough to get my hands on her dough." Marquise shook his head. "I ain't proud of none of that, babe. I was stupid. Only thinking about myself."

Terelle rubbed her temples. She stared at Marquise's face, trying to make some sense of what he was telling her. "I'm so confused. You're talking in circles," she said, exasperated. "First of all, you were employed—I got you that job at the nursing home so you could have your own money, to keep you out of the game."

"I tried to leave it alone. I really did. But I couldn't. I couldn't stack no real money working at that nursing home."

"If you were patient, we could have put our money together. Eventually, we would have been able to acquire all the material things we wanted."

"I know that now, but..." Marquise's voice trailed off in disgust. "But when they finally made me an offer to handle some weight, I jumped at the chance. I didn't need Kai anymore, she was high maintenance and too much trouble. So, I tried to dump her. But by then, shorty was out of control. Shorty was whack, babe."

"Nobody told you to fuck with that crazy chick!" Terelle shouted, her anger taking her voice up several octaves. She felt the piercing stab of Marquise's betrayal as keenly as if it had happened only yesterday.

"I know, babe. I'm so sorry," he said sincerely. "I tried to break up with her, but shorty started threatening some crazy shit the minute I tried to step off. She came looking for me over Jalil's crib, threatening everybody—you, me, and Ayanna. She told Ayanna she was going to call the Section 8 officials and get her thrown out. Ayanna was so scared, she told me I had to leave. Once I left the crib, Kai told me if I didn't go with her, she was going to send the cops to our place and have you arrested for receiving stolen property."

"I know. Ayanna called me after you left, she mentioned that the chick who abducted you was looking for an expensive watch."

"Yeah, the one I told you Joko gave me. I lied, babe. Kai gave me that watch, but she insured it in her name. She was going to have you arrested and I couldn't let that happen, babe, so I got in the ride with her."

"I know, Marquise," Terelle admitted, lowering her voice, concentrating on calming herself down. Getting herself worked up wasn't good for the rest of her recovery. "I have a copy of the voicemail you left for me," Terelle said gently, concentrating on keeping her anger contained.

"Yeah, I left you that message so you'd know that despite how it looked, I really did love you," Marquise said, recalling the words he'd left on Terelle's answering machine. "But she was determined to have her way. She wouldn't let go, so I decided to ride it out with her 'til she bought me a new truck. I figured after I got my hands wrapped around the steering wheel, I was going to scoop you and my baby girl up, and flee Philly—with the Jamaicans' drugs."

"You stole the Jamaicans' drugs?" Terelle's eyes were wide with fear.

Marquise cleared his throat. "Yeah. Real stupid, huh? I planned to make a connection in some hick town where no one would ever think about looking for me. Then, me and you were gonna ride out into the sunset. Move to another country. But the fed boys had been doing surveillance on the Jamaicans. They knew I was involved, so they swooped down on me at the hospital. I was dirty. Having drugs on me was a violation of my probation. They gave me a choice: snitch or do time. Big time!" Marquise shook his head. "Damn, I messed up."

Terelle shook her head, too. "I wonder what would have happened if I'd heard your message before I went out looking for you."

Marquise squinted in confusion. "You were looking for me the day I got hit?"

It was Terelle's turn to scowl. "Yes."

"Okay, now I'm confused. What are *you* talking about? I'm glad you didn't find me; they probably would have shot you, too. The feds told me they were on to my scheme. They were shooting at Kai, too. Damn shame what happened to her, but there wasn't a damn thing I could do about it. She brought that life sentence on herself. I thought her parents would use their dough and buy her out of that bogus charge. Never thought she'd have to actually do the time."

Terelle was too ashamed to speak, but it was time to divulge her secret. Finding her voice, she asked, "Are you ready to hear what really happened?" Terelle's voice was soft and shaky.

"I know what happened," he said adamantly. "I accepted being in the program. Figured I'd outsmart the feds, sneak out, scoop up you and Keeta and be out! But I outsmarted myself. I never counted on you buying that whack story that I was dead. Never took into account that hearing that kind of news would push you over the brink. You fell apart before I could get to you, babe, but I never gave up on our love. I snuck in that mental hospital, whispered in your ear, every chance I got. And you finally heard me, Terelle. Now that we have a second chance, I have to figure out a way to get out of this program."

Terelle mulled over his words. "What kind of program were you in, Quise? A drug program?"

"Naw, a witness protection program—with the feds. That's how I got the information."

"I'm confused, Marquise. Why are you in a witness protection program?"

"I just told you. I was under surveillance when I got shot." Marquise's voice faltered. "I was bangin', you know, with the Jamaican drug boys, trying to get in the fast lane. They finally let me handle some weight."

"How'd you get the money for weight?"

"I got some of it from Kai. The Jamaicans let me owe them the rest of the money. You know, they let me have it on some I.O.U. shit. With some crazy high-interest rates. I knew you wouldn't be down with me trying to sell the product, so I was gonna stiff the Jamaicans and take off with the product. Get rid of it after I skipped town."

"Quise, I can't believe you allowed yourself to get involved with those ruthless people."

"Yo, that stupid way of thinking is behind me now. I'm just trying to bring you up to date—right my wrongs with you." Marquise's eyes pleaded for understanding. "I want you to understand how things went down. Like I said, when the feds caught me dirty, the evidence they had could have sent me upstate for twenty years or more."

"I see," Terelle said, not seeing at all.

"The weird part is, I don't know how the Jamaicans found out, but somehow they knew the feds were gonna pop me and more than likely offer me a deal if I cooperated. Wasn't like I was in the major league or nothing, but I had some information the feds could use to take down the big boys. And that's why the Jamaicans hit me."

Terelle stared at Marquise. Nervously, she began forming in her mind the words that would reveal the truth. The secret that was so disturbing she'd lost her mind. And lost their daughter.

"After the feds scooped me up at the hospital," Marquise continued, "they pretended I was dead, faked a death certificate, gave me a new identity, and let Kai take the fall. I'm pretty sure they're gonna let her out after the Jamaicans go to trial."

Buying time before she admitted to the truth, Terelle turned to Marquise. His disclosure was startling. Did the feds really believe the Jamaicans had shot Marquise? Oh God, would she be arrested when the truth came to light? Then, it hit her. Marquise had been duped by the feds.

# Chapter 14

K ai had been luxuriating in Parker's hotel room for two days. Parker often mumbled discontentedly that he needed his space. He constantly complained about the expensive meals and other services Kai had charged to his room, but Kai didn't care. She didn't intend to budge until Parker provided all the information she'd requested.

So far, he'd gathered choppy leads, but nothing useful—no exact addresses for Melissa Peterson or the Montgomerys. He had, however, learned the whereabouts of Terelle Chambers. It turned out the little ghetto girl was convalescing in Spring Haven mental hospital. Kai never imagined that the underprivileged Terelle could afford residency at the exclusive mental health facility. Before she'd gone to prison, Kai had experienced a meltdown and had spent a few weeks at Spring Haven. How the hell, she wondered, could Terelle Chambers afford such expensive treatment?

Kai had never experienced a second of guilt over falsely accusing a Spring Haven employee of rape. Now, knowing that the facility was treating her nemesis, Kai felt even more justified in having been awarded close to a million dollars for their wrongdoing. Of course Kai had never fully benefited from the money. Her biological mother had skedaddled with all the money in her bank account and Kai seriously doubted if the crude woman had even a penny left. When she caught up with that biological bitch, nothing short of murder would satisfy her.

Settling the score with Terelle was not a top priority. Kai preferred to collect the money owed her before paying the slumbering Terelle a surprise visit. But Terelle was not going to enjoy the peaceful passing Kai had originally planned for her. Oh, no! There'd be no compassionate smothering with a pillow. She'd grip that thug chick by the shoulders and shake her into awareness. Kai wanted Terelle to fully experience every ounce of her hatred. For what she did to Kai, Terelle deserved to lose fingers, an eyeball, a toe or two. Oh hell, why not emulate Daddy dear and perform free surgery for the poor, disadvantaged slut. Giving Terelle a hysterectomy and a double mastectomy seemed like the charitable thing to do. Yes, Terelle was going to pay dearly for her crime.

The carnage and bloodshed Kai would leave behind would be so Charles Manson-like, the entire city of Philadelphia would quake in fear. Any officials of the law who came looking for Kai would be shit out of luck. Before the idiot police force could put two and two together and point their incompetent fingers in her direction, Kai would take her millions and flee to a remote exotic land where she could sit back and sip pastel-colored exotic drinks while the natives lined up to indulge her kinky sexual desires.

There was a tingling going on inside her kitty. Oddly, vengeful thoughts intermingled with kinky fantasies served as a powerful aphrodisiac. Her kitty purred like crazy, it refused to calm down.

Kai patted her cat as if to say, *okay, all right, I'll take care of you*. She checked the time. Parker wouldn't be back from the day's seminars at the convention center for at least five or six hours. *Crap!* Even getting poked with his little cock was better than self-administered release.

She was briefly disappointed, but instantly perked up when she realized there was hope for her dilemma. She'd visited the hotel's hair salon, fitness center, several lounges and restaurants, and of course, she was a regular at the Martini Bar, but she hadn't gotten around to enjoying the hotel's Exotica Spa.

There were a scattering of brochures on top of the desk in Parker's hotel room. She skimmed through them and quickly located the Exotica Spa brochure. Damn, the spa required an appointment. Kai picked up the phone and pressed two buttons. "I'm a guest in room nine-oh-five; I'd like to make an appointment to get a massage. Sometime this afternoon, if possible."

"You're in luck," said the cheery voice of the spa's receptionist. "Someone just cancelled. I have a one-fifteen appointment available. She was scheduled for the deluxe package."

"What's included in the deluxe?" Kai asked.

"A facial, body scrub, body wrap, foot bath, and a full body massage."

"Mmm, sounds yummy. By the way, who gives the massage?"

"Our technicians are all highly skilled and certified—"

"Male or female?" Kai interrupted.

"Uh, it's your choice, of course, but your appointment is with Connor. He's male," the receptionist added, keeping the sunshine in her voice.

"Okay, see you in a few."

Connor reminded Kai of Reece, the Spring Haven employee she'd accused of rape. Like Reece, Connor was medium height, broad shouldered, and handsome. Amazingly, he also had platinum-colored hair and beautiful green eyes, exactly like Reece.

Connor's experienced fingers sank into the muscles of Kai's back.

"Ow!" she complained.

"Sorry. The deep tissue massage can be painful, but the healing benefits are worth the initial discomfort," Connor told her in a velvety voice.

"I can think of a more sensitive area that could use some deep tissue massaging. Catch my drift?" she asked, turning onto her back and flinging off the towel. Nude, Kai separated her thighs, inviting Connor to pleasure her center.

"Oh! I'm sorry. I didn't realize you wanted a sensual massage," Connor responded in a professional tone.

"Does that translate to deep tissue fuck?"

"It certainly does, madam. We are more than delighted to provide deep penile penetration if you'd like."

Kai gave Connor a dazzling smile and spread her pussy lips for him.

When Connor unzipped his pants, he pulled out a decent-sized tool. Kai closed her eyes in near ecstasy. It wasn't huge; but it was attractive, with a nice shape and even coloring.

Connor slathered his penis with a warming lubricant. Wearing the serious expression of a craftsman at work, he drove his cock in and out of Kai's kitty with precision and expertise. Hitting the right spots, Connor filled her with a succession of unrelenting penile thrusts until Kai reached a powerful orgasm. She screamed in surrender, emitting long, strangled cries of passion.

With a warm, wet towel, Connor, still serious—his manner reminiscent of a physician caringly tending to a patient—dabbed the outside of Kai's pussy. Gently, he separated the soft pussy petals and used the warm towel to soothe the delicate flesh. Kai moaned softly as Connor inserted a towel-covered finger to soak up her juices.

Lucky for Connor, his performance was magnificent. He wouldn't meet the same fate as Reece. Reece had been such an abominably bad fuck, he'd left Kai no choice but to take legal action against him and the hospital that employed him.

"You were great," Kai complimented. "Thanks a bunch!"

"You're quite welcome, madam."

Feeling drowsy, Kai snuggled into a curled position atop the massage table. "I guess I could use a power nap."

"I'll get you a warm blanket," Connor offered. He went to a cabinet and returned with a soft blanket. "When you're ready, press the button," Connor said, pointing to an overhead button. "Jorge will come right in to administer your foot bath."

"There's more?" she asked, bolting upright and wearing a dreamy smile.

"It's all part of your deluxe package."

"Does Jorge give a sensual foot massage?"

"Most definitely. And Sergio will provide a superior body scrub and body wrap. Our premier aesthetician, Emily, is scheduled to give you a facial."

Kai frowned at the mention of a female name. "Nix the facial."

"As you wish," Connor said respectfully.

Perhaps the day would come when Kai resumed an interest in pussy. Right now, keeping her kitty filled up with hot cum was at the top of her to-do list.

"I'll make sure Jorge and Sergio are aware of your preferences. Just press the button when you're ready."

Kai could certainly live the rest of her life like this—and she fully intended to. She smiled a thank you, making a mental note to add a big tip for Connor and company—courtesy of Parker, of course.

# Chapter 15

"After we get married," Marquise said, unaware that Terelle had just experienced a startling revelation. "We could probably leave the federal program. If we get in Philadelphia's witness relocation program, we could keep our identities, wouldn't have to change Keeta's name or anything. The only problem," he said, crinkling his brow, "is the city program is run by the district attorney's office and it doesn't provide no real protection. All they do is move you around the city from one ZIP code to the next. The Jamaicans will kill us if we stay in Philly."

Terelle couldn't believe what she was hearing. The feds had really deceived Marquise. "Baby, listen to me…the feds aren't protecting you. They lied to you. The Jamaicans didn't shoot you."

"What? How would you know?"

It was time to confess. Terelle swallowed. "I was there."

Marquise's brows knitted in confusion.

"I saw you and that social worker. In the garage. You were down on your knees—eating that bitch's pussy."

Marquise drew in a sharp breath. "Aw, damn," he blurted, his voice filled with passionate remorse.

"We followed you—me and Saleema followed you and Kai Montgomery to Dave and Buster's." Terelle grimaced, disgusted by having to verbalize Kai Montgomery's name. "We were hiding behind a car in the underground garage," Terelle continued. Speaking in a soft voice, she painfully relived the day that changed her life. "When I saw you put your face between that bitch's legs, I lost it."

The revolting scene of Marquise down on his knees giving Kai head flashed across her mind. The memory was so obscene, Terelle shuddered.

"I wasn't eating her pussy!" Marquise protested.

"Stop lying, Quise. Damn! I said I saw you!"

"Aiight, aiight. I know how it looked. And I admit, I had my face down there, but I wasn't doing nothing. I was trying to talk myself into it, but I felt like a chump being down on my knees like that. I told myself, 'Man, get the fuck off your knees. Fuck that trick!' I couldn't let shorty pimp me like that, so I stood up and bent shorty over the hood of her car. Then the lights went out. Can't remember getting shot or nothing. Next thing I knew, I was in the hospital surrounded by the feds. But I'm so, so sorry, babe." Marquise's voice broke in the midst of his apology. "Can you forgive me?" Anxiously, he chewed on his bottom lip.

Too choked up to speak, Terelle nodded her head.

Marquise changed the tense moment by flashing a bright smile. "The only person I ever went down on is you! Today was my first time, babe."

Terelle couldn't keep from grinning. "You did it like a pro," she said, blushing at the memory.

"Been watching porno flicks while I've been in the program. Got my game tight," he said, laughing.

Terelle laughed. "You're still crazy, Quise. Damn, I love you. But, baby, you have to listen to me." Terelle's voice became serious.

"Those feds are not trying to protect you; they've been lying to you. They've been using you to get at the Jamaicans."

"How do you know they're lying?"

"I know they're lying because…"

"Because what?"

Terelle swallowed hard. "Because *I* shot you, Quise!"

"Fuck outta here," he said in disbelief. "You're scared to death of guns."

Tears welled and began to stream down her face. "I shot you, Quise." Her voice trembled, her body shook. "It was an accident, baby. I was trying to shoot that half-white bitch. When I saw you bent over, banging her like she had the best pussy in the world, the rage that went through me took away my fear of guns. I grabbed Saleema's heat, aimed it straight at Kai's fuckin' head," Terelle confessed, her voice taking on an angry timbre. "But all of a sudden, you raised your head! The bullet with that bitch's name on it, hit you." Terelle covered her face in horror. Marquise wrapped his arms around her. "Oh, Quise. I thought I killed you. I lost my mind over the thought of losing you." More bitter tears poured down Terelle's face.

Murmuring soothingly, Marquise pulled Terelle closer. "It's aiight, babe. I deserved that hit. I deserved all the misery I've been living with. I'm just sorry that because of my dumb ass, you went out like that. I'm mad as hell that you and Keeta had to pay for my mistakes."

"You don't understand…you can't testify, Marquise," Terelle said, her words muffled against Marquise's chest. She lifted her head and spoke clearly. "The feds are not gonna protect you. Can't you see? They didn't know or care who shot you. They lied to you, making you believe it was the Jamaicans. After they get your testimony, they're not going to care what the Jamaicans do to you."

Gnawing nervously on his lip, Marquise's dark-brown eyes bore into Terelle's. "You're right, babe," he agreed.

"So, what are we gonna do?"

"I don't know; I'm tryna think." He chewed on his lip. Concern distorted his handsome features, while his eyes darted about worriedly. In deep thought, Marquise rose from the bed, pacing with long strides inside Terelle's small bedroom.

"I gotta get outta the program. Go in hiding somewhere. Can't stay in Philly. The Jamaicans are dangerous people; if they find out I'm still alive, they'll come after me." He paused. "They'll come after you…" Marquise gulped in fear. "And Keeta." Marquise turned dead-serious eyes on Terelle. "Babe, we gotta grip up Markeeta. All of us gotta get the fuck outta Philly."

Looking anxious, Terelle wrung her hands. "Oh, my God. We can't let anything happen to Keeta!"

"I know, babe. I know."

"Saleema has legal custody of Markeeta. As far as Children and Youth Services are concerned, Markeeta's father is dead and her mother is a disabled lunatic."

"You're in your right mind now. And I'm damn sure not dead, so what's the problem?"

"Yeah, *we* know that, but Saleema thinks I'm crazy. She's trying to keep Markeeta. She's planning to get married to some white dude and take Keeta to the Cayman Islands. I kept insisting that you came to see me in the mental hospital, but she didn't believe me. She thinks I'm too crazy to be a fit mother."

"Fuck what Saleema thinks," Marquise bellowed. Looking like a wild man, he banged the top of Terelle's bureau. "Yo, I'm not dead and you're not crazy. Now, that's the muthafuckin' facts. We gon' get our baby girl. Call Saleema right the fuck now and tell her to pack Keeta's stuff. Saleema gotta be smoking dope if she thinks I'm gon' sit back and allow her to take my baby girl to some fuckin' island. Hell fuckin' naw. It ain't sweet like that!" Marquise punched his open palm as if ready to wage war against Saleema and anyone else who tried to stand in his way.

"Calm down, Quise. We're gonna get Markeeta back. With you in the flesh, standing by my side, it shouldn't be a problem convincing Saleema that I'm not crazy. But we have to hurry up before she takes off for the Caymans."

"When's she supposed to be rollin'?"

"Soon—a few weeks," Terelle said, shaking her head miserably.

"Man, I'll whip Saleema's and her man's ass. I ain't nevah liked that bitch, noway. I take back all that good shit I said earlier. Saleema can kiss my black ass. I ain't letting her and one of her freak-ass tricks raise my daughter!"

"But Saleema has legal rights to Keeta. Suppose she refuses to give her up?"

Marquise's face twisted into an awful grimace. "I ain't tryna hear that shit, Terelle. Saleema's gon' give me my daughter."

Terelle drew in air. "In my heart, I don't think Saleema has been trying to hurt me. Her intentions have been nothing but honorable. She thought I was too crazy to look after Keeta's best interests and that's why she kept her from me. She's trying to do the job she knows I would want her to if I were thinking clearly."

"But you are thinking clearly, babe. You're aiight, now. Ain't nothing crazy about you."

"Let's be reasonable, Quise."

"Fuck being reasonable," he shouted. Marquise gave Terelle

an evil look. "Fuck Saleema, aiight? Markeeta's our daughter. If we have to snatch her, then that's what the fuck we'll do."

"Quise?"

"What?"

"Will Keeta and I have to change our identities if we go on the run with you?"

"Hell, yeah! We can't put our real identities on blast if we want to live."

Terelle looked distraught. "That's going to be so confusing for her. She's already attached to Saleema. If we snatch her and give her a new identity, she's going to be more confused than ever. Do you think that's fair to Markeeta? Do you think disrupting our daughter's life, deliberately risking her life just so we have her with us, is fair? Do you think putting her in harm's way is good parenting?"

"Whatchu tryna say, Terelle?"

Terelle swallowed. She swiped at her teary eyes. "You know what I'm saying, Marquise."

"Sounds like you don't think you're capable of taking care of our daughter. I disagree. Look, I got my game tight; can't nothing stop me from taking care of mine." He nodded his head emphatically. "Believe that!"

Terelle responded with silence and a skeptical expression.

"We're a family, babe," he said cajolingly. "We have to stick together."

"My capabilities are debatable. I've applied for social security because I'm certifiably mentally ill and considered physically disabled, also."

Marquise leaned back, his face creased in disagreement. "Ain't nothin' wrong witchu! Aiight," he said with outstretched hands,

"I admit, you could stand to put on a little weight here and there, but other than that…how you figure you're physically disabled?"

"I haven't been released from physical therapy yet. It's just a technicality, but it's documented that I'm mentally and physically disabled."

"Aiight, aiight. But we both know that's some bullshit they put down on paper."

"Quise, you're deliberately missing my point."

"What's your point?" He shrugged his shoulders in exasperation.

"What I'm trying to say is…" Terelle blinked back tears. "I'll go to the end of the earth with you, Marquise. You know that. But I can't…I refuse to drag Markeeta into our mess. She's safe with Saleema. If the Jamaicans decide to come after her, she'll be safe and sound and out of the country."

"I'm not leaving our daughter behind; we can't run without her, babe." In an obvious panic, Marquise gazed around desperately. "She's just a child; children adjust to all kinds of shit. As long as we're with her, showing her love, she'll be aiight."

"It's not that simple. She doesn't even know us anymore. Suppose she doesn't adjust?"

Perplexed, Marquise tilted his head to the side. "I kept my eye on Keeta for the past two years. I always knew she was safe. Fuck outta here; I'm not letting her go to no damn Cayman Islands. I can't have my baby girl a million fuckin' miles outta my sight. How I look letting some wacko trick and a triflin' ho take my daughter that far away?" He snorted in contempt and angrily smacked his empty glass off the top of the bureau. The carpet muffled the sound of the glass hitting the floor and also prevented it from shattering.

Though Marquise appeared to have matured—and he had in

many ways—it was still painfully clear to Terelle that he had not mastered any control of his irrational, volatile temper.

"Saleema's out of the sex business," Terelle offered in a calming tone.

Marquise sucked his teeth and then gave a loud and malicious guffaw. "Who's to say she won't go back to her old whoring ways if money gets tight?"

Sudden anger burned Terelle's face. "Just like you and me, Saleema didn't have anyone looking out for her. She started turning tricks around the same time you started hustling and she was still tricking when she was forced to become a parent to our daughter. I didn't see you breaking down her door trying to get Keeta away from her while you were hiding out," Terelle shouted. "Saleema didn't know how to be a mother; she didn't have any parenting experience, but my girl got creative. When she realized that selling her body wasn't bringing in enough to take care of both herself and our daughter, she started her own outcall service. You can call her every name in the book, but Saleema did the best she could. Her life was turned upside-down because of me and you, because of our bullshit. You refused to get a grip—you continually allowed your dick to lead you around by the nose, and I was so stupid, I took your shit until I couldn't take it anymore." Terelle eyed Marquise closely. "You let a slut bitch who didn't even know the meaning of love take us all down, and you have the nerve to call Saleema out of her name."

Marquise flinched as if he'd just received a succession of hammering blows.

"Running an outcall service was illegal, but my girl had to get creative and business savvy so she could make sure our daughter got a proper education. Profits from her sex trade business paid for Markeeta's private school and that fancy mental institution I was wasting away in for two years. So, don't be trying to assassinate my best friend's character just because you're angry and frustrated. Saleema did what she had to do so she could hold it down for our daughter! She kept Markeeta safe and loved when neither of her parents could do shit for her!"

During Terelle's tirade, Marquise head was hung low. When she finally paused, Marquise raised his head. "I feel about this small." He positioned his thumb beneath his index finger, leaving very little space between his two fingers. "Are you finished making me feel like shit?" he inquired, contrite.

Terelle nodded, her facial expression turning from angry to compassionate. "All I'm saying," she said softly, "is that you and I have both made some bad mistakes. But Markeeta is innocent. I've seen how well-adjusted and happy she is. Saleema has done a damn good job of raising her." Terelle looked at Marquise intently.

"True," he admitted.

"I refuse to uproot Markeeta and drag her all around to God knows where with us. We don't even have a plan. All we know is that we have to run. For our lives! We can't reclaim our daughter until this shit is over and we're absolutely certain that we can give her a safe and stable home."

# Chapter 16

"Nine hundred and twenty-five dollars!" Parker yelled, waving a statement with the hotel's letterhead. "I just stopped at the front desk to pick up my messages and this is what I'm greeted with—a goddamn spa bill for over nine hundred dollars."

Kai rubbed her eyes, and lazily straightened her body from its curled position. She propped herself up on an elbow and delivered a series of sighs, then narrowed her eyes in a manner that was designed to inform Parker that she didn't appreciate being rudely awakened from her late-afternoon nap.

"What the hell did you get done? Cosmetic surgery?" Parker continued ranting. He was red-faced and breathing hard. "This has to stop, Kai. You're costing me an arm and a leg. I feel like you're taking advantage of me." Parker huffed and puffed some more. "I can't deal with this. I really need you to leave. You have to go—right now!" Parker yelled.

"That's not a problem," Kai said calmly as she swung her legs over the side of the bed. "Did you get the information you promised to get for me?"

"I certainly did," Parker told her, his words coated with contempt. He tossed several pages of computer-printed pages at her.

"Here's everything you need on the Montgomerys. That

woman—Melissa Peterson—is locked up for a number of charges including extortion. Seems she was trying to shake down the Montgomerys. You can pay your *mother* a visit at her new place of residence, Sybil Brand Women's Prison in California."

Kai took note of the fact that Parker's lips curled maliciously when he spat the word *mother*. He had personally berated her with the unkind reminder that she was the natural spawn of gutter trash. Her birth mother was a black ignoramus, who had no clue how to outmaneuver rich, white people. *Crap!* What a dumb bitch Kai had for a mother.

Kai gave a bitter chuckle and kissed good-bye all hope of ever retrieving the money Melissa Peterson had swindled from her.

*Way to go, Mom. What an embarrassment you continue to be. You should have stayed in your lane and kept up your small-time hustle— prostituting and hoodwinking your incarcerated daughter.*

Kai threw her legs over the side of the bed. She'd been napping after her romp with Connor, Jorge, and Sergio. Oh, the things Jorge did to her feet! Sliding his cock in and out between her toes had sent sparks to her kitty. The edible body wrap that Sergio applied and digested… Kai got chills just thinking about him nibbling exotic fruit from her nipples and between her legs. Kai had learned a thing or two today.

She felt a tingling in her pleasure center. Crap! She was fuckin' horny again. If she weren't so disgusted with Parker, she'd suggest a farewell fuck. After dressing quickly, Kai searched the contents of her purse, making sure all her cash was there as well as the paper with Parker's personal information.

"By the way, honey," Kai said as she sauntered toward the door. "You were in such a rush this morning, you left a folder behind." She pointed to a folder lying atop the desk.

Parker gasped in shock. His eyes shot downward to his briefcase, which was on the floor, propped against the legs of the desk chair. "That folder should have been in my briefcase; how'd it get over there?"

"Beats me!" Kai shrugged. She blew Parker a kiss and slammed the door. She'd actually lifted the folder from his briefcase as he slept the night before. After getting him drunk, she'd used his camera to take lots of compromising pictures, downloaded them to his laptop and later printed the pictures in the hotel's computer center. She'd also made copies of his personal information, which she'd lifted from his briefcase. A girl never knew when she'd be required to drive a hard bargain. Should that time occur, having a little leverage would certainly give her an edge.

"Can you get me a cab?" Kai asked the doorman after exiting the hotel.

"Sorry, ma'am. I can't leave my post. You can go inside and have the front desk call one for you."

"How long will that take?"

The doorman shrugged. "Depends… could take up to an hour. You'll probably make out better if you flag one down on Market Street or walk around the corner. They're usually several cabs sitting outside the Convention Center."

She sighed, sucked her teeth, and rolled her eyes. "Thanks for nothing," she muttered. For Kai, hailing a cab seemed as foreign as sticking her thumb out to hitchhike. It was as unfamiliar and distasteful as descending the putrid-smelling stairs of the Broad Street subway. Prior to being incarcerated, she'd driven a luxury car. Damn, she missed her Benz. Her parents had no doubt made a nice profit on the sale of her car. No way was she running out into traffic, waving her hands like a dumb schmuck. She'd watched reruns of *Sex and the City*; she'd noticed how week after week, Carrie and her friends still hadn't mastered the art of flagging down a cab without giving up a large portion of their dignity and self-respect.

Prancing along Market Street, Kai spotted a caravan of parked cabs—most of them yellow, some were dark brown, maroon, and tan. She plopped herself into the backseat of the first cab she approached. "The airport," she said, and then gave a sigh of relief when the African driver nodded.

"Okay," he said good-naturedly as he pulled away from the curb and slowly merged into traffic. "My name is Trevor," the driver said cheerily.

*Whatever!* she thought with a smirk and then rolled her eyes. However, despite her annoyance at the cabbie's uncalled-for self-introduction, Kai couldn't help giving a sigh of relief. Her search for a taxi hadn't been as much of an ordeal as she'd expected.

"I'll take the quick route," the driver said, flashing pearly white teeth.

Kai could see his face in the rearview mirror. She'd gotten into the cab without actually looking at his face. To her surprise, the cab driver was very handsome. He had angular features, full, sensual lips, high cheekbones, and a pair of dark, deep-set eyes that blazed with passion as they appraised her.

Marquise Whitsett was the first black man Kai had ever fucked. After Marquise—after being in the slammer and all—she'd given her body to two other black men. Hell, she'd fallen hard for that no-good Mookie, but despite her sexual dalliances with them, black men still seemed strange and forbidden—an unfamiliar species to whom she was sexually attracted but with whom she felt absolutely no kinship.

To hell with her curly hair and olive complexion and to hell with her black biological mother! Kai was raised in a white community by white parents. In her heart she felt like a white girl. Anyone who thought otherwise could simply kiss her ass.

"We'll be at Philly International in no time at all," Trevor announced.

Kai liked his accent. It had a sexy, velvety quality like the African actor in the film *Blood Diamond*, which, unfortunately, she was forced to view in a crowded room with a pack of funky female prisoners.

She'd never fucked an African before, but had developed an interest when she'd heard her fellow inmates extol the physical attributes of African men. The inmates had claimed that Africans were all hung like horses. Certainly, *all* African males couldn't be well endowed, common sense told her. It had to be a myth.

"So, tell me," she said, leaning forward flirtatiously.

"Tell you what?" the driver asked and suddenly flooded the cab with roaring laughter. The sound was jolting—as loud and thunderous as if the radio had been suddenly turned to full blast. Kai was shocked. She hadn't said anything funny. Had she been in a particularly sour mood, Kai would have resented such uncalled-for merriment. But she had started to feel pretty good. Sexually inquisitive and aroused, she squeezed her thighs together and asked breathily, "Is it true that you guys have really big ones?" Prepared for another assault of ear-splitting mirth, Kai quickly reared back. She was tempted to cover her ears with her palms to protect her eardrums from the driver's deafening laughter.

"That's a myth!" the driver said and then released another loud guffaw. "The connection between penis size and African ancestry is erroneous."

Her lips scrunched together in disappointment.

"Not all Africans have big ones—but I do!" he boasted without laughter.

Kai beamed; her stomach clenched in excitement. "Forget the quick route. Wanna fuck me in your cab?"

"No! Not in my cab. The sex smell would be very bad for business."

"Do you want to get a room or something?" she asked irritably.

"No, no. Very bad for business. I can't leave my cab unattended."

"Well, where the hell do you want to do it?"

"Outside—in the wilderness," he said casually. Too casually for such an outlandish suggestion.

"Wilderness! We're not in Africa, buddy. We're in Philadelphia. Now, tell me where the heck do you expect to find any wilderness in a heavily populated city?"

"There is such a place," the driver said self-assuredly. "It's not too far from the airport."

She gave his proposal some thought. Though she doubted that the cabbie would be able to find any "wilderness," the idea of fucking outside in some out-of-the way, woodsy area was stimulating. Kai pinched her stiffening nipples in anticipation of getting sexed Zulu-style outside.

## Chapter 17

Fifteen minutes later, about a mile from the airport, Trevor pulled into the Tinicum woods.

"Despite its urban location, the Tinicum National Wildlife Refuge provides a home to a variety of wildlife," he told Kai, sounding like a tourist guide. He flashed another sparkling smile.

"What kind of wildlife?"

"Deer, fox, raccoons, opossums..."

Frowning, Kai looked around. "Lock the doors," she demanded. "I refuse to leave the *refuge* of this cab. No way I'm going out there," she said firmly.

"You'll be safe with me."

"The sun's going down; this area looks dark and ominous..." Kai paused, hugging herself. "This is definitely not my flow. I don't see how I can get aroused if I have to worry about being mauled by a wild animal."

On cue, Trevor delivered hearty laughter. "You're safe here. Trust me. Come!" He opened the driver's side door, got out, and walked to the back of the cab and opened the trunk. He appeared at the passenger window, grinning and holding a folded blanket that he'd gotten out of the trunk. "No harm will come to you. I promise. Come, please," he repeated, his large hand outstretched.

"Don't you want to show me your lovely vagina?" he cajoled in a sexy, silken voice.

Kai's kitty went into a spasm and purred like crazy.

"A beautiful woman such as you must possess a fine-looking and sweet-smelling flower. I bet it's soft and pink inside."

His unusual form of flattery and the lilt in his voice were causing Kai to cream her panties. If his dick lived up to the sexiness of his voice, Kai would be a goner. She suddenly understood why the ultra-blonde model dropped babies like a rabbit for that scarred-up African singer. African men were sexy and shameless seducers.

"Come now, show me your flower," Trevor insisted. "I'm very anxious to see it."

*Mmm.* Trevor was talking dirty but the words came out sounding melodic and sweet. Her kitty stopped purring and started to roar. Against her better judgment, Kai unlocked the door.

"Ah, what a beauty," Trevor said as he took Kai's hand, assisting her out of the cab. He released her hand and walked around, surveying the wooded area.

Kai noticed that Trevor held his carriage in an erect, regal manner. He selected a spot and spread the blanket in the midst of high grass and tall weeds. Trevor was taller than Kai had realized, and muscular, with an incredibly broad chest. He kept his shirt on but shed his pants without compunction, as if he were in the privacy of his own bedroom.

Kai's eyes were fixed on the big bulge inside Trevor's underwear. She eagerly waited for him to give her a glimpse of his big groin muscle.

When he stuck his hands inside the opening of his boxers, Kai gasped in shock. And revulsion. Trevor unfurled a long penis—

nearly half the size of a man's arm. He was well endowed, indeed. But he was uncircumcised. Yuck! There was an abundance of excess, loose foreskin hanging over the tip of his giant penis.

Kai grimaced and looked away.

Oblivious to Kai's revulsion, Trevor began to stroke his unattractive appendage. Using a full-fist grip, he retracted the foreskin as his hand glided up and down the length of his penis. His dick grew disturbingly large. It became so engorged, it took on the appearance of a strong and sturdy tree branch.

Kai gawked in horror and fascination.

"What's wrong? Have you never been loved by a penis in its natural form?"

She hadn't. However, with the foreskin pulled back, the cab driver's dick was no longer repulsive. It was dark and arched upward like an unsheathed, mighty sword. Trevor polished his dick with the pre-cum that oozed from the enormous head. His weapon shimmered and pulsed. It was the biggest, most perfectly formed, most beautiful fucking mechanism Kai had ever beheld.

Silently, reverently, Kai disrobed and lowered herself upon the blanket. Kai sensed the African would be an unimaginative lover. He'd assume that the girth and length of his dick exempted him from having to bother with tenderness or creativity. Kai's thoughts turned briefly to the sexy male trio who'd pleasured her at the Exotica Spa. Connor, Jorge, and Sergio were all extremely caring and creative.

So what! She didn't care. The beast between Trevor's legs would give her a hard, rough ride—a fuck she wouldn't soon forget. She gazed at his darkly pigmented, spear-like weapon and found her pussy pulsing out of control. A man who possessed such magnificent machinery did not need to be inventive. Her fear of wild animals disappeared as Kai lay spread-eagle, waiting for the African to ravage her.

While continuing to stroke himself, Trevor knelt down on the blanket. His weapon was aimed toward her face. "Look at how your beauty arouses my manhood." The hole in the center of his giant knob widened as more pre-cum pumped out.

Without planning to, Kai propped herself up with her elbows. She licked her lips involuntarily.

"Try it," Trevor offered. He flashed a broad grin as he inched closer. "Open your mouth; it's very tasty."

He was an obnoxious and cocky bastard, Kai decided, but God help her, she couldn't deny that she wanted to taste the creamy fluid that trailed down his sturdy black shaft. Refusing to completely obey, but desiring the taste of his elixir, she parted her lips—slightly.

Trevor smoothed back the coils of hair that partially obscured her face. "Your beauty should never be concealed," he told her as he guided his slippery knob to her lips.

Hit by a sudden pang of sexual hunger, Kai moaned as she opened her mouth wide, determined to suck every ounce of cum out of his dick.

"No, no, no," Trevor admonished softly. "Don't behave like that. Are you a whore?"

"No," Kai responded in a whisper, her tongue flicking out, capturing the moisture Trevor had deposited on her lips.

"Then act like a lady, not a whore. A whore is a disgusting type of person, don't you agree?"

Kai nodded helplessly. She was shocked at her reaction. She should have been cursing this black bastard out instead of agreeing with him. What the hell was wrong with her? *I'm horny!* Yes, she was horny and willing to do whatever it took to get the dick! She'd curse his ass out after she reached an orgasm.

"A lady performs fellatio politely and slowly. She sucks a penis with poise and dignity." He spoke softly, seductively as he slid his dick past Kai's lips, touching her nose with his slick and fragrant tip.

Trevor smelled masculine. He emitted a powerful, musky scent.

Oh, God! Kai felt light-headed and woozy. She was so intoxicated by his scent, she had to fight the urge to open her mouth wide and swallow his dick. She pursed her lips. It wasn't likely that Trevor would approve of any tendencies toward greed.

"A lady takes very small, dainty sips of a man's ejaculation. Do you agree?"

"Right," Kai readily agreed.

"A whore is a perverted person," he said in a harsh voice. "She guzzles down semen until her belly is full—until she's drunk with pleasure," he explained, angrily distinguishing the differences between a lady and a whore. Trevor took a breath. "I prefer to be in the company of a lady. Are you a lady or are you a whore?"

"I'm a lady," she said meekly. Her blatant lie made her cringe. Obviously she was a slut and a whore, who did she think she was fooling?

"You can't be a lady with tainted blood. I can tell you're of mixed race. There's a ball of confusion inside you. You're a wild child. Wanton. Untamed."

Trevor had a point. She was confused, no doubt about it, and she'd already admitted to herself that she was slightly insane. But it hadn't occurred to her that her mental problem stemmed from being of mixed parentage.

"I am a purebred black man." There was pride in Trevor's voice.

"In other words, I am a pedigreed animal and you are just a mutt." He gave Kai a sympathetic smile and shook his head sadly.

Kai dropped her head in shame. She hated being a mutt. She tried so hard to act superior and white but Trevor saw right through her. Damn him.

A myriad of emotions plagued her. First of all, the tables had turned and Trevor was obviously in control of this completely bizarre scene. But instead of running from the absurd scene, she found herself mesmerized by Trevor's superior attitude and hypnotized by his big, black dick, which swung like a pendulum. Kai salivated and battled badly with the overwhelming desire to saturate his hard, dark flesh with her juicy mouth and pussy. But she knew if she displayed any tendencies associated with whorishness, Trevor would swiftly retrieve his dick and self-righteously stuff it back inside his boxer shorts.

She sucked the tip of Trevor's dick and licked his length in a prim and proper manner. After close to an hour of this "ladylike" behavior, Kai got so aroused by his low moans and exotic love language, she lost her head and gave him a thorough tongue lashing that resulted in loud, undignified slurping sounds.

Trevor disengaged his dick from her mouth and wagged a reproachful finger. "You'll get no more of this Grade A meat until you learn to mind your manners."

Feeling deprived, she gave a small whimper. She wanted and needed more.

Trevor reinserted his penis and Kai, completely conscious of conducting herself properly, sucked quietly. Gracefully, she swallowed tiny portions of the pre-ejaculatory fluid. She behaved so well and with such refinement, Trevor became overly aroused. He forced the full length of his heavily veined dick inside her mouth and down her throat. Kai was being strangled by a big dick. Her mouth was stretched wide and gaping in anxious anticipation of the delicious flooding inside her mouth that would precede the pussy pleasure Trevor could provide.

Trevor released a generous amount of creamy fluid, some of which spilled out of Kai's mouth and ran down her chin. Reflexively, she raised the back of her hand up to her chin.

"No, don't use your hand; that is not proper etiquette." Taking several long, proud strides, Trevor rushed toward the cab. He opened the front passenger door and rustled around inside the glove compartment.

The African returned to the blanketed area where Kai remained on her knees with sperm dribbling down her chin. He handed her a greasy yellow napkin, which was emblazoned with the logo of a fast-food restaurant. "Dab your lips," he instructed and handed Kai the crinkled napkin.

Kai accepted the soiled napkin and murmured, "Thank you."

"You've been a fine lady," he complimented after she wiped away all signs of his hot lust.

Trevor got down on the blanket with Kai. "Lie on your back and spread your legs for me."

Happily obliging, Kai spread her legs wide.

# Chapter 18

Kai turned up her nose at all who had the misfortune of being in close proximity as she sashayed down a pathway inside the airport. Unburdened by luggage, carry-on or otherwise, she swung her arms and her hips as if she were on the catwalk during Fashion Week in New York.

Her designer-wear was oh, so two years ago and her glittery diamonds and other sparkly jewelry remained secured inside the prison vault, but it didn't matter. Emulating a supermodel, Kai held her head high and strutted her stuff.

Her sassy walk wasn't the ostentatious runway strut she would have preferred had she been physically able, but after being nearly gutted by the African's tree trunk-sized dick, she couldn't quite manage a full-fledged strut. Under the circumstances, Kai did the best she could to announce to the world that she was happy to be *FREE!*

Yes, she was feeling herself. Getting good dick had a way of making a woman feel like she could conquer the world. Prepared to wage war against her parents, Kai felt invincible. Perhaps it was the African's semen, some of which seeped into the crotch of her panties.

Trevor's big dick had nearly split her in two, but what he'd given her was worth the sweet pain. The African had pumped power into her pussy and she wasn't about to waste another drop. Tightening her vaginal walls to securely store the warrior cum inside her body, Kai made a decision to withhold from urinating during the five-hour flight to Los Angeles.

She acknowledged that her thought processes were not rational. "What the hell do you expect?" Kai asked herself out loud. Heads turned in her direction. Kai responded by stopping in her tracks, and placing an indignant hand on her slender hip, which was jutted out excessively. She rolled her eyes and sucked her teeth at the onlookers until they figured out it was best to be on their way instead of standing around gawking at her.

Had she not been the crazy bitch that she was well aware of being, she would have realized that her intimidating behavior could result in being taken into custody by the TSA. But Kai did not possess clear, rational thought, so she did what she wanted to do, telling herself that she'd get herself checked out by an expensive psychiatrist after she'd collected her dough. There had to be something she could take for whatever was wrong with her.

The money she'd finagled from Parker, along with the wad of cash she'd stealthily slipped out of Trevor's pants pocket, allowed Kai to purchase a first-class ticket to Los Angeles. The cab driver should have known that her services were not free.

Feeling entitled, Kai boarded the plane and took her assigned seat. Ah! The air smelled fresh, the passengers were attractive, and everything about first-class was bright and appealing. It was time to resume her prominent position as a card-carrying member of the good life!

With her cum-filled kitty clenched tight, Kai ordered a martini, hoping the level of sodium would help her retain water and prevent her from having to urinate.

Taking advantage of the increased leg room provided in first-class travel, Kai stretched out her long legs, giving a sigh of satisfaction as she reclined her seat. Being in such a comfortable environment, she selected mental imagery that would produce pleasure. Smiling to herself, she relived her experience with Trevor and made a mental note to find out where African men hung out in L.A.

Next, her thoughts drifted to Mookie, her prison boyfriend. Even though he'd ultimately wronged her, he'd sexed her down good while he was in the slammer.

When her thoughts turned to Marquise, Kai sat straight up. Though the African and Mookie both were fabulous fucks, neither could hold a candle to Marquise. She drew in a deep breath and shook her head. There was no point in getting all warm and fuzzy over a dead man.

Kai took a swig from the martini glass and then made an imaginary toast to her deceased lover. She giggled to herself as she remembered how her convict friends used to speak of pouring out a lil' liquor for deceased friends and loved ones. She wondered how the airline would react if she suddenly got the notion to pour out a lil' liquor for Marquise. Being that she was crazy, Kai decided to find out for herself. She held out her arm and tilted her glass, watching with great interest as the liquid splashed out onto the floor in the aisle.

A flight attendant materialized, cloth in hand. Stooping while looking up and gracing Kai with a *don't worry about it* smile, the attendant quickly mopped up the mess.

"Stop!" Kai implored the flight attendant. Holding her palm out like Diana Ross singing "Stop in the Name of Love."

"It's okay, I don't mind," the woman said, mistakenly thinking Kai was willing to clean up her own mess.

"By the way," Kai said, her face sad and forlorn. "I'm not totally black, ya know, so quite naturally, I wouldn't know all the rules. But…" she took a deep breath, "if I'm not mistaken, when someone pours out a little liquor for a fallen brother, it's customary for the liquor to soak for a few minutes, maybe hours, but I'm really not sure." Kai shrugged.

The flight attendant gave Kai a look of bafflement, then her facial muscles relaxed as if she'd suddenly been enlightened to the fact that she was dealing with a nut. "Oh. I'm sure it's okay if the liquor is cleaned up right away," the white flight attendant said indulgently.

Kai wore an affected puzzled expression. "Like I said, I'm not totally black, so I don't actually understand their ways and customs."

The flight attendant feigned an understanding smile and hurried away.

Throughout the episode, the other first-class passengers did not dignify the barbaric and distasteful situation with as much as a glance.

Clutching the computer print-out Parker had given her as if it were a map to an Old-World treasure chest, Kai rushed inside a taxi parked outside LAX. The sun hadn't gone down yet; it was still daylight in Los Angeles. Without giving the driver so much as a glance, Kai barked out the Rodeo Drive address. She didn't have time for any more sex games with cab drivers. She was all about business. Once her bank account was brought up to date, there would be plenty of time for kinky sex with strangers.

Reeking of stale semen, Kai entered a large and luxurious waiting room, which was impressively decorated in various shades of lavender, amethyst, cream, and gray. The walls were plastered with her father's numerous credentials. Since many of the dates were fairly recent, Kai could only surmise that at least a dozen of the certificates hadn't been acquired as a result of rigorous training. Really, how does a general surgeon suddenly put up a plaque and declare himself qualified to perform cosmetic surgery? By attending a couple of expensive, weekend-long classes, Kai presumed. Classes that her money had paid for, no doubt.

Ignoring the clients who waited in the lobby area, Kai walked around in a circle in the middle of the room. She observed the posh environment with amazement and indignation. She focused on the reception desk and didn't know which was more beautiful, the prestigious, curved desk, which was made of a mixture of walnut wood with cherry finish or the flawless, blonde beauty who sat perched behind it.

"May I help you?" Judging by the annoyance in her tone, the young blonde must have asked the question several times, but Kai, shocked and outraged over the gall of her father, hadn't heard the receptionist until now. "If you're here for an appointment, I'm sorry to inform you that Dr. Montgomery does not accept walk-ins."

Looking mean and crazy, Kai traipsed across the room and approached the desk. "I don't need an appointment," she snarled as she mimicked the neck twist the girls in prison utilized to emphasize their point.

Intimidated, the blonde recoiled, but quickly composed herself. "The doctor has a two-year waiting list, but I can give you a list of referrals if you'd like." The receptionist spoke in a tone as stern as she could manage under the highly unusual circumstances.

"My name is Kai Montgomery. I'm Dr. Montgomery's daughter."

The receptionist grimaced and shot Kai a look of disgust and disbelief. "You're Dr. Montgomery's what?" she asked, giving Kai a sweeping look of disapproval.

"Are you deaf? I said, I'm his daughter!" Kai jabbed the air with a finger. "Tell my father I'm here." Kai wanted to yank the snotty receptionist up by the collar prison-style, but she'd save that gesture for her adopted mother. That bitch was in on the scam, too.

Kai leaned in close. "Listen, I don't care if my father is in the middle of performing surgery. For all I care, he can be back there." She nudged her head at the closed set of double doors behind the desk, "removing a matching set of luggage from beneath the eyes of some saggy old broad." She paused for effect. "I don't care what the fuck he's doing," Kai exploded, now waving her finger in the woman's face. "You tell *my* father that I said for him to get his thieving ass out here right now, before I barge in there and smack that scalpel out of his hand!"

Obviously upset, the blonde flushed. Her embarrassed eyes darted desperately around the waiting room, sending silent words of apology to Dr. Montgomery's hoity-toity clientele. She took a deep, furious breath, straightening her shoulders in a manner that would convey she had the situation under control, but then quickly turned up her nose, pursed her lips, and started coughing from Kai's stench. Too bad she'd inhaled so deeply.

The blonde pushed a button on the elaborate telephone console. "Sorry to bother you," she whispered loudly into the phone. "Would you please tell Dr. Montgomery there's a young woman here to see him? She claims she's his daughter."

A few minutes later, another blonde who could have easily passed for the older sister of the receptionist appeared from behind the double doors. A lab coat lent professionalism to expensive attire that shouted, *spoiled, pampered bitch*. Kai was green with envy; her father paid the woman well. A pink gold-and-diamond, Cartier bracelet peeked beneath the sleeve of the blonde's lab coat, a sparkly reminder of the jewelry and wealth Kai no longer possessed. She yearned to have her life back.

The blonde gave Kai a fake smile and beckoned her to follow. Seeming entirely too self-assured, efficient, and way too satisfied with her life, the blonde irked Kai. Kai had to resist the urge to grab a handful of pale hair and give the woman a hard head yank.

"How are you?"

Refusing to engage in meaningless chatter, Kai ignored her.

"I'm Michelle Llewellyn, Dr. Montgomery's assistant," the woman said with pride as she ushered Kai into an examining room. "Dr. Montgomery is in the middle of a procedure. He'll be with you shortly. Can I get you something? Coffee? Bottled water?"

"Wanna know what you can get for me? You can get my father, bitch," Kai spat. "I didn't come to California to sit around waiting like one of his over-the-hill patients."

The smug smile fell from Michelle's face. "He'll be with you shortly," she said and hurried from the examining room.

Kai refused to sit down. She glanced impatiently at the minute hand on the wall clock. If her father didn't have his ass in there in exactly five minutes, she fully intended to throw a monumental temper tantrum.

Philip Montgomery, tanned and handsome, materialized in three minutes.

*Daddy!* Kai's heart fluttered. She suddenly wanted to hurl herself in his arms. Distant memories of sitting on his lap, being kissed, cuddled, and adored, flitted across her mind. Once upon a time, she'd been daddy's little princess. But the DNA test that revealed he was not her natural father had stripped her of her title and pushed her off his lap—off her throne.

"Kai," her father said. He forced a tight smile. The lack of warmth in his voice and in his eyes infuriated Kai.

"Hello, Father; remember me?" Having no idea how awful she looked and smelled, Kai put a hand on her hip and assumed a haughty stance.

A flicker of a grimace crossed her father's face. "I was with a patient. You shouldn't have come barging into my place of business without an appointment," he said, irritated.

Kai felt mortally wounded. The glimmer of hope that her father hadn't actually abandoned her was instantly dashed. Showing a tough exterior, she said, "What a way to greet your long-lost daughter. I take it you're not happy to see me?" She shook her head, feigning regret.

"Look, there's no point in dancing around this issue. You're not my daughter and you damn well know it."

Kai flinched.

"When your mother came skulking around here trying to squeeze money out of me, she told me she'd paid you a visit and given you the details of your birth. So I assume you tracked me down and traveled this far because you want to collect the inheritance my mother left you."

"That would be correct...genius," Kai said sarcastically.

"You're not entitled to that money," he said sneeringly.

"Yes, I am! I upheld my end of the bargain—graduated college, worked at that horrible nursing home..."

"You don't get it. I adopted you with the mistaken belief that you were my own child. My mother was aware of that. It was also her decision that I forgo a paternity test at that time. The acknowledgment that I even suspected being your natural father would have humiliated my wife and the rest of my family."

"So why'd you go against her wishes and take that damned DNA test?"

"For my own sake, I needed to know. I waited until my mother had passed away."

"And after taking the test, you began to treat me like garbage," Kai said challengingly.

"You're not my daughter. I don't know who you belong to, but after I learned the disgusting news, it sickened me to have to uphold my obligation to raise you," Philip Montgomery said cruelly. "And now, I absolutely refuse to continue to enrich the life of another man's child."

"You adopted me; legally I'm your daughter. You can't just toss me out like garbage."

Kai's father gave her a snide look that made her cringe. "You're an adult; get a job." He dug in his pocket and pulled out a few bills. "Here, this is all the cash I have. That'll get you air fare back to Philadelphia." Philip Montgomery pressed the cash inside Kai's hand. "Take the money and go."

Furious, Kai tossed the money in her father's face. "I came here to claim my rightful place, my rightful inheritance. I want my money or the whole town will know about your questionable credentials."

Her father laughed at Kai. "My credentials are authentic. Now, listen to me, young lady." He pointed a finger. "I had to call the authorities on your blackmailing mother; don't force me to call them on you. Haven't you had your fill of prison?"

His threatening words put her tantrum on pause. She glared at him, squared her shoulders, and stormed out of the examining room.

In the corridor, she happened upon Michelle Llewellyn. Prison life had taught her to take advantage of every situation. As Michelle fixed her mouth into another fake smile, Kai used her shoulder, knocked against the blonde, and caused her to crash into the wall. Kai's intuition told her the bitch was fucking her father…getting money that should have been racking up interest in a bank account in Kai's name.

"What happened?" she heard her father ask his paramour.

"She bumped into me…by mistake, I think!" Michelle replied, confused.

Kai didn't look back. Her mental wheels were already churning, coming up with a way to put plan B in motion.

# Chapter 19

"I don't have much to pack. That's a small blessing, I guess," Terelle said, looking in the mirror as she grabbed a handful of thick, long hair. She needed a perm badly, but that would have to wait. In the meantime, she tried to tame her tangled tresses with a nylon brush. "I'm going to have to give Aunt Bennie some kind of explanation." She looked at Marquise, waiting for some input.

Marquise sat on the edge of Terelle's bed. He rubbed his forehead thoughtfully. "Leave her a note. Just say you have to bounce. Tell her you'll call her to let her know you're aiight." He gnawed on his lip in thought. "I gotta get in touch with my man, Jalil; he might be able to help us out."

She turned around and faced Marquise, fixing her eyes on him questioningly.

"Jalil's cool. He knows," Marquise responded to her inquisitive gaze.

Terelle's heavy lashes blinked rapidly. "He knows what?"

"He knows everything. His uncle works in the housekeeping department at Spring Haven; that's how I got in and out without signing in."

Terelle furrowed her brows. "Both Jalil *and* his uncle knew you were alive?"

Marquise shrugged. "Yeah, they knew. And I ain't gon' lie, Jalil told his girl, too."

Terelle winced. "Ayanna knew?"

"Yeah, but Jalil got on her about running her mouth and giving up information like she did back when Kai came to her crib…"

Mentioning Kai's name was not a good move. Terelle bristled, gave Marquise an evil look, and spun back around. Now, facing the mirror, she raked the brush through her hair with an angry vengeance.

"My bad, babe. I know shorty's name sets you off. My bad," he repeated. He rose, stood behind Terelle, watching her through the mirror. His intently focused eyes asked for forgiveness. "For real, though, you don't have to worry about Ayanna saying anything."

"I'm not worried about that! I'm in a state of shock at finding out that once again, everybody and their mother knew something I didn't know."

"Aw, babe. It wasn't like that." Easing up closer, Marquise placed his hands on her shoulders. Gently, he tried to turn her toward him, but she stiffened.

"Who else knew you were in hiding?"

"Nobody."

"You sure?"

"Babe, I don't have any reason to lie to you," he said, his tone begging her not to be upset with him. "Come on, Terelle. Don't take it that way. After the feds relocated me, I tried to get at you, but your phone was disconnected. I didn't know what to think. I flipped out."

She turned around, tilted her head toward Marquise. "Why didn't you call Saleema?"

"I didn't have her number on me. Me and Saleema always had beef, so it wasn't like I knew her number by heart."

Terelle put her chin in her hand, gave some thought to what he'd said.

"I had to find out what was up, so I put a call through to Jalil. When he told me what had happened with you, I knew it was my fault." Marquise scraped his teeth against his bottom lip. "I felt like such a fuck-up. I was a step away from just giving up and losing my mind, too." Marquise sighed deeply at the terrible memory. "Then Jalil came at me with the information about his uncle working at the hospital where you were at. I couldn't believe that stroke of good luck."

Terelle nodded. She walked over to the bed and sat down, all fight gone.

"His uncle gave me access to the side door where there wasn't no cameras or nothing. I woulda ended up a nut case if I didn't get to see your pretty face. I woulda been spaced-out like this—" Marquise made his eyes grow large, his body became comically rigid and he stretched his arms out in front of him like a zombie. "It wouldn't have been a pretty picture if I ended up being a patient in the room across the hall from you, now would it?"

Terelle found herself smiling. Marquise's ability to bring humor to their dire situation reminded her of one of the many reasons she loved him. "So, what do you think Jalil can do for us?"

"I don't know. All I can do is let him know about the situation. Jalil's my man; I know he'll do whatever he can to help us out."

"Should we be straight with Saleema—you know, let her know you're alive and well?"

"Naw, babe. She don't need that information; it might put Keeta in danger. Like you said, we gotta look out for our daughter's safety."

Looking upset, Terelle massaged her temples. "I have to tell Saleema *something*. We'll never get Markeeta back if I run off without an explanation." Things were moving so swiftly, Terelle's head was spinning.

Marquise sat on the bed next to Terelle. "Call Saleema, make up something that will buy us some time."

"How much time?"

"We're probably gon' need about three or four months after the case for this whole thing to blow over."

Terelle's face crumpled. "We have to leave Keeta for that long?"

Marquise nodded. "But we'll get through it and we'll be stronger—as a family."

"How'd you come up with that time line?"

"I'm just guessing, babe. I figure when I don't show up to testify, they'll realize I'm not a snitch… they'll leave us alone if I make arrangements to pay them back for the product I stole. Then, we'll only have the feds to worry about." Marquise paused. "But the feds—man, they can be real dirty when they want to. Who knows what those dudes are capable of? They might put a hit out on my ass for reneging on my end of the bargain."

"If that's the case, what makes you think it'll ever blow over?"

"It has to," he said, injecting strength in his tone. "In time, the feds gon' have to take their focus off of me. Shit, they're gon' need all their concentration for the next dumb hustler who comes through," Marquise said, shaking his head at his own stupidity.

It was Terelle's turn to console Marquise. She rubbed his wide back in a circular motion, ran her hand up his neck, and caressed the hair at his nape. "We're gonna get through this. I know we are. Way back in the seventh grade, I fell in love with you. I put all my future happiness in your hands. I loved you then and I love you now, but I'm tired of waiting for happiness to arrive in the future. It's time to be happy now. You're alive, we're together, and Markeeta's safe and loved. The odds were stacked against us, but we survived."

Marquise beamed. He dropped a quick, grateful kiss on her lips. "Damn, you know how to make your man feel good." He kissed her again. "I love you, girl. I gotchu. You heard me? I ain't nevah gon' let nothin' happen to you. Believe that!"

Looking determined to handle things, Marquise went downstairs to call Jalil.

Jalil was truly a friend indeed. After being told of their plight, he made Terelle and Marquise an offer they couldn't refuse. It turned out that his grandfather, who had passed away a few months ago, had lived in the rural South. The grandfather left his home to Jalil.

"The place is situated in the back woods of South Carolina. It's nothing more than a shack," Jalil admitted. "But it's got running water and everything. I haven't even called the different utility companies to turn shit off yet."

"The back woods sounds like a good chill spot to me," Marquise said.

"Yeah, ain't hardly any people around. My Paw Paw lived like a hermit. I used to visit when I was a little kid, but man, once I got some age on me, you couldn't pay me to go down there. Me and my Paw Paw touched base the few times he made trips to Philly," Jalil said with a chuckle.

"From what I hear, the house needs a lot of fixing up before I can even think about trying to sell it," Jalil continued. "So, for real, for real, you and Terelle would be doing me a favor by staying there; I won't have to be worrying about vandals breaking in and messing the house up worse than it already is."

"Thanks man, I appreciate it," Marquise said.

"But, there ain't no buses or nothing that go there, man. Y'all gon' be in the boonies, for real."

Marquise scratched his head. "Think you could rent me a car? I'll pay for it."

"Man, even if I did rent you a whip, how you gon' return it? The crib is out in the sticks; ain't nothin' around, dawg. Nothin' but dirt road and trees and shit. Besides, I don't even know how to give you directions; I only know how to get there by memory. Chill, man. I gotchu. I'll take a day off work and drive you there."

"Yo, man. That's whassup; thanks."

"Ayanna's probably gon' want to come along for the ride, so be prepared for her yakkity yak all the way down I-95." Jalil and Marquise both laughed.

"Aiight, man, I'll see you soon. Good looking out," Marquise said and hung up the phone.

A few hours later, Marquise and Terelle, along with Ayanna, were sitting in Jalil's car, parked in the lot of the Sunoco gas station on Fifty-Second Street. Jalil was outside the car, pumping gas, preparing for the nine-hour trip to the back woods of South Carolina.

Marquise, assuming the co-pilot position, sat up front in the passenger seat. He flipped through Jalil's CDs. Terelle and Ayanna shared the backseat. Having so many children had put a lot of extra weight on Ayanna since Terelle had seen her last. Ayanna, wearing high-heel lace-up sandals and a skin-tight denim skirt with ruffles at the bottom, looked to be about a size twenty-two. The extra weight didn't seem to bother her and Terelle had to admit, Ayanna still had a pretty face.

As Jalil predicted, Ayanna ran her mouth nonstop and they hadn't even left Philly yet. "My cousin's babysittin'. She never kept the kids overnight, she don't even know what she's in store for," Ayanna said, laughing. "My bad ass kids are gonna drive that poor girl to pulling out all her hair extensions. Let me tell you what my next to the youngest did last night…"

Terelle tuned Ayanna out. She didn't want to hear what she was talking about. Hearing about Ayanna's children was making Terelle feel heartsick. She decided she must have been delusional to think she could pick up and leave town without setting eyes on her baby for the next three or four months.

Bending at the waist, Terelle hugged herself as she fought back tears.

"You all right, Terelle?" Ayanna asked, scooting closer to Terelle.

Marquise looked over his shoulder. "What's wrong, babe?"

"I feel sick," Terelle murmured.

"Is she 'bout to throw up, man?" Jalil asked, from outside, peering through the window with a petrified look on his face.

"No, I'll be all right. I just need some air," Terelle said weakly, blinking back tears.

Marquise quickly got out of the car and opened the back door for Terelle. Before her feet hit the concrete, Terelle burst into tears. Leaning against the outside of the car, Marquise pulled Terelle against him, circling his arms around her. "What's the matter, baby?"

After filling the tank, Jalil screwed the gas cap on. Trying to give Marquise and Terelle a little privacy, he hurriedly got back behind the wheel.

Terelle's chest heaved against Marquise's. Marquise patted her back. "I can't do it," she sobbed. "I can't do it," she repeated, her voice stronger.

"Can't do what—leave Keeta?" Marquise whispered, his voice calm and steady in her ear.

Sobbing softly, Terelle nodded. "I know we can't take her with us, but I don't want to leave without seeing my baby one more time. We're her parents, Marquise," she cried. "We can't leave town without telling our child that we love her."

"Don't you think seeing me might upset her?" Marquise asked, deeply concerned. "How healthy will it be for her to see the father she believes is dead?"

Terelle lifted her chin. "Markeeta needs to know that we love her. I'm not going anywhere until I tell her."

Marquise looked at Terelle. "You sure about this, babe?"

"I have to follow my heart. Suppose something happens to us."

"Ain't nothing gon' happen—" Marquise snapped.

"But suppose it does," Terelle snapped back. "If something happened to us, wouldn't you want our daughter to know that she was truly loved?"

Marquise swallowed. "You wanna call Saleema and ask her to bring Markeeta to meet us here?"

Swiping away tears, Terelle nodded.

"Yo, Jalil," Marquise shouted. "Let me hold your cell phone, man."

# Chapter 20

**O**h, Lord. Please don't tell me I'm gonna have to have my girl put back in Spring Haven, Saleema thought after hanging up the phone. Terelle had been crying hysterically, and it was hard for Saleema to make out much of what she was saying. However, Terelle clearly got across that she wanted Saleema to bring Markeeta to a damn mini-market parking lot on Fifty-Second Street, right next to the overpass on Lancaster Avenue. She said she wanted to tell Markeeta good-bye.

Truth be told, Terelle was easier to deal with when she was in that trance state. It broke Saleema's heart seeing her girl all screwed up like that, but had she known Terelle was going to wake up and become such a nutty pain in the ass, Saleema would have preferred she stayed in the coma, or trance, or whatever the hell kind of state she'd been in. Mind you, if Terelle had awakened in her right state of mind, Saleema would have helped her get on her feet and would have gladly turned Markeeta over to her. Well...not gladly. She would have reluctantly turned Markeeta over because she loved the child like she was her own. But she would have done the right thing for both Terelle and Markeeta.

But Terelle was still buggin', still talking crazy. Still bringing up Marquise's name every chance she got. If Saleema didn't protect Markeeta from Terelle, Markeeta would probably turn out as loony as her mother.

The only reason Saleema was even bothering to indulge Terelle's retarded-ass request was because she had some documents she wanted Terelle to sign. Saleema was no longer satisfied being Markeeta's guardian. She wanted Terelle to sign over her parental rights so she could legally adopt Markeeta.

Terelle was never going to get her act together. She'd always be delusional when it came to Marquise. It would be over Saleema's dead body that she would let Markeeta live in poverty with a spaced-out, mentally ill mother. It simply wasn't going to happen, not in this lifetime. She'd brought Markeeta too far to allow Terelle's crazy ass to damage Markeeta's young psyche. Saleema was willing to hold off her move to the Cayman Islands and her pending nuptials until she'd accomplished her goal of adopting Markeeta.

Saleema swerved her brand-new Lexus LX around the numerous potholes that dented the strip known as Fifty-Second Street in west Philly. Sure, she was born and raised in the worst section of southwest Philly, but that didn't mean she had an unwavering allegiance to the 'hood. Saleema had a much better life now; if she wanted a dose of 'hood reality, she could always rent a DVD to find out what her peeps were up to.

Now, her best friend was screaming like a crazy banshee and insisting that she bring her child—yes, Saleema thought of Markeeta as *her* child—to some ghetto-ass parking lot, where Markeeta's innocent eyes would have to observe her mother in a full-fledged bout of insanity.

The only reason Saleema had brought Markeeta along was so that Terelle could literally kiss her daughter, good-bye!

Saleema sucked her teeth as she wheeled into the A Plus parking lot. The same lazy-ass crackhead who'd been posted outside the store for the last few years was still out there begging for spare change. Now, that didn't make any damn sense. She didn't want to be accosted by him or the drunk who was wobbling around, barely able to stand on his feet, yet had the nerve to stagger up to people, asking if he could pump their gas. Saleema caught a glimpse of another hustler and quickly averted her gaze. This one was carrying a bucket of filthy water and was hell bent on smearing up windshields for a dollar.

She parked her shimmering SUV in the cut near the air pumps. She narrowed her eyes in an evil-ass glare, defying any of those derelicts to come anywhere near her whip.

Sticking her head out the window, she impatiently searched for Terelle. She refused to un-strap Markeeta from her car seat to go looking for Terelle inside the store.

*Aw shit, here comes this bastard with his bucket of nasty water*, Saleema mused, irritated. She wanted to reach for her burner, which was tucked inside her purse, but she opted to scare him off with a can of pepper spray. She reached over to the glove compartment but catching a glimpse of a bizarre sight, she froze, her arm stretched out in midair.

Grinning, the man ogled the beautiful SUV. "That's a nice ride, shawtie. Let me clean it up for you real quick," he said as he pulled a dirty, dripping rag from the bucket.

Saleema gasped, then yelped, covering her mouth with terrified, bugged-out eyes. Markeeta screamed from the backseat; she began to struggle wildly to get out of her car seat.

Startled by the yelling inside the SUV, the car washer dropped his bucket of water. Getting the bucket refilled must not have been an easy endeavor for his eyes filled with remorse as the purplish-colored water streamed across the concrete.

"What the fuck is wrong with y'all?" the man wanted to know, returning his attention to Saleema who was now trying to calm Markeeta down. Markeeta had unlocked the strap that secured her in the car seat and quick as a wink, she'd climbed out of the child seat and was now yanking on the locked back door.

"Stop it, Keeta!" Saleema screamed and then looked over her shoulder at the surreal scene that had Markeeta losing her mind.

On the other side of the parking lot, Terelle had bolted out of a dark-colored car. There was no hint of weakened limbs as Terelle dashed across the asphalt with Marion Jones-like speed.

Unbelievably, keeping pace with Terelle was none other than… Marquise! In the flesh! And he looked exactly like Markeeta. Exactly. Just bigger and…hmmm, without hair. Saleema noticed his braids were shorn.

Saleema would have loved the luxury of passing the fuck out from the sheer shock of witnessing a dead man sprinting toward her in broad daylight, but with Markeeta going berserk, Saleema had to keep her head together.

Markeeta had given up on trying to unlock the door, but had determinedly managed to get the car window down halfway and was trying to climb out, all the while, screaming at the top of her lungs, "*Daddy!*"

The plaintive wail of their daughter enlivened the couple with what appeared to be superhuman speed. Within seconds, Terelle and Marquise had nearly reached Saleema's Lexus.

Thinking her friend too far gone to even kiss her child goodbye, Saleema would never have shown up had Terelle mentioned Marquise's name. But here he was in the flesh.

Not knowing if Terelle and Marquise planned on kidnapping Markeeta, Saleema tumbled over the car seat and landed in the back on top of Markeeta. Protectively, she scooped Markeeta up and held the child in a tight, protective embrace.

"Let me go, let me go," Markeeta screamed, scratching and clawing at Saleema like her loving guardian was her mortal enemy. Markeeta yelled louder than ever, "*Daddy!*"

Crying and limping as she ran, Terelle didn't make it the full distance. She dropped to the ground in a crying heap just before reaching the back passenger door. Markeeta's reaction was too much for her fragile mental state, Saleema assumed, but she wasn't sure if Terelle was crying tears of joy or sorrow over the fact that Markeeta hadn't mentioned her name.

Calmly, Marquise opened the door and gently took his daughter from Saleema's arms. He swooped Markeeta into the circle of his arms, held her high in the air, then brought her down to eye level, adored her with his gaze, and then kissed her cheeks, her hair, her arms, her hands and fingers, all the while murmuring, "Oooo, baby girl, baby girl! Do you how much Daddy missed his baby girl? I love you, Keeta. You know that, right?" Marquise kissed Markeeta's lips.

Nodding her head vigorously, Markeeta kissed her father back. She hadn't seen the man in two years and yet she tightened her tiny arms around her father's neck like she was holding on to a life raft.

The shock of it all was too, too much for Saleema. Slumping down, she joined Terelle on the grimy concrete. Pressed against her best friend, her head hung low, Saleema boohooed, her sobs a combination of confusion, frustration, and defeat.

❖❖❖

"I told you he was alive," Terelle whispered fiercely to Saleema. Her misty eyes were focused in the direction of the most heart-warming and beautiful scene she'd beheld since Markeeta had warmed up to her daddy two and a half years ago, back when Marquise had first gotten out of jail.

"What is going on, Terelle?" Saleema demanded. She was in too much shock to peep the irony that she and Terelle were back on the dirty ground together as they'd been in the Dave and Buster's parking lot on the day Terelle shot Marquise. She was also in too much of a stupor to realize she was ruining her pale-blue Versace cropped pants.

"He's on the run from the feds. I'm going with him. We need you to watch Keeta for us until we can get this shit straight." Terelle sniffled, knowing she wasn't making much sense. But giving Saleema too much information was not a good idea.

"I've been raising that child, playing the role of mother for two damn years and you want me to start watching her—like I'm suddenly her damn babysitter?" Saleema sounded angry. She shifted her position like she was ready to get up, bum rush Marquise, and yank Markeeta from his arms.

"I know you didn't realize this day would ever come, but it has..." Terelle trailed off and observed the father and daughter reunion scene. Her heart was so filled with love and gratitude, it didn't even matter that Markeeta continued to ignore her. She understood. Markeeta perceived her as sickly, crazy. But, as sure as she was of her own name, she knew that the day would come when Markeeta would learn to love and trust her again.

"As my best friend in the whole world, Saleema, I'm begging you to watch my daughter until me and her father come back for

her. I promise you, we'll give her the lifestyle she deserves."
Feeling Saleema's pain, Terelle began to cry harder. She embraced her friend, hugged her tight. "I love you, Saleema. And I know you love me. That's why you've been protecting Markeeta. No one in my whole family has ever shown love like you have, girl." Terelle placed her hands on both sides of Saleema's head and turned Saleema's tear-stained face toward her own. Looking intently in her friend's eyes, Terelle said, "Keeta's my daughter, Saleema. She belongs to me and Marquise. You've got to stop fighting us."

"But...," Saleema sputtered.

"You see Quise over there loving up his daughter. Do you still think I'm crazy?"

"No, but..."

"But, nothing! You're talking to me, Saleema. The real me!" Terelle held Saleema in an intense gaze. "And this is real talk. When me and Quise get ourselves together, you gotta give us our daughter back," Terelle said sternly. "I don't want no shit outta you. I forgive you for treating me like your worst enemy; I know you thought you were protecting Keeta. But from now on, you gotta have my back. I don't want to have to fight you for my daughter; do you hear me, Saleema? We've been friends forever, I love you like a sister, but don't play with me. I will hurt your little ass over my child." Terelle gave a little laugh, but she was dead serious.

Sniffling and wiping away the tears that rolled down her face, Saleema laughed, too. "Look who's calling somebody little."

"Not for long, bitch." Terelle chuckled. "I'm 'bout to get my weight back up. I got my man back!"

Wincing, Terelle gripped the bumper of the Lexus, using it to pull herself up. Her frail body had been put through hell. It felt like every muscle screamed in pain. But she disregarded her aching muscles as she watched Markeeta hugging her father as if they'd been separated for only a day. Limping badly, Terelle rushed toward the two people she loved more than life itself.

But before she could wrap her arms around her family, she was stopped in her tracks by jarring music—reggae music, which poured from the speakers of a black Magnum with tinted windows. Terelle's heart took a dive. The car made her think of a shark, and though the music that emanated from within was a dance-happy, lilting Caribbean melody, it had the same effect as the eerily dramatic music from the movie *Jaws*.

Terelle's eyes met Marquise's and then shot to Saleema's face. "Get Keeta, Saleema."

Jumping up, Saleema reacted quickly. She raced toward Marquise and tried to take Markeeta from his arms. Markeeta screamed and clung to her father. Marquise bit down on his lip, his face contorted in emotional anguish. His eyes darted wildly from the black Magnum to his daughter's face. "You gotta go with Saleema," Marquise whispered, handing his daughter over to Saleema.

Saleema tried desperately to pull Markeeta away from Marquise.

"Stop!" Markeeta yelled as she kicked her leg out at Saleema, landing a small foot in Saleema's stomach.

"Oh, my God." Saleema grabbed her stomach and turned help-lessly toward Terelle. "What's wrong with her? I can't believe she went off on me like that!"

Markeeta's emotional outburst was shocking to Saleema, who knew her to be a calm and well-adjusted child. But Terelle under-stood Markeeta's sudden personality change. Watching her daugh-ter was like watching herself. Terelle was also typically calm and low-key. But when it came to defending her relationship with

Marquise, she turned into a scratching, kicking, fighting, murderous warrior.

There wasn't time to explain. Terelle was frightened that the occupants of the Magnum were Marquise's mortal enemies. She shot Marquise a frightened look. "We have to go, Quise. Put Markeeta down; she'll be all right!"

But Marquise stood in place, gripping his daughter, chewing on his bottom lip and looking helpless.

Two seconds later, Jalil's car shot across the lot and screeched to a crooked stop directly in front of Marquise and Markeeta. "Come on, dawg. It's time to roll out!"

In utter shock and bewilderment, Saleema gawked at Terelle, silently demanding an explanation for the sudden commotion.

"Markeeta. Stop it!" Terelle said sharply, suddenly assuming the role of mother. While Marquise stood stock still and doing nothing to help the situation, Terelle risked being her daughter's adversary forever. She peeled each of Markeeta's fingers away from Marquise's shirt and roughly yanked her away, handing the kicking and screaming child she loved over to Saleema.

Jalil pushed open the passenger door. "Get in, dawg!"

Marquise gazed at Markeeta, his expression tortured.

"Quise, let's go," Terelle insisted.

"No! Daddy! Don't leave me," Markeeta wailed. She punched Saleema, fought like she was a grown woman as Saleema struggled to get her inside the LX.

Inside Jalil's car, Marquise and Terelle watched helplessly through the back window, as Saleema tussled with Markeeta, trying to strap her inside the child seat.

The LX finally pulled out of the lot and raced north.

Jalil pointed his car south.

# Chapter 21

Her father was a cold-blooded bastard. After placing his daughter on a pedestal for her first nine years of life, he cruelly, maliciously began treating Kai like she was invisible. She'd been so confused by his emotional abandonment, so traumatized; she had to undergo therapy. The sessions began when while she was still in puberty and had continued up until that fateful day when she was carted off to jail.

Damn, she missed her therapy sessions. She'd always felt so justified in behaving badly whenever her therapist helped her uncover one of the reasons she was such a screwed-up young woman.

Kai could recall one particular session when she'd experienced an epiphany—or at least she'd thought so at the time. She was fourteen years old when her psychotherapist tried out a new technique. Using regression therapy, she took Kai back to the day her life had changed. Under hypnosis, Kai relived an important event that occurred when she was only nine years old. Sitting on her father's lap, watching TV with the back of her head pressed against her daddy's chest, Kai purred like a kitten while her father stroked her curls. He loved her curly hair, he always told her that. Her mother said her father had discovered that caressing her hair and massaging her scalp was a surefire way to calm Kai down whenever she resisted sleep as a baby.

Her father's large fingers massaged her scalp on the day she was kicked from the throne. His fingers were so loving and soothing, she'd felt compelled to reciprocate the pleasure, and since her hand just happened to be placed near his thigh, that was the body part she innocently caressed. Something long and hard sprang up beneath her small hand. It frightened her. She yelped; her father pushed her off his lap. He gave her such a hard shove, she slid across the shiny parquet floor.

He couldn't have meant to push her so hard, she thought to herself when her butt hit the floor. Her father adored her; he worshipped the ground she walked on, that's what he'd always said. She was his princess! So why was he standing up now, glaring at her while she rubbed her sore behind?

"For as long as you're under my roof, don't you ever do a thing like that again," her father had said, pointing an incriminating finger at her. Just before he stormed from the family room with his face etched in fury, Kai noticed that the thing that boys have between their legs was pressing against the fabric of his pants. Like his finger, her father's penis pointed angrily at her, too!

Back when she was fourteen, when that memory had been un-blocked, Kai had felt deeply humiliated and tainted. She'd blamed herself for her father's alienation. But today, she knew better. Her father's dick got hard because she was a sexy bitch then and she was a sexy bitch now. No man could resist her.

With that thought planted firmly in her mind, Kai Montgomery began to put together a back-up plan. She was not going down without a fight. Her father owed her and she intended to collect. She wanted to get her status back; she wanted to be reinstated as a wealthy physician's daughter. Kai absolutely refused to live her life being perceived as half-black, orphaned, and poor.

Being uncharacteristically frugal, Kai bought a cheap but sexy sundress and sandals, a pair of sunglasses, and a hat. She needed somewhere to stay and discovered that even motels that advertised as being cheap were quite pricey in Beverly Hills. But she needed to shower and change clothes, so she forked over the cash.

But there was still another dilemma. She needed transportation, however, a cheap rental would bring her unnecessary attention. Driving a Honda or a Ford would make her stick out like a sore thumb here in elite Beverly Hills.

So, Kai put her superior fellatio skills to good use and gave the manager at a rental center that specialized in exotic and luxury rentals the best blow job he'd ever had. He made copies of her photo ID and she promised to return the luxury car in three days.

Kai had sucked dick to obtain a top-of-the line black Benz with low mileage and that was in pristine condition. The feeling of driving the big Benz was indescribable. The model she'd driven prior to being incarcerated paled in comparison to the looks and performance of this fine automobile.

Getting a taste of the good life she'd had and lost was extremely painful for Kai. Her plan simply could not fail. If it did, the law would have to come after her because Kai knew she'd never be able to relinquish this luxurious Mercedes Benz. Not in three days—not ever. If she didn't get the money she was entitled to, she'd go out and suck as many dicks as required to get her hands on a gun. She decided she'd prefer to be involved in a shoot-out with the police before lowering her standards and wheeling around in an ordinary car.

Disguised in shades and wearing a floppy hat, Kai blended in with the incognito celebrities in Beverly Hills. Undetected, she tailed her father to a small, bungalow-style home—the love nest he used for sexual dalliances with his assistant, Michelle.

Inept fellow that he was, Parker hadn't been able to obtain the home address of the mansion her father shared with her mother. Not a problem. Kai was certain she'd have the keys to the mansion and more in time. Meanwhile, Kai kept her eyes on the bungalow, watching with the focused intensity of a cat waiting to pounce on prey.

Much sooner than expected, Michelle burst through the door. The pretty assistant looked upset. Oh! She was crying, wiping away tears. Lover's spat? More than likely, Kai told herself.

Philip Montgomery appeared in the doorway. Michelle turned and threw a set of keys at him and then roared away in a beautiful Porsche. *Bitch!*

Oh well, there was no time to dwell on jealousy. Taking advantage of another spur-of-the-moment opportunity, Kai waited a few minutes and then rushed to the front door and pressed the bell.

Apparently expecting Michelle, her father swung the door open instantly. Kai flung herself into his outstretched arms. It didn't matter that those open arms had been intended for someone else.

"Daddy!" she cried, shedding manufactured tears. "I'm so sorry for the way I acted in your office." She embraced him, her arms wrapped around his neck.

"Kai!" he said sternly. "What are you doing here?" Philip Montgomery tried to remove Kai's arms from around his neck.

"I followed you. I have to tell you how sorry I am for being the wretched burden I've been on you my entire life. But I can't help it if I still love you. I'll love you until the day I die; you're the only father I ever knew."

Her father was stiff and uncomfortable with Kai's outward display of emotion and confession of endless love. He cleared his throat. "Kai, I want you to get a grip on yourself. You have to go back to Philadelphia. Your mother and I have started a new life. You're all grown up now. We paid a lot of money to get you out of that legal entanglement. We feel we've done our part. Now, I'll pay your living expenses in Philadelphia if you promise to leave Los Angeles tonight."

Kai's arms fell away from his neck. Her head dropped as she wept bitter tears. "I'm baring my soul to you, Daddy. I don't want your money. It's never been about money. I always demanded money from you because I was so angry that you took your love away. Daddy," she said, looking in his face, blinking tears from her lashes, "you broke my heart."

Ah, that guilt-trip arrow hit him right in the heart. She could sense her father softening a little, so she took a chance and wrapped her arms around his waist. She loved the smell of the expensive fragrance he wore and was seriously looking forward to shopping for fragrances and trinkets for herself on Rodeo Drive.

"You used to love me, Daddy. Don't you remember when I was your little princess?"

Her father emitted a soft groan of anguish. He remembered, she could tell. "Please Daddy, don't send me away," she added, hoping to increase the intensity of the guilt-trip. "I want to stay— just for a little while. Please." She raised her tear-stained face upward. The look in his eyes gave her a glimmer of hope.

"I know I'm not your real daughter; I know you had to force yourself to stop loving me. Didn't you, Daddy?"

"Yes," he admitted in a strangled voice. "I loved you, Kai… It's just that…"

Aw shit, she was getting to him, tugging at his heart strings. "I understand," she said, cutting off his words. "I just need one thing from you."

"How much do you want?" he asked, his voice filled with compassion as he unwittingly entwined his fingers into her curly, abundant hair.

She had the bastard in the palm of her hands. He couldn't resist her hair. "I just want to be your little princess, one more time. Okay, Daddy?" she asked in the smallest, most innocent voice she could produce.

She reached up and kissed his cheek. "I love you, Daddy," she whispered as her lips moved to his mouth. Hesitantly she brushed her lips across his. Then she waited a few moments before testing him with a full lip kiss. "I miss my daddy; I want you back. Please," she whimpered.

"I'm sorry, Kai. I can't do this…" He backed away.

But she took his hand. "I want to sit on your lap; I want you to play in my hair. Show me how you used to love me, one more time. I promise you, I'll leave tonight. Can I please sit on your lap, Daddy?"

Like a man entranced, Philip Montgomery walked over to a chair—a very rich-looking, barrel-shaped chair, which was covered in a plush, velvety, cherry-red fabric with an extra large seat cushion for added comfort. There was also a matching pillow. The adjacent sofa was identical in color and fabric. Her father's assistant/mistress had good taste, but the bitch could kiss this hideaway good-fucking-bye. This richly appointed love nest belonged to Kai now.

Music flowed softly in the background. She could smell a wonderful aroma emanating from the kitchen. Michelle had been setting the tone for a romantic evening with Kai's father. Tough! Kai was taking advantage of the staged romantic ambiance. She'd eat the meal later.

Kai sat on her father's lap. Without prompting, he ran his fingers through her hair. She pulled up her sundress. She didn't have on panties; she hadn't bothered to waste her precious few dollars on new underwear.

Philip Montgomery inhaled sharply when he realized his adopted daughter was bare-assed. His gasp became a helpless groan. He didn't resist as Kai swiveled into his lap. Seemingly in search of a comfortable position, she wiggled her butt around until she located his bulge. Kai backed up and captured his fabric-covered penis. Using glute muscles, she maneuvered the hard shape of his dick into the space between her bare butt cheeks.

Next she dropped the straps of the sundress and reached for her father's hands. This time, he tried to stubbornly resist her, but she roughly pulled his hands from her hair and placed them on her small, perfectly shaped breasts. He moaned in anguish as he kneaded her breasts and pinched her nipples.

"I love you," she whispered as she ground her butt against his cock. "Tell me you love me, Daddy. Tell me I'm still your little princess."

"You're my…" His harsh breathing interrupted his speech.

Kai slipped her hand behind her back and unzipped his pants.

"This is insane," he said weakly.

"It's okay, Daddy. No one will ever know."

He groaned when she fondled his penis and pulled it out of his pants.

"Kai. Honey. We shouldn't…"

*Honey!* It had been years since she'd heard him address her using such an endearing term. She felt so confused. She loved him. But she hated him, too. The powerful emotions of love and hate battled against each other. Needing to win the war, Kai put a shield around her heart. "Tell me you love me, Daddy," Kai insisted, her voice cold and gruff.

"I love you," Philip Montgomery uttered breathily as Kai pushed down on his erection.

Chapter 22

Life was sweet. Well… it was sweeter than it had been in quite a while. She had successfully seduced her father. He'd gotten rid of his blonde mistress and Kai was now living in the bungalow. Many nights, he stayed with her instead of going home to her mother. Yes, her father was pussy-whipped.

Once again, she was driving a Benz and due to Philip Montgomery's generosity—and guilt—Kai had lots of high-tech gadgets, designer clothes, and plenty of disposable income. She should have been happy. But she wasn't because despite his surface generosity, her father wasn't charitable enough to fork over the millions from her trust fund—the millions that he owed her.

Considering how happy she and her kitty cat made Daddy, his stubborn refusal to go against his deceased mother's wishes felt like a stinging slap in the face. An additional insult was his refusal to publicly declare that she was his adopted daughter.

"You're not my natural daughter, Kai. I can't give you the money," he kept telling her, making her angry, forcing her to cut off his access to her kitty.

But her adopted father was a shrewd man. He knew the key to her heart. When she got upset with him, refused to sleep with him, he'd buy her a trinket. Something so breathtakingly beautiful and outrageously expensive, she simply couldn't stay angry.

Kai's existence was kept a secret from the members of her father's social circle and her adopted mother didn't have a clue that Kai was living in Beverly Hills. Something had to be done. She'd be damned if she'd live out her life as her father's paid sex toy.

When she heard his key in the lock, Kai rushed to the barrel chair. She usually greeted him naked, but this time she wore a very tight thong that gave just a glimpse of her hair-free private parts.

A few years back, Kai had sported a Brazilian bikini wax, with a patch of triangular-shaped hair. That look had whipped the thoroughly thugged-out Marquise into shape. Being behind bars for two years had kept her out of the loop of what's in and what's out. How embarrassed was Kai when, planning to seduce her father into complete submission, she'd gone to a salon earlier that day and requested a Brazilian, her voice haughty and defiant?

The receptionist turned her nose up. She looked at Kai like she was from Mars. "A Brazilian, with a patch of hair? Ohmigod! That's sooo five years ago. Going completely bare is trendy among celebs today."

Keeping up with the day's trends, Kai had her kitty shaved clean. She was sure Daddy would love it.

With her feet planted on the chair cushion, her legs parted, Kai gave Philip Montgomery a crotch shot designed to weaken his resolve. The pussy flesh that was visible had no signs of hair follicles or skin discoloration. Like a little girl's vagina, Kai's kitty was small, smooth, and unblemished. Having a clean-shaven kitty added validation to her little-girl routine. Her father loved her as a child and Kai would be damned if she'd ever lose his love again.

With her eyes closed, she smiled. The rustling sound of her father coming out of his clothes was music to her ears, a lover's symphony. Well, to be perfectly honest, it wasn't music Kai heard; it was the sound of cha-ching, cha-ching—money in the bank!

In less than a minute, he was on his knees, lapping at the slip of fabric between her legs. It felt so good, Kai pulled the thong to the side, allowing him full access to her most private part.

With puckered lips, he placed kisses all over the smooth, clean area. He stopped kissing to briefly observe her vagina. "Honey! I love this look. It's so attractive," he exclaimed. "Mmm," he moaned and began to lick her vulva up and down. Next, he used his tongue to spread open Kai's sticky inner lips. He slid his tongue into her slit while his lips anxiously sucked her clit. "Your tight cunt is making Daddy erect."

Daddy was hard and Kai was dripping wet. She'd have to bargain with him later; right now, her kitty was burning with desire. The fire that raged between her legs needed to be extinguished, quick! Kai eased out of the chair and down to the floor. Invitingly, she opened her legs. Fortunately, Kai didn't need the full length of a dick to come. After he slipped the head inside her tight hole, she clenched her muscles and held it in a vise-like grip. With his knob gripped tight and locked in place, Kai rotated her pelvis until she brought herself to a speedy orgasm.

"Oh, Daddy," she said, releasing a satisfied sigh.

Overcome with passion, Philip Montgomery attempted to invade her space with a few more inches, but Kai blocked his entry by pulling back, making his stiff appendage slip out.

"It hurts," she said, her voice a painful whimper. "I got this wax job for you—to please you. I didn't know it would hurt like this. It's burning so bad...Daddy, I really can't take anymore." She looked near tears. Her father looked frantic and horny.

"I won't hurt you, honey," he promised, trying to get her to lie prone.

Getting out of the missionary position, Kai sat up. "Yes, you will. It really hurts."

"What do want me to do, honey? I'm all worked up," he said desperately. "If I kiss it and make it better...if I promise not to hurt you, can I put the head back in?"

Philip Montgomery, a highly esteemed surgeon, was nothing more than a lustful pervert—like most men. She beamed in victory. Then she smiled in sincere recollection of the times her father kissed her boo boos, kissed away her pain, back when she was really a little girl.

After he'd reinserted the knob of his cock, Kai asked again if he loved her.

"Yes, I love you, honey," he said and pushed in an inch.

Kai yelped, pretending to be in great pain. It was the high-pitched squeal of a hurt child.

"I'm sorry, honey," he said, breathing hard.

*Sick bastard.* "How much money did Grandmother leave me?"

"Millions, honey. But you're not—"

"How many millions?"

"I can't give you that information, honey. It's a private matter," he said gently.

"Okay," Kai said, her tone of voice sad and disappointed. "You're hurting me," she whined and wriggled uncomfortably. "Take it out!"

"Give me a minute, honey. I'll take it out in a minute," he said, breathing and thrusting hard, forcing a few more inches inside her tight, shaven vagina.

"I said you're hurting me. Take it out!" she screamed, as if in the midst of a tantrum.

"Okay, honey. Okay. If you let me finish, I'll give you a million dollars. That's fair, isn't it?" It was his dick talking, getting him into trouble—had him making promises he'd later regret.

"Let's go in the bedroom," he suggested.

She thought about his proposal. Getting a million dollars out of her father was a very good start.

"All right," she said, still using a childish voice.

Once inside the bedroom, Kai stopped acting like a child. She pushed Philip Montgomery onto the bed. Straddling him, she fucked him like the full grown woman she was.

Late that night, after her father left, Kai took a picture of her pretty pussy and sent it to his cell phone. Next, she sent him a text message: *Deposit $1,000,000.00 into bank account for Kai.*

Seven days later, she had her own bank account with a deposit of a cool million. Having her own money elevated her self-esteem, but increased her restlessness. Sex with her father was getting boring. It just wasn't kinky enough for her taste. Besides, she was beginning to feel as if the walls were closing in on her. It was Saturday night—a perfect night to go out on the prowl.

Kai found what she was looking for.

To hell with sitting at home and waiting for her father like a good little girl, Kai put on lip gloss, dressed up, and hopped in her new Benz. She cruised to an African restaurant on Wilshire Boulevard that she'd found after diligently searching the internet.

Bouncing merrily out of her car, she handed her set of keys to the extremely good-natured and courteous valet.

Feeling beautiful, she strutted inside the restaurant. Heads turned in her direction and Kai detected no malice or envy. Instead, she saw only admiration and appreciation of her stunning beauty.

The atmosphere inside the restaurant was vibrant and alive. She was glad she'd decided to leave the tomb that was her home.

"Dinner for two?" a round-faced, dark-brown woman asked.

"No, just one—me," Kai said, smiling as she admired the restaurant's décor with its colorful images of African folk art. The woman led her to a table in the rear and then returned with two bowls—one filled with water and the other empty.

"Allow me to wash your hands," the woman said, smiling sweetly as her luminous eyes glanced at the empty bowl.

Kai wasn't taken aback. She'd read that this hand-washing ritual was part of the custom, since most Africans enjoyed using their fingers instead of eating with utensils. She placed her hands inside the empty bowl and the woman poured a stream of cool water over Kai's fingers. It was soothing and sensual.

Unfortunately, sexual activity with females had gone out of fashion for Kai, otherwise she would have been angling for a way to introduce the woman's sweet face to her clean-shaven kitty cat.

After perusing the menu, she ordered chicken stew, which was served with a flatbread, mashed potatoes, fresh peas, and collard greens that were thinly cut and sautéed with onions and tomatoes. The meal was scrumptious. Kai made quite a display of openly sucking the spicy flavors from her fingers. With each finger that she licked and sucked, she cut her eyes at the diners and workers as well, curious to see who among the crowd found her finger sucking particularly arousing.

Every eye in the restaurant was riveted to her table. She couldn't blame them for watching her. She was, after all, an extremely sexy bitch. Kai laughed softly. Possessing a million dollars was quite an ego boost. She recommended that anyone going through a difficult period should figure out a way to acquire a large sum of money. The one million dollars her father provided certainly gave her a new lease on life. She was finally beginning to feel like her old self again.

As the evening progressed, Kai noticed the music had changed. A handsome African DJ had cranked up the music, changing the soothing tones to pulsing jungle beats. Couples moved toward the dance floor. In no time at all, the floor was packed.

African dancing was enthusiastic and unrestrained. Instead of relying on just their arms and legs, Africans seemed to fluidly move all of their body parts with wild abandon. Men danced with men as well as with women. Watching them dance was a complete turn-on. Just as she made flirty eye contact with a man whose sensual moves caught and held her attention, her cell jangled.

Oh, crap! It was her stupid father. She started to ignore his call, but being that she now had the upper hand in their relationship, she decided to amuse herself by engaging in a conversation with her pussy-whipped, asshole of a father.

"Hi, Daddy," she yelled above the loud music.

"Hi, honey. I was worried when I got here and you weren't home. Where are you?" He sounded sullen. Kai didn't care.

"In a restaurant," she said nonchalantly, knowing full well he expected her to be at the bungalow when he came home from his clinic.

"I, uh, I brought food, your favorite…"

"Oh! Sorry. I wanted to try something ethnic."

"What?"

"I'm tired of regular American food; I was in the mood for ethnic cuisine," she said, chuckling at her clever metaphors.

"Honey, I can't understand a word you're saying."

"Hold on, Daddy. I'm going somewhere quiet." Kai left the main room and went inside the restroom. "Can you hear me now, Daddy?"

"Yes," he said, sounding relieved. "How long will it take you to get home?"

"Home?"

"Yes, home. Why are you repeating everything I say?"

"Because I don't consider that bungalow as home. Wouldn't home be the place where you and Mother reside?"

"Stop being ridiculous. I told you your mother thinks you're in Philadelphia."

"Shouldn't we let her know that I'm here?" There was a long pause on her father's end. Irritated, Kai broke the silence. "Oh, forget it. I'll talk to you later." She clicked a button on her phone, disconnecting the call.

A few seconds passed and her cell rang again.

"Yes, Daddy."

"Honey, I gave you the money. Can't you be reasonable?"

"You gave me a pittance of the money I was left. I'm in therapy again," she lied. "And my therapist said I'm experiencing abandonment issues."

"You didn't say anything about us, did you, honey?"

"No, Daddy."

"Good. Good, girl," her father said with a sigh. "Kai, honey. I don't want to hurt your feelings, but I have to be honest with you. Miranda never wanted anything to do with you. I forced you on her, insisted that we adopt you. She…well, after a while, we both wanted to be free of you," he said. "Of course, I've changed my feelings toward you, so honey…can't you be satisfied having me? Involving Miranda will cause tension. We're happy together, aren't we, honey?"

"No! I'm not happy. Mother doesn't have to love me, but it's not fair for her to get away with kicking me out of her life. It's not fair, Daddy, and you know it. Take me home with you," Kai insisted. "You're the breadwinner," she added. "What do you care what Mother thinks. Her concerns didn't matter when you brought me home as an infant; her feelings should be of little consequence now."

"I can't spring this on Miranda tonight. It's insensitive."

"You're absolutely right, you should be more sensitive. So why don't you go on home and be with your wife? I thought you wanted me; but it seems you don't. I guess I should seriously consider going back to Philly."

"No!" he blurted. "Don't leave, honey. Give me a little time to sort things out."

"All right, Daddy. Call me after you tell Mother that your daughter is coming home." *No more calls from Daddy*, Kai thought with a giggle, and turned off her phone.

She'd scored a touchdown with her father. It was only a matter of time before she moved into the mansion. Though she couldn't dance a lick—had no rhythm whatsoever—she mimicked dancing by wiggling or shaking her tiny ass. Feeling triumphant and motivated by the beat of the drums, Kai shook her ass like crazy as she exited the restroom.

It took only a few seconds for the man she'd made eye contact with earlier to spot her. Eyes gleaming, he rotated his pelvis in time with the music, beckoning her with gyrations, gesturing for Kai to dance with him.

She worked her way through the throng. The African put an arm around her waist and pulled her so close, they were groin-to-groin. Kai didn't have to move a muscle. Propped up by his arm, she allowed him to grind against her, hard. If he was packing like the African cab driver, this man was carrying a weapon of mass destruction inside his pants. Her interest was definitely piqued.

"My name is Sebastian; may I buy you a drink, pretty lady?" he asked with a broad smile when the song ended.

Sebastian was full of himself; Kai could tell. He thought his offer should have her cumming all over herself. "No, thanks. I'm rich; I don't need hand-outs."

Sebastian burst into laughter. "Then maybe you should buy *me* a drink!"

"I prefer to buy some cock."

He laughed heartily. "What I have is not for sale. I like to give it to pretty ladies such as you."

"Well…I'll need to have a look at what I'm getting." Sebastian was sexy and whatever was pressed against her on the dance floor felt impressive, but if he didn't measure up to Trevor, she had no interest in his goods.

*Trevor!* She'd had a freaky good time with him. She still had his card and intended to look him up when she returned to Philly. "In the meantime…" Kai's eyes traveled down to Sebastian's crotch.

"In the meantime, what?"

"In the meantime, I need to know how well you're hung," she said with a straight face.

His eyes widened in shock. "I can't show you here on the dance floor," he said modestly.

"Okay, let's go. We'll have privacy inside my car. I'll drive somewhere where we can be alone. You can take it out and show me. If you're well endowed, I'll take you home with me. If you're not, I'll bring you back to the restaurant. Fair enough?"

"That's fair," he said, laughing.

Kai drove to a secluded spot and Sebastian eagerly unzipped his pants and displayed his penis. It was huge. Like a cobra. Kai licked her lips in anticipation.

"So what do I get in exchange for my big machine?" he wanted to know.

"I'm going to let you treat me like your personal whore." Kai was truly looking forward to a repeat of the experience she'd had with Trevor. Though Sebastian seemed a bit mild mannered, she hoped that was just a ruse. She wanted rough, degrading sex. Her pussy dripped in anticipation.

Sebastian looked embarrassed. "I'm too much of a gentleman. I would never treat a pretty lady like a whore."

*Oh, crap!* Disappointment washed over Kai. *Crap!* She'd left the bungalow in search of bold, black Zulu beef. She sure wished she could twitch her nose and replace Sebastian with Trevor. Trevor was a master at treating a woman like gutter trash. Trevor had rammed her hard and without tenderness or compassion. He'd left her pussy gutted and flooded with his creamy milkshake. It had taken a couple of days for her vaginal walls to tighten up to their normal size.

"Let me see between your legs," Sebastian suggested softly.

*Mmm.* There was hope that the sexual energy that had flowed between them could be reignited. Feeling optimistic that Sebastian had toughened up and was prepared to talk dirty and treat her like scum, Kai turned toward the passenger seat and drew up her legs. Smiling proudly, she pulled her thong to the side, eagerly showing off her cute little hair-free, kitty.

Sebastian reared back, his face twisted into a grimace. "Why on earth did you remove all your pubic hair?"

"Don't you like it?" Kai's smile twitched in uncertainty.

"No! Your vagina looks disgusting without hair. I could never touch you; I'd feel ashamed—as if I were having intercourse with a child."

"Oh, fuck you, you heathen," Kai blurted angrily. This was ridiculous. These African men went from one extreme to the other. She'd be damned if she was going to waste her time with Sebastian's primitive, puritanical ideas. "Get the hell out of my car!" she screamed in outrage. She reached over and pushed open the passenger door.

Sebastian looked around worriedly. "You promised to take me back to the restaurant."

"Pretend like you're back in the Motherland, being pursued by a wild animal. Run, motherfucker, run! Sprout wings, fly! I don't care how you get there, but you'd better get your worthless ass out of my car."

Sebastian stared at Kai, eyes wide with incredulity. Kai pulled out her cell phone. "Get out or I'm going to call the police."

At the word *police*, Sebastian's eyes looked ready to pop out of his head. He jumped out of the car and ran like hell.

Furious with dumb-ass Sebastian, Kai sped all the way home. To hell with getting a speeding ticket; she defied anyone to fuck with her tonight. She screeched into the driveway of the bungalow.

Her mouth dropped open when she noticed a light glowing.

*Daddy's home*, she thought with a smile. His car was parked in the garage in the back. He'd stayed—he'd waited for her to return, which meant he'd had a change of heart and was willing to see things her way.

Kai raced to the front door. Philip Montgomery flung it open.

"Daddy!" she shouted. Thrilled to see him, she jumped in his arms and wrapped her legs around his waist. After being snubbed by the African, her adopted father's white penis and his appreciation for her pretty pussy was more than welcome.

Chapter 23

Kai sat in the passenger seat of her father's Rolls. Her Louis Vuitton duffle bag was in the back, stuffed with enough changes of clothes to last for at least two days.

"I want you to brace yourself. Miranda's appearance is…well, it's startling."

Kai scrunched up her face. "What do you mean by startling? What happened to her?"

Her father cleared his throat. "As you've guessed, I was having an affair with my assistant, Michelle. But that's over," Philip Montgomery quickly assured Kai, patting her hand. "While it was going on, Miranda and I had some knock-down, drag-out fights."

"You and Mother fought physically?" Kai couldn't imagine her dignified adopted mother throwing a punch.

"No," he said, shaking his head. "But we used some pretty cruel and cutting words." He stopped for a red light and turned to Kai. "Honey, I love my wife. I always have."

"Don't you love me?"

"I love you, too, you know that. It's just not the same. Miranda is going through a very difficult time and we're going to have to cool it—"

"But, Daddy…," she whined.

He patted her hand. "I know, honey. We'll meet up at the bungalow from time to time. For your mother's sake, we have to respect her home, okay?"

"Does this mean you're going to start up with Michelle again? If that's the case, you can just turn this car around and take me to the airport and have my Benz shipped to Philly."

"No, no. Michelle resigned. She's working for another surgeon. I hear they're heavily involved."

"Do you miss her?" Kai eyed him intently.

"Not at all. No one holds a candle to you."

"Except Mother," she said, pouting.

"Honey, it's different with her. She's my wife; I have a respectful love for her."

"That's a bunch of crap. If you respected her, you wouldn't have cheated with your assistant."

"I made a mistake. I'm only human."

"What about us?"

He gave her a look of bewilderment. "We're not cheating. What we have is special. There's no word to define it." He reached out and traced her lips with his fingertips. "I love you, you're my favorite girl."

Kai smiled, somewhat satisfied with his response. Sexing him regularly was the only way she'd ever soften him enough to get him to turn over the money she'd been promised since she was a child. Like hell, she'd respect her mother's home. She didn't notice anyone showing any respect for her when they left her to rot in jail. Not once had her father told her he was sorry for the two years she'd spent behind bars. He didn't express any outrage over the incompetent way the lawyer he hired had handled her case. He didn't even bother to make up an excuse for not writing or visiting. If not for the money he and his wife left on her books, it would have been hard to believe that Kai had ever had any family at all. She felt her adopted father had forced her into becoming his mistress instead of allowing her to claim her rightful place as his darling daughter. And for that unforgivable transgression, Philip and Miranda Montgomery were going to pay dearly.

The opulent home was quiet. Not tranquil, not peaceful. Quiet. Unsettlingly quiet. Like a tomb. Kai sensed there was no joy inside these walls. Her parents obviously had money to burn but they certainly weren't enjoying it. Her father would rather reside in a small bungalow than sleep here. Kai couldn't blame him. But she was here now, she'd liven things up. When Kai was around, there was never a dull moment.

"Miranda's recovering from cosmetic surgery." He shook his head. "A botch job she had done in Switzerland. She's not healing well. She's taking a lot of medication and it makes her drowsy. Wait here while I go talk to her," her father said, leaving Kai alone in the dimly lit atrium. She scanned her surroundings. Her parents had always been wealthy but judging by the looks of things—the art work, lush greenery, they were really rolling in dough now. Absently, she wondered why her mother went all the way to Switzerland for a face lift.

About twenty minutes later, she heard her father's footsteps on the marble tile. "She's awake, she's lucid," he said, his voice hushed, "but not for long. She became so upset when I told her you were here, I had to give her a sedative to calm her down."

"Should I wait to see her in the morning?" Kai's voice was hushed as well. The quiet house seemed to demand that every word uttered be softly spoken.

"No, she wants to talk to you. Let's hurry before the medication sets in."

Kai nodded in understanding. With her face creased in insincere concern, she followed her father up an impressive staircase.

Miranda Montgomery lay in bed. Her face was bandaged like a mummy's. Through the gauze, slits had been made for her eyes, nose, and mouth. She looked awful. Worse than awful, she looked monstrous. Kai could only imagine what hack-job horror lay beneath the bandages..

Feeling suddenly enlightened, Kai concluded that her mother, desperate to compete with her husband's young assistant, didn't trust her husband or any of his friends to surgically improve her fading beauty so Miranda slipped off to Switzerland, telling her new Beverly Hills friends that she was going away for a little R&R.

"Hello, Mother," Kai whispered. "How are you feeling?" Though her words came out dripping with concern, her face was twisted in disdain.

"Why did you come here, Kai?" Miranda asked coldly.

Kai quickly manufactured tears. "I came to spend time with my family."

"We were never a family," her mother said in a harsh murmur.

"You're the only family I ever had." Kai's voice was weak. She turned her head toward her father; her eyes were pained. He rubbed her arm sympathetically.

She took a deep breath. "Mother, I know I was a difficult child—"

"*Difficult* is putting it lightly. You don't fool me, Kai. I've known you since you were three weeks old. You want something. What is it? Money?" Miranda turned to her husband. "Tell her, Philip... your mother put certain conditions on that money."

"She knows that, Miranda. There's no point in making her feel worse by rubbing it in."

Kai released a sniffle. "Mother—"

"Clearly, you've managed to wrap my husband around your finger again. Like mother, like daughter," Miranda spat. Her eyes peeking through the gauze bandage were glinting with anger. "Philip," she said to her husband, "I can't believe you'd do this to me. Why can't I have some peace in my life? Send her back to whatever hellhole she crawled out of. I don't want her around. I never wanted her around..." Miranda Montgomery became so overwrought, she tried to get up, lifting herself with her elbows. But being groggy and weak, she collapsed back into the down-filled pillows.

"Calm down, Miranda. Working yourself up is not good for your recovery. Kai is just here for a visit. Let's try to be civil, all right, dear? She's our adopted daughter; let's behave like a civilized family, shall we?"

"I've done that already. Held my head high and allowed your bastard child to call me Mother. The abuse I took from..." Miranda's words trailed off.

"You're talking out of your head," Philip Montgomery said.

Miranda snorted. "You humiliated me...made me raise the daughter of a black prostitute. Pretending to be liberal-minded..." Her voice was badly slurred by the medication that was taking effect.

"Your accusations are uncalled for. Kai is not my daughter; we both know that. Giving an underprivileged child a good home was the charitable thing to do," Philip Montgomery reasoned.

Kai's ears burned; she recoiled. *Underprivileged. Charitable. Black prostitute. Bastard. Illegitimate.* The brutal slurs caused her to blank out for a second.

"All those years...you thought she was your own flesh and blood...you adored her; but I hated her." Miranda's voice, formerly softened by medication, was now strengthened by hatred and became hard, razor sharp.

Kai squirmed at the hatred and the discomfort of having to control the urge to slap her mother senseless, rip away the mummified bandaging, and expose her ugly, disfigured face.

Ever conniving, Kai pretended to be distraught with hurt and humiliation. Weeping bitterly, she turned and sought solace from her father. Falling into his arms, Kai cried, "Daddy, it hurts so bad to now know that everyone hated me. How could all of you—my birth mother, you, and Mother—how could all of you despise an innocent baby?" she wailed.

"I never despised you, honey. Honestly. I loved you; I just hated the idea that your real mother had tricked me into thinking you were my own child." He tightly enfolded his weeping daughter in his arms, comforting her while his wife, fighting her medication, continued to mutter insults.

"Aren't I your favorite girl?" Kai asked, weeping openly. Wracking sobs shook her body.

"Shh. Shh; it's okay, honey. Your mother doesn't mean a word she said; she's medicated—talking out of her head."

"I meant every word," Miranda said acidly. "Get her out of our bedroom."

"Miranda, be reasonable." He looked at Kai. "She really doesn't mean any of those words, honey."

Unconvinced, Kai continued to cry. Feigning emotional distress, she flapped and flailed her arms about. In the midst of thrashing, she took a calculated risk and pretended to accidentally stroke his crotch. She felt him tense and braced herself, expecting him to swat her hand away. But he didn't move. He swallowed audibly, a sign that he couldn't resist Kai's touch. Her lips, pressed against his chest, curved into a smile.

Her father was so vulnerable, so easy to seduce. Men were so pathetic. Even with his wife lying in bed before them, he could not resist her. She rubbed in a circular motion, until she felt his manhood become rigid. Then she gave it a firm squeeze until the bulge grew harder and lengthened inside her hand.

A familiar tingly sensation coursed through her and settled inside her kitty cat. Feeling hot and amorous, she tilted her head for a kiss.

"Not here…"

She silenced him by pressing her lips against his and felt him melt from her kiss, which prompted her to become even more daring. She probed inside his mouth. Giving in, Philip Montgomery returned the kiss with hungry urgency, exploring with his tongue, and feeding from the sweetness of her mouth.

Immensely pleased with the progress she was making, Kai boldly backed him into a corner, dropped to her knees, and hastily unbuckled his belt.

The clicking sound alerted Miranda. "What's going on, Philip?" his wife asked. Her shaky voice was barely audible. She turned her head side-to-side and stretched open her eyes, trying to locate her husband.

"Nothing's going on, dear," he said, his voice husky from lust as he allowed Kai to ease down his pants. He shot a quick, wary look at his wife. Her eyes were closed. Her lashes fluttered as she wrestled with the drowsiness that had overtaken her.

His pants and underwear were now gathered around his feet on the floor. At first Kai circled the head of his cock with a moistened thumb, and then she began to torture it with a tongue that was hot and demanding.

Wanting to cry out in helpless passion, Philip grabbed Kai's hair with both hands to steady himself.

Kai cupped his scrotum and nipped it softly with her teeth. "Daddy," she whispered, "can I lick your balls?"

"Aggh! Yes!" he groaned as he went into an automatic squat position, legs gapped as he offered her a mouthful of testicles.

"What's wrong, Philip?" his wife murmured, twisting, trying to get a glimpse of her husband and Kai. "Why are you making those noises?"

"I stubbed my toe," he said hoarsely. "I'll be in bed soon," he assured her between lustful, panting breaths. "Go to sleep. You need your rest, dear."

"Where's Kai?" Miranda whispered suspiciously.

"In one of the guestrooms," he groaned as Kai blew cool air on his nut sac. Her tongue alternated licking one ball and then the other.

Miranda's babble faded into the background, becoming a low, nonsensical hum, which Kai and her father easily tuned out. Caught up in the frenzy of deceit and lust, their passion was at an all-time high. Kai brazenly tore out of her clothes and then spitefully flung her bra on the bed.

Philip Montgomery, worked up into a hot, sweaty fever, didn't notice the frilly, pink push-up bra that lay at his wife's side.

On the floor, beside the bed, Kai changed position and got down on her hands and knees.

"Fuck me, Daddy!" she cooed, pushing out her butt, enticing him to penetrate.

With no regard for his wife's consciousness or lack thereof, Philip Montgomery hastily joined Kai on the floor, panting as he slid his hot flesh inside her. Growling, he drove his hardness in and out until he reached a jarring, pulsing climax.

Through sheer will, Miranda Montgomery raised herself. Her eyes were stretched open in shock. Horrified, she stared at the distorted, shadowy figures crouched down on the floor.

Her husband and adopted daughter writhed and moaned, their naked bodies so close they seemed fused together. Fucking like wild animals, the two were oblivious to everything except their raw passion. Kai talked dirty, arousing her father to the point where he'd forget they were on the floor fucking next to the bed where his wife lay.

Feeling eyes upon her, Kai jerked her head in the direction of the bed. Amused, she observed her mother's raised, trembling figure. Through gauzy slits, her mother's eyes blinked in disbelief. Her lips were parted in shock and disgust but she was too groggy to make any audible sound. The wheezy sounds of her agitated breathing went undetected by her husband.

As his body shook from the final tremors of the gushing orgasm, Philip Montgomery moaned and gasped, murmuring Kai's name.

Kai gazed at her mother defiantly, and then spread her lips into a gleaming, victorious smile.

# Chapter 24

I nside a smartly furnished guestroom, Kai lay curled in her adopted father's arms. Though he slept soundly, Kai couldn't get a wink of sleep. Plotting and planning on how to get her dough was keeping her awake. She wanted her money, dammit. If her little performance in her parents' bedroom didn't bring in a truckload of cash, then she should just throw up her hands and give the hell up. There were no more shenanigans up her sleeve and her bag of tricks was completely empty.

Huffing in frustration, she turned her back to her father and moved away from him. On cue, he scooted up behind her. *Oh, crap!* Even while asleep, he yearned for her closeness, draping an insistent arm around her slender waist.

Kai was infuriated. As clingy and needy as he'd become, her father sure had a lot of nerve being insufferably stubborn. Her asshole of a father still flat-out refused to relinquish her inheritance. *Why? Because his mommy said so. Goddamn momma's boy!* Ugh! Kai loathed weakness. Her father maintained his ridiculous allegiance to his dead mother's wishes, which is why she had forced him to bring her face-to-face with her adopted mother. She needed an ally who wasn't a blood relative to the dead grandmother. Yes, in her admittedly warped mind, she was convinced she would turn her rivaling mother into a collaborator.

It seemed that no sooner had sleep finally claimed her, when her father inched up on her ass, sticking her butt cheeks with an early morning erection. For crying out loud, she hadn't even washed last night's gook out of her kitty. Feeling a fresh sense of rage, Kai closed her legs, blocking his entry to her kitty. She was quickly losing all respect for him; she'd held him in higher esteem when he'd stood up to her at his clinic. Kai supposed he'd lost his balls the moment she'd started licking them, which was the first time she'd seduced him inside the bungalow.

Eventually her father gave up his senseless poking in the dark and fell back into a deep sleep. Kai fell asleep as well. When she awakened at eleven in the morning, her father was gone. He'd scampered off to his clinic, leaving behind a batch of semen that slid out of her kitty and pooled in a circle on the expensive bed linen. *Thieving bastard!* She got out of bed and pulled a clingy sleep shirt out of the Louis Vuitton duffle bag.

Kai found her mother, looking as mummified as the night before, reclined on a chaise lounge inside her bedroom and being catered to by a Mexican maid. The curtains were drawn to keep out the sunshine. Kai sat across from her mother while the maid poured a cup of tea.

"Cup of tea for you?"

"No thanks. A cup of Joe for me. I need a heavy dose of caffeine in the morning."

The maid smiled broadly and began to pour another cup of tea.

"No! Coffee. *Café!*" Kai said irritably.

"Ah! *Café,*" the maid said, finally deciphering what Kai had said. Then, she gazed at Miranda Montgomery, silently asking permission to indulge Kai's request.

Her mother sat up, blew the steaming brew, and then took a

sip of tea. She sighed and then nodded her head. "Go ahead, Concetta. Make our guest a pot of *café*."

In a flash, the Mexican woman named Concetta exited. She politely closed the door behind her.

Kai's mother was draped in a checkered Burberry robe and matching pajamas. *How boring*, Kai thought. No wonder Daddy has to stray.

"Did you find the little present I left on your bed?" Kai asked with a smirk.

Her mother put down her tea cup with a clatter and slumped down as if sucker punched. "You've always been underhanded and conniving; what else is new under the sun?" Miranda Montgomery spoke from an awkward, reclined position.

"Stop talking in circles. Did you find my pink bra?"

"Yes, Concetta uncovered your vulgar attempt to extort me. You're just like your real mother—a natural-born slut." Miranda sighed. "I hope you don't think that I would ever suspect Philip—"

"Of having the hots for his daughter?" Kai said, completing her mother's comment. "Or were you going to say he wouldn't stick his cock into a black woman? We both know that whatever way you put it, it's a lie."

Miranda sighed. It was a rattled, defeated sound. "My husband is a good man."

"He's faithful, right?" Kai said sarcastically.

"Yes, he's faithful."

"Take your head out of the sand, Mother. How exactly do you suppose I was conceived?"

"You're not his daughter," Miranda said, raising her voice.

"No, I'm not his biological daughter, but I'll always be his favorite girl. Catch my drift, Mother?"

Miranda blinked. "To think that I changed your diapers, clothed you and got you ready for school…" She waved her hand in exasperation. "And even dealt with that wild hair of yours."

"Yes, Mother," Kai said softly as she dredged up another painful memory. "You dealt with my hair by chopping it off. Sent me to school looking ugly and disfigured…"

"I cut it neatly," her mother said in protest.

"I looked like a freak," Kai said softly as she traveled down memory lane, recalling going to school with her hair choppily shorn by the hands of an angry, jealous woman. "In the name of duty…you took care of me."

"You're right, Kai. I was motivated by duty and love. Love for my husband, whom I continue to love to this day."

"Funny how things have a way of coming back around." Kai's voice had a haunted sound.

"What do you mean?"

"You ruined my hair, disfigured me. You succeeded in getting rid of all those curls that Daddy loved to run his fingers through. Oh, he still does, by the way." Kai gave her bouncy curls an arrogant flip. "Ironically, you're the one disfigured now. Yes, I know about your pathetic attempt to find youth in Switzerland." Kai gave a malicious giggle. "Look at me, I'm young and beautiful— and I'm still Daddy's little girl." Kai said the last three words using a sultry tone, hinting at an illicit relationship between her and her father.

"That's a sick and disgusting insinuation, young lady."

"All right, Mother. Suit yourself. Pretend like you don't know what's going on. Is that what you did when Daddy was hot and heavy for my natural mother? I guess you looked the other way until you had to face his living and breathing infidelity—me!"

Miranda opened her mouth, stretching the gauze in wide protest.

"Oh, save your breath! I know I'm not his birth daughter. It doesn't matter because I have something that you'll never have. Don't act shocked. You knew about his affair with his assistant. Isn't that why you went sneaking off to Switzerland to try to buy back your youth?"

Miranda's eyes grew large.

"Yes, Daddy tells me everything. We're very close, you know. He feels sorry for you, Mummy…" Kai gave a spiteful laugh. "Did I say, 'Mummy?' Excuse me, that was a slip of the tongue. I meant to say, 'Mother,' but you know…your look is so…uh, Egyptian…"

Miranda shuddered at the insult. "I will not be offended in my own home; I want you to leave, young lady." Angry and intending to show that she meant what she said, Miranda sat up straight.

"Daddy said I could stay," Kai snarled, her lip curled defiantly. "Daddy's so handsome and fit; it must be awful trying to compete with all those younger women throwing their panties at him."

"Must you be so vile and disgusting?"

Kai shrugged. "Just keeping it real."

"Keeping it real!" Her mother spat out the words. "Would you kindly refrain from using prison jargon in our home?"

Kai smirked. "So how'd the surgery turn out? What does your face look like beneath those bandages?"

Hunching over, Miranda hugged herself and then held her mummified head in anguish. "This can't be happening—not again. It can't be," her mother moaned.

"Mother, puh-leeze. Instead of all this, 'Oh, woe is me crap,' you should be thanking me."

Miranda's snort indicated that she disagreed.

"Seriously, Mother. You should be thanking me for running off the assistant Daddy was banging," Kai said and then rose from her seated position and crossed over to her mother.

"Keep away from me, Kai," her mother said warily.

"Though I'd love to slap your face for cutting my hair and all the other sneaky things you did when I was just a helpless child, I'm not going to lay a hand on you, Mother."

Kai towered over her mother, who was slumped on the chaise lounge. "I have something to show you. Something that's going to make you green with envy. Wanna see?" Kai taunted as she began to slowly inch up her cotton nightshirt.

Her mother shrank back. "Concetta!" she said, yelling for the maid, but the volume of her voice was muffled by the gauze around her mouth. Miranda trembled and struggled for breath as Kai began to unveil her hair-free cunt.

Kai advanced closer. "Do you want to see the tight, smooth vagina your husband adores?"

Grimacing, Miranda turned her face away and reared back, pressing into the chaise lounge, as if attempting to disappear inside the cushion.

"Look at it, Mother!" Kai demanded, her face twisted into a mask of hatred as she dropped the nightshirt so she could physically turn her mother's face forward.

Her mother struggled, tried to pull away. "Stop it, you're hurting me!"

"I'll rip off those bandages; I'll mess up that botch-job even worse than it already is if you don't take a good, long look at my pussy!" With one hand, Kai grabbed the back of her mother's bandaged head, yanked it forward and held it in place. With the other hand, she tugged up her nightshirt, exposing her waxed-clean vagina once more. "Too bad you don't have a pretty pussy like this. You can try to get your wrinkled face surgically fixed but there's nothing you can do about that tired-looking old cunt. It's stretched out of shape. Hanging. Cavernous. Wide as the Holland Tunnel. No cosmetic surgeon in the world is skilled enough to duplicate this. There's just no way for you to get your saggy snatch fixed."

Bitter tears filled her mother's eyes.

"There's no time for tears, Mother. You have to get busy; you have to do something to save your failing marriage." Kai paused and took a deep breath. "Oh, by the way, you weren't dreaming last night. You saw exactly what you thought you saw—Daddy and me down on the floor—fucking next to your marital bed."

Kai let go of her mother's bandaged head and used both elbows to keep the nightshirt hitched up. Then, stepping a little closer, she opened her pussy lips. Kai's parted pussy was eye-level and only inches away from her mother's face. "Do you recognize your husband's scent?"

Her mother shoved her hard. "Get away from me, you stinking slut."

Kai was thrown off balance, and her hands fell away from her vagina; the nightshirt fell down. "I'm Daddy's slut. Did you catch a whiff—did you sniff his cum?" Kai nodded and gave her mother a knowing look. "Daddy's going to keep coming back for more as long as my kitty stays tight, smooth, and young." Kai sauntered back over to the chair that faced the chaise lounge and sat down.

The maid returned and knocked on the bedroom door. With her legs crossed primly, Kai, acting as the woman of the house, said, "Come in." Though her mother's mouth was hanging open sadly, she was at a loss for words.

As Concetta poured coffee for Kai, Kai spoke to her mother in upbeat, conversational tones. "Did you know your husband has a picture of my kitty? He carries it around with him in his cell phone; he looks at it while he's working. Yes, he's probably looking at my cute little kitty right now."

Concetta, apparently able to pick up a little English, smiled fondly at the words, *cute little kitty*.

"That will be all, Concetta," Miranda said after the maid finished pouring Kai's coffee. When the maid left the room, Miranda asked her daughter, "How much will it take to get rid of you forever?"

"How much did my grandmother leave me?"

"Ten million," Miranda said in a hollow voice.

"I want it."

"Philip used some of it to set up his practice."

"How much is left?"

"I'm not sure, maybe half."

"Five million?"

"More or less."

"Daddy's been making money hand over fist; I want all of it."

"I'll see what I can do."

"Daddy can't help himself. He'll probably leave your bed and join me in my room as long as I'm in this house," Kai said threateningly. She looked over at her parents' bed. "Is your bed king-sized?"

"Larger," her mother said tonelessly. "It's custom made."

"Hmm. So, if it happens that I become afraid of the dark…" She paused thoughtfully.

"I'm tired; where are you going with this, Kai?"

"You know how I used to climb in the bed with you and Daddy when I had bad dreams when I was a little girl. I'd hate to have to join you two at this age." Kai darted her eyes at the bed.

"Though I must say, that bed is really big. It looks like there's plenty of room for me."

Miranda brought her hand to her head and sighed wearily.

Kai's fingers fluttered to her chest. "Honestly, Mother… I'm amazed at the way Daddy behaves when I'm around. He loses all sense of reason and self-control. If I wanted him to, he'd fuck me—"

"Stop it, Kai! You're making me nauseous."

"Really, Mother…I'm certain he'd throw caution to the wind and lick my kitty and my ass with you lying right beside him in bed."

The mummy mask hid her mother's expression, but Kai could tell by her mother's blinking eyes that she was repulsed, broken-hearted, and defeated. Miranda reached for a silver container and shook out a pill. "I'm in a great deal of pain; I would like to recover in peace." She tilted her head backward and swallowed the pill. "I'll make sure you have the money, but it's going to take a few days. In the meantime, I want you to gather your belongings and vacate my home."

Kai *tsked* and rolled her eyes heavenward. "I can't do that. Daddy wants me to stay and that's what I intend to do. I'll leave when ten million dollars is deposited in my bank account." Kai rose. She walked over and placed an understanding hand on her mother's shoulder. "There, there, now. Don't fret. I'm sure you'll have this matter settled in no time at all. Once you've handled your business, you'll be rid of me. This little home wrecker will be out of your hair," Kai said in a child-like, sing-song chant, pointing at herself with both index fingers. Then, her voice became deadly and low. "If I were you, I'd double up on those pain pills or tell Daddy to double up on the dosage of whatever he uses to knock you out at night. Trust me, you don't want to hear the sounds of passion that will emanate from my room tonight." Kai shrugged. "Who knows, we might bring our fuck fest back to the master bedroom!"

"I said I'd get the money for you. Why do you insist on staying where you're not wanted?"

Giving the question some thought, Kai dramatically pressed a finger against the side of her chin and tilted her head in thought. "Frankly, I don't trust you," she responded. "You swindled me out of my inheritance once. How can I be sure you won't try it again? So…I'll be sticking around for a while." Kai stuck her hand on her hip. "I'm going to act extra sluttish when Daddy comes home tonight. I have to keep my daddy happy—make sure he keeps coming back for more."

Miranda covered her gauzed face with her hands and shook her head repeatedly. "Why? Why? Why are you doing this to me?"

"Because I hate you," Kai said simply. "I hate Daddy, too," she admitted with a shrug. "But, I make allowances for him because he's handsome and sexy. And he's a damn good fuck!"

# Chapter 25

K ai had matured. After manipulating her parents and succeeding in collecting her full inheritance, the old Kai would have embarked on a whirlwind shopping spree. Trust, she'd get around to it eventually, but right now, there were pressing issues that required her immediate attention.

Melissa Peterson was off the hook for the time being. Kai's revenge was on hold because her dumb slut of a mother was locked up at Sybil Brand Women's prison.

But Terelle Chambers was available and that bitch had some explaining to do. Terelle could fool the staff at Spring Haven with her emotional breakdown stunt, but she couldn't fool Kai. Crazy recognized crazy. If that ghetto bitch was faking her condition, Kai would know right off the bat.

She'd never formally met Terelle, but since she'd taken a murder rap for the shrewd ghetto girl, it seemed fitting that she have a face-to-face sit-down with her old foe.

Most likely, Terelle would lie prone and pretend to be totally spaced out, but Kai would jolt her out of her self-imposed stupor by whispering, *"Hello, Terelle. Remember me? I'm Kai Montgomery."* If stating her name didn't have the effect of a high-voltage jolt from a stun gun, then Kai would kick the conversation up a notch by dreamily sharing her memories of the good times she'd spent with Marquise. *Your fiancé loved sexin' me doggy-style. He said he was mesmerized by my light skin tone, my curly hair, and my cute, white-girl ass. We'd be fucking like rabbits right now if you hadn't murdered him.*

Hearing those words, the hot-headed, murdering little thug girl would jump right out of her faked-out trance and start swinging at Kai. At that point, Kai would slap the shit out of the bitch, and demand that the hospital staff call the police. Terelle deserved worse than prison time. Nothing less than a lethal injection, would compensate for killing off the best dick Kai had ever had.

Her vengeful musings were put on pause when she entered the lobby of Spring Haven. Carrying a bright bouquet of flowers, Kai gave a faint smile. This place brought back fond memories.

The smile slipped from her face when her thoughts wandered to her birth mother. Kai took a deep, angry breath, and then exhaled slowly. Eventually, her mother would be released from prison and Kai would be waiting for her outside the prison gate. Boy oh boy, right after that bitch caught a whiff of sweet freedom, Kai's hired henchmen would snatch her up and deliver her to Kai.

The bitch had fucked Kai over and Kai intended to fuck her back. She'd do it with a long, thorny rose stem. She had many wonderfully torturous scenarios in mind. If Melissa had known what Kai now knew, her greedy, conniving ass would have taken the money Dr. Montgomery offered before Kai was born and gotten a damn abortion.

That stupid bitch was going to rue the day she listened to her money-hungry, whore-pimping aunt, Addie Mae. Melissa allowed her aunt to talk her into giving birth to Kai for the sole purpose of blackmailing her trick, the esteemed young doctor, Philip Montgomery.

Kai's thoughts returned to the present. "I'd like the room number for Terelle Chambers," Kai told the smiling woman who sat at the information desk. "She's really bad off—nonverbal, catatonic—but I just want to sit and hold her hand. Hopefully, these flowers will provide some comfort and have an uplifting effect." Kai was really pouring the bullshit on thick.

The woman looked surprised. "I don't even have to look her up on the computer," she said and produced a bright smile. "Miss Chambers was released. She's one of our success stories."

*Released!* The word echoed in Kai's mind, making her feel lightheaded. The news was so completely unexpected, she felt woozy and off-kilter. She wasn't sure if she should be delighted or distraught. Choosing happiness, Kai returned the woman's smile. With Terelle on the outside, Kai could exact some unsupervised personal justice before turning her in.

The enforcers of the law obviously weren't even trying to find Marquise's real killer, so Kai felt it was her personal responsibility to track Terelle Chambers down. When she found her, she planned to tie her up, naked and spread eagle. She'd clamp her lips shut with a staple gun, whip her with a wet leather belt, push thumbtacks in all ten fingertips. Finally, she'd smear Terelle's pussy with grape jelly and unleash a swarm of bees.

After torturing Terelle for a few agonizing days, Kai would then conduct a citizen's arrest and drag the gun moll into the police station with her own bare hands.

"Do you have an address for Miss Chambers?" Kai graced the woman with another lovely smile. Being beautiful had its perks. Some people seemed to thoroughly enjoy the fact that she was not only gorgeous, but also well bred, refined, and articulate. "I flew in from California, having no idea my dear friend had been released. Terelle's family is not very stable. There was no one I could call."

The woman nodded sympathetically, which encouraged Kai to continue. For the most part, Kai was winging it; she had no idea what kind of family Terelle had. "Not having any contact with her terrible relatives, you can't imagine how ecstatic I feel knowing that my dear, dear friend has overcome her condition. I just want to wrap my arms around her neck and give her a tight hug," Kai said theatrically.

"It's against the rules," the woman said in a conspiratorial whisper, "but some rules are meant to be broken. My gut tells me you're a wonderful person—flying in from California to sit next to someone you didn't expect to even know you were there. For your information," the woman continued, "Terelle Chambers made a miraculous recovery. She left here talking clearly and walking on her own."

*Hmm. Walking and talking on her own!* That might make it more difficult to subdue the tramp, but where there was a will… "That's wonderful! I can't wait to see her. What's her address?"

The woman gave Kai a wink. "Just a minute." She clicked a few buttons on the computer keyboard. "We wouldn't want those gorgeous flowers to wilt. I'm sure Miss Chambers will be thrilled to see you," she said as she jotted down the address on a yellow Post-It.

Kai snooped around the front of the house, trying to look

through the narrow slits in the blinds, attempting to see if there was any movement inside the house, hoping to find Terelle home alone.

Kai didn't see a woman peering through an upstairs window. She heard, however, heavy footsteps running down the stairs, but before she could sprint to her car, the front door swung open. A dykie-looking woman gawked at Kai. "What the hell?" the woman muttered.

Busted, Kai smiled and cleared her throat while she tried to think of a lie that would gain her entry. "I'm a friend of Terelle's and…"

The woman gave Kai a murderous look. "I know who the hell you are. And you're damn sure not a friend of Terelle's." Standing in the doorway, the butch-looking woman glanced over her shoulder. "Sheila!" she yelled to someone inside the house. Kai hoped she wasn't yelling for another manly dyke. She wasn't physically capable of dealing with two burly women.

"I sat in that courtroom every day during your trial. How'd you get out of prison? Now it makes sense why my niece took off without a reasonable explanation. Those people from the district attorney's office must have called and told her they let you out of jail. Terelle knew you'd be coming after her."

A much more attractive woman with blonde locks—who was no doubt, the butch's bitch, appeared in the doorway, looking puzzled. Her perplexed gaze quickly shifted to a hardened glare. "What's she doing out of prison?"

"Her daddy's rich, so I guess she's above the law."

Oh, crap! How'd these two intruders enter the scenario? She hadn't planned on any intervention. She thought she'd be able to fuck Terelle up to her heart's content in peace and in private.

Kai thought about bolting, but changed her mind. "I didn't come here to start trouble. Honestly," Kai said, using her sweetest tone of voice. "I came to talk to Terelle; I want to give her my side of the story. Obviously, I'm innocent or they wouldn't have released me from prison."

"Look, get your funky ass off my porch," Terelle's aunt said, advancing menacingly toward Kai. "You tried to steal Marquise from Terelle and when you couldn't have him, you shot him like a dog. You even ran over his legs, you heartless killer!" Her voice cracked with emotion.

"I didn't kill him. Terelle did!" Kai said defiantly, but wisely took a few steps back.

Terelle's dykie aunt took a deep breath and frantically fanned her face with her hand and looked at her lover. "You better get her outta my face, Sheila. I swear to God, I'm gon' knock the shit outta this bitch if she don't take her ass away from 'round here."

Sheila glowered at Kai. She stepped forward and placed her hands on Kai's shoulders and twisted her around. "Let me help you turn your ass around."

"Don't put your hands on me," Kai shouted, jerking away from the woman's grip. "Touch me again and I'll have you both arrested. I'll have this drug house shut down," she shouted nonsensically for good measure. "You two lesbos are absolutely right—my father's rich and yes, I'm above the law." She scoffed and gave her hair a haughty toss, and then strutted down the front steps to her precious Benz that her father had obediently shipped to her.

"Ain't that some shit? Lawd, money sure can talk. I can't believe they let a killer get out after serving only a few years," Sheila said to Terelle's aunt. "Can you believe it? Our people just can't get justice."

"Go get a pen, so I can jot down her license plate number!" Terelle's aunt said. "Hurry up, before that bitch pulls off!"

When Sheila returned, pen and paper in hand, Kai's Benz was no longer in sight.

"Did you memorize the numbers on the plate?" Sheila asked.

Looking fretful, Aunt Bennie wrung her hands. "I only got the first three letters. I was too upset to concentrate." She shook her head solemnly. "I'm gonna call the police and give them the numbers I got off her plate. I'm gonna let them know that the murderer they let out of prison is after Terelle."

"Bennie," Sheila said softly. "We can try to get some help from the police, but I doubt if they're gonna do anything. What can they do? Kai didn't actually threaten Terelle."

"Well, she doesn't have to threaten her, that crazy look in her eyes said it all!" Aunt Bennie took a deep breath. "I wish my niece would give me a call. That bloodthirsty lunatic has gotten a taste of getting away with murder and I don't think she's going to stop." Aunt Bennie looked close to tears. "Did you see that look in her eyes?"

"Yeah," Sheila responded. "That woman is stone cold crazy!"

"Oh, Lawd, I wish Terelle would call so I can warn her," Aunt Bennie cried.

# Chapter 26

"What happened to your hat?"

Marquise touched his head. A look of surprise crossed his face. "It must be somewhere in the parking lot. It probably fell off while I was struggling with Keeta."

Now that she thought about it, Terelle couldn't recall seeing Marquise wearing his baseball cap during his turbulent reunion with their daughter. "Quise, I don't think you had it on while you were with Keeta."

"Yes, I did. I said it must have fell off my head. Look, I don't know what happened to it. Why you stressin'? You think the feds or the Jamaicans can track us by my scent?" Marquise laughed, trying to lighten the tense mood.

Terelle shrugged and pretended to let it go. She had an uneasy feeling that she couldn't explain. She didn't like the idea of Marquise leaving anything behind. The possibility that the Jamaicans or the feds might have possession of his personal property didn't sit well with her. Losing his hat seemed somehow to make him as vulnerable as he'd be if someone who worked roots had gotten hold of a strand of his hair. Terelle shuddered involuntarily.

"You cold, babe?" Marquise put his arm around her.

She snuggled next to him. His warmth made the bad feeling, like someone was walking over her grave, disappear.

Early the next morning, garbed in bedroom slippers, a robe, and with an ugly, nylon sleep cap on her head, Kai sat behind the wheel of a nondescript rental car, staking out the back of Terelle's aunt's house. She watched the two lesbos come out of the house. Terelle's aunt double-locked the front door. The butch and her bitch walked to the curb, kissed, got in separate cars, and drove away.

*Goody!* Kai pulled out of her parking space and drove around the back of the house. She pulled out her cell and pushed numbers. "Hello? My name is Terelle Chambers and I need a locksmith. This is an emergency; I'll double your fee and give you a tip if someone can get over here right away." After giving the locksmith the address to Terelle's aunt's house and instructing him to come to the back of the house, Kai sat back and waited.

She didn't know exactly what she was looking for, but common sense told her that the clue to where Terelle had run, lay somewhere inside her aunt's house.

Forty-five minutes later, a white van pulled up. Kai jumped out of her rental, waving her hands like the lone survivor of an air disaster, flagging down the rescue party.

"Thank God!" she said breathlessly. "I was sound asleep and I thought I heard my cat crying to get in. I went downstairs and opened the door to let her in; when she didn't come in, I stepped outside to look for her." Kai touched her chest with the palm of her hand. "I was half asleep—I wasn't thinking when I closed the door. This is so embarrassing."

The sleepy-looking locksmith didn't require Kai's long explanation. He yawned throughout her practiced spiel. He took a look at the back door. "Aw, that's a piece of cake," he said and walked lazily back to the van. He returned with a satchel of tools and Kai was inside in less than twenty minutes. The locksmith didn't even bat a suspicious eye when Kai conveniently pulled his fee, plus tip, from the pocket of her robe.

Alone in the house, she scrunched up her nose in disdain as she wandered from one tacky room to the other. The house lacked style and personality. Unattractive brown-colored, wall-to-wall carpeting covered the floors and the stairs. The walls were decorated with floral prints in plastic frames, purchased from Wal-Mart, Kai was certain. The furniture in the living room, kitchen, and dining room was cheap and outdated. A hideous China cabinet took up most of the space in the small dining room. The wood-grain eye-sore didn't have one piece of China inside. Instead, there were several photographs of the two ugly lesbos that were situated around a huge glass punch bowl, replete with a plastic ladle. And there were all sorts of ceramic figurines and objects on display. Tacky, tacky, tacky! These underprivileged people needed to be shot for showcasing their bad taste.

Making her way toward the stairs, Kai pursed her lips. She felt personally offended to have to search the ghetto-fabulous abode.

Kai climbed the stairs. Assuming that the largest bedroom belonged to the lesbians, Kai passed it by and stuck her head in the middle room. That room was filled with junk, and it seemed to be used for storage. She hoped she wouldn't have to look through that mess to find whatever it was she was after. And just what did she hope to find, she asked herself? She shrugged. Some sort of clue. Surely, someone was lending Terelle a hand. Perhaps she'd jotted an address or telephone number on a piece of paper. Kai entered the last bedroom, which she assumed had been Terelle's, and immediately began yanking open bureau drawers. She searched for what felt like hours. Aside from a correspondence from the Social Security Administration, which at least provided Kai with the ghetto girl's social security number, Kai came up empty-handed.

Terelle was a boring bitch. Kai couldn't find any other correspondence, no journal, nothing of interest. Frustrated, she plopped down on Terelle's bed. She yanked off the sleep cap and twirled her hair as she became lost in thought.

Then it hit her. People usually kept their secrets under the mattress or beneath the bed! Excited, Kai leaped up and pulled the mattress off the bed. Nothing! Crap! She put the mattress back in place and then got down on her knees, lifted the dust ruffle and snooped under the bed. It was dark under the bed, but Kai could make out an object. Something lying out of reach—something that didn't belong under there.

Lying flat on her stomach, she stretched her arm and fingers, trying to grip the thing that her keen instinct told her was evidence that would lead her to Terelle.

Fuck it! Kai got up, raced downstairs to the kitchen, and returned with a broom. With one, hard sweep, she brushed the object out from under the bed. And she could hardly believe what her eyes beheld. In fact, it took several long moments to accept that her eyes were not deceiving her. With something akin to reverence, she brushed her fingers across the brim of a red-and-black baseball cap before gently lifting it off the floor.

She scrutinized the cap, which was emblazoned with a logo of a team that Marquise, in his words, loved to rock. She caressed it as if the baseball cap was a long-lost lover. Kai turned it over and brought it close to her face. She took a quick sniff, then closed her eyes as if enraptured and inhaled deeply. Granted, Marquise had a powerful male scent, but could it emanate so flagrantly after two years? She took another deep whiff. His scent was very strong. Overpowering. Fresh!

*Marquise!* Kai whispered. *Marquise, you're alive!* It all made sense now; her sudden release from prison; Terelle's miraculous recovery and abrupt departure. Marquise was alive and that ghetto bitch had better get prepared for a showdown because Kai was going to track her down. And once she did, there was no telling what she was liable to do. If Terelle put up too much of a fight, Kai would have to switch into crazy mode, rip Terelle's pussy out like she'd done to Terelle's homegirl, Taffy. A woman with a shredded pussy would be of no use to any man.

Kai licked her lips, imagining getting sexed by Marquise. Kai's kitty purred and salivated with excitement. *Oh, Marquise!* Yes, she'd do anything to get that dick back. She'd lie, cheat…and kill! Fuck shredding Terelle's pussy, Kai was going to have to kill that bitch. No doubt about it. If she wanted to keep Terelle permanently out of the picture, Terelle would have to die.

Before Marquise even thought about sulking or grieving over his thug chick, Kai would show him her bank account and promise to buy him all the baseball caps, sneakers, urban wear, and bling his ghetto heart desired.

He'd probably be really upset with her for a while, so she'd let him work off his anger by sexing her rough and hard. Hell, if she thought it would make him happy, she'd offer him some chocolate pudding. Yes, for Marquise, she'd explore the mystery of anal sex. For the love of her life, she'd endure the pain. Had she just referred to Marquise as the love of her life? Grinning, Kai nodded her head in response to her own question. Not only did she love Marquise, she intended to bear his child.

*Chapter 27*

**S**hortly after comforting Terelle, Marquise began to gnaw at his bottom lip. His calm demeanor was gone. He was breathing so hard, his shoulders and chest heaved. He clutched his head between his palms, and rocked back and forth. Marquise was grieving—feeling the loss of the daughter he'd only been allowed to hold in his arms for a few minutes, and Terelle didn't know how to comfort him.

Quiet and tense, Jalil and Ayanna sat up front. Terelle imagined they were wracking their brains trying to come up with consoling words. But Terelle doubted she'd ever smile again—not until she was smiling and gazing into her daughter's pretty, brown eyes.

How was it possible to hurt in so many ways? Along with her own sorrow, her raw, excruciating pain, Terelle hurt for Marquise and for Markeeta. She wasn't striving for jewels, exotic cars, or massive wealth. What she craved was peace…to live in peace and harmony with her family. Something so seemingly simple was the hardest thing in the world for Terelle Chambers to attain.

She cut her eye at Marquise. He was bent at the waist, his head hung so low it was practically in his lap. Her man was falling apart. Their precious daughter was somewhere screaming for her daddy. The mental image of Markeeta fighting and screaming was gut wrenching, unbearable. Would the suffering ever end? Why was it that she could never keep a grasp on happiness for very long? Why was every aspect of her life shrouded in misery?

Clenching her teeth, Terelle tried to fight the crushing sorrow but couldn't. It was too much to bear. A pool of tears filled Terelle's eyes. She sat very erect and still. She didn't raise her hand to wipe away the tears. She didn't even try to blink them away. With her eyes wide open, hands limp at her sides; she stared fixedly at the road ahead, allowing the tears to fall from her eyes. She stiffened her shoulders, trying to be strong, but peace beckoned, calling her name. She heard a buzzing inside her head and felt herself slowly drifting away; going back to that in-between state of consciousness where she couldn't fully feel the pain.

Drifting. Unaware that Marquise had managed to pull himself together and was sitting up. She was floating. Unaware that her teary eyes stared into space. Unaware of everything except the peace that seduced her—until Marquise's hand touched her cheek and tenderly wiped her tears away.

"Babe," he whispered, bringing her back. He eased her head downward until it lay upon his shoulder. Enveloped in Marquise's strong arms, Terelle sobbed softly.

Up front, Jalil turned up the music.

In the back, Marquise caressed Terelle's arm. "It's okay, baby. Go 'head and cry. Let it all out."

Terelle cried harder. Louder. He squeezed her tighter. "I'm not gon' let you down," he whispered in her ear. Then he cupped Terelle's face and tilted her head upward until her eyes met his soul-deep gaze. "We gon' get through this, babe. Trust me. I'm not gon' let you down." He paused, gnawed at his lip, and stared at her intently, urging Terelle to believe.

"You gotta have some faith in me. You heard me?" Marquise said. "Me, you, and Keeta, we ridin' out! Into the sunset, baby. The three of us, together. A family. Forever."

Terelle sniffled and shuddered with emotion. Too choked to speak, she nodded her head vigorously, telling Marquise that she truly believed.

Chapter 28

"You're a private detective. What do you mean, you can't help me?"

"I can't… I, uh…" Parker stammered. "I'm in the middle of a big case."

"Is that so," Kai said.

"Yeah, I swear, I'd help you if I could, but I'm really swamped right now."

"I see. Okay, well…" Kai paused for effect. "It might interest you to know that I did a little detective work of my own." She heard Parker take a gulp of air.

"Oh, yeah?" He tried to sound nonchalant, but his anxiety was obvious.

"Turns out, you're a married man with three kids. Didn't you tell me you were single?"

"I lied. Geeze, sue me for fuck's sake. I was at a convention, for crying out loud. What man doesn't have a little fun when he's away from the wife and kids?"

"Speaking of kids…did you know your oldest son, Parker, Jr. has a MySpace page?"

"Hey! Leave my family out of this. I could have you arrested for threatening—"

"You must not know about me." There was an unmistakable warning tone in Kai's voice. "I've already done time for a crime I didn't commit. Murder! Did you know that?"

Parker gulped again. "No," he said in a tiny voice.

"Hmm. You're a piss-poor detective. But despite your deficiencies, I think you can handle my problem. By the way, don't even think about reporting me. The justice system still owes me a big paycheck. They've been avoiding me like the plague. They wouldn't dream of digging me up over the likes of you and your silly little accusation. So, where were we? Oh yes, we were discussing Parker, Jr.'s MySpace page. Too bad he doesn't require permission before comments are posted. I have my cursor positioned on the send button. Parker, Jr. is a click away from receiving the first picture taken from a batch that unfortunately does not shed a favorable light on you. I plan to begin my smear campaign by posting a photo of you all dolled up in my frilly lingerie on your eldest son's Myspace page. When word gets out, Parker, Jr.'s page will get thousands of hits."

Parker gasped audibly. "He's just a teenager! For Chrissakes, have a heart. I mean… Geez…what do you want me to do?" he asked. Parker was upset, talking fast. His Bostonian accent was so thick; Kai could barely understand his plea.

"I'm afraid this job won't be as easy as before. This one is really going to be a stretch; you're going to have to come out of your comfort zone. You can't just flip open your laptop to locate the fugitives I'm looking for."

"Fugitives!"

"Yes. A real Bonnie and Clyde-type duo. You're probably going to have to get down and dirty with this one—visit rough neighborhoods, have up-close and personal conversations with the poor and disenfranchised, enter squalid crack houses…"

"I'm not sure if I'm—"

"I'm sure that portfolio I'm carrying has oodles of unflattering photos of you and me. Your wife is sure to recognize the picture of your cock. I took that shot while you were asleep—tied a little pink bow around it. And just in case she's not certain the cock belongs to you, I also took a full body shot with the bow in place. And there are plenty more. With my hidden camera, I captured you sucking my tits, nibbling on my clit…"

"Okay, okay. I'll do it."

"Thought so," she said smugly. "Don't even think about changing your mind or the Roxbury Parent Teacher Association, of which your wife is president, will get thumbnails of you in a variety of compromising positions."

Even though Parker had reluctantly agreed to help her find Terelle and Marquise, Kai was too impatient to wait for a report. She twirled her hair and racked her brain trying to remember something, anything that could help her locate her man.

Merion Avenue! Marquise had once hidden out on the 4800 block of Merion Avenue after being thrown out of his apartment by Terelle. Kai had rescued him from that rundown hell hole. She'd taken him home with her and showered him with the best life had to offer…and that's when he was shot. By Terelle? Maybe not. It didn't make sense that he'd run off with the woman who shot him. He wasn't dead but he'd most definitely been shot. Kai saw the blood. Marquise's blood had spilled out of his head and onto the concrete in Dave and Buster's underground parking garage.

Kai didn't like thinking about that incident. It was creepy the way his body had slumped over while he was preparing to fuck her pussy. She remembered the sound of his bones crunching under her tires and her blood ran cold.

She shook away those unpleasant thoughts and steered the rental toward Merion Avenue. If she was lucky, the chick who'd rented the place had managed to keep the section eight she was so deathly afraid of losing.

Kai banged on the door like she was the head of the Philadelphia Police force.

"FBI, open up!" Kai laughed to herself. She was only kidding, but it worked. The door swung open. A passel of stair-step children, several in disposable diapers, stared at her with large, frightened eyes.

"Yes," said the trembling voice of a teenager. The lean teenager held a baby on her narrow hip.

Kai looked around. The furnishings looked familiar. Not much had changed. "Are you the woman of the house?" Kai said, using a crisp, authoritative voice. She knew this teenager wasn't the section eight dweller, but asking her made her FBI cover more credible, Kai thought.

"No, she ain't here," the young girl said.

"What's your name, young lady?"

"Tyneesha Burton," the teenager said, nervously shifting the baby to her other hip.

"Tyneesha, I'm with the FBI and we're looking for Marquise Whitsett."

"Why y'all looking for Quise? He's dead!" Tyneesha shouted abruptly. She looked at Kai like she was crazy.

"We have evidence that he's alive and if you don't want to be implicated, I'd advise you to cooperate."

"But, I don't know nothing." Tyneesha poked out her lips in frustration. "Quise got killed, that's all I know," she said adamantly. "Damn, I just got out of the youth detention center; I ain't tryna get in no more trouble."

Kai stared the girl down and came to the conclusion that Tyneesha Burton didn't have any useful information; she really believed Marquise was dead. *Oh, crap!*

"You won't get in trouble if you provide honest answers," Kai said, not really knowing what to ask next. She needed to sit down and think! There had to be a way to find out where Marquise and Terelle were headed. "May I have a seat?" Kai asked.

The girl gave a long sigh and finally nodded. Kai entered the house, moved toys and other objects aside, and sat on the sofa. "Who is the owner of this house?"

"My cousin and her boyfriend live here," she blurted and then covered her mouth as if she'd given too much information. "I mean…um, just my cousin lives here."

"Section Eight housing is federally funded. If it's determined your cousin has someone living here whose name is not on the lease, she could be looking at some serious jail time." Kai didn't know squat about Section 8, but she recalled how upset the mother of all these little rascals was when she came here looking for Marquise two years ago.

The teenager looked frantic; her eyes misted over. "My cousin's gonna kill me for opening up my mouth. Please don't tell her I told you about Jalil. But, for real, for real, Jalil don't stay here all the time," Tyneesha added.

*Jalil!* Kai remembered that name. Jalil was the name of Marquise's best friend. "You're trying to protect your cousin Ayanna. That's not a wise choice, so if I were you, I'd start talking."

Tyneesha frowned. "Talkin' 'bout what?"

"For starters, you can tell me what kind of car Ayanna and Jalil are driving. I'll need the make, model, and color of the vehicle. The plate number would be helpful, if you have that information."

"Jalil drives a blue Mitsubishi."

Kai wrote the information down. Perhaps Parker would have some use for it. "Now, I want you to be really honest. Do you know the whereabouts of Ayanna and Jalil?"

"No, ma'am. I don't know where they at. Ayanna said something important came up and they had to go down South for a few days."

"Have you spoken to your cousin since she left?"

Tyneesha nodded. "She calls all the time to check on the kids."

Kai narrowed her eyes. "Is your cousin a good mother? Tell me the truth—does she ever abuse her kids?"

"No, I never saw her abuse 'em."

"She never spanks any of her children?"

Tyneesha shrugged uncomfortably. "Every once in a while, I guess. But she don't hit 'em with nothin' that would abuse 'em; she mostly uses her hands."

"Get your cousin on the phone."

She sighed audibly and pulled a bright pink cell phone off a clip attached to the waistband of her jeans. Still huffing, she flipped open the phone and pressed a button. "Ayanna," she whispered, "there's some lady here; she wants to speak to you."

Kai took the phone. "I'm with the FBI, Ayanna. Listen to me carefully. Don't scream or yell or draw any unnecessary attention to yourself. You are harboring a fugitive. If you don't want to end up doing a long stretch in jail, you'll do exactly as I tell you." Still winging it, Kai paused to collect her thoughts. "Go somewhere private and call me back. I'll give you ten minutes. I'm here at your home where your minor children are being supervised by a juvenile offender…" Kai glanced at Tyneesha; the teen's expression suggested that she didn't appreciate being referred to as an offender. *Too bad!* Kai clicked the Off button and waited for Ayanna to call back.

In less than ten minutes, Tyneesha's cell phone blasted a snippet of a horrible hip-hop song. Ugh! Ghetto music! It was the kind of music Marquise used to listen to. She hoped his taste had improved.

"Um…this is Ayanna. Nobody's with me," said the trembling voice over the phone.

"Ayanna, trying to protect Marquise Whitsett is going to screw up your life. Be smart, Ayanna, don't lie to me."

"Okay," she said, sounding defeated.

"Where are you?"

"Right now, I'm in the bathroom. We pulled off the highway so I could call you; I told 'em I had to use the restroom."

"Is Terelle Chambers with you?"

Ayanna was silent.

"Ayanna?"

"Yeah, she's with us. But, seriously, I ain't know Quise was no fugitive or nothing. My fiancé only told me Quise was in some kind of protection program. For real, that's all I know."

Hmm. Things were starting to add up. Marquise had been hiding out in the witness protection program, which meant he had crucial evidence that would land someone—probably a drug lord—in jail. Kai figured her sudden release from prison was connected to Marquise's expected testimony. Apparently, he'd had a change of heart about his court appearance and was now on the run. Interesting. Maybe Terelle hadn't shot him, after all. Maybe Marquise had been the victim of a drug deal gone wrong. Oh, what the hell did it matter? He was alive and kicking, and hopefully still in tiptop shape in the sex department.

Yes, the pieces of the puzzle were coming together. Kai was getting a much clearer picture, but she'd get the exact details from Marquise himself once they were reunited.

Realizing she'd been lost in thought and silent for quite a while, Kai blurted, "You could end up in prison if you don't tell me the whereabouts of Marquise Whitsett." She took a deep breath, exhaled, and then added, "By the way, we've been advised that your boyfriend, Jalil, lives with you. That's a federal offense." She wanted to laugh when Ayanna gasped. Kai didn't know nor cared about the penalty for violating the Section 8 housing code. That she could threaten Ayanna with jail time gave her malicious pleasure. To shake Ayanna up even more, Kai added, "We've also been made aware that you physically abuse your children—"

Ayanna sucked in a startled breath. "I don't abuse my kids!"

"You don't spank your kids?"

"Yeah, I spank 'em, but I would never abuse my children."

"Hitting minor children with your hands is considered abuse, so it looks like you're going to be hit with a number of charges if you don't cooperate with this federal investigation."

"I am cooperating; I called you back, didn't I?" Ayanna shouted, sounding a bit too feisty for Kai's taste.

"Excuse me, I don't like your tone. I can have Tyneesha Burton and your four children taken out of here and placed in foster care with the snap of my fingers. Is that what you want?"

"No, ma'am," Ayanna whispered over the phone, sounding appropriately docile and subdued.

"I didn't think so." Tickled pink that Ayanna was such a ding-bat that she actually believed she was talking to a federal agent, Kai bit the inside of her lip to suppress an eruption of wicked laughter. She was very proud of her performance. If her every move weren't being witnessed by Tyneesha and the four children she would have jumped up, clicked her heels, and taken a bow.

But, keeping it professional, she continued, "What's your present location?"

"Um, we're driving through Virginia right now."

"Your destination?"

Ayanna gulped. "South Carolina."

"Where in South Carolina? I need an exact address."

"I don't know the address; I ain't never been down there before. Jalil's grandfather left him that house and he's letting Marquise and Terelle stay there 'till everything blows over."

"Can you be more specific? Who's Marquise running from?"

"To be honest, I really don't know. All I know is everybody thinks Quise is dead and he needs somewhere to hide out for a minute."

Ayanna was such an idiot—really intellectually challenged. Boy, Marquise had to be really desperate to share such important information with her dumb ass. Hopefully, Kai would get to him before whomever he was running from did.

"I'll call you in a few hours. In the meantime, do your best to get the address from Jalil. But don't say anything stupid," she warned. "Don't say anything that will make him suspicious. If something happens and we lose our target, I'm holding you responsible. You'll be going to jail."

Knowing she would soon be reunited with the man who'd given her the best sex of her entire life made Kai's kitty twitch with anticipation!

# Chapter 29

"Pull over at the next rest stop, Jalil."

"Why?" Jalil asked, clearly annoyed.

"I gotta pee!"

"Again? Whassup with all this peeing? You pregnant?"

"Hell, naw." Ayanna sucked her teeth. "Stop playin'; you know I got my tubes tied." She shook the bottle of spring water she'd been sipping on. "It's all this water I been drinking."

"Well, stop drinking it. Whassup? You dying of thirst or something?"

"Stop buggin', Jalil. People s'posed to drink a lot of water. It's good for you."

"Yo, leave that water alone. All this running to the bathroom is cutting into the time. North Carolina is a long-ass state to drive through. We ain't never gon' get through it if you keep taking bathroom breaks."

"My bad," Ayanna said.

"North Carolina ain't no joke," Marquise added from the back. "Feels like we've been rolling through this jawn for a coupla years. My ass is starting to hurt."

"Then you need to stand outside the car and stretch your legs when we pull over," Ayanna told Marquise, and then pointed to a sign ahead. "Look, Jalil. There's a rest stop coming up."

"Damn," Jalil muttered and pulled into the far right lane. "And who keeps calling you? You better not be creepin' with no knucklehead nigga!"

"Yeah, right!" she said sarcastically. "That's Tyneesha calling. She's checking in. Letting me know what's going on with the kids."

"What we paying her for if she gotta report every move the kids make?"

Ayanna gave Jalil a hateful look. "I can't speak for you, but I'm a good damn parent. I need to know where the kids are and what they doing every hour. A good parent can't never be too responsible," she chastised.

Even though the constant, blaring ring tone from Ayanna's cell phone was getting on Terelle's last nerve, she had to give the woman her props. Ayanna was a concerned parent and a good mother, despite her numerous deficiencies.

"I have to go to the bathroom, too," Terelle said.

"You do?" Ayanna asked, giving Terelle a worried gaze.

"Yes," Terelle said.

"Me, too," Marquise joined in.

"Dang!" Ayanna blurted.

"Dang!" Terelle repeated, twisting her neck, annoyed and combative. She'd whip that bitch's ass for trying to give her man attitude.

"Don't go there, babe," Marquise warned, placing a calming hand on Terelle's shoulder.

"I'm just saying," Ayanna said with a nervous chuckle. "You know, the way Jalil was blaming me for slowing us down, I'm just surprised that now, all of a sudden, everybody has to go." Ayanna smiled dumbly and held up her hands.

Jalil parked. Everyone, including Jalil, went inside the food and rest area.

Twenty minutes later, the two couples, carrying an assortment of munchies, strolled back toward the car.

"Aw shit!" Ayanna blurted. "I'll be right back. I think I left my wallet inside the stall." Before anyone could say a word, Ayanna was trotting back toward the steps and double doors.

"Is it me or is Ayanna trippin'?" Jalil asked.

Marquise's shoulders rose and fell in silent response. Terelle's eyes shot skyward.

"Damn, can't take her nowhere. I don't know why she's buggin', y'all," Jalil said apologetically.

Terelle's mind was already on overdrive. Every passing motorist was suspect as she looked over her shoulder in fear of the feds or the Jamaicans. Now Ayanna was behaving curiously, causing Terelle to feel even more uneasy. Instead of cautiously looking over her shoulder, maybe she should be cutting her eyes to the right and left.

Something wasn't right. She couldn't put her finger on it. A host of negative emotions filled her with quiet apprehension—a dreaded sense that all was not well in the world. There was no sense in agitating Marquise with her vague feelings and doom. So she kept her concerns to herself and suffered in silence.

At the crack of dawn, Jalil announced, "Yo! Wake up, y'all; we at the crib."

The chorus of crickets and other night creatures intermingled with the sound of tires crunching over a gravel road. Terelle lifted her head from Marquise's chest, stretched, and rubbed her eyes. The small, wood-frame house hung in the background, half hidden by tall grass and a tangle of weeds. Terelle studied the shabby-looking structure in silence. Obviously, the desolate place had been left untended for quite some time. The screen door hung off a rusty hinge; the porch sank in the middle. The house was so rickety it appeared to perilously lean to one side. There was an ancient-looking, rusted Chevy pickup parked next to the house. The truck looked like it had been sitting in the same spot for about fifty years. Still, Terelle felt immensely welcome. And safe.

She inhaled the clean, early morning air. *Home, sweet home!* She smiled for no apparent reason other than that the little shanty had good vibes and was so far out in the boondocks, she was certain no one would ever track them down.

Marquise gawked. "Damn, where we at?" There was an amused chuckle in his sleepy voice. "Yo, we out in the sticks, for real. Look at the crib," he said, pointing at the small house in amazement. "That jawn is little as shit. Real talk. Yo, I'm a couple inches taller than the crib," he exclaimed, taking long strides toward the dilapidated wooden front porch steps.

"This is Cordova, South Carolina, dawg. Ain't nobody gon' sniff you out down here. Don't no buses, trains, trucks, or nothing come through here. It's so dead around here, my Paw Paw got excited the year they put a stop sign up at the split in the road."

"Stop playing!" Marquise said.

"That's fucked up," Ayanna said, yawning. "What, they ain't never had no stop signs around here before?"

"Never needed none," Jalil responded. "Don't that many cars be driving down that road."

Groggy, Ayanna stuck her legs out of the car. When the soles of her high-wedged sandals hit the gravel, her ankle turned. Jalil caught her before she hit the ground.

"Damn! They ain't got no pavements out here?" Irritated,

Ayanna kicked a pile of gravel. "Can't even walk straight in this hick town."

"Uh-huh, that's what you get...tryna be cute! You so hard-headed. I told you not to wear those heels," Jalil chastised.

"Whatever!" Ayanna gave Jalil a hand flip and rolled her eyes.

Ahead, Marquise stopped and waited for Terelle to catch up. When she did, he caught her off guard by bending down and swooping her up in his arms. Terelle let out a surprised squeal.

"We at the love shack, baby. Gotta carry you over the threshold." Cradling Terelle in his arms, Marquise did a funny, jerky dance down the dirt path that led to the ramshackle front door. He stopped every few seconds to give Terelle a kiss.

Wobbling in the heels, Ayanna shuffled beside Jalil. She completed a wide-mouthed yawn and then shook her head at Marquise. "Umph, some people don't never change. Even after your brush with death, you still crazy, Quise," Ayanna murmured and gave a tired chuckle.

No one laughed with her. Jalil jabbed her in the side and gave her a stern look.

"What?" Ayanna asked, rubbing her side.

Ignoring Ayanna, Marquise kissed Terelle on the cheek and then started acting even sillier in an attempt to lighten the suddenly tense atmosphere.

"Bump that rump," Marquise said, holding Terelle and bouncing her booty in the air in time to the music in his head. He danced her up the rickety steps.

"I can't; I ain't got no rump to bump," Terelle complained, laughing.

"You can have some of mine!" Ayanna offered, her hands running over her ample ass.

"Yo, that's mine," Jalil reminded Ayanna, licking his lips as he eyed her big behind. "You can't give none of that away. And you better not be breaking off no knucklehead nigga."

"Give it a rest, Jalil. I ain't breaking off nobody but you, boo."

"Aiight, now! Lemme find out!"

Ayanna sighed loudly.

"That's aiight, babe. Don't even worry about your tiny little butt," Marquise told Terelle. "We down South now. We gon' fatten you up with some Southern-style cooking." He shot Jalil a questioning look. "What do they eat down here, dawg? I know they ain't down with no hoagies or Philly cheesesteaks." Marquise eased Terelle out of his arms while Jalil fiddled around in his pocket, examining different sets of keys.

"Naw, they don't know nothin' 'bout that. They eat a lot of pig's feet. Ham hocks and shit like that," Jalil responded.

"Eeew!" Terelle and Ayanna screeched in unison.

"Yo, don't knock it 'till you try it," Jalil said confidently. "I ain't gon' hold you; ain't no shame in my game—I fucks with some pork." Jalil laughed. "You don't know? Shit, my Paw Paw could burn when he started pulling out skillets and pots and pans. He could make a pig's tail taste like a juicy piece of steak. He said his peoples were raised on pork, but after they up North, they got all uppity and started acting like they was too good to eat pork." Jalil pondered for a second. "Shit, that's probably why he left me this property; I was the only real muthafucker in the family."

Ayanna snorted. "Umph! You call this property? Seems to me like your Paw Paw was playing a practical joke, leaving you some shit like this!" She laughed, then continued. "Ain't nothing wrong with pork—you know, like spare ribs, bacon and shit like that—but pig's feet...that don't even sound like something people should eat."

"Man, my Paw Paw could take a pot of pig's feet and make it

taste like a gourmet meal. And don't get me started about his hog maws." Jalil licked his lips as he fit different keys in the locks.

"Hog maws! Aw, fuck that. You done lost me now, dawg," Marquise blurted. "What the fuck is a hog maw? Whatever it is, it sounds nasty like a muthafucker." Marquise twisted his face in revulsion.

"I know, right?" Ayanna agreed, frowning.

Terelle snickered. "My gran used to stink up the house whenever she cooked chit'lins and that other stuff. Early in the morning, the fumes from Gran's chit'lins would wake me and my mom up. We'd be holding our breaths and gagging while my mom rushed around getting us dressed. Then me and my mom would jet out of the crib, take a couple buses, and go to South Philly and binge on Pat's cheesesteaks."

Terelle smiled at the memory, and then grew quiet. She hadn't allowed herself to mentally dwell on her drug-addicted mother. Too painful. The vivid recollection of whipping her mother's ass—kicking her in her frail ribs—greeted Terelle with the harshness of being hit upside the head with a bag of skeleton bones. All the repressed anger at being neglected as a child by her mother had surfaced when her mother reported Marquise's death. She never would have lifted a hand to her mother had she been thinking rationally.

"You and your mom missed out on some good eating," Jalil said, after finally finding the right key and pushing open the creaky wooden door.

The musky smell of mold and mildew filled Terelle's nostrils, shifting her thoughts away from her mother.

"Dayum!" Marquise blurted. "Smells like somebody been cooking hog maws up in here."

"Told you it wasn't the Four Seasons or nothing," Jalil said.

"Yo, dawg. Me and my baby are soldiers. We can hang. Right, babe?" Marquise hugged Terelle comfortingly. "We gon' get down with the get down. Ain't nothing a little Spic and Span can't handle." Wearing an exaggerated expression of confusion, Marquise wondered out loud, "How we gon' get some Spic and Span up in this dip? Where the stores at around here?"

"Man, ain't no stores around here. We have to go into town to pick up some odds and ends."

Marquise reared back. "Say what?"

Terelle punched him in the arm. "Listen to you, trying to talk all countrified."

"I am countrified," he proclaimed with a thick Southern accent, which made Terelle burst into laughter. "We down home now, baby." He slumped his shoulders and dragged his legs lazily, giving his interpretation of a country walk. Jalil and Ayanna joined in the laughter.

"Do you know how to cook real soul food, Jalil?" Terelle inquired. "'Cause I gotta get my weight up."

"I can burn. You'll see. You gon' be fat as Ayanna after you eat my Southern cooking."

"Watch it," Ayanna cautioned. "I thought you said you liked my weight."

"I love it, baby! Terelle's gon' be p-h-a-t—looking good, just like you."

As Marquise and Terelle roamed about and inspected their new home, Ayanna took on a serious expression and pulled Jalil to the side. "After we take them to town, we gotta bounce back to Philly."

"I thought we were gon' stay down here for a few days—take a vacation."

"Vacation! Stop playin'." Turning her nose up, Ayanna looked around the shabby quarters. "We out here in the sticks, camping out in this musty, broke-down, log cabin. How the hell is this a vacation?"

"Ain't nobody twist your arm and make you come down here. I was prepared to bring my man and Terelle down here by myself."

Indignation flickered across Ayanna's face. "I ain't think it was right for you to rush out and leave me for days in the house with the kids."

"It was a tense type of situation for Quise…he didn't want too many people involved, being that he's on the run and all. Besides, I knew you wouldn't like it down here in the boonies—that's why I was trying to ride out solo. But, you started trippin', talking 'bout I don't never take you nowhere. You guilt-tripped me into bringing you down here, now you wanna bounce." Jalil shook his head.

Ayanna poked out her lips. "It ain't my fault we gotta go back."

"Whose fault is it?"

"Nobody's. Tyneesha called and told me the baby was running a temperature. That's what I been worrying about and that's why I was back and forth on the phone with her. I was trying to tell her what to do to bring the baby's fever down."

"Why didn't you tell me the baby was sick?"

"We were just a couple hours away from here when it got really high. Wasn't nothing we could do, so I told her to go to the store and buy some Children's Tylenol. The last time she called, she said the baby was sleeping but she was still warm."

"What does she mean, she's still warm? Is she using a thermometer or just guessing?"

"I didn't ask her."

"Get Tyneesha on the phone, let me talk to her."

"No! She's been up with the baby for hours. Let her get some rest."

"Aiight. Let me run Quise into town. I gotta get a couple hours of sleep, and then we'll head back to Philly."

Ayanna breathed an audible sigh of relief.

## Chapter 30

Marquise and Jalil returned from town, loaded down with bags from Piggly Wiggly.

"Uh-uh, y'all gon' stop playin'. Y'all did not go out and find a store called Piggly damn Wiggly. What did y'all buy? Hog maws and a bunch of different types of pork?" Ayanna asked, scowling at the grocery bags.

"Yup," Marquise teased. "I'm down with Piggly Wiggly. We need some of them jawns up in Philly."

"He messin' with you, Ayanna," Terelle said. "It's a regular supermarket like Acme or Pathmark."

"How do you know?" Marquise inquired. "Up until now, you never traveled outside of Philadelphia."

Laughing, Terelle put her hand on her hip. "That's what you think? Humph! I'm down with Piggly Wiggly my damn self," Terelle said, joking.

"Lemme find out," Marquise said, laughing as he gave Terelle a sidelong glance.

As Ayanna continued to eye the bags suspiciously, her ring tone blared. Jalil yanked the cell phone from her grasp. "Did you take the baby's temperature?" he yelled into the phone. "What! She ain't sick? Ayanna said the baby had a high fever." Jalil gave Ayanna an evil look and handed her the phone. "Tyneesha said the baby's not sick. Don't let me find out you lying and tryna get your creep on with some knucklehead nigga."

Rolling her eyes and muttering under her breath, Ayanna aligned the mouthpiece with her lips. "Girl, why you got Jalil trippin'?"

Alight with interest, everyone's eyes were focused on Ayanna. Ayanna squirmed under the spotlight. "How the baby doing?" she said into the cell phone. "Oh, she's feeling better?" Ayanna smiled sheepishly.

"Yeah, aiight. I got something for your ass," Jalil yelled. "Lemme find out. Your lies done backfired on your ass, so I guess we ain't gotta bounce back to Philly now."

"Hello! Hello! Damn, the phone went dead." Ayanna shook her cell phone, pushed buttons repeatedly. "My fuckin' phone went dead. How am I s'posed to see about my kids?"

"It's hard to keep a signal down here," Jalil explained. "It'll come back on. But like it or not, baby, you stuck out here in the sticks for the next coupla days," he said, cutting an eye at Marquise.

Marquise gave him an "I ain't in this mess" look, then averted his gaze.

"Aw, this is some bullshit." Ayanna continued to fidget with her phone. "You mean to tell me I can't use my phone?"

"I said, the signal goes off and on. You'll be aiight."

Terelle and Marquise cleaned up the place. Pouting, Ayanna watched TV, repeatedly checked her phone for a signal, and dozed off and on.

Jalil fixed a huge Southern breakfast that included fried chicken, fried potatoes, grits, pancakes, bacon, and eggs.

After stuffing themselves, the two couples immediately passed out. They slept for seven hours straight.

Terelle was the first to wake up. When her eyelids fluttered open, she gasped at the shock of finding herself in a strange bedroom. On cue, Marquise slid his arm around her waist and pulled her close. Even under those dire circumstances, waking up in bed with her man was a little bit like heaven. She snuggled next to him, enjoying his warmth until her wayward thoughts insisted on conjuring up disturbing images of Markeeta's tiny mouth stretched into a scream.

Trying to shake away the unpleasant recollection, Terelle eased out from beneath Marquise's arm and found her way to the bathroom. She emptied her bladder and then went outside and took a seat on the raggedy porch. She needed to be alone to think. On blind faith, she'd followed Marquise to God's country—no neighbors, no telephone, no way to stay in touch with Saleema. She shook her head, hoping Marquise had some kind of plan in mind. She was yearning for her baby and couldn't be certain how long she'd last in the back woods of South Carolina.

She looked heavenward in hope of enlightenment. The sun was setting, leaving a streak of dark red across the blue sky. It was a lovely sight but failed to shed illumination on her weighty problems.

Bent at the waist, with her elbows pressed into her knees, her palms cupping her cheeks, Terelle wondered if Markeeta was doing okay. Was her daughter sitting and staring into space, traumatized by losing her father for the second time in her life, or was she over it already and happily out on a shopping spree with Saleema? Terelle could only hope Markeeta was resilient and had bounced back with ease.

"You okay, babe?" Marquise asked. He cautiously cracked open the unstable screen door and slipped outside.

Moments later, Jalil and Ayanna joined them. "Damn, it's too quiet out here," Ayanna grumbled. "Go get me a chair, Jalil. I ain't sitting on this raggedy-ass porch. I might get a splinter in my ass."

"Aiight! Damn, you a pain." Jalil turned around and reached for the handle of the screen door. A moment later, the sound of tires crunching over twigs and gravel echoed ominously.

Marquise's mouth dropped open. Terelle's eyes grew wide in alarm. Ayanna clamped a hand over her mouth; her eyes darting around with dread. Astonished, Jalil spun around. "What the fuck!"

"Where's the fuckin' burner I bought?" Marquise shouted as the approaching headlights lit the darkening wooded area.

"You hid it in the truck, in the glove box," Jalil reminded him.

Terelle's brain was on overload. Dangerous people had tracked them down. Marquise had gone to Piggly Wiggly and bought a gun! No, that didn't make sense, but he had managed to get one just the same. Markeeta! Oh, God, Markeeta. Would she ever see her daughter's face again?

Marquise's pounding footsteps crashing on the wobbly wooden steps brought Terelle's mind into focus as the car came into view.

But it wasn't the dreaded Jamaicans or the feds.

Behind the wheel of a shiny black Mercedes Benz was none other than Kai!

"Ohmigod!" Ayanna screamed. "That's that same crazy bitch who came to my crib looking for Quise, a couple of days before she shot him and ran over his legs!"

"Quise!" Terelle hissed through clenched teeth, glaring at Marquise as if he'd given Kai a personal invitation.

"How the fuck..." Jalil clamped his lips shut mid-sentence and then glowered at Ayanna.

"I ain't fuckin' know," Ayanna said defensively. "She told me she was with the FBI and was gon' take the kids from us. She made me tell her where we was at."

"I thought that bitch was still locked up!" Marquise fumed. He stomped down the steps so hard, a plank of wood caved in. When he reached the ancient Chevy pickup, he hesitated briefly, and then jerked away in anger. "I don't need no fuckin' gun! I'm gon' smack the shit outta that bitch and bash her head in with my muthafuckin' fist."

Kai sat in her Benz, cool as a cucumber, undaunted by Marquise's obvious fury.

Marquise stormed over to the driver's side. Kai lowered the window. The beaming smile she set on Marquise's face sent Terelle into a whirlwind of spitting and kicking rage.

"Uh-uh. No, she didn't bring her skank-ass down here to grin up in my man's face." Terelle was breathing fire. "Where my shoes at; I'm about to put my foot all the way up that ho's yellow ass." She whirled toward the door, but unwilling to take her eyes off Marquise for more than a few seconds, she jerked back around. "Fuck it, I don't need no shoes!" She ran down two steps, then stumbled and lost her balance when she reached the third step, which had been cracked by Marquise's body weight.

Jalil raced forward and grabbed Terelle by the arm. "Come on, Terelle. Tighten up. Let Quise handle this."

Breathing hard, blowing out hot air like flames from a dragon, Terelle tussled with Jalil. She desperately tried to break away, but Jalil held her in an iron-tight grip. Restrained by Jalil's arms, Terelle watched helplessly as Marquise argued with Kai. She couldn't make out what he was saying; the distance between them made his words indistinguishable. Terelle did, however, make note that Marquise hadn't lifted a hand to smack the shit out of Kai, as he'd promised.

Incensed, Terelle tried to break Jalil's hold. She'd bash that bitch's head in her damn self. She scanned the stony ground and spotted a nice-sized brick. If she could get her hands on the brick, it would make a perfect weapon to go upside that heifer's head with. "Let me go, Jalil!" Terelle struggled desperately. "Let me the fuck, go!"

"No! Marquise got this, Terelle." Jalil tightened his grip on Terelle.

In the blink of an eye, Marquise was no longer barking into the open driver's side window. To Terelle's horror and utter amazement, Marquise was making long strides to the passenger side. A second later, he was inside the car and Kai was backing up and turning around at breakneck speed.

Shocked, Jalil's arms fell limp at his sides. Terelle made her get-away and zoomed down a couple of steps. She hopped over the cracked, rotted strip of wood and ran with her arms flailing, mouth open wide as she wailed Marquise's name while she chased Kai's car into the twilight.

"Marquiiise! What the hell is wrong with you? Marquiiise!" She stumbled over a fallen branch, her body crashed down to the ground. Engulfed by a choking cloud of dust kicked up by the car's tires, Terelle gnashed her teeth and tried to call Marquise's name, but the only sound that came out was a weak, strangled scream. "Why, Quise? Why?" she murmured as she helplessly watched Kai shoot down the dirt road like a bat out of hell.

Sprawled out on the ground, Terelle kicked her feet in anger, pummeled the dirt with angry, balled hands. She beat the ground with all her might, punched the gravel, pounded the tiny pebbles and stones, until her torn and bleeding fists unfurled in defeat and despair.

# Chapter 31

"We gotta help Quise," Terelle cried. "Hurry up, Jalil." Terelle tugged on the door handle of Jalil's car. "We gotta try to catch up with them before it gets real dark."

"We ain't going after that crazy-ass bitch!" Ayanna poked out her lips and folded her arms. "Fuck that! Call the cops. Let the police handle it. I got four kids to worry about, I'm not trying to get my legs run over or get shot in the head."

"Please, Jalil," Terelle begged, her lips trembling.

"No!" Ayanna spoke for Jalil. "Marquise is a grown-ass man. Ain't nobody tell his dumb ass to get in the car to try to reason with that throwed-off chick. He done dealt with her enough times to know she got real slimy ways. Quise shoulda just slapped the shit outta her like he said he was and sent her on her way. But, no! He had to climb his ass in her car. Shit! What the fuck was he thinking?" Ayanna sucked her teeth in disgust. "Quise's dumb ass must like getting fucked up by that bitch!"

"Who you calling a dumb ass? What the fuck were you thinking when you gave her directions and led her straight the fuck to us?" Terelle snapped, stepping toward Ayanna, lips twisted angrily, neck rotating challengingly, informing the bitch that she was two seconds from going upside her damn head.

"I was thinking about my kids," Ayanna replied, wisely backing away from Terelle.

Terelle glowered at Ayanna and then turned to Jalil. "Jalil! We gotta go after him. There's no telling what Kai might do!" Terelle insisted, her face streaked with dirt and tears.

"Yo, Terelle. Ayanna's probably right. This is over my head. We gotta drive into town and find a police station."

"We don't have time for that," Ayanna shouted and pulled out her cell. "I'm calling 9-1-1!" She flipped the phone open. "Damn. Still ain't got no signal." She looked at Jalil. "What we gon' do, Jalil? We gotta get back to Philly."

"That bitch kidnapped Marquise. Y'all just gon' leave him down here with her?" Terelle asked, looking at Jalil and Ayanna in bewilderment.

Ayanna sighed in exasperation and then shook her head disgustedly. "Ain't nobody kidnap Marquise. It looked to me like he walked around to the passenger side and got in of his own free will. That bitch must have some good pussy—"

Terelle reared back in indignation. "I don't believe you just came out your mouth like that. I should whip your ass for saying some shit like that."

Ayanna held her arms out, defiant. "Bring it, with your bony-ass self! I ain't scared of you."

Terelle charged toward Ayanna. Jalil grabbed her, lifted her off the ground. "Stop it, Terelle. This situation is fucked up, but y'all two can't start fighting and carrying on. Come on, y'all calm down so I can think."

Terelle stopped struggling and Jalil lowered her feet to the ground.

"She's gonna kill him. I know she is," Terelle said, crying. "She doesn't want me and Marquise to be happy; she never did." Terelle covered her face in anguish. "Oh, my God. My poor, baby. Markeeta's losing her daddy all over again. How did one bitch get so much power over my happiness?" Sobbing pitifully, Terelle shouted, "I'm never gonna be happy. Never. Never. Never. Never. Never. Never!" she cried, stomping her right foot each time she spoke the word.

Ayanna gawked at Jalil. "Oh shit! Is this how she starts off? Is she 'bout to have one of them nervous breakdowns?"

Looking stunned, Jalil held his hands out helplessly. "I don't know." He frowned toward Terelle. "Come on, Terelle. Calm yourself down. You're starting to scare the shit out of me and Ayanna."

"Never, never, never, never, never…" Terelle continued, still stomping with each repetition of the word.

"We gon' find Quise." Jalil spoke in the tone of voice one would use with a child or a very unstable adult. "It's gon' be aiight. Okay, Terelle?"

But Terelle didn't look up; she seemed oblivious to his appeasing words as she stared down at the foot that stomped the ground. The stomping and one-word mantra took on a rhythmic quality as she began to alternate between her right and left foot. "Never, never, never, never, never…"

"Aw, this is fucked up," Ayanna complained. "She's starting to piss me off. Do something, Jalil. I'm not with this crazy shit."

"I tried. She won't stop."

"Terelle, cut that shit out," Ayanna yelled. "Quit it, now!"

But Terelle continued the stomping mantra.

"Jalil! Do something. She's going crazy; we gotta get her an ambulance or something." Ayanna rolled her eyes at Terelle and

Jalil. "See, I knew I shoulda stayed my ass in Philly. Listen to me, Jalil." Ayanna pointed her finger for emphasis. "The minute we find somebody to come out here and get her, we're out! I'm not playing with you, Jalil. This is too much. I wanna go home!"

Throughout the stomping and the shouting, Terelle was fully cognizant, in complete control of her mental faculties. But she was filled with rage—rage that she intended to unleash on Kai. Until she wrapped her hands around Kai's throat, she'd have to keep her internal furnace flaming high. Fuck Ayanna. And fuck Jalil, too. She wasn't getting in any damn ambulance. No one was carting her off to a goddamn mental hospital. Never again!

Still repeating the mantra, Terelle stomped over to the broken-down Chevy and tried to yank open the door. The old, rusted door groaned painfully, a creaky plea to be left in peace. She scrambled across the stained and tattered cloth front seat, turned the old-fashioned knob that opened the glove compartment and there it was...the gun Marquise had the foresight to purchase while he and Jalil were out shopping at Piggly Wiggly. How'd he get it? It was probably bought illegally and Jalil wouldn't want to keep an unregistered gun in the car, which explained why Marquise had left the gun in the old truck. Terelle held the gun without fear. She'd pulled a trigger before and she was about to do it again.

With a bullet hole between her eyes, Kai Montgomery would have no choice but to leave Terelle and her family alone.

"Whatchu doin', Terelle? Put that gun down before you hurt somebody." Looking determined to wrestle the gun from her hand, Jalil rushed toward Terelle.

Mumbling as she walked, Terelle didn't aim the gun directly at Jalil, but just raised it a bit, making it clear the gun was not merely a prop.

Terelle was well aware that from Jalil's and Ayanna's perspective, she seemed crazy as a loon. But though she was desperate to find Marquise and she was beyond livid with Kai, in her heart of hearts, Terelle Chambers knew that she was perfectly sane.

As Terelle grew closer, Ayanna covered her mouth in horror and then scurried across the dirt path and crouched behind the trunk of a big oak tree.

"She's crazy, Jalil! Duck! Run for cover," Ayanna implored Jalil from behind the safety of the large tree.

Walking fast and chanting, gun pointed outward, Terelle came within a foot of Jalil. With his hands raised high in an "I surrender gesture," Jalil darted out of Terelle's way.

Terelle proceeded to speed-walk past Jalil and Ayanna who were now both huddled behind the oak tree. Hit with a sudden thought, she stopped and began to backtrack.

"Give me your phone, Ayanna."

"It don't work! You know we can't get no signal."

"Give me your fuckin' phone!" Terelle screamed, jabbing Ayanna in the chest with the deadly gun.

Ayanna quickly produced the phone. "Here! Take it! Damn!"

There was no point in jacking Jalil's car. Terelle had never learned to drive. It was pitch black now, and with just a little moonlight to illuminate the road, she set off on foot to find her man.

# *Chapter 32*

With smirking satisfaction plastered on her face, Kai wheeled the Benz with one hand and with the other hand, she kept the gun held low, pointed at Marquise.

"I'm not stopping until we get where we're going, so eat!" Kai demanded, nodding her head toward the bag of sourdough pretzels she'd brought along for their trip.

Marquise broke a piece off the pretzel, took a bite, and then threw it out the window in disgust.

Kai shrugged. "You know, you should be a little more respectful of the environment. Oops! Pretzels are bio-degradable, so even though it's childish and wasteful to toss it, I guess it's okay. Marquise, you're going to need all your strength to fuck me the way I intend to be fucked."

Marquise's jaw tightened. "I'm not touching you!" He bit another piece, didn't chew it, spit it out the window.

"You're so disrespectful. Here I was considerate enough to bring you something to eat and you won't show the least bit of appreciation. Now, eat the damn pretzel!"

"Fuck no!"

"You can't make love to me if you don't have any strength."

Marquise breathed out heavily and stared out the window. "I'm not going to touch you."

"No?"

"Hell, no! Fuck those pretzels. And fuck you!"

Kai shrugged. "Suit yourself. I'll just have to cut off your balls and shoot off your dick. And since you're currently legally dead, I know the justice system won't be coming after me. How the hell can they dare put me on trial for killing you again? I already have a multi-million-dollar lawsuit pending for my false imprisonment. Believe me, the justice system will not fuck with Kai Montgomery again."

Unnerved by talk of castration, the flicker of anger that had gleamed in Marquise's eyes went out like the glow of a doused candle. Kai smiled, satisfied to see that her words had such a powerful effect. Yes, it was thrilling to know Marquise took her warning seriously.

"Could you make yourself useful?" Kai asked Marquise. "The MapQuest directions are under the visor on the passenger side."

Marquise ignored Kai's request. Silently and anxiously, he chewed his bottom lip. Ever so often, he lifted his downcast eyes and stared out the window as the Benz sped along the dark, isolated road. There were no street lights, no traffic lights, there wasn't even a stop sign in view.

"Okay, suit yourself." Kai brushed a tangle of curls from her face. "I was always a bright child, you know. Having a photographic memory, I never had to do homework or study for tests," she rambled.

"Whatchu telling me that for? I don't give a fuck what kind of child you were," Marquise growled. "Right now your brain is scattered like a muthafucker—that's all I know."

"Hey, did we just pass Magnolia Street?" Kai slowed as she approached a hard-to-read street sign.

"I don't know!"

"Oh, this is Cannon Bridge Road. Okay, I have to turn right when we get to Old Edisto Road." Kai took her eyes off the road and turned her gaze on Marquise. "Here, honey, eat something. We'll pick up some groceries tomorrow. I can't stop anywhere tonight. You understand, don't you?" Kai smiled sweetly and pushed the bag of pretzels toward Marquise.

"I said, I don't want no fuckin' pretzels!"

Kai gave Marquise an indulgent smile and reached over and stroked his crotch with the nozzle of the gun.

Marquise froze. He gawked at the gun, muttered something incomprehensible and inched away. "Yo, get that jawn away from my dick," he finally rasped, giving Kai a look of pure hatred.

"As I was saying," she continued with an exasperated sigh as she returned the gun to her own lap, "I memorized the directions, so I don't need your cooperation." She turned her head toward Marquise. "Besides, you're probably illiterate. If we rely on your reading skills we'll end up in west Jablip." Kai cackled with laughter. "West Jablip! That's so funny. Do you get it?" She paused and then further explained. "We're already in east Jablip, but if we depend on your ability to read the MapQuest directions, we'll get so lost, we'll find ourselves even deeper in the sticks." Shaking with laughter, she took her hand off the steering wheel and slapped Marquise on the shoulder, trying to coax him into joining in the merriment of her clever witticism.

Marquise kept his shoulders erect, his expression stoic.

Apparently utilizing her gift of memory, Kai turned right on Old Edisto Drive.

Enraged, Marquise flung the cellophane bag of pretzels out the window.

Kai ignored his tantrum. "We still have about five or six miles before we get to Magnolia Street." When they reached it, she turned. Coming out of the isolated back roads, she drove up a ramp that led to I-26 W to Columbia.

"Hey, we passed through Columbia on the way here. Where you taking me, back to Philly?" Marquise wondered, appalled.

"That's for me to know and you to find out. Why should I give you any information? After two long years of thinking you were dead—thinking you were ashes inside an urn—I don't even get so much as a kiss. All you've been doing is griping from the moment you set eyes on me. Didn't you once tell me that I gave you the best sex of your life?"

Disgusted, Marquise flung his head back, banged it furiously against the leather headrest. "Man, I ain't nevah said no shit like that. I can't believe you still stuck on that same dumb shit. Whatchu tryna prove? Where do you think this is gonna lead us? I ain't feeling you like that, shorty." He gestured with a pointed finger. "From the gate, I couldn't stand your stuck-up ass. The only reason I even dealt with you was for the dough you was willing to throw my way." He paused. "My biggest mistake was getting into a sexual relationship with you. Yo, it wasn't worth it. None of it was worth losing my family."

"Your family!" Kai scoffed. "I hate it when you refer to that ghetto girl and your illegitimate child as your *family*. A real family consists of two educated professionals with 1.2 well-cared-for children. That hairy nurse's aide you call 'family' doesn't even shave her legs. That poop-scooping girlfriend of yours is nothing more than an incubator for a pack of unplanned pregnancies. I can assure you that if I allowed you to continue that sordid relationship you'd end up saddled down with a pack of snotty-nosed, kinky-headed kids, living in substandard housing for the rest of your life. You'd be so exhausted; you'd probably require

Viagra before you reach the age of thirty. And quite frankly, Marquise, I detest men who have to rely on Viagra to get a hard dick. So instead of complaining, why aren't you thanking me for sparing you from such a dismal future?"

Marquise shook his head. "Whatever, shorty. So where we going? And how long you plan on keeping me there?"

"A friend rented us a little cottage. It's in a remote area; we'll have absolute privacy. And we can stay there as long as we like. Hell, we'll stay there until I overdose on your love."

"I ain't got no love for you."

Kai frowned. "Then, we'll be there until I O.D. on your sex."

"I'm a changed man; you can't tempt me with your freaky sex tricks. I'm a one-woman man. The only female I plan on sexin' down is my girl, Terelle."

Kai gave Marquise a snide look. "I prefer not to have to use force, but I'm not above forcing you to fuck me if that's what it takes to make you realize how good we are for each other."

"You talkin' crazy. How you sound threatening to force me to sex you?"

"Forcing you is not my preference. In fact, I'm ninety-nine-percent certain that once we get back in bed together, all those old feelings will return. If you want to keep your balls attached, you'll do your best to conjure up those old feelings, okay, sweetheart?"

Marquise punched the dashboard.

"Temper, temper!" Kai teased. "Do me a favor, save some of that passion for me. I want you to dog me, baby. Fuck me long and hard."

Marquise grunted in disgust.

"I hope you don't plan on being stupidly stubborn for too long.

Hopefully, you'll come to your senses quickly and realize that it's in your best interest to marry me instead of scary/hairy Terelle." Overcome by a sudden, bright idea, she took her eyes off the highway to look at him. In that brief moment, she almost slammed into a truck.

"Yo, keep your eyes on the road before you get us both killed. Damn!"

"Fuckin' trucks think they own the highway," she muttered. "We can get married down here," she blurted cheerfully. "Nothing elaborate. A justice of the peace and after we're married, we can buy a home, wherever you'd like." Kai beamed at Marquise. "Did I mention that I'm independently wealthy?" She nodded enthusiastically. "Yes, I finally got my inheritance."

Marquise was expressionless.

"Millions and millions of dollars, all mine! Yours too, if you cooperate."

"Yo, you can't buy me! I'm not feeling you or your dough!"

"We'll see about that."

Twenty-six miles later, Kai merged onto the Charleston Highway. After being held captive for almost an hour, Marquise groaned deeply when Kai exited the highway and turned down a dark, desolate, country road.

The sound of the flowing Edisto River could be heard as Kai silently forced Marquise at gunpoint to enter the well-kept little cottage. Holding a gun in one hand and her Louis Vuitton duffle bag in the other, she gestured for Marquise to open the unlocked door.

"Strip naked," she ordered Marquise after marching him into the small, quaint bedroom.

He drew back, scowling at her as if she'd lost her mind.

"I took a crash course in removing bullets while I was in jail. A sharp knife and some alcohol is all I need to take a bullet out of your ass. The only problem I can see, is that your rhythm will be off while you're serving me dick." Kai was lying, but it sounded plausible to her ears.

Marquise made an exasperated sound and then removed his clothes.

Kai unzipped the duffle bag and took out a monstrous set of leg irons and a heavy-duty pair of handcuffs.

"Yo!" Marquise protested as she gestured with a wave of the gun that she expected him to lock up his feet. But he did it. He had to obey or endure the feeling of hot lead buried in his ass.

"Put your hands behind your back."

He complied with her request, mumbling a string of profanity that was so low, Kai couldn't decipher one single word. But judging from his expression and the emotion attached to the presumably vile words, it was obvious that Marquise was not pleased. After he wore himself out, Marquise dropped his head in anguished surrender.

"Lie down!"

"How the fuck am I gon' lay down with my hands behind my back?"

"Oops!" Kai unlocked the handcuffs and then cuffed him with his hands held in the front. "Marquise," she said in a dreamy tone. "Never in a million years did I think this day would be possible." She ran her gaze up the length of his long, magnificent body. "You standing here handcuffed and naked is like a fantasy..." Kai shivered. "Looking at you gives me goose bumps. Having you all to myself is a dream come true."

Shackled like chattel, Marquise stood naked. Though it was a humiliating situation he stood tall, head held high and proud, face savage and intense as he angrily gnawed on his bottom lip.

Kai moved closer. "Marquise, you are my most cherished fantasy. Don't you realize how much I love you?" she murmured as she dropped to her knees and placed the gun on the floor.

She cupped his balls and reverently kissed them, and then slowly licked his scrotum until his unwilling dick finally began to rise, grazing her chin and lips along the way.

"Oh, Marquise," she sighed as she watched his resolve dissipate. The tender tongue bath she'd just given him made him lengthen somewhat. "I want to see it grow until it's as big and beautiful as it was the last time we fucked." She fondled his member. It pulsed at her touch. "See! It still loves me, Marquise." Kai's lips turned down. "But I want you to love me, too." She pouted. "Tell me, please. Please say you love me," Kai begged, looking up at his face.

Marquise's dick went suddenly limp. He smiled in triumph. "I hate your fuckin' ass," he told her spitefully.

"No, you don't. You don't hate me. You're just upset. But I know how to make it all better." Kai pressed her cheek against Marquise's flaccid dick and then gently caressed it with her chin, her lips, her nose—her entire face. When it grew to its full, thick, length, Kai licked and separated her lips, welcoming Marquise inside her moist mouth.

Though his stiffened dick throbbed against his will, Marquise didn't move a muscle toward Kai's open mouth.

"Please." Her warm breath tickled the head of his dick. "Let me suck it."

The tip of his dick brushed across Kai's lips. She instantly covered his dick with desperate, pleading kisses. She licked the thick veins that pulsed through his hard length, shining his dark flesh with the moisture from her tongue.

"Put it in," she begged. "Fuck my mouth hard and then shoot cum all over my face."

Marquise grunted. Unable to maintain his resolve, he roughly pushed the head of his dick into the warm space between Kai's parted lips.

Kai moaned in satisfaction. After the uninspired sex she'd put up with from her pussy-whipped, white adoptive father, she was more than ready for some hardcore, rough, black thug sex.

Her mind skipped down memory lane and recalled the time when Marquise had spent the night with her in her upscale apartment on the waterfront. Marquise had been so furious with her, he'd picked her up and body slammed her onto the bed.

Mmm. It was a delicious memory. The sex they'd shared that day was incredible. Marquise had yanked her around, choked her, and then tried to fuck her to death. Umph, umph, umph. He'd been seconds away from slapping the shit out of her and whipping her ass, when he had a change of heart and plunged his angry dick deep into her kitty, making it purr from the stabbing pain. Anger had an amazing way of heightening sexual pleasure, Kai fondly recalled.

Kai kicked the gun across the room. She stood up and quickly removed her clothes. "After you shoot your first load, I'm going to help you recharge, so you can shoot the next load up my ass."

Marquise was getting more worked up, more excited. Kai could tell by his heavy, erratic breathing.

"I wish I could trust you enough to take the cuffs off. Baby, when we get back to where we used to be—you know, in love and sexually inseparable—I want you to throw me around like you did before." Kai closed her eyes in ecstasy, overwhelmed by the erotic memory. "Do you remember when you choked me?" she asked, her voice a low, sensual whisper.

Marquise bit down on his lip, yanked at the handcuffs.

"Take 'em off," he prompted seductively. "I'll choke the shit outta you if you take these jawns off me."

Kai shook her head. "Not yet. I don't trust you, Marquise." She paused and excitedly ran her fingers through her hair. "But it's just a matter of time before we're back like we used to be. I can feel the sexual tension between us. Can't you?"

Marquise nodded.

Kai smiled. "When I take those handcuffs off, I want to be certain that you love me again. After you admit your love, I want you to get real tough with me. Rough me up like you did before. But take it up a notch. Degrade me, hurt me. Pull my hair…spit on me…kick me…And then punish my pussy. Fuck my kitty like you hate it. Violate me, rape me." She looked at him tenderly. "And then tell me you love me."

"Fuck that! I ain't telling you shit, you crazy bitch," he said with disgust.

"Hate, love…they're both strong emotions. I'll accept hatred until you're able to admit that it's really love that you feel. So go right ahead, my darling, tell me how much you hate me, because I'll know in my heart what you're really feeling is love."

Marquise's mind raced. How the hell was he going to get out

of this sick situation? Naked and back on her knees, Kai gazed up at Marquise with what she thought was a beautiful expression of love and undying devotion, but to Marquise, she looked like a stone cold nut—a complete lunatic.

Marquise turned up his nose at Kai. "You a sick ass, do you know that?" he taunted. But if he ever planned to escape, he'd have to play his part. So Marquise forced his cuffed hands down on top of Kai's head. With the handcuffs pressed into her mop of curly hair, he held her head in place as he rammed the full length of his erection inside her mouth.

"Fuckin' bitch," he muttered as he pushed his steely rod, banging into her gums and her fleshy inner cheeks.

"I hate your fuckin' guts," Marquise snarled.

"Tell me again," she moaned in ecstasy, her whispered words caressing his dick...

"I hate you!" he growled through clenched teeth while winding his fingers into her hair. Marquise yanked a mass of curls with such loathing he pulled a hank of hair out at the roots.

As if enraptured by the sweet pain, Kai moaned and tried to get a suction grip on his dick, but Marquise refused to allow her the pleasure of having his dick trapped between her greedy lips. Thrusting hard and fast, he took control, escaping her puckered lips as he drove his saliva-slick member past her tongue and tonsils. He kept up the frenzied momentum until he felt resistance when his slamming dick hit the back of her throat.

Kai gagged. Her eyes burned and watered, but she took the punishment, telling herself Marquise's ramming thrusts were an expression of his passion. She allowed Marquise to forge ahead, forcing himself deeper, as far as his dick would go.

She gurgled in response. It was a strangled mixture of pleasure and pain. In Kai's mind, Marquise was showing her love, as he tried his best to choke the life out of her, using the only available weapon—his iron-hard dick.

His orgasm pulsed through him, he pulled back so he could aim and spray her face, but he changed his mind, grabbed a handful of her hair and pumped harder.

"Deep throat it, bitch," he growled as he plunged deeper into her throat.

Marquise's large fuck muscle blocked her passageway. Kai struggled to breathe. There was so much dick shoved down her throat, she couldn't even contract her throat muscles to swallow. While Kai's mouth was gaped open, Marquise sent jets of hot semen sliding down her throat.

# Chapter 33

Terelle hobbled along the dark, stony road. She lost her balance and tripped twice, twisted an ankle and scraped a knee, but she continued on her aimless trek, refusing to be slowed by the pain, relying on the moonlight to illuminate the way. The stark fear that Marquise was in imminent danger kept her moving quickly along. Where was she going? She really didn't know, she just had to keep moving.

Jalil and Ayanna had tried to convince her to get in their car, but Terelle no longer trusted them. Had she not heard Ayanna mention the words *ambulance* and *nervous breakdown*, perhaps she wouldn't have pointed the gun at the couple, insisting that they leave her alone and be on their way. "Go the fuck back to Philly," she yelled as Jalil pleaded with her to get into his car. There wasn't a chance in hell she was going to let those two have her committed while Marquise was somewhere being tortured by that raving lunatic, Kai Montgomery.

Jalil slowly drove alongside her, urging her to get into the car.

"I'm not playing with y'all," Terelle said in a threatening tone. "You don't want to help me find Quise, so ride the fuck out!" Then Terelle shot a warning bullet into the dark sky. Ayanna screamed and Jalil pressed his foot down on the gas pedal and sped away.

*Punk asses!*

Now alone with no clue where Kai had taken Marquise, Terelle had to admit that finding her beloved without the assistance of law enforcement was pretty much hopeless.

Calling the police would undoubtedly blow Marquise's cover, but at least his life would be spared. Kai was going to kill him; of that, Terelle was certain. She gazed at the cell phone, pressed a button. Nothing. Still no signal. Feeling defeated, she hung her head. Then something in the road caught her attention. An oddly shaped stone? She bent and picked it up. Oddly, it was a hard pretzel, with a small portion bitten off.

After a few seconds, she felt enlightened. Her heart pounded, her eyes welled with tears of joy. Marquise! He'd left her a sign. He hated hard pretzels, and would only eat soft Philly pretzels. He'd tossed it out the window to let Terelle know Kai had driven him along this path.

Holding the pretzel piece like it was a golden nugget, Terelle picked up her pace, eyes downcast, looking for more clues as she excitedly trotted along the dark road. After picking up a few more scattered pretzel pieces, Terelle came to an area that wasn't quite as desolate. There were signs of life, moving traffic, a highway.

The cell phone beeped as it suddenly sparked to life. Startled, she dropped it. At her feet was a practically full bag of sourdough pretzels. Big, hard, nasty pretzels; the kind Marquise would never eat.

Crying, she pressed numbers in the cell phone. "Saleema," she cried when her friend answered.

After inquiring about Markeeta and being assured that her daughter was all right, Terelle sniffed through the entire telling of the absurd kidnapping.

"Where are you right now?" Saleema had obviously recovered

from the chaos she'd been dragged into the day before. She was now back to her cool, take-charge self.

Turning her gaze to the discarded bag of pretzels and then up to the street sign, Terelle said, "I'm in Cordova, South Carolina. I'm sitting on the curb, on Old Edisto Drive."

"Scroll through the numbers. Make a call to the last person Ayanna talked to. If it's Kai's number, maybe you'll hear Marquise in the background. If we're really lucky, Quise will have his hands on that bitch's phone and answer the call his damn self. It's worth a try," Saleema told Terelle.

After hanging up, Terelle pushed the number and got Ayanna's cousin, Tyneesha. She hung up on the teenager and quickly called the next number on the list of incoming and outgoing calls.

That call went straight to a computerized voice mail. Dispirited, Terelle called Saleema and reported her findings.

"Give me the number."

Terelle rattled off the number she suspected belonged to Kai.

"Don't worry, we're going to find that yella muthafucker. And this time, I'm gonna put my foot up her ass," Saleema said with laughter.

"I wish I could laugh with you, but I'm so afraid for Marquise, ain't nothing funny right now."

"He's aiight," Saleema said with certainty. "That bitch is tryna get her fuck on; she ain't gon' hurt Quise."

Terelle winced. "Marquise wouldn't cheat on me, Saleema. He really is a changed man."

"You're right," Saleema said, but her tone contradicted her agreeable words. Terelle could tell that Saleema didn't think Marquise was capable of changing his doggish ways.

"I can track her down at her exact location, but she's going to have to turn her phone on."

"Really? How?" Hope filled Terelle's voice as well as her large, luminous eyes.

"There's so much new technology out, you wouldn't even believe the shit you can do nowadays. There's that GPS shit…"

"What's that?"

"Global Positioning System. You'll need to track the person with a computer, which isn't a problem, but I prefer to use LBS—"

"Which is?"

"Location Based Services. A lot of cell phones come with the chip. So, obviously, LBS is more convenient for us. The service is offered on most handheld devices. Damn, Terelle, you've been out of the loop for so long, it feels weird having to explain everything to you."

"Sorry."

"It's not your fault. It's just, you know, weird. I'll school you— bring you up to date on all the good shit that's available—after we rescue Quise."

"Okay," Terelle said with a smile in her voice. Saleema sounded so self-assured, Terelle was starting to feel better by the second.

"I know that siditty heifer has a hi-tech handset. We'll find her. Sit tight and don't even worry about it. If we can't locate her with my phone, my fiancé has access to all types of shit that's not available to the public. One way or another, we're gonna find that yella bitch. Now, get up off that curb and take your ass to a restaurant or something."

The only thing in view were the headlights of the few motorists who passed through, but she looked around anyway. "There's nothing here, Saleema. I'm in the sticks. But I'll be all right."

"Terelle, it's gonna take at least two to three hours to get to you. You can't sit outside on the curb like a refugee."

"I'm fine! See you soon." Comforted by the knowledge that Saleema would be there in a few hours, Terelle eased back and rested on her elbows. Then she picked up the bag of pretzels and pressed it next to her heart.

*Hang in there, Quise.*

"I need you to get me a private plane," Saleema told her wealthy fiancé.

"Why? Where do you want to go?"

"South Carolina. Terelle needs me," Saleema said and then recounted the story Terelle had told.

"Saleema, this seems a bit risky. The young woman is unstable, you said so yourself. How do you know she isn't making all this up; she could be delusional. Besides, it sounds too dangerous to get involved in. If your friend is being honest, then her predicament is a matter for the police."

Saleema gave him a look of disbelief. "Oh, it's like that?" She gestured with a freshly manicured finger. "Oh, so now you think you have the final word on what's best for me?" She rubbed her forehead wearily. "You know what? Just fuckin' forget I asked you anything."

"Honey, I have your best interests at heart."

"Oh, really. Well, I'm glad you're exposing your control issues before we walk down the aisle. So, check this out...I'm going to take Markeeta to her Aunt Bennie's house. The wedding is off. I'll pack my and Markeeta's things after I get back."

He stood up abruptly, wrung his hands anxiously. "Saleema, don't be upset with me. You know I'd never try to control you."

"Then make the arrangements, dammit."

"Consider it done."

"Thank you," Saleema said and hurried to Markeeta's bedroom.

He pulled out his cell phone but before he pushed a number, Saleema stopped abruptly and turned around. "Make sure I have a rental car when the plane lands. Nothing fancy. An economy car."

He frowned, perplexed. "Why do you want to rent an economy car?"

"I plan to get in and out of that Godforsaken place as fast as possible. I don't want to draw a lot of unnecessary attention to myself. The last thing I need is for some country bumpkin to take notice of a big, shiny luxury car."

"I see," he said, nodding in understanding, but his voice held a measure of concern.

"I'm going to be fine. Trust me," Saleema said reassuringly. "I always look out for number one."

Markeeta was in her room rearranging the furniture inside her dollhouse. "Keeta, sweetie. I have to take you over to your Aunt Bennie's for a couple of days."

"Why?"

"I have some business to take care of. Something really important. I'll only be gone for a day or two. Three days at the most. I want you to be a real good girl until I get back, okay?"

"Okay." Markeeta agreed. "Are you going to bring my daddy back? He told me he was coming back for me."

Saleema stared at Markeeta, speechless. Markeeta believed that Saleema could make anything happen. Now, it was up to her to make good on the promise Marquise made to his daughter.

Saleema pondered Markeeta's question for a bit and then nodded her head with conviction. "Yes, Keeta. As a matter of fact, I am

bringing your daddy back. I'm bringing your mommy back, too."
Saleema knelt down to Markeeta's level. "Your mommy loves
you very much, Markeeta. She's been through a lot and all I'm
asking is that you give her a chance to show you how much she
loves you. Can you do that for me, Markeeta?"

Markeeta nodded. "I don't want Terelle to cry again."

"Keeta?" Markeeta looked up. "Don't call your mother by her
first name."

"Are Daddy and Mommy going to live with us?"

Saleema breathed a sigh of relief. Everything was falling into
place. She smiled sadly. Her work was done, it was time to let
Marquise and Terelle finish raising their daughter. It was going
to break her heart to return Markeeta to her parents, but it was
time to let her go.

With firm conviction that she could make good on her promise
and safely reunite Marquise and Terelle with their daughter,
Saleema smiled. "No, sweetie," she said. "Your parents are going
to have their own place. You're going to live with your parents.
Are you ready for that? Is that okay with you?"

"Uh-huh. I love my daddy and my mommy." Markeeta gave
Saleema a big grin. "And I love you, too."

# Chapter 34

**H**ornier than ever after being force-fed hot cum, Kai licked her lips and tried to will Marquise's limp member back to a state of arousal.

"Is it okay with you if I take a break and rest for a minute?" Marquise asked, his chest still heaving from the violent orgasm.

"I guess." Disappointment turned down the corners of Kai's mouth.

Marquise tried to shuffle over to the bed. He looked down at the shackles with revulsion. "Man, take this bullshit off my feet. Who do you think you got up in here, Kunta Kinte or somebody?"

"Is he that runaway slave who got his foot chopped off?"

Marquise winced. He made an exasperated sound and flopped on the bed and lay on his back.

Looking frustrated and desperate, Kai stood, raking her hands through her hair. As her eyes darted about, she nervously began to twirl hair around her finger. It was difficult to think straight when her pussy was rapidly pulsating in need of some dick.

Like a sneaky feline, Kai sidled alongside the bed and then sat perched next to Marquise. She gently touched his shoulder. "How long do you have to rest?" she asked in a quiet voice.

"Don't you ever get tired!" Marquise bellowed. "What's wrong with you? You brought me here against my will…" He blew out an angry burst of air. "Can't a nigga get some fucking rest before you start working yourself up for round two?"

Anger flickered in Kai's eyes. "It's impolite to leave your sex partner hanging."

"You ain't my fucking sex partner!"

"Whatever! The fact is, I graciously allowed you to release your load in my mouth. I had hoped to make love to you with my lips and swallow your cum at a leisurely pace. But you were so damn rude you rammed your big dick down my throat. I felt like I was going to choke to death or drown."

Marquise snickered. "Didn't you say you liked it rough?"

"Yeah, I do. However, I was hoping for a little tenderness after you got all that aggression out of your system."

"My bad."

"Assuming that expression means that you're sorry, why don't you make an effort to make it up to me?"

He gave Kai a sneer, which she chose to ignore.

"Marquise," she said, pouting. "My kitty's throbbing for an orgasm; would you mind licking it until you're feeling up to par?" She gave him a slight smile. "Be a gentleman and suck my kitty until, you know…" Her eyes swept downward toward his flaccid member. "Until you've recovered and regained your erection?"

Wearing a frightful grimace, Marquise struggled into a sitting position. "Yo, I ain't no fuckin' gentleman and you damn sure ain't no lady. Wanna know what you are? You a smut bitch. You act just like a nasty-ass alley cat, always scrounging around, scratching' and scheming while you sniffin' out a nigga's dick. I already told you, I ain't sticking my jawn in your stank pussy!"

The stinging slap that landed on Marquise's cheek was not

premeditated. It wasn't even an angry response to being told her kitty held an odor. The violent gesture was the result of having a pussy on fire, while a red-blooded, living and breathing human being in close proximity refused to douse the flames.

Livid, but shackled and unable to whip Kai's ass, Marquise slumped backward. His head banged against the headboard, but he was too fuming mad to feel the pain.

"You're going to fuck me, Marquise. I didn't drive all the way to fucking South Carolina just to swallow your seed. Now, what's the problem? What do you need to help get it back up?" Kai looked around. "Maybe there's porn lying around. Do you think dirty pictures will help? That's what clinicians offer sperm donors when they need a shot of cum in a cup." Kai walked briskly around the bedroom, frantically yanking open drawers, looking under the mattress and under the bed.

Unable to bear the sight of crazy-ass Kai plotting on his dick, which was getting softer and smaller by the minute, Marquise squeezed his eyes closed and screamed inside his mind. Meanwhile, his dick, having its own will to survive, was steadily shrinking in a desperate effort to disappear from Kai's deranged view. By the time Kai's head popped from beneath the bed, Marquise's penis had withered to less than half its original size. Needing to know what was happening around him, Marquise opened his eyes, but was sorry he'd done so.

Kai took one look at Marquise's rapidly decreased phallus, and her mouth dropped open in shock. She abruptly closed it, giving Marquise a threatening look that indicated that he should expect a slow and agonizing death. Then, quite suddenly, Kai smiled. Her face lit up as if she'd been struck by a wickedly brilliant idea.

Feeling tired and hopeless, Marquise lowered his eyelids. Kai flitted around the bed. He could feel her presence at the foot of the bed. She caressed his bound feet. The wormy feeling of her fingers tickled. Marquise's feet wiggled uncomfortably. She sank down to her knees on the floor and began to cover the soles of his feet with moist kisses.

Marquise shuddered. "That shit feels real slimy," he mumbled.

"Relax. Enjoy." Kai kissed the tops of his feet and all ten of his toes. She was working overtime, trying to get his dick hard. Every so often, she'd stop kissing and glance up to see if she'd made any progress. But, Marquise's penis, in a state of siege, had coiled into a tight, miniature ball.

Kai snaked her tongue in and out between Marquise's toes.

Still no response; his dick remained limp as a wet noodle. "Yo, you got my flesh crawling," he finally said. His face was contorted as if in excruciating pain.

"Fuck it!" Kai shouted and got up off her knees. Furious and in severe throes of sexual frustration, she smacked Marquise's left foot so hard, the chain that dangled between his shackled feet rattled and squealed in protest.

"You gon' stop putting your hands on me anytime you get good and muthafuckin' ready!"

"Shut the hell up, you limp-dick, bitch!" Kai exploded.

Marquise sighed and closed his eyes again.

"Look at me!" Kai demanded.

"Man, fuck you! I'm not tryna watch you while you're thinking up ways to get my jawn hard."

The mattress sank. Marquise opened his eyes. "What the fuck you think you doin'?" In disgusted amazement, Marquise gasped when Kai squatted over his iron-bound feet. He tried to kick, tried to move his feet from side to side. He even tried to lift them up so he could kick her in the pussy, but he couldn't budge his feet from their shackled position.

Kai's lips were drawn in hostile determination, her eyes glazed with a look that held no compassion. Marquise could only defend himself by tightly curling his toes.

"Uncurl your toes or I'll cut off every one of them."

Marquise straightened out his toes.

Kai rubbed her slit up and down the top of his foot until it was sloppy wet. Then she eased her dripping kitty up to the tip of his big toe. "Ahh," Kai sighed pleasantly as she pushed down on his stiff toe. "This little piggy…" she began to chant tauntingly as she gyrated on his toe. Suddenly, she stopped all movement. "The hell with one little piggy, my kitty needs a lot more."

Greedily, Kai stretched her vaginal lips wide open. She pulled in four of the toes on his right foot and would have clenched her walls around the small toe as well, but it was too short to provide pleasure.

Deliriously euphoric and writhing in ecstasy, Kai's fingers gripped the bedspread as she bounced up and down and rode Marquise's stiffened toes. Feeling herself coming close to her climax, Kai lifted up. Wanting to prolong the freaky sexual experience, Kai switched over to Marquise's left foot and then back to humping his right foot. She kept up the freaky rotation with abnormal speed and sexual gluttony.

Kai was out of hand. Her behavior was so disgusting and gross, Marquise had no choice but to try to hurry Kai along. He undulated the big toe on his right foot and used it to stroke her clit as hard as he could.

Sighing as if enraptured, Kai stopped switching from one foot to the other and dedicated her pussy to the toes on Marquise's right foot. The veins in her forehead began to protrude. Perspiration trickled from her face down to her neck and pooled inside her cleavage. Suddenly, she stopped moving. Close to reaching an orgasm, Kai's back became rigid. She grunted and squeezed her legs tightly together.

She squeezed her thighs so close together, they seemed locked. Straining, she moaned with pleasure as Marquise firmly pressed the warm, fleshy part of his toe against her swollen clit.

Kai took in a sharp breath and then exhaled. She gave a long, squawking sound as she reached a shuddering climax. Finding Marquise's feet no longer useful, she dismounted and toppled over onto the bed.

Flat on her back, chest heaving, heart rate still pumping from the powerful orgasm, Kai smiled blissfully.

"Yo, shorty. Whatchu gon' do? You gon' lay on your ass forever?"

She raised her head. "What do you want me to do?" she asked, her voice a euphoric whisper.

"Go get a rag or something," he barked, wiggling his toes in anger and disgust. "You was real disrespectful with your moves. I don't appreciate the way you handled that shit. At the end…" He shook his head and bit down on his bottom lip. "At the end, you got real dirty with it. You ain't have to spray pussy juice all over my feet. What you was doing, marking your territory?" He screwed up his face, wriggled his toes again. "Damn, my toes feel all sticky and shit. Get a rag! My jawns is starting to stick together. This is fucked up and nasty!" Marquise scowled at his feet and then stared daggers at Kai. "Would you please go get something and wipe your slimy scum off my muthafuckin' feet!"

Lazily, Kai eased off the bed and sauntered into the bathroom. Marquise could hear the sound of running water. She returned with a washcloth.

"Wipe off your own fuckin' feet," Kai hissed and threw him the wet cloth. He managed to catch the soggy washcloth before it plopped down on his chest, but with cuffed hands he couldn't do anything except hold it.

She put a hand on her hip. "You have a lot of nerve barking orders at me as if I'm the one who's enslaved."

He shimmied into a sitting position. He was fuming mad and the veins popped out at the sides of his neck. "I ain't your fuckin' slave!" Marquise snapped, unbelieving that he'd been referred to as her slave.

Kai's eyes leisurely roved over the shackles and chains that confined Marquise. "Oh, no? You're not my slave?"

"Fuck no!"

"When you learn to treat me with respect, I'll give you your freedom."

Marquise held up his cuffed hands in exasperation. "You got me confused. First, you tell me to dog you—you said you wanted me to treat you real greasy—now you're saying I gotta respect you if I want to get this iron off my hands and feet."

Kai's lips turned up at the corners, forming into a merciless smirk. "Being that you're my slave, the way I treat you depends entirely upon my mood."

"Yo, I'm sick of looking at you. What is it gon' take to get through to you—I'm not interested in you or nothing about you!"

"There may be times when I want to feel your love in a rough, passionate way," she continued as if Marquise hadn't said a word. "At other times, I may want it sweet and tender." Smiling whimsically, Kai droned on but Marquise was no longer listening.

With his chin digging into his chest, he frowned down at his sticky toes, groaned and stared off in thought.

"Whatever the case, I have to be able to trust you. If I know that you love me; if I can believe in my heart that you won't leave me, then I'll unlock the handcuffs and the shackles on your feet."

*Unlock!* Marquise looked at Kai with renewed interest. "I'm not gon' leave you. You know how me and you was, ain't nothing changed," he said in response to her proposition. His expression was now warm and sincere, his voice gentle. "I was just mad about the way you came at me with the gun and shit, while my girl Terelle was around."

"Stop referring to her as your girl!" Kai shouted. And then, she opened her mouth wide and screamed like a lunatic. She abruptly closed her mouth and then shot a look at Marquise. "Do you see what hearing her horrible name does to me?"

"Yeah, I can dig it," he muttered. "So, look, shorty. Um, I mean, Kai…baby. You gon' wipe my feet off or what?" He perused her naked body; his eyes traveled up and down leisurely and then focused on her bare genitalia. Marquise grazed his teeth against his succulent bottom lip, melting Kai's anger with his sexiness.

Lust flickered in Kai's eyes, then she blushed. She shifted her feet, changing her posture from an angry combative stance to that of a demure little girl. "Ask me nicely."

Marquise nodded his head toward his feet. "You gon' wipe my feet off for me, baby"? His voice was low and throaty, seductively motivating Kai to thoroughly clean her vaginal juices off his feet. "Can I get a little lotion?" he asked after she'd finished. "My jawns is feeling kind of dry."

Kai strutted to the front door.

"Where you going?"

"I'm going out to the car to get the rest of my luggage. The lotion and other toiletries are packed in one of the bags." She blew Marquise a kiss. "Be right back," she said and then pointed at Marquise. "And you are going to get the most sensual foot massage you ever had in your life."

"You dat bitch, I know you gon' handle shit—you gon' work it like I'm somewhere in paradise."

Kai beamed at the compliment, threw on Marquise's oversized shirt, and traipsed toward the front door.

"Hurry up. My dick needs some more attention."

Kai took a look at his thick phallus, which was now standing up rigid, but slightly bent. In an instant, she had a vivid memory of how Marquise's crooked dick could locate her G-spot without difficulty. She drew in a sharp, lustful breath and raced to the car.

# Chapter 35

Terelle was asleep, sitting on the concrete with her back against a telephone pole. She'd been in the midst of the sweetest dream—she and Marquise and Markeeta frolicking at the most beautiful beach. In reality, Terelle had never been to a beach. She'd never left the 'hood in her life. But the dream seemed so real; she could feel the warmth of the sun hitting her wet body as she and her family jumped over waves, splashing one another, reacting as if fun in the sun was a familiar experience.

But in an instant, night fell. Dark creepy night. And she was running and calling Marquise and Markeeta. She ran into a dank, dark cave and heard chains rattling and could hear Marquise yelling as if he were being tortured. Then Markeeta's voice came from another direction, screaming, *"Daddy! Mommy! Where are you; I'm lost!"*

"Terelle!"

Terelle jolted awake. "Saleema!" she cried, then rose and rushed inside the small, nondescript rental car. "Thank you, Saleema. Thank you so much," Terelle said, strapping her seatbelt into place.

Saleema gazed at Terelle before pulling off. "You look a hot mess. You look like you've been to hell and back." She shook her head in sympathy, then said, "I took care of everything. I know exactly where that bitch is at."

"Where?"

"About thirty miles from here. She's hiding out in another little hick town called Dixiana. I have the directions. There's one problem, though…"

Terelle turned curious eyes on Saleema.

"I didn't have time to get a gun. Along with my foot, that crazy bitch might need some hot lead up her ass. "

Terelle raised her top, revealing the gun tucked in her waistband.

"Aw, shit. You gangsta, now!"

"I'm about my business," Terelle bragged, chuckling while trying not to allow her deep concern to show on her face. The nightmare had her spooked, but she didn't want Saleema to know how badly she feared for Marquise's safety.

"How's Keeta?"

Saleema beamed the brightest smile Terelle had seen in a very long time. "Keeta's ready to pack her bags so she can live with her mommy and daddy."

Hit by an unexpected jolt of emotion, Terelle covered her face as she burst into tears. She cried loud, body-shaking sobs. Finally, she looked up at Saleema. With a steady stream of tears pouring from her eyes, Terelle asked, "Did she really say, 'mommy,' or are you just trying to make me feel good? Tell me the truth, Saleema; I can take it."

"Well, she called you by your first name, but I got with her little butt about that. So she changed it up and referred to you as mommy. Really, Terelle, I wouldn't lie about that."

Sniffling, Terelle wiped her eyes and pulled at the glove compartment. "Do you have any tissues?"

Saleema gave her a look. "Yeah, in my Lexus. I didn't have time to stock this Camry with a bunch of supplies." Saleema dug into her Fendi bag. "Here." She handed Terelle a wad of tissues.

"Thanks," Terelle said, and blew her nose.

"Aiight, you ready to go kick some ass?"

"Girl, you just don't know. This time, when I aim at that bitch's head…I'm not going to miss."

Saleema and Terelle stared at each other briefly and then Saleema followed the printed directions that led her to I-26 West.

Kai returned carrying another Louis Vuitton duffle bag. She pushed an oversized suitcase with her foot.

"I'd offer to give you a hand, but…" Marquise raised his cuffed hands.

Kai gazed over at him. "I'm sorry, Marquise. I'll take them off as soon as I'm sure I can trust you."

"These jawns is tight and they starting to hurt," he complained.

Kai smiled. "I know a way to take your mind off the discomfort."

"What's on your mind? You want to ride big daddy's dick?"

Kai dropped the duffle bag and quickly pulled off Marquise's large shirt. She rushed over to the bed and attempted to straddle him.

"Yo! Hold up. I wanna make love to you, baby; I'm not trying to bust a quick nut. Bring those sweet, little titties down here. Rub 'em against my lips."

Kai purred and smashed her breasts against his face.

"Kai," he whispered. "Yo, slow down, baby. You already got me at a disadvantage with my hands and feet locked up. Let me love you with my tongue the way I want to, aiight? Let me do this."

"Can't we skip the foreplay?" she whimpered, her kitty bubbling over with lust.

"Naw, we gon' do this my way, aiight?"

"Okay," she reluctantly agreed.

"Now, lean down and let me suck on your left tit."

Kai did as she was instructed. Her pussy was clenched up in agony as Marquise alternated between nibbling and flicking his tongue against her nipple.

"Let me bite on the right nipple."

Obediently, Kai tried to feed Marquise her right nipple, but he ignored it and buried his face in her cleavage, inhaling her, licking the perspiration between her breasts.

"Oh, God!" she moaned, throwing her head back, as her eyes rolled deliriously into the back of her head.

Marquise nipped her delicate, rose-colored bud. Kai yelped in pleasure and pain. He held her nipple captive between his teeth while his tongue scoured the sensitive flesh, thrashing it with long, hard tongue strokes.

Kai pulled her nipple out of his hungry mouth. "I can't take anymore. Fuck me, Marquise. I need some dick."

"Uh-uh. Come on, baby. Let me do this. Bring that ass up here close to my face. You think I forgot how to make your pussy cry? Naw, I ain't forget. I gotchu, baby. Gimme some pussy. You got my hands tied, but I'm resourceful. I'm gon' suck the skin off your clit with my lips and then I'm gon' dig out the cream that's covering your pussy walls." Marquise gazed at Kai's helpless expression. "I'm gon' do all that with no hands, baby. Now, sit on my face and let me work on you."

"I don't want to cum like that. I miss your dick."

"It's all good. I'm gon' give it to you in a minute. Be patient. Is that aiight with you?"

Kai shivered as she nodded her head. She was so horny, she made tortured, whimpering sounds. Finally, giving his hot, bulging phallus one last lingering look, she scooted up toward his face.

Kai positioned her ass and pussy over Marquise's face. She was so hot, so close to spilling her juices, her thighs trembled as she tried to clamp them against Marquise's cheeks.

"Raise up!"

"Why?" she asked, confused.

"I don't eat food in the dark and I don't eat pussy without seeing what I'm about to eat."

Kai released the grip she had on his face and reluctantly lifted her butt.

"Spread your pussy for me."

Her trembling fingers delicately parted her vaginal lips.

"Aw, shit. There it go, there's that pretty pink pussy. Mmm, baby, your pussy lookin' good as shit. Spread it open wider."

Moaning, Kai stretched her pussy lips.

"Yeah, baby, I'm gon' put my thick inches all the way up in that pink shit."

"Marquise!" Kai moaned his name.

"Come on, baby, hold it together. Don't cum on yourself yet."

"All right," Kai whispered, trying to stay strong.

"Dip your finger in it." He shrugged. "I can't do shit with handcuffs on."

"I know, I'm so sorry, Marquise."

"Shh." Marquise silenced her. "It ain't about nothing. We gon' get through this together. I'm your man; you're my bitch. I gotta play my part and prove to you that I'm the only muthafucker you gon' ever need in your life. You heard me?"

"Yes, darling."

"Yo! Shut the fuck up with the corny, 'darling' shit. If you gon' ride with me, you gon' have to represent like a bitch in heat. At all times. Now, how you gon' act?"

At this point, Kai's kitty had ceased purring and was hissing, spitting, and ready to roar. "I'm...," she murmured, so horny she could barely speak.

"What? Speak up. I can't hear that soft shit you talkin'."

"I'm your bitch in heat," she said in a stronger voice. "Forever," she added.

"Aiight. Now, finger fuck yourself. Fuck your finger the same way you gon' rock on this hard dick."

Kai winced with desire. Slowly, she inserted a finger, creating slurping sounds as she probed deep inside her pink tunnel.

"Umph," Marquise grunted. "Rock on that finger. Act nasty like you did when you fucked my toes."

In response to his command, Kai rotated her finger. She worked on herself so intensely, her breathing became harsh, her tongue lolling out of the side of her mouth.

"Naw, that ain't gon' get it. Get up off me, bitch."

"Why?" she shouted and cut an eye at his dark, pulsing manhood. She wanted to touch it. She wanted to trace her fingers along the veins that ran up and down his length. She wanted to taste it, suck it, fuck it. Desperately, she reached out.

"Not yet. Stand up. Put your foot up on the bed. Yo, if I see that thick cream running down your leg, my shit's gonna stand straight up like a soldier ready to go to war. You heard me, bitch?"

Kai nodded sadly.

"Soldiers invade and conquer shit. They take over territory; take whatever they want. I'm gon' fight until I draw blood; I'm not gon' stop battling until I own all that pink area between your legs." He nudged his chin toward her vagina. "Can't stop until I own that territory."

"Marquise, you don't have to fight for it. It's already yours, my kitty belongs to you," Kai said blissfully.

"Naw, I don't want nothing easy like that. I'm a beast. Grrrr!" He clenched his teeth and growled. "I like to fight and rip shit apart. That's my nature, mami. After I stake my claim on that pussy; I'm gon' fuck it 'til it bleeds. You ain't gon' be able to walk for a week."

Kai closed her eyes and moaned. His crude words were a sweet serenade.

"Now, stand up and get real freaky with it." Marquise paused and looked at Kai curiously. "You're my freak, ain't you?"

"Of course!" Kai said, sounding insulted. "You know I am."

"Oh, aiight. Well, act like it. Let me see you fuck yourself."

With clumsy, lust-driven movements, Kai rolled off Marquise and landed on her feet. She stood next to the bed. Marquise turned on his side, licking his full lips in anticipation of Kai's freak show.

Kai placed a bare foot on the bed and raised her hand to give self-administered pleasure.

Marquise kissed the top of her foot. Kai moaned; her hand dropped helplessly to her side. "Stop," she pleaded. "You're going to make me cum."

He gave her a seductive look and then brushed his lips against her ankle, kissing and biting first her ankle and then the top of her foot.

Kai cried out; her hips bucked forward in desire.

"Aiight, baby. Go 'head. Suck on your finger before you stick it in. I want your shit real juicy and wet."

Kai slurped on her finger, holding Marquise in a crazed gaze. The corners of her mouth were pooled with drool. She thought she looked sexy, but she was making a spectacle of herself. She was the perfect image of a lunatic getting her freak on.

"Damn! You seeeeexy!" Marquise egged her on. "Get freaky with it, hump on it like a dog."

Again, Kai did his bidding. With both feet on the floor now, she hunched over like a humpback, throwing her narrow hips in high gear.

"Is it real wet?"

"Uh-huh."

"Show me your finger."

She extracted her finger and held it up for his inspection.

"Naw, fuck that. It ain't sticky enough. You need some help?"

Kai nodded.

"Bring your ass back over here and throw your leg up on the bed."

Kai rushed to the side of the bed. Marquise pressed together his two middle fingers and pushed them inside her dripping tunnel. Gently, he eased the two fingers in and out. Kai gasped harshly. She moaned as if in pain.

"See how your pussy is opening up for me?"

Kai inched closer, tried to snatch up a few more inches, but Marquise withdrew his magical fingers. "You almost ready. When your juice starts drippin' off my fingers, I'm gon' glide my dick right up in it. Once I'm inside…umph!" He shook his head. "It's not gon' be all nice and romantic; it's gon' be straight triple X." He nodded. "Smutty, hardcore sex. I'm gon' do some real damage, tear that pink shit up. There's gon' be a whole lot of mayhem and violence going on between your pussy walls."

Marquise plunged his fingers inside her tunnel. Kai's face took on a savage look. She arched her back and emitted animal-like sounds as he rammed his fingers in and out.

"Yeah, baby," he said in a voice that was a low, sexy rumble. "I'm gon' split that pussy open, leave it gutted, ripped up—raw meat."

Kai's breathing became erratic. Animal lust jolted through her. "Ohmigod. I'm cumming. Marquise. I love you. Oh God, I love you, Marquise," she screamed as her body smashed into his finger. "Do you love me? Please, please, tell me."

"Damn right," he said, his voice a sexy and low baritone.

A soft moan escalated to a long and loud cry as the spasm began to course through her, shaking her torso with pure pleasure and then causing her entire body to convulse. Screaming a jumbled mixture of incoherent rambling, Kai reached her second climax.

She collapsed on the bed, curled behind Marquise. Her head rested against his back, an arm looped around his shoulder, a hand rubbed his other shoulder.

"You finished?" Marquise asked.

"No, I could never get enough of you." The warmth of her smile lit her eyes.

"Baby."

"Hmm."

"I want to hold you. Go get the key so I can put my arms around you," he said tenderly. Kai murmured softly but didn't make a move.

Marquise abruptly sat up, his expression was stone, his voice gruff. "Unlock all this shit so I can fuck you the way I want to. You gotta trust me, Kai. When I'm sexin' you, I want to dig my fingers in your waistline, pull your hair, and spank that red ass."

Aroused again, Kai closed her eyes dreamily and exhaled.

"Don't front on me. You know you like it when I manhandle you."

"I do."

"Trust me, baby. Go get the key," he insisted.

"Okay, I'll get it," Kai said breathily. She turned toward him and tenderly kissed him on his lips.

Marquise kissed her back. "You gon' be my good girl, now?" He gave her an intense look.

Kai was overwhelmed with emotion. She'd never been a good girl before, but she was willing to try. Marquise kissed her again, this time giving her tongue. He worked his fingers into her hair, grabbed a handful and pulled it, tightening his grip with each tongue thrust. Marquise put so much effort into the kiss, sucking her tongue so hard and relentlessly, Kai writhed until she rolled off the bed and hit the floor.

"I want you to be a real good girl and go get that key," he said, his voice coated with syrupy seduction.

Kai tried to stand up, but her knees felt wobbly, like rubber. They buckled.

"Crawl, baby," Marquise encouraged.

Too weak to walk, Kai took Marquise's advice and crawled over to the duffle bag that contained the key. She felt a lump form in her throat. At first she couldn't pinpoint why she was starting to feel so emotional. Then it dawned on her. No one had ever loved her before. Her birth mother hated her and gave her away. Her adoptive mother was ashamed of her. Her adoptive father used her as a fuck toy. All the men and women she'd ever fucked just wanted her for her remarkable beauty.

But now, for the first time in her life, she was going to find out what love was truly about. It was as if Marquise had risen from the dead, broke through the barriers of heaven and hell, to teach her how to love.

"Hurry up, baby. Get the key," Marquise cajoled.

Naked, Kai crawled faster toward the duffle bag. When she reached it and extracted the key, Kai cried tears of joy. She kissed the key that would set Marquise free. He possessed the best dick she'd ever had; he was the true love of her life. And in just a few moments, he would be free to fill her up with his thickness, free to spank her ass for keeping him shackled for so long.

Marquise Whitsett would be free to teach Kai how to feel worthy of receiving love.

Kai unlocked the iron restraints on his feet.

Marquise rotated his ankles for a few moments and then gleefully rubbed together the soles of his feet.

Smiling, pleased to give him such joy, Kai hurriedly inserted the key and turned the lock, releasing his wrists from the tightly binding handcuffs.

Giddy with love and joy, Kai fell on top of Marquise. She kissed him firmly on the lips. His arms made a tight, possessive circle around her waist.

In an instant, he flipped her over. Maliciously, his big hands tightened around her neck. "I gotchu now, bitch!" he spat through teeth that were clenched together in rage.

# Chapter 36

"Where are we?" Terelle asked, looking around the dark back road, worry etched in her face.

"Lost," Saleema replied calmly.

"I thought you had all this advance technology. What do you mean we're lost?"

"I told Franklin to get me a no-frills rental; I should have told him to make sure the car had a navigational system. But chill, I can use my cell," Saleema said, taking out her cell phone and pushing some buttons. "Oh, okay, I made a wrong turn about ten miles ago."

"Ten miles!"

"Ain't no thing. Just have to back up and turn around."

"Oh, God!" Terelle moaned. "Hang on, Quise, please."

"I'm telling you, Terelle. Quise is from the streets. He's got inbred survivor skills. He ain't gon' let that yella bitch get the best of him, not again. Uh-uh," Saleema emphasized, shaking her head.

"I hope you're right. Now, hurry, Saleema."

Twenty minutes later, Saleema pulled into a wooded area, parked, and turned off the ignition. "We have to walk from here. Can't let that heifer hear the motor of the car. Do you want me to carry the gun?"

Terelle shook her head adamantly. "I got this."

The two best friends, covered by the cloak of darkness, crept along a bumpy path until they saw a soft glimmer of light that led them to a one-story dwelling. Unlike the shack Jalil's Paw Paw left him, this little house appeared to be in pristine condition. It was a cute little cottage, adorned with flowers and lush foliage. But knowing that an unspeakable crime was being committed inside, Terelle saw the attractive abode for what it really was, a despicable death trap.

The sight of Kai's black Benz parked in the driveway made Terelle gasp. Her heart lurched inside her chest. The Benz gave her the same creepy feeling she got whenever she saw a funeral hearse.

"Shh! We have to be real quiet."

Terelle nodded. Her trembling hand covered her mouth. "How are we gonna get in?" she inquired, her words muffled by her hand.

"Let's creep to the back. If we're lucky, we should find at least one unlocked window."

Terelle and Saleema crept up to the darkened window. It was low enough to peek inside without having to stand on their toes. Squinting through cupped hands pressed against the glass, Saleema and Terelle gazed into a dark kitchen.

"I can see the living room from here. That light is coming from another room—the bedroom, I guess."

"I hear noises." Terelle looked frantic. "Sounds like I can hear Quise. He's alive!"

"Yeah, I heard him, too."

Terelle tried to push the window up, but it wouldn't budge. She looked at Saleema with mounting anxiety. "I'm about to pull this gun out and smash out this windowpane."

Saleema tried the window. "It's not locked, Terelle. It's just stuck. We have to push it up together. Quietly," she said firmly. "We don't know what kind of weapons that bitch is holding. We'll be two dead asses if she comes barreling through the kitchen armed with an AK-47."

Terelle and Saleema worked together and quietly pushed the window up, raising it just enough to shimmy their slender bodies through. Carefully, Terelle and then Saleema slid over the kitchen sink and eased their feet down to the tiled floor.

"Now what?" Saleema asked as she and Terelle stood huddled together, trying to get their bearings and adjust their vision to the darkness.

"Get down," Terelle said, pulling the gun out of her waistband and cocking the hammer. "In case she's strapped, we'll stand a better chance if we crawl to the living room and try to scope out what's going on in the bedroom."

The trek on their knees seemed to take forever. Terelle could hear the low, crazy-sounding rumble of Marquise's voice. Was Kai torturing him slowly?

At last they reached the living room and could clearly see inside the lit bedroom. Bracing herself for the worst, Terelle peered inside the bedroom.

She let out a yelp of surprise, jumped to her feet, and screamed, "Quise! How could you?"

Startled, Marquise rolled off Kai. From Saleema's vantage point, his dick was limp. Kai was limp, too. Her head lolled to the side. Her complexion appeared bluish. She looked dead. Saleema and Terelle stood rooted in the doorway, both unwilling to go near Kai.

"Babe!" Marquise sounded tortured. "I lost control of myself;

I ain't know what I was doing. I think I killed her." He grimaced and looked over at Kai's still body.

Uncomprehending, Terelle shook her head. "What the hell are you saying, Marquise? You fucked her to death?"

"No," he shouted, then pointed at the iron manacles that lay on the floor. "After she unlocked that shit, after I was free, I was so mad, I choked her ass." Marquise fumbled around for a pulse and looked up with a sickly expression "She's dead!" he exclaimed. Frowning, he scooted away from Kai as if death was contagious.

"You have nursing training; go check her out and see if she has a pulse," Saleema told Terelle.

"Hell, no! I'm not touching her. She's dead. Look at her!" Terelle started shaking and whimpering. Marquise abruptly stood up, unconcerned about his nudity. He was prepared to walk across the room to comfort Terelle.

Frowning at the sight of his penis, Saleema turned her head. She bent down, picked up Marquise's pants off the floor, and tossed them to him.

Marquise dressed hurriedly and rushed to Terelle's side. "It's over, babe. Don't cry, please. I'm so sorry you had to go through this shit again. But it's over, now!" he murmured, trying to console Terelle.

Terelle couldn't stop trembling nor could she stop the tears that fell from her eyes. She didn't give a shit about Kai's death. Her tears were simply a reaction to the emotional roller coaster she'd been on.

"Look, ya'll. We ain't got time for all this lovey, dovey shit. We gotta make sure she's dead and then get rid of her body." Saleema noticed Kai's duffle bags and luggage. "We gon have to take her stuff deep in the woods somewhere and burn it. We can't leave anything behind."

"What do you think we should do with her—burn her up with her clothes?" Terelle's eyes were wide and frantic.

"Hell, no, bones don't burn. Don't you watch TV? They're always using forensic evidence in court. Bones and teeth and shit always talk for the murder victim." Saleema gave a impatient sigh.

"Yo, I ain't murder her; that shit was self-defense," Marquise protested

"Aiight, whatever." Saleema waved a hand dismissively. "Anyway, this bitch is about to be fish food. I already know where we gon' take her. I checked it out on the map. There's a swamp—it's not too far from here. Once we throw her in, she won't ever resurface."

"You sure 'bout that?" Marquise asked. "You know, do fish swim in a swamp?"

"It's just an expression. But, trust me, a swamp isn't like a river. Once she gets entangled in all the muck and mud, ain't nobody gonna be able to pull her back up."

"Are you sure? How do you know?" Terelle exclaimed, voice rising fearfully.

"I'm positive. I watch all the true crime shows."

Terelle was irritated by Saleema's nonchalance. "This isn't a TV show, Saleema. This is reality and I don't want to end up behind bars over that bitch!"

"Calm down, Terelle. I got this. For real."

Marquise looked doubtful. "What about her car?"

Saleema shrugged. "Leave it here. Somebody rented her this cabin, let them worry about ditching her car."

"Suppose they report her missing?" Terelle inquired, her pitch rising an octave.

"Fuck it. She's missing. What they gon' prove?" Saleema glanced over at Kai's lifeless body and flinched. "Wrap her up in that sheet,

Quise. You're gonna have to either drag her or carry her to my car. We can't leave her here." Saleema was decisive and definitely in charge. "You never know who might come snooping around and discover her while we're out getting the car."

Marquise bit his lip and nervously began to perform the unpleasant task of wrapping Kai in the sheet. Then the three friends made their trek down the dark road. Saleema carried the twin Louis Vuitton duffle bags and Terelle dragged the rolling suitcase. Marquise, face contorted miserably, carried Kai's corpse. When they reached Saleema's rental car, she and Terelle threw Kai's luggage in the trunk.

Marquise tried to ease Kai's body into the confined space, but he was so shaky and nervous, the sheet-covered body tumbled out of his hands. Terelle and Saleema both winced at the soft but hideous thud of Kai's head clunking against the floor of the trunk.

All three stared worriedly at each other for a few seconds and then quickly pulled themselves together and rushed inside the rental car. Saleema revved the engine and roared away.

# Chapter 37

As expected, in the hours before dawn the swampland was deserted, quiet, and deathly still. There were no rustling sounds of animals scurrying, no leaves blowing in the breeze. Having a corpse in the car seemed fitting in this eerily quiet, macabre atmosphere.

Marquise's complexion was ashen and gray; he looked close to breaking. "Come on, Quise. Don't fall apart on me now," Saleema said firmly. "We have to get her into the swamp."

"I'm aiight, I'm aiight," he responded, but his voice quavered and held an odd tone. He didn't sound convincing.

Terelle gave Marquise a concerned glance. "Take her out of the trunk, Quise. I'll help you drag her down to the swamp."

Together, Marquise and Terelle, each pulling one of Kai's ankles, began the creepy trudge toward the swamp. With Kai still wrapped in the sheet, they dragged her across the dark, marshy terrain.

Holding a long-barreled flashlight that she'd thoughtfully brought along, Saleema illuminated the way through tall grass and down to the eerie swamp. As they lugged Kai along, the sheet began to unravel, exposing Kai's naked body, which was a sight Terelle had a hard time stomaching.

Finally, they reached the muddy bank and sloshed into it until they were ankle-deep in the muck. Terelle wanted to ditch Kai right then and there, but to rid themselves of her body forever, she knew they'd have to pull Kai deeper into the dreary water.

"Grab her by the arms; it'll be easier that way," Saleema suggested, sounding almost casual, though the trembling hand that held the flashlight suggested otherwise.

Taking Kai by the arms, Terelle and Marquise waded through the thick murky water, pulling and tugging Kai's body. They let her go when at last, they reached the knee-deep section of the swamp.

But Kai didn't go under. She sort of floated on the top. Terelle looked back at Saleema for guidance.

"Push her under," Saleema yelled from the bank. Terelle couldn't do it; she'd had enough of the ink-colored, bug-infested bayou. Marquise had to finish the job. Swatting giant-sized mosquitoes, Terelle turned away and trudged toward the slippery bank. Midway, she heard an unbelievable sound. Saleema heard it, too. The light of the flashlight wavered like crazy as Saleema, with shattered nerves, tried to steady the flashlight and zoom in on Marquise.

Terelle's terror-stricken gaze followed the light that shone on Marquise. She couldn't believe her eyes. Apparently, neither could Saleema. She dropped the flashlight and the swamp went dark.

"Pick up the flashlight, Saleema!" Terelle screamed as she tried to quickly tread through the oatmeal-thick quagmire toward Marquise. He was tussling with a snarling Kai, who had amazingly and vigorously come back to life!

The shaky beam from the flashlight once again lit what had now become a mushy battleground. Marquise was trying to force Kai's head into the murky shallow water, but Kai wouldn't go down.

Damn! Never dreaming she'd need it, Terelle had left the gun in the car. Kai wasn't going down easily and Marquise needed something with some weight to knock Kai upside her stubborn head. "Help us, Saleema!" Terelle yelled. The flashlight Saleema held was the heaviest object they had access to. "Bring the flashlight!"

"Okay." Saleema had no choice but to try to pull herself together. Terelle needed her help. Ignoring her shaking body, she raced as fast as possible toward Terelle. As soon as Saleema was in Terelle's reach, Terelle yanked the flashlight from her hand and quickly treaded toward Marquise and Kai. When she got close, she didn't hesitate for a second. Eyes filled with murderous contempt, Terelle bopped Kai upside her skull. Kai swooned but somehow determinedly kept her dazed and rubbery body upright.

"Bitch!" Terelle screamed. Swinging the flashlight with all her might, Terelle bashed Kai in the mouth, busting her lips, knocking out teeth. Kai screamed in anguish, her hands flew up and protectively covered her mouth.

Kai's blood spattered on Marquise's arms, and mingled with the muck and mud that caked on his shirt and his weary limbs. Mentally and physically fatigued, he released his grip on Kai's arm. "Fuck it! This bitch won't die; and I can't kill her again. I ain't built like that," he muttered exhaustedly. "Leave her out here. Let's go." Looking haggard, like a war-weary soldier who's been in combat for too long, Marquise withdrew his support. He scrubbed at his mud-and-blood spattered arms, and then, zombie-like, he treaded past Saleema and stiffly headed toward the bank and the car.

Stunned, Saleema watched as Marquise walked woodenly to the car. Then she quickly refocused her attention to the disaster in the muddy water. Saleema gasped in horror as Kai floundered about in the sloshy marsh with blood gushing and running between the fingers that covered her mouth. Suddenly, Kai flopped down, landing on her butt.

Terelle advanced toward Kai. She raised the flashlight, prepared to strike again.

"Come on, Terelle," Saleema yelled. "Quise done lost it, girl. He flipped out. Fuck this bitch. She can't survive out here. Come on, let's go."

The flashlight wavered in Terelle's shaky grasp. "If we leave her out here alive, I'm gonna be looking over my shoulder for the rest of my life." She raised the flashlight higher, intending to crack Kai's skull wide open.

Seeing the flashlight poised to strike again, Kai sprung up out of the water and tried to wrestle the flashlight away from Terelle. Judging from her angry expression and the way her lips folded inward to form the letter *b*, it seemed Kai intended to call Terelle a bitch, but with missing upper and lower teeth, the slur came out indecipherable.

"Help! Saleema!" Terelle screamed at the top of her lungs. Kai was outrageously strong. Terelle was amazed at her strength and vicious determination. Swiftly, Kai maneuvered behind Terelle and pulled her into a vise-like headlock and tried to force her beneath the water. "Saleema!" Terelle gurgled.

As fast as she could, Saleema trekked through the oozy marsh. She gawked at an object in the distance. "Look!" Saleema called out and pointed at a floating log.

Struggling to free herself from Kai's powerful headlock, Terelle was able to glimpse the submerged tree trunk. Her incredulous eyes darted toward Saleema. *Why the fuck would Saleema point out a damn piece of wood, instead of helping me kill this crazy bitch?* Terelle struggled and managed to loosen Kai's chokehold. "Hurry up," she sputtered. "This psycho bitch is trying to take me under!" Kai's weight on Terelle's neck and shoulders was overwhelming. Terelle had to lock her knees to remain upright.

Saleema, with her mouth agape and wearing an expression of terror, was frozen in place. Baffled, Terelle followed Saleema's gaze. Oddly, the floating log was picking up speed and there was something extremely disturbing about its swiftness. Suddenly, Terelle realized it wasn't a log at all. Recognition of what was speeding toward her sent a surge of adrenaline through Terelle's body igniting the primitive flight or fight instinct, which increased her strength one hundred fold. Terelle drew her elbow forward and then delivered a rib-cracking blow to Kai's left breast. Kai howled and involuntarily released Terelle. Stumbling, Kai lost her balance.

Hurtling toward Saleema, Terelle managed to evade the menacing dark log and pulled her stunned friend toward the drier land.

Saleema and Terelle, now safely on the muddy bank, watched Kai flail to regain her footing. They watched with horrified fascination as the log floated closer to Kai and then began to surface, revealing itself to be a living creature—a large, wild alligator.

Seconds after Kai managed to stand upright, she saw the predator speeding toward her. Horrified, she tried to run. The alligator shot up from the water, opened its jaws and clamped down on one of Kai's muddy thighs.

Saleema screamed as the wild gator twisted in a frenzy, rolling over and over, holding Kai's mangled limb locked inside its bone-crushing jaws.

With an amazing burst of energy, Kai squirmed and fought

until she was free. Arms flaying, she struggled to swim, clawing at the water desperately. But her sluggish swimming was no match for the speedy alligator. In a flash, Kai was captured between the gator's sharp teeth again.

Crying, pacing in circles several feet from the edge of the swamp, Saleema blabbered incoherently. She closed her eyes, unwilling to witness Kai's last grotesque moments. Her hands covered her ears in an attempt to block out the blood-curdling screams.

But Terelle fixed unblinking eyes on Kai's tortured face.

"Help me!" Kai gave a gurgled cry.

Terelle turned a deaf ear to her adversary's plea. "Fuck you, bitch!" Terelle spat. If she went anywhere near the deceitful bitch, she knew Kai would try to pull her in and give the gator a double treat.

And if by some miracle Kai survived the gator's clenching jaws, Terelle knew the crazy woman wouldn't rest until she succeeded in destroying Terelle and her family.

Shining the beam of the flashlight, Terelle watched without blinking as Kai's mouth stretched into what would be her final scream. It was a horrible sound. Still, Terelle held her enemy in a steady gaze.

Quite abruptly, Kai became still. Her wide, frantic eyes focused on Terelle's face. Her lips spread into a detestable, bloody grin.

With a mighty jerk, Kai's entire body was yanked beneath the swamp water, and pulled down to a dark, muddy grave.

The surface of the thick, gloomy water rippled, bubbled briefly, and then became peaceful.

# Chapter 38

Finally, Terelle dropped the flashlight and released a peal of hysterical laughter.

Saleema pulled her hands away from her ears. Grimacing, she looked at Terelle. "Is it over?" Terelle kept up the maniacal, crazy laughter that echoed throughout the swampland.

"Shut the hell up," Saleema shouted. She picked up the flashlight and shot the beam in the area of the water where she'd last set eyes on Kai. "Is she dead? Did it kill her?"

Terelle nodded, continuing the insane laughter until tears ran from her eyes. Soon, she was laughing and crying at the same time. Saleema gave her a sad look that expressed her understanding. After all Terelle had been through, she was entitled to laugh, cry, dance naked and muddy through the swampland, if that's what she wanted to do.

Terelle gagged. She made choking sounds, vomited, and then collapsed, splayed out on the ground sobbing and calling out her daughter's name.

"Keeta's okay, Terelle. You know she's safe with Aunt Bennie."

"Kai was an evil bitch, Saleema. To the bitter end, she hated me. Wanted to pull me into the muddy swamp with her. She wanted to kill me. She probably would have killed Keeta, too, if she thought my child stood in the way of her having Marquise. Evil is so powerful. It's such an ugly thing. I don't ever want Keeta to experience anything except love, joy, and peace. Oh, Saleema. How am I going to protect my daughter?" Terelle cried.

Saleema turned to her best friend. "Listen to me, Terelle. You are going to drive yourself crazy if you think you can protect Markeeta from all the evil in the world. She's going to have to stand on her own two feet. The best thing you can do is make sure she's prepared. You have to make sure she gets a better chance than you and I got. Quise, too. The three of us were throwaway kids. We didn't have any guidance." She shook her head. "We had to raise ourselves. So, me and Quise tried to ease the pain by chasing after a dollar. You tried desperately to get some love by creating a family, but Quise was too young, too wild to give you what you needed."

Sitting there in the swampy mud, Saleema started to cry. Terelle joined in. Saleema wiped her tears with the back of her hand. "But, look at us, Terelle. The three of us are still standing. This cruel world tried to beat us down, but we made it, girl. We survived. Since we were little kids, me, you, and Quise have had a bond of love and friendship. And to this day, we still have a bond. Markeeta. I love her just as much as you and Marquise do. So I have to give you some advice and you'd better listen to me." Terelle gazed at Saleema. "The best thing you can do for Keeta is give her unconditional love, education, and guidance. Your job is to prepare her for this world, make sure she's fully equipped. I know you can do it, girl. When our baby reaches adulthood, I want her to be a whole person. I don't want her walking around half-blind, fumbling around—shattered and splintered like we were."

Saleema held her hand out toward Terelle. "Let's go."

Hugging each other, the two women trudged toward the car, but suddenly stopped in their tracks. The sheet that had concealed what they'd believed was Kai's lifeless body lay on the ground. It was an ugly reminder of the horrid events of the night.

Wearing a repugnant expression, Saleema picked up the sheet, bunched it together. "This gets burned with the rest of her shit." Pressing a button on the keyless remote, Saleema popped open the trunk.

"Oh, God. I hope Quise is all right." Suddenly remembering how Marquise had walked away from the struggle with Kai, Terelle rushed toward the passenger door to comfort him and hopefully snap him out of his traumatic state.

Saleema flashed the beam of light inside the trunk and snatched the handle of one of the duffle bags. She unzipped it, intending to quickly stuff the sheet inside. "Terelle, come here. Come, quick!" she called urgently.

Terelle had her hand on the handle of the passenger door. Marquise was hunched over in the backseat, hands covering his face, crying in the dark. She'd have to deal with whatever bad news Saleema had discovered inside the trunk later. Right now, Marquise's needs were of far more importance. "Wait a minute, Saleema." Terelle rushed to Marquise's side.

"She's dead, Quise," Terelle told him as she pulled his hands away from his face.

"Until today, I have never been involved in taking nobody's life. Not even while my young, dumb ass was out there on the streets. I ain't never had the stomach for murder."

"You didn't kill her, Quise." Terelle wiped his tears away.

"No, I tried to kill her. Thought I did, but obviously I fucked it up. Then, I walked off like some punk-ass and let my girl finish the job," he groaned.

"I didn't kill her, either." Terelle saw the question on Marquise's face.

"Who killed her? Saleema?"

"None of us!"

Marquise tilted his head, not understanding.

"A wild gator came from out of nowhere. Me and Saleema ran; we got the hell out of that swamp, but Kai didn't make it."

"A gator?" Marquise shook his head. "Now, you're making shit up," he said, his eyes filled with woe and weariness.

Terelle tilted his chin upward. "Would I lie to you? Kai was evil—so evil she was trying to pull me down under, as if she had a right to have beef with me. Like I stole her man!" Terelle spoke with chilling hostility as she brushed away an errant lock of hair. "Anyway, we saw the gator swimming toward us, real fast. Like I said, Saleema and I escaped, but Kai wasn't fast enough. The alligator bit the shit out of her and dragged her under water. It was hard to watch, hard to listen to her cry for help, but I kept my eyes on her until the bitter end, had to make sure that bitch was dead."

"I heard the screams. Felt like I was going to lose my mind if she didn't shut the fuck up. I thought you were pounding her in the head, fucking her up unmercifully with that long-ass flashlight."

"I tried, but she was strong as an ox. Bitch tried to choke me to death. For a minute I thought I was going to lose the battle and end up on the bottom of that muddy swamp!"

"She had me handcuffed—my feet, my hands," Marquise said, his head lowered as he recounted his ordeal with Kai. "Mentally,

I had to stay a hundred steps ahead of her just to get myself free. Then I snapped. I wasn't really trying to kill her." He shook his head with incredulity. "It don't even matter now." He was briefly quiet and then looked at Terelle. "I can't believe we're out here in the swamps with alligators and shit. It feels like I'm in the midst of some never-ending nightmare."

"No, the nightmare is over; this is a new beginning, Quise. For me and you. And Keeta."

"Terelle," Saleema called persistently from the back of the car.

"Go see what she wants, Quise. I can't take anymore," Terelle admitted glumly.

Marquise reluctantly got out and walked to the back of the car. Saleema was rooting around inside a piece of luggage. "Look!" she said, awe in her voice.

Marquise peered inside. Saleema aimed the flashlight beam inside the duffle bag.

"Dayum! Look at all those stacks! I thought that bitch was lying about having a lot of cheddar!"

Saleema picked up a bundle of one-hundred-dollar bills and handed it to Marquise. "It looks like every stack is wrapped with a $10,000 strap. And look, Marquise," she said, shining the light closer. "There's a whole lot of stacks—looks like millions!"

Marquise's mouth dropped wide open, momentarily speechless.

Then in unison, Saleema and Marquise yelled, "Terelle!"

# Chapter 39

That night in the swamp had a life-altering effect on Saleema. She called off her wedding, gave away all her designer clothes, and got rid of her fake hair and fake nails. With her cut from Kai's trust fund, Saleema moved into a mansion and opened her doors to dispirited, homeless young women.

In addition to providing free room and board, Saleema hired competent educators, psychologists, and lecturers who assisted her in providing guidance for her charges on their individual journeys of rediscovery and self-love.

Without Saleema's intervention, the flocks of castaways would have been easy prey for all the wolves in sheep's clothing who were ready to pounce on innocent young girls without financial means or family support. Saleema fully intended to turn her girls into strong and independent young women who would recognize game in an instant, who would never settle for anything less than being treated like a woman of worth.

How many couples honeymooned with a child in tow? Terelle wondered, though she wouldn't have had it any other way. Smiling, she looked over the balcony of the luxurious villa she and Marquise had rented and couldn't help pinching herself as she watched her *family*—her husband and their daughter—splashing in their private pool. Markeeta's happy, high-pitched squeals echoed up to Terelle's ears. Knowing Markeeta would be content to stay out in the pool for the next several hours, Terelle tucked an extra container of sun block inside the large straw bag she was packing.

Marquise's abandonment of the witness protection program and his unwillingness to testify at the trial were not criminal acts. The government's withdrawal of protection didn't matter because the Jamaicans got off scott–free. They never considered Marquise a threat because they still believed he was dead.

Still, instinct told Terelle it was best to extend their honeymoon and to stay in Canada indefinitely. At the moment, there were too many bad memories for her at home in the States.

Along with the sun block and other odds and ends, she stuck a *How to Speak French* CD and CD player in the bag. Of course, settling down in Montreal would have to be a family decision, she told herself as she descended the stairs. She and Marquise and Markeeta would discuss it over dinner tonight.

"*Bonjour!*" she greeted her beautiful family.

"*Bonjour,* Mommy," Markeeta replied with smiling enthusiasm.

"Whaddup!" Marquise greeted.

Yes, Marquise would be the stubborn holdout. Kicking and screaming, he'd resist learning to speak French, but Terelle Chambers Whitsett knew without doubt, she held the key to Marquise's heart, and though it might take a minute, he'd eventually come around.

# ABOUT THE AUTHOR

Allison Hobbs was raised in suburban Philadelphia. After high school she worked for several years in the music industry as a singer, songwriter, and studio background vocalist. She eventually attended Temple University and earned a Bachelor of Science degree. She is the national bestselling author of *Pandora's Box, Insatiable, Dangerously in Love, Double Dippin'*, *The Enchantress* and *A Bona Fide Gold Digger*. Hobbs currently resides in Philadelphia. Visit her at www.allisonhobbs.com and www.myspace.com/allisonhobbs or email her at pb@allisonhobbs.com

EXCERPT FROM

# a bona fide gold digger

BY ALLISON HOBBS

AVAILABLE FROM STREBOR BOOKS

## chapter one

**H**ad her guard been up, Milan Walden would have sensed something was amiss. She would have noticed while gliding into her reserved space that there were more cars than usual in the company parking lot. But, seduced by the unseasonally springlike weather and still basking in the afterglow of a succession of mini orgasms and one major, body-quaking orgasm the night before, Milan felt lighthearted and carefree. It was February, but her mind was already on a new summer wardrobe, a new hairstyle with bronze highlights, and perhaps a new car. Something sleek and elegant—a Jag or a Ferrari. And breast implants.

Smart, competent, and accomplished, Milan damn well deserved a bigger set of boobs. But with her low tolerance for pain, she doubted she could suffer through surgery or the agonizing healing process afterward. So, on second thought, she decided to forgo breast augmentation altogether. She'd start wearing bras with more padding to give the illusion of a bigger bustline. Her extra dollars would be spent on something totally unrelated to pain— like the pricy anchor pendant, with its brilliant round diamonds that swung from a delicate platinum chain, that she'd been coveting at Tiffany.

After a successful nine-month stint as the executive director of Pure Paradise Renewal Center and Day Salon, twenty-six-year-old Milan Walden was earning a six-figure salary and would soon be eligible for a substantial salary increase. The board of directors was decidedly pleased with Milan's inventive ideas and vigorous campaigns to promote the spa's beauty and wellness services. They were particularly impressed with the quarterly profits.

Under Milan's helm, profits at Pure Paradise had tripled in nine short months. Business was booming! Though the wealthy elite were the target market, Milan had innovatively devised beauty renewal and well-being programs to fit the budgets of women from all economic brackets.

Of course, Milan had the good sense not to integrate the well-to-do with the hopeless bottom feeders. No, no, no. The streamlined programs for those of modest income were scheduled on specific days and time slots, and upon arrival, the less fortunate were herded down to the lower level—unseen by discriminating eyes.

Milan looked forward to her performance review. Certain that her salary would more than double, she smiled wistfully as she envisioned indulging herself with all the fabulous material things money could buy.

*Not bad for a gangly black kid from the Raymond Rosen housing projects*, she thought with smug satisfaction as she breezed through the automatic sliding glass doors. She caught a glimpse of her reflection as she passed the mirror that hung above the security station and had to admit that she looked damn good.

Impeccably swathed in a textured well-cut pantsuit and a pair of beaded mules, carrying a colorful trendy leather briefcase, and sporting an expensively coiffed hairstyle, Milan had used her fashion and beauty sense to change her ugly duckling status to that of a beautiful swan.

She was brimming with pride and absolutely pleased with her life as well as the glorious sunny day, which she perceived as a divine design to complement her charmed existence. She failed

to notice the serious expression of the usually smiling and solic-
itous security guard as she whisked past him.

When she approached the company's reception area, the
woman who sat behind the desk greeted Milan with a strained
smile and a weak "Good morning." The woman was Milan's exact
age. She had a nice figure and appealing facial features, however,
being a lowly receptionist was probably as far as she aspired.
The poor envious creature would never come close to reaching
Milan's level of success. Feeling superior, Milan smirked at the
receptionist as she briskly walked past. *Don't hate!*

A few moments later, as she floated toward her secretary's desk,
Milan couldn't imagine why, though she could smell the overpowering and sickeningly sweet fragrance of potpourri that always
wafted throughout Pure Paradise, she was unable to detect even
a hint of the wonderful aroma of her morning cappuccino.

Her secretary, Sumi, who also served as the center's tour
guide for prospective clients, was completely incompetent, but
being a young and flawless Eurasian beauty, Sumi was excellent
advertising for Pure Paradise. Desperate women in their forties
seeking to stave off the destruction of time flocked to Pure Paradise,
where they were promised youth and rejuvenation with massage
therapy, aromatherapy, yoga, Pilates, facials, seaweed wraps,
colonics, and even journaling sessions, for pity's sake! What a
crock!

Thankfully, a sucker had been born every minute during the
wild sixties. Bless those grungy, down-with-the-establishment
hippies for prolific breeding and for producing such materialistic
and narcissistic offspring.

"Sumi," Milan hissed, banging her chic, lime-colored Italian
leather briefcase on Sumi's desk. "Where's my cappuccino grande?
You know I can't begin my day without my caffeine fix."

A look of extreme discomfort crossed Sumi's pretty face.
"Someone snatched it," Sumi explained, her voice an apologetic
whisper.

"Someone snatched it?" Milan echoed. "Who?" she screeched.

In search of a cappuccino thief, she whirled around and assessed her secretary's work area in anger and disbelief.

Sumi pointed toward the executive office—Milan's office. Just as Milan cut her eyes in that direction, the door flew open. A stern-faced board member emerged from Milan's office and beckoned her.

Utterly surprised, Milan's jaw dropped. "Good morning, Mr. Billings," she said, quickly composing herself. "What a wonderful surprise," she continued in an unnaturally high-pitched voice.

"Yes, good morning, Milan." He gave her a tight smile and then with a pompous lift of his chin, he said, "We'd like to have a word with you."

*We?* Milan mouthed the word as she turned her head to meet the wide, doe-shaped eyes of Sumi. She grasped the handle of her briefcase and glared at her secretary, willing the frazzled girl to enlighten her.

"The board," Sumi finally responded. "They're all in there."

"All of them?"

Sumi nodded gravely.

*What the hell?* With panic mounting, Milan cleared her throat, donned a twitchy smile, and walked woodenly toward Mr. Billings. Wheels turned quickly inside her head and then it dawned on her—the board wanted to reward her for her amazing accomplishments. They probably wanted to present her with a monetary bonus a few months before her scheduled performance review. A genuine smile now replaced the painful spastic grin. With a feeling of great relief, Milan traipsed inside her spacious office and offered a cheery "Hellooo," animatedly waving a hand at the board members as if they were all the best of friends.

❦

Six entirely caucasian Pure Paradise board members were convened. They all sat stiffly on the sofa, settee, and two chairs. The board's chairperson, Dr. Kayla Pauley, an attractive and fashionable, forty-something dermatologist, sat behind Milan's desk, wearing a classy Norma Kamali jacket and sipping the stolen cappuccino. Milan was reminded of how much she disliked the sickeningly self-assured Dr. Pauley. Still, she gave a delighted smile that welcomed the insufferable woman to her desk—and to her badly needed morning java.

Milan cast a hopeful glance at a male board member who sat in one of the cushy chairs. Not only did he refrain from offering her a seat, the man had the gall to give Milan a look of contempt and then fixed a pleasant gaze on Dr. Pauley.

Irritation coursed through her body and threatened to make an appearance on her face, but she shook off the feeling and graced the board members with another forced smile. She supposed their solemn expressions and the stifling doom and gloom atmosphere was merely a façade, a necessary preface to glad tidings.

Dr. Pauley set the container of cappuccino upon the desk. "Good morning, Milan. I guess you're wondering why we're here." Dr. Pauley leaned forward in Milan's executive chair and began shuffling papers.

Milan nodded absently as she glanced disapprovingly at the bloodred lip prints left on the cup. *Her* cup! Despite the monetary compensation she was about to receive, Milan couldn't help feeling violated. Why did Dr. Pauley have to ruin the moment by brazenly guzzling her cappuccino and sitting at her desk?

"It's been brought to our attention," Dr. Pauley began slowly, "that you haven't been...how should I put it?" She paused briefly and then exclaimed with an extravagant wave of her hand, "Milan, we've discovered you haven't been forthcoming."

*Say what?* Milan kept her bright smile frozen in place, for surely she had mistaken the word *forthcoming* for *rewarded*. Of course the board was gathered to show how much they appreciated her. Her performance at Pure Paradise was stellar. They couldn't possibly have convened to accuse her of—what? Theft? Embezzlement? Why did white people always think blacks were prone to steal? How dare they even suggest that an intelligent, attractive, polished, and educated woman such as she would take something from Pure Paradise?

*Hmm.* On second thought, she had pocketed dozens of those cute little pastel-colored bottles of Hawaiian hand lotion. Sudden fear made her heart pump a trillion beats per second. *Oh hell!* she thought with relief and calmed down. The product was included in the gift bags—giveaways for new clients. *You can't steal something that's being given away.* She had a notion to inform the stuffy board members of that fact, but held her tongue. In Milan's opinion, the real thief was Dr. Kayla Pauley, the coffee-snatching, desk-stealing hussy.

Without a doubt, the board had made a mistake, and Milan was prepared to loudly protest any wrongdoing on her part. "Exactly what are you trying to say?" Milan inquired. Her broad smile morphed into a don't-mess-with-me-before-I've had-my-coffee scowl.

Taken aback by Milan's sudden intimidating presence, Dr. Pauley drew back and nervously reshuffled the papers.

"Milan," Mr. Billings said, rising from his position on the settee. "It's come to our attention that you falsified your credentials."

Milan's mouth went dry. Her rising panic escalated to full-blown terror. She swallowed and took a peek at the papers on her desk. She squinted at her resume, scrutinized it as if there was some kind of mistake. But her name was right there in bold letters as well as her educational background. There were other papers on the desk. One was embossed with the University of Pittsburgh logo and another boasted the Temple University logo.

"There is no record of your ever receiving a bachelor's degree from Pitt or an MBA from Temple." Now emboldened, Dr. Pauley leaned forward. "Milan, your position requires a degree from a four-year college at the least. Our records indicate that your education is limited to a high school diploma," Dr. Pauley said, shaking her head and scanning the papers in annoyance. "Unless you can provide the proper documentation, we're going to have to terminate you immediately."

Dr. Pauley's words were chilling. Milan's knees, damn them, knocked together uncontrollably. She hadn't heard what she thought, had she? She definitely needed a moment to process the information. She stammered, "I know I don't actually have a degree, but obviously I'm a strong, dynamic leader. My experience speaks for—"

Before she could utter another word, Royce, the security guard, appeared. He glowered at Milan briefly and then said gruffly, "Come with me, Ms. Walden."

Milan's jaw dropped. "You're kidding!" She twirled on her heels and faced the group of six. "Is this necessary? My accomplishments here have been huge," Milan said, fighting for survival, trying to reason with the board. "I put in thirteen-hour work days and I've made this company a small fortune." She paused to catch her breath. "And now you're treating me like a common thief."

"Please leave the premises, Milan, or security will have to forcibly remove you," Dr. Pauley said, unmoved by Milan's outburst. Slowly and gracefully, she picked up the phone. "Sumi, please pack up all Milan's belongings."

Milan opened her mouth to further defend herself, but she felt faint. The words necessary to halt this travesty of justice escaped her.

Smiling wickedly as she swiveled toward Milan, Dr. Pauley said, "We'll forward your belongings to your current address. Hopefully, that isn't a fabrication as well."

The next three minutes were a blur of embarrassed gasps, chuckles, and outright slurs from subordinates who apparently felt Milan had it coming. A minute or so later, she sat inside her car, stunned and trembling, but very reluctant to leave Pure Paradise. Driving away obliterated her chance of being available should the board come to their senses and reconsider their absurd decision to fire her. As far as Milan was concerned, keeping her around—college degree or not—made good business sense.

Royce had brusquely escorted Milan through the sliding doors and returned to his station. From his vantage point, he could see that she was making no attempt to vacate the company parking lot. The once-friendly security guard stepped outside. With an angry expression, he motioned for Milan to get moving.

Could the day get any worse? Her mind was spinning, her head throbbed, and she felt queasy. She really needed something to calm her down. She imagined Dr. Pauley and realized that what she needed was a goddamn cup of coffee!

Blinking back tears, she pulled herself together, turned on the ignition, and careened out of the lot. The car, seemingly on automatic pilot, was pointed in the direction of the nearest Starbucks.

## *chapter two*

"**D**id you get ghetto on that heifer?" Milan's sister, Sweetie, wanted to know after Milan related her harrowing ordeal. Dropping batter-covered wing dings into a pan of sizzling oil, Sweetie spoke with her back to Milan.

"No, I didn't get *ghetto*," Milan spit out the last word. As her sister damn well knew, Milan had long ago redefined herself and had shed the skin of a person who resolved issues by behaving in a manner as abhorrent as *getting ghetto*. She now possessed well-honed sophistication and was a savvy businesswoman. Her mother and her sister still embraced their ignorance and lack of sophistication, but in no way did the word *ghetto* apply to Milan.

Sweetie tossed in the last wing ding and turned around. "Well, what did you do? I'm waiting to hear how you whipped that ass." With her face screwed up and clearly exasperated, Sweetie folded her arms as she waited for Milan to respond.

"What could I do?"

Sweetie gawked at Milan. "Please tell me that you at least grabbed that wench by the collar and smacked your coffee out of her hand."

"Get serious, Sweetie. You know I wouldn't disgrace myself like that."

"Hmph! If that heifer had come at me like that, her ass woulda been wearing that damn espresso."

"Cappuccino," Milan corrected.

"Whatever! Did you whip that ass?" Sweetie repeated.

Milan sincerely loved her sister, but Sweetie had to be the most hopelessly ignorant and thoroughly ghettoized person she knew. The two sisters were like night and day. They had nothing in common.

Sweetie had no ambition. She was out of shape and her wardrobe was a fashion disaster. How her sister could walk around in a pair of low rider jeans with a roll of flab hanging over the waistline was beyond Milan. Sweetie was satisfied being a sloppy-looking, stay-at-home wife and mother. She and her husband, Quantez, had two bad-behind boys spaced only ten months apart, and judging by the way her sister loved to brag about her sex life, it wouldn't be long before baby number three was conceived.

In Milan's opinion, the only thing Sweetie had going for herself was her pretty face. She didn't need a drop of makeup, not even lipstick. Her glamour routine was simple: moisturizer and lip gloss. Milan had to work hard to be glamorous and couldn't help thinking that God had given the wrong sister the natural beauty.

Breaking off her thoughts of envy, Milan said, "Sweetie, I just lost the best job I've ever had and all you can think about is whether or not I retaliated with physical force. I need to focus on finding another job. A good job that pays as much or even *more* than I earned at Pure Paradise." Milan fell silent briefly, and then looked at her sister intently. "Sweetie. There's a possibility that the board might spread malicious rumors about my education."

"Rumors?"

"You know what I mean. After all the energy I put into my career, I could end up blackballed. The board could inhibit my earning power; they could prevent me from ever working again."

"Oh, please, how can a few people stop you from ever working again?"

"Those few people have a lot of power. They're well respected in the spa industry. But besides that, I don't know what I'm going to tell Mom. I need you to help me come up with a story." Milan shook her head mournfully. "She's going to be absolutely distraught when she finds out I lost my prestigious position."

Sweetie nodded in sad agreement. "Yeah, she's gonna miss all those freebies. Did you grip up some gift bags for us before you split?" she teased, making light of Milan's situation.

"I don't give Mom just the free gift bags. Ever since I've had the job, I've showered both you and Mom and your kids with expensive gifts."

"And we appreciate it, but Mom gets a big kick out of getting all that free stuff," Sweetie explained, giggling as she spoke.

Not seeing any humor in being unemployed and possibly having her future earning power opposed, Milan grabbed her briefcase and stood. Stepping over several Fisher Price toys she recognized as part of the plethora of Christmas gifts she'd purchased for her nephews, Milan announced, "I'm leaving! How can you be so insensitive? I can't think of any reason why you'd think it appropriate to poke fun at a time like this." Pointing a French-manicured finger around Sweetie's disorderly living room, Milan confronted her sister. "What's the problem, Sweetie? Are you jealous because I didn't screw up my life the way you screwed up yours? Two kids back-to-back, living in low-income housing—"

"Excuse me!" Sweetie said, interrupting Milan. "My life is

not screwed up. I have a hard-working husband who loves me enough to pay all the bills, including the day care bill for our two kids so I can have some free time for myself."

"Your husband earns—what? Thirty...thirty-one thousand a year?" Milan tsked at the absurdity of such a meager salary. "You sound like a fool bragging about the pittance Quantez is bringing in. You should be out looking for a job so you can help make ends meet around here." She looked around her sister's house with her nose turned up. "And you shouldn't be bragging about sending your children to that subsidized, ghetto day care center while you're sitting on your butt, not even making an attempt to elevate yourself or your family."

"My husband does not want me to work. And anyway, Miss High and Mighty, what the hell do *you* have?" Sweetie asked, her face scrunched up in hostility. "I'll tell you what you have— a bunch of nothing, that's what! Nice clothes and an overpriced apartment and that's it. But you know what your problem really is?"

"No, but I'm sure you think you're in a position to tell me."

"You need some dick," Sweetie said in a deadly calm voice. "How long have you been humping that fifteen-hundred-dollar penis?" Sweetie asked and then gave a burst of loud, malicious laughter. "Girl, I remember when you called me to brag about the price you paid for a damn vibrator." Sweetie's shoulders shook from laughter. "Anytime a woman brags about the amount of money she spent on some battery-operated dick, you know her life is fucked up. *My* life, however, is just fine. Let me remind you, I have a fine-ass husband and two gorgeous kids who *looove* me."

Milan inhaled sharply.

Sweetie's dark eyes sparkled with mischief. "With all your important *this* and expensive *that*, how come you don't have a man? How come you're sitting up in my crib, crying on my shoulder? Oops! I forgot. Unlike me, you don't have a man to hold you tight. There's nobody at your crib to take your troubles to. You wanna know why? Because there's not a man on the planet who would find you loveable enough to even listen to your bull-shit."

Milan realized her sister's words were designed to cut deeply, but she honestly did not feel any pain. No, there wasn't a special man in her life—her choice. With her all-encompassing career goals, there was little time left to emotionally invest in a man. Yet, her sex life was completely gratifying. But how could she expect someone as closed minded and unsophisticated as Sweetie to understand her hedonistic lifestyle?

"It's not like I *can't* get a man; but honestly, emotional attachment is the last thing on my mind. And marriage?" she said with a scornful snort. "You know my career comes first. I don't have time for a relationship with a man or anyone else for that matter. As you well know, I don't even have time for girlfriends."

Sweetie folded her arms. "Well, that's a damn shame, 'cause now you don't have nothin'. No job, no man, and not one even one girl-friend. Umph!" Sweetie screwed up her face and shook her head.

*Ow!* Now, Milan winced. Damn shame that she didn't have a single friend, male or female. But at what point during her rise to the top was she supposed to take the time to cultivate friendships? In her current predicament, she could use some meaningful advice from a cultured and educated best friend. Instead, she had to listen to Sweetie pontificate about life lessons—how Milan should take this setback as a lesson in knowing one's place in life. Sweetie droned on and on as if it were the perfect time for Milan to embrace an existence similar to hers, with a poorly paid husband and a couple of snot-nosed brats hanging on to her skirt tail. *No thanks!*

Milan shook her head. She should have thought twice before she spoke disparagingly of Sweetie's husband. Sweetie became a monster over the slightest criticism of Quantez. Now on a roll, Sweetie viciously continued to cut Milan to shreds.

"You were married to that damn job and now you ain't even got that. I hate to tell you this, Milan, but every time you said the words *executive director*—which was about a thousand times in every conversation—me and Mommy wanted to throw up. I'm sorry those people kicked you out the way they did but at least now I don't have to hear about Pure Paradise every day of my life. Without your job and snooty job title, you ain't shit. So, whose life is really screwed?"

Being informed of her worthless status was jolting and the only thing she could think to say was, "You and Mommy talk about me behind my back?"

"Every day!" Sweetie said with a vindictive grin.

"How could Mommy talk disapprovingly of my carefully planned lifestyle when you and Quantez live like *this*?" Milan looked around the cramped and untidy quarters with an expression of revulsion.

Offended, Sweetie sucked her teeth. "We got a roof over our heads and food—" Sweetie closed her mouth abruptly. "I don't have to explain my life to you. You said you were leaving, so get the hell out." She walked to the door, twisted the knob and yanked the door open.

"You don't have to tell me twice." Milan moved toward the door with her nose turned up. When one last insult formed in her mind, she turned around suddenly. "By the way, since you have so much *free time*, how come your place smells like pissy diapers?"

"Get out!" Sweetie shouted at her sister and held the door wide open.

Milan huffily obliged. Sweetie slammed the door behind her.

Being thrown out of the upscale Pure Paradise was extremely humiliating, but being ejected from Sweetie's little shack of a home was degrading as hell. Her own sister's rejection seemed to foreshadow the coming of terrible times, as if this was an ominous warning that dire circumstances loomed close by.